BEANS, BOURBON, AND BLOOD

T0109789

BEANS, BOURBON, AND BLOOD

WILLIAM W. JOHNSTONE

AND J.A. JOHNSTONE

PINNACLE BOOKS
Kensington Publishing Corp.
www.kensingtonbooks.com

PINNACLE BOOKS are published by

Kensington Publishing Corp.
900 Third Avenue
New York, NY 10022

All Kensington titles, imprints, and distributed lines are available at special quantity discounts for bulk purchases for sales promotion, premiums, fundraising, and educational or institutional use.

Special book excerpts or customized printings can also be created to fit specific needs. For details, write or phone the office of the Kensington Sales Manager: Kensington Publishing Corp., 900 Third Avenue, New York, NY 10022. Attn. Sales Department. Phone: 1-800-221-2647.

PINNACLE BOOKS, the Pinnacle logo, and the WWJ steer head logo Reg. U.S. Pat. & TM Off.

First Kensington Books hardcover printing: June 2024
First Pinnacle Books mass market printing; August 2024

ISBN-13: 978-0-7860-5071-0
ISBN-13: 978-0-7860-5072-7 (eBook)

10 9 8 7 6 5 4 3 2 1

Printed in the United States of America

Chapter 1

Luke Jensen reined his horse to a halt and looked up at the hanged man. The corpse swung back and forth in the cold wind sweeping across the Wyoming plains.

From behind Luke, Ethan Stallings said, "I don't like the looks of that. No, sir, I don't like it one bit."

"Shut up, Stallings," Luke said without taking his gaze off the dead man dangling from a hangrope attached to the crossbar of a sturdy-looking gallows. "In case you haven't figured it out already, I don't care what you like."

Luke rested both hands on his saddle horn and leaned forward to ease muscles made weary by the long ride to the town of Hannigan's Hill. He had never been here before, but he'd heard that the place was sometimes called Hangman's Hill. He could see why. Not every settlement had a gallows on a hill overlooking it, just outside of town.

And not every gallows had a corpse hanging from it that looked to have been there for at least a week, based on the amount of damage buzzards had done to it. This poor varmint's eyes were gone, and not much remained of his nose and lips and ears, either. Buzzards went for the easiest bits first.

Luke was a middle-aged man who still had an air of vitality about him despite his years and the rough life he had led. His face was too craggy to be called handsome, but the features held a rugged appeal. The thick, dark hair under his black hat was threaded with gray, as was the mustache under his prominent nose. His boots, trousers, and shirt were black to match his hat. He wore a sheepskin jacket to ward off the chill of the gray autumn day.

He rode a rangy black horse, as unlovely but strong as its rider. A rope stretched back from the saddle to the bridle of the other horse, a chestnut gelding, so that it had to follow. The hands of the man riding that horse were tied to the saddle horn.

He sat with his narrow shoulders hunched against the cold. The brown tweed suit he wore wasn't heavy enough to keep him warm. His face under the brim of a bowler hat was thin, foxlike. Thick, reddish-brown side-whiskers crept down to the angular line of his jaw.

"I'm not sure we should stay here," he said. "Doesn't appear to be a very welcoming place."

"It has a jail and a telegraph office," Luke said. "That'll serve our purposes."

"Your purposes," Stallings said. "Not mine."

"Yours don't matter anymore. Haven't since you became my prisoner."

Stallings sighed. A great deal of dejection was packed into the sound.

Luke frowned as he studied the hanged man more closely. The man wore town clothes: wool trousers, a white shirt, a simple vest. His hands were tied behind his back. As bad a shape as the corpse was in, it was hard for Luke to make an accurate guess about his age, other than the fact that he hadn't been old. His hair was a little thin, but still sandy brown, with no sign of gray or white.

Luke had witnessed quite a few hangings. Most fellows who wound up dancing on air were sent to eternity with black hoods over their heads. Usually, the hoods were left in place until after the corpse had been cut down and carted off to the undertaker. Most people enjoyed the spectacle of a hanging, but they didn't necessarily want to see the end result.

The fact that this man no longer wore a hood—if, in fact, he ever had—and was still here on the gallows a week later could mean only one thing.

Whoever had strung him up wanted folks to be able to see him. Wanted to send a message with that grisly sight.

Stallings couldn't keep from talking for very long. He had been that way ever since Luke had captured him. He said, "This is sure making me nervous."

"No reason for it to. You're just a con artist, Stallings. You're not a killer or a rustler or a horse thief. The chances of you winding up on a gallows are pretty slim. You'll just spend the next few years behind bars, that's all."

Stallings muttered something Luke couldn't make

out, then said in a louder, more excited voice, "Look! Somebody's coming."

The town of Hannigan's Hill was about half a mile away, a decent-sized settlement with a main street three blocks long lined by businesses and close to a hundred houses total on the side streets. The railroad hadn't come through here, but as Luke had mentioned, there was a telegraph line. East, south, and north—the direction he and Stallings had come from—lay rangeland. Some low but rugged mountains bulked to the west. The town owed its existence mostly to the ranches that surrounded it on three sides, but Luke knew there was some mining in the mountains, too.

A group of riders had just left the settlement and were heading toward the hill. Bunched up the way they were, Luke couldn't tell exactly how many. Six or eight, he estimated. They moved at a brisk pace as if they didn't want to waste any time.

On a raw, bleak day like today, nobody could blame them for feeling that way.

Something about one of them struck Luke as odd, and as they came closer, he figured out what it was. Two men rode slightly ahead of the others, and one of them had his arms pulled behind him. His hands had to be tied together behind his back. His head hung forward as he rode as if he lacked the strength or the spirit to lift it.

Stallings had seen the same thing. "Oh, hell," the confidence man said. His voice held a hollow note. "They're bringing somebody else up here to hang him."

That certainly appeared to be the case. Luke spotted a badge pinned to the shirt of the other man in the lead, under his open coat. More than likely, that was the local sheriff or marshal.

"Whatever they're doing, it's none of our business," Luke said.

"They shouldn't have left that other fella dangling there like that. It . . . it's inhumane!"

Luke couldn't argue with that sentiment, but again, it was none of his affair how they handled their law-breakers here in Hannigan's Hill.

"You don't have to worry about that," he told Stallings again. "All I'm going to do is lock you up and send a wire to Senator Creed to find out what he wants me to do with you. I expect he'll tell me to take you on to Laramie or Cheyenne and turn you over to the law there. Eventually you'll wind up on a train back to Ohio to stand trial for swindling the senator and you'll go to jail. It's not the end of the world."

"For you, it's not."

The riders were a couple of hundred yards away now. The lawman in the lead made a curt motion with his hand. Two of the other men spurred their horses ahead, swung around the lawman and the prisoner, and headed toward Luke and Stallings at a faster pace.

"They've seen us," Stallings said.

"Take it easy. We haven't done anything wrong. Well, I haven't, anyway. You're the one who decided it would be a good idea to swindle a United States sena-tor out of ten thousand dollars."

The two riders pounded up the slope and reined in about twenty feet away. They looked hard at Luke and Stallings, and one of them asked in a harsh voice, "What's your business here?"

Luke had been a bounty hunter for a lot of years. He recognized hard cases when he saw them. But these two men wore deputy badges. That wasn't all that unusual. This was the frontier. Plenty of lawmen had ridden the owlhoot trail at one time or another in their lives. The reverse was true, too.

Luke turned his head and gestured toward Stallings with his chin. "Got a prisoner back there, and I'm looking for a place to lock him up, probably for no more than a day or two. That's my only business here, friend."

"I don't see no badge. You a bounty hunter?"

"That's right. Name's Jensen."

The name didn't appear to mean anything to the men. If Luke had said that his brother was Smoke Jensen, the famous gunfighter who was now a successful rancher down in Colorado, that would have drawn more notice. Most folks west of the Mississippi had heard of Smoke. Plenty east of the big river had, too. But Luke never traded on family connections. In fact, for a lot of years, for a variety of reasons, he had called himself Luke Smith, instead of using the Jensen name.

The two deputies still seemed suspicious. "You don't know that hombre Marshal Bowen is bringin' up here?"

"I don't even know Marshal Bowen," Luke answered honestly. "I never set eyes on any of you boys until today."

"The marshal told us to make sure you wasn't plannin' on interferin'. This here is a legal hangin' we're fixin' to carry out."

Luke gave a little wave of his left hand. "Go right ahead. I always cooperate with the law."

That wasn't strictly true—he'd been known to bend the law from time to time when he thought it was the right thing to do—but these deputies didn't need to know that.

The other deputy spoke up for the first time. "Who's your prisoner?"

"Name's Ethan Stallings. Strictly small-time. Nobody who'd interest you fellas."

"That's right," Stallings muttered. "I'm nobody."

The rest of the group was close now. The marshal raised his left hand in a signal for them to stop. As they reined in, Luke looked the men over and judged them to be cut from the same cloth as the first two deputies. They wore law badges, but they were no better than they had to be.

The prisoner was young, maybe twenty-five, a stocky redhead who wore range clothes. He didn't look like a forty-a-month-and-found puncher. Maybe a little better than that. He might own a small spread of his own, a greasy sack outfit he worked with little or no help.

When he finally raised his head, he looked absolutely terrified, too. He looked straight at Luke and said, "For God's sake, mister, you've got to help me. They're gonna hang me, and I didn't do anything wrong. I swear it!"

Chapter 2

The marshal turned in his saddle, leaned over, and swung a backhanded blow that cracked viciously across the prisoner's face. The man might have toppled off his horse if one of the other deputies hadn't ridden up beside him and grasped his arm to steady him.

"Shut up, Crawford," the lawman said. "Nobody wants to listen to your lies. Take what you've got coming and leave these strangers out of it."

The prisoner's face flamed red where the marshal had struck it. He started to cry, letting out wrenching sobs full of terror and desperation.

Even without knowing the facts of the case, Luke felt a pang of sympathy for the young man. He didn't particularly want to, but he felt it, anyway.

"I'm Verne Bowen. Marshal of Hannigan's Hill. We're about to carry out a legally rendered sentence on this man. You have any objection?"

Luke shook his head. "Like I told your deputies, Marshal, this is none of my business, and I don't have the faintest idea what's going on here. So I'm not going to interfere."

Bowen jerked his head in a nod and said, "Good."

He was about the same age as Luke, a thick-bodied man with graying fair hair under a pushed-back brown hat. He had a drooping mustache and a close-cropped beard. He wore a brown suit over a fancy vest and a butternut shirt with no cravat. A pair of walnut-butted revolvers rode in holsters on his hips. He looked plenty tough and probably was.

Bowen waved a hand at the deputies and ordered, "Get on with it."

Two of them dismounted and moved in on either side of the prisoner, Crawford. He continued to sob as they pulled him off his horse and marched him toward the gallows steps, one on either side of him.

"Just out of curiosity," Luke asked, "what did this hom-bre do?"

Bowen glared at him. "You said that was none of your business."

"And it's not. Just curious, that's all."

"It doesn't pay to be too curious around here, Mr. . . . ?"

"Jensen. Luke Jensen."

Bowen nodded toward Stallings. "I see you have a prisoner, too. You a bounty hunter?"

"That's right. I was hoping you'd allow me to stash him in your jail for a day or two."

"Badman, is he?"

"A foolish man," Luke said, "who made some bad

choices. But he didn't do anything around here." Luke allowed his voice to harden slightly. "Not in your jurisdiction."

Bowen looked levelly at him for a couple of seconds, then nodded. "Fair enough."

By now, the deputies were forcing Crawford up the steps. He twisted and jerked and writhed, but their grips were too strong for him to pull free. It wouldn't have done him any good if he had. He would have just fallen down the steps and they would have picked him up again.

Bowen said, "I don't suppose it'll hurt anything to satisfy your curiosity, Jensen. Just don't get in the habit of poking your nose in where it's not wanted. Crawford there is a murderer. He got drunk and killed a soiled dove."

"That's not true!" Crawford cried. "I never hurt that girl. Somebody slipped me something that knocked me out. I never even laid eyes on the girl until I came to in her room and she was . . . was layin' there with her eyes bugged out and her tongue sticking out and those terrible bruises on her throat—"

"Choked her to death, the little weasel did," Bowen interrupted. "Claims he doesn't remember it, but he's a lying, no-account killer."

The deputies and the prisoner had reached the top of the steps. The deputies wrestled Crawford out onto the platform. Another star packer trotted up the steps after them, moving with a jaunty bounce, and pulled a knife from a sheath at his waist. He reached out, grasped the dead man's belt, and pulled the corpse close enough that he could reach up and cut the rope. When he let go, the body fell through the open trap and landed with a soggy thud on the ground below. Even from where Luke was, he could smell the stench that rose from it. He didn't envy whoever got the job of burying the man.

"How about him? What did he do?"

"A thief," Bowen said. "Embezzled some money from the man he worked for, one of our leading citizens."

Luke frowned. "You hang a man for embezzlement around here?"

"When he was caught, he went loco and tried to shoot his way out of it," Bowen replied with a shrug. "He could have killed somebody. That's attempted murder. The judge decided to make an example of him. I don't hand down the sentences, Jensen. I just carry 'em out."

"I suppose leaving him up here to rot was part of making an example."

Bowen leaned forward, glared, and said, "For somebody who keeps claiming this is none of his business, you are taking an almighty keen interest in all of this, mister. You might want to take your prisoner and ride on down to town. Ask anybody, they can tell you where my office and the jail are. I'll be down directly and we can lock that fella up." The marshal paused, then added, "Got a good bounty on him, does he?"

"Good enough," Luke said. He was beginning to get the impression that instead of waiting, he ought to ride on with Stallings and not stop over in Hannigan's Hill at all. Bowen and those hardcase deputies might have their eyes on the reward Senator Jonas Creed had offered for Stallings's capture.

But their horses were just about played out and really needed a night's rest. They were low on provisions, too. It would be difficult to push on to Laramie without replenishing their supplies here.

As soon as he had Stallings locked up, he would send a wire to Senator Creed. Once he'd established that he was the one who had captured the fugitive, Bowen wouldn't be able to claim the reward for himself. Luke figured he could stay alive long enough to do that.

He sure as blazes wasn't going to let his guard down while he was in these parts, though.

He reached back to tug on the lead rope attached to Stallings's horse. "Come on."

The deputies had closed the trapdoor on the gallows and positioned Crawford on it. One of them tossed a new hangrope over the crossbar. Another deputy caught it and closed in to fit the noose over the prisoner's head.

"Reckon we ought to tie his feet together?" one of the men asked.

"Naw," another answered with a grin. "If it so happens that his neck don't break right off, it'll be a heap more entertainin' if he can kick good while he's chokin' to death."

"Please, mister, please!" Crawford cried. "Don't just ride off and let them do this to me! I never killed that whore. They did it and framed me for it! They're only doing this because Ezra Hannigan wants my ranch!"

That claim made Luke pause. Bowen must have noticed Luke's reaction because he snapped at the deputies, "Shut him up. I'm not gonna stand by and let him spew those filthy lies about Mr. Hannigan."

"Please—" Crawford started to shriek, but then one of the deputies stepped behind him and slammed a gun butt against the back of his head. Crawford sagged forward, only half-conscious as the other deputies held him up by the arms.

Luke glanced at the four deputies who were still mounted nearby. Each rested a hand on the butt of a holstered revolver. Luke knew gun-wolves like that wouldn't hesitate to yank their hoglegs out and start blasting. He had faced long odds plenty of times in his life and wasn't afraid, but he didn't feel like getting shot to doll rags today, either, and likely that was what would happen if he tried to interfere.

With a sour taste in his mouth, he lifted his reins, nudged the black horse into motion, and turned the horse to ride around the group of lawmen toward the settlement. He heard the prisoner groan from the gallows, but Crawford had been knocked too senseless to protest coherently anymore.

A moment later, with an unmistakable sound, the trapdoor dropped and so did the prisoner. In the thin, cold air, Luke distinctly heard the crack of Crawford's neck breaking.

He wasn't looking back, but Stallings must have been. The confidence man cursed and then said, "They didn't even put a hood over his head before they hung him! That's just indecent, Jensen."

"I'm not arguing with you."

"And you know good and well he was innocent. He was telling the truth about them framing him for that dove's murder."

"You don't have any way of knowing that," Luke pointed out. "We don't know anything about these people."

"Who's Ezra Hannigan?"

Luke took a deep breath. "Well, considering that the town's called Hannigan's Hill, I expect he's an important man around here. Probably owns some of the businesses. Maybe most of them. Maybe a big ranch outside of town. I think I've heard the name before, but I can't recall for sure."

"The fella who was hanging there when we rode up, the one they cut down, that marshal said he stole money from one of the leading citizens. You want to bet it was Ezra Hannigan he stole from?"

"I don't want to bet with you about anything, Stallings. I just want to get you where you're going and collect my money. Whatever's going on in this town, I don't want any part of it."

Stallings was silent for a moment, then said, "I suppose there wouldn't be anything you could do, anyway. Not against a marshal and that many deputies, and all of them looking like they know how to handle a gun. Funny that a town this size would need that many deputies, though . . . unless their actual job isn't keeping the peace, but doing whatever Ezra Hannigan wants done. Like hanging the owner of a spread Hannigan's got his eye on."

"You've flapped that jaw enough," Luke told him. "I don't want to hear any more out of you."

"Whether you hear it or not won't change the truth of the matter."

Stallings couldn't see it, but Luke grimaced. He knew that Stallings was likely right about what was happening around here. Luke had seen it more than once: There was some rich man ruling a town, and the surrounding area, with an iron fist, bringing in hired guns, running roughshod over anybody who dared to stand up to him. It was a common story on the frontier.

But it wasn't his job to set things right in Hannigan's Hill, even assuming that Stallings was right about Ezra Hannigan. Smoke might not stand for such things, but Smoke had a reckless streak in him sometimes. Luke's hard life had made him more practical. He would have wound up dead if he had tried to interfere with that hanging. Bowen would have been more than happy to seize the excuse to kill him and claim his prisoner and the reward.

Luke knew all that, knew it good and well, but as he and Stallings reached the edge of town, something made him turn his head and look back, anyway. Some unwanted force drew his gaze like a magnet to the top of the nearby hill. Bowen and the deputies had started riding back toward the settlement, leaving the young man called Crawford dangling limp and lifeless from that hangrope. Leaving him there to rot . . .

"Well," a female voice broke sharply into Luke's thoughts, "I hope you're proud of yourself."

Chapter 3

Luke knew he should probably keep riding. Instead, he reined in and looked over at the woman who stood at the end of the boardwalk in front of the businesses to his right.

As he did that, a wagon rattled past on his left. From the corner of his eye, Luke saw that the man driving the rig wore a black suit and a black top hat.

The local undertaker, on his way up to the top of Hangman's Hill to retrieve the body that had been cut down. Had to be. That was going to be a mighty unpleasant task.

Luke turned his attention to the woman who had spoken to him. She was worth paying attention to. Blond, in her late twenties, pretty, and well-shaped, in a long brown skirt and a white long-sleeved blouse.

"You need a coat if you're going to be out in weather like this, ma'am," Luke said.

"I'm too hot under the collar to get chilled."

She looked angry, sure enough, as she gazed at Luke with intense blue eyes. He sensed that her anger wasn't directed solely at him, though. She seemed like the sort of woman who might be mad at the world most of the time.

Then she looked past him, up the hill, and sick dismay crept over her face.

"They hanged him," she said softly. "They really did."

"Friend of yours?" Luke glanced at her left hand and saw the ring on her finger. "Not your husband, I hope."

"What?" The woman looked confused for a second, then gave a curt shake of her head. "No, of course not. I barely knew Thad Crawford. Well enough, though, that I refuse to believe he was a murderer, no matter what the judge and jury said."

"Well, I didn't know the man at all, so I didn't feel like getting shot over something bound to happen, anyway. If that's what's got you upset with me, you're off the mark, lady. There was nothing I could do."

She glared at him for a few seconds, then said, "I suppose you're right. Verne Bowen and his men would have killed you if you'd tried to interfere, and Thad Crawford would still be just as dead."

"Seems like the only logical way to look at it," Luke drawled.

"But I don't have to like any of it."

"No, ma'am, you don't. Neither do I."

She blew out an exasperated breath, shook her head,

and turned to go back into the building behind her. Luke looked at the words lettered on the front window: HANNIGAN'S HILL CHRONICLE.

So the blonde had something to do with the local newspaper. Maybe he would pick up a copy of the current issue while he was in town, Luke mused. He wondered if it would have something to say about the hangings.

He heeled the black horse into motion again. He hadn't thought to ask the woman where the marshal's office was, but he didn't need to. He had already spotted the squarish stone building in the next block on the left, with a sign over the door that had Marshal Verne Bowen's name on it.

"That was a pretty woman, even if she was mad as a hornet," Stallings said. "You should have introduced me."

Luke grunted. "Not likely. I don't reckon she would've had any interest in meeting a swindler. Anyway, I don't know her name, so I couldn't have introduced you, could I?"

"I suppose not. I wouldn't mind seeing her again, though."

"Give it up, Stallings. It's your weakness for women that got you caught in the first place, remember? If you hadn't bedded that ranch wife while her husband was away, and then ran out on her, she wouldn't have been mad enough to put me on your trail."

"Well, she should have been smart enough not to believe me when I told her I'd take her to Cheyenne. I don't want to get tied down like that."

"So now you're tied, anyway," Luke said. "At least, your hands are."

Stallings just sighed. Luke hoped that would shut him up for a few minutes.

On the way to the marshal's office, they passed a frame building that sat by itself on the corner of one of the side streets. The sign on the awning over its porch read: MAC'S PLACE—GOOD EATS.

Luke's stomach responded instantly to the thought of a hot, well-cooked meal. Years of riding lonely trails had given him the ability to whip up biscuits, beans, and bacon, as well as boiling coffee, but after the long ride, an actual meal, maybe a steak, a heaping helping of potatoes, some greens, and a bowl of deep-dish apple pie, sounded mighty good. He would come back here after he got Stallings locked up, he told himself, and see if Mac's Place lived up to the sign's claim.

They stopped in front of the marshal's office. Luke swung down from the saddle and tied the reins of both horses to the hitch rack. He pulled his bowie knife from the sheath on his left hip, behind the holster that held a Remington revolver rigged for a cross-draw, and cut the rope that bound Stallings's wrists to the saddle horn. He left the rope around the confidence man's wrists in place.

Something flickered in Stallings's eyes. Luke figured he was thinking about making a try for the knife. He was ready to grab Stallings's arm, jerk him out of the saddle, and dump him on the ground if he made any sort of suspicious move.

Then Stallings sighed, grasped the horn, and dismounted without trying anything as Luke stepped back. Whatever wild urge had gone through him for a second, he had thought better of it.

Luke took hold of his arm and steered him onto the boardwalk. The door to the office was unlocked. It was furnished like dozens of other small-town lawman's offices Luke had been in—a scarred desk with a leather chair behind it, racks on one of the walls holding rifles and shotguns, a map of Wyoming on another wall, some ladder-back chairs, and a Franklin stove in the corner. To the right of the desk, an open door led into the cellblock in the rear of the building.

Marshal Bowen had said that he would be back soon, but Luke didn't see any point in waiting for the lawman to return. He marched Stallings through the cellblock door. The iron-barred cells were on the left. All four of them were empty, their doors standing open.

"One's as good as another," Luke said. He put Stallings in the first one and clanged the door closed behind the fugitive.

"What about these blasted ropes?" Stallings asked. "They've just about rubbed my wrists raw."

"Stick your hands through the bars."

Stallings did so. Luke drew his knife again and cut the bonds. Stallings sighed in relief as the pieces of rope fell away. His wrists did look a little sore, Luke noted, but that didn't generate any sympathy in him.

"When am I gonna get something to eat?" Stallings asked as he rubbed his chafed wrists. "It's been a long time since breakfast this morning, and we were on pretty short rations, too."

"I'll talk to the marshal when he gets here. He may have some arrangements already made for meals to be delivered to prisoners. If not, I'll see about sending something in for you."

"Better not wait too long. I might just starve to death, and then how would you claim that reward?" A startled look appeared on Stallings's face as if he had just thought of something. "Wait a minute. That bounty the senator offered for me, it wasn't, uh, dead or alive, was it?"

Luke had to laugh. "No, they don't usually put dead-or-alive bounties on cheap swindlers like you, Stallings. All I had to do to earn it was apprehend you."

"Well, that's a relief, anyway. Don't forget about the food."

"I won't," Luke said as he heard the front door of the office open and close again. Somebody had come in, and he figured it was Marshal Bowen.

He walked out of the office and stopped short as he realized the new arrival wasn't Bowen at all.

Instead, a woman stood there just inside the door, and she looked good enough to make Luke catch his breath.

Chapter 4

Thick auburn curls fell around an attractive face dominated by a pair of green eyes. Her skin was creamy and the low-cut blue gown she wore displayed a considerable amount of it, including her shoulders and the upper swells of her bosom. The dress nipped in at the waist and then swelled again around the curve of her hips. It was the sort of outfit designed to take a man's breath away in a saloon—or a boudoir—but it looked a bit out of place in the dingy office of a small-town marshal.

She frowned in confusion, cocked her head slightly to the side, and said, "You're not Verne."

"No, ma'am, I most definitely am not," Luke said.

"I thought he'd be back by now. The hanging's over, isn't it?"

"It is. The marshal and his men were headed back this way the last time I saw them. I'm a little surprised they haven't shown up by now, too."

"Verne probably stopped at Hannigan's office. The deputies are back. Some of them came into the Lucky Shot a few minutes ago. When I saw them, I figured Verne was in his office."

"The Lucky Shot would be one of the local saloons, I take it?" Luke guessed.

"You'd take it right. It's my place. I'm Irish Mahoney."

Since she had given him her name, it seemed only fitting that he introduce himself. "Luke Jensen," he said. "It's a pleasure to meet you, Miss Mahoney. Or is it Mrs.?"

"It's Miss," she said. "And my name is actually Iris, but with this hair"—she gestured toward the auburn curls—"and a last name like Mahoney, people started calling me Irish and it stuck. Are you waiting for the marshal, too, Mr. Jensen?"

"That's right. I asked him if it was all right for me to lock a prisoner in one of his cells, and he said it was. I went ahead and put the fellow back there."

"You're a lawman, too?"

"Not exactly."

"Oh." She nodded. "Bounty hunter."

"That's right."

"We don't get many of those passing through here. Do you plan on staying long?"

"Just long enough to send a telegram, pick up some supplies, and spend the night in a real bed."

"Come on down to the Lucky Shot later on, if you want," Irish Mahoney said. "We can help you out with the last of those things." She paused, then added boldly,

"We can even arrange for you to have some company, if that's what you want."

He refrained from asking if that company might be herself, although he couldn't stop the thought from going through his mind. If that was the case, he might be tempted, but he had never been one to pay for female companionship and didn't see any real reason to start now.

Before either of them could say anything else, the door opened and Marshal Verne Bowen came in, carrying a Winchester. He stopped and frowned.

"What do you want, Irish?"

"Can't I just stop by and say hello to a friend?" she asked.

"You know I'm always glad to see you." Bowen glanced at Luke and added, "Can't say the same for you, Jensen. Where's your prisoner?"

"I already put him in the first cell back there," Luke explained. "Since they were all empty, I didn't figure it mattered. But you can move him, if you want."

Bowen stepped past Irish and came over to the desk. He laid the rifle on it and said, "He's fine where he is. How long do you plan on leaving him here?"

"Just overnight. I'm going to send a telegram, pick up some supplies, and head out tomorrow."

Irish said, "I told Mr. Jensen he could get a good night's sleep at the Lucky Shot."

"You two introduced yourselves, did you?" Bowen said.

"It seemed like the polite thing to do," Luke said. "I appreciate the loan of your cell, Marshal. If I can repay the favor . . ."

Bowen waved that off. "Forget it. Like you said, the cells are empty right now. If you want him fed, though, you'll have to see to it yourself. I'd suggest you go down the street and talk to McKenzie. His prices are reasonable."

The marshal was probably talking about Mac's Place. Luke had intended to stop in there, anyway, so when he did, he'd see about having supper for Stallings delivered to the jail.

"I'm obliged to you, Marshal." He nodded politely to Irish Mahoney and pinched the brim of his hat. "Ma'am, it was a pleasure to meet you. Maybe I'll stop by your establishment later."

"You do that, Mr. Jensen," she said. "First round is on the house."

As Luke opened the door to step out of the office, he heard Irish say behind him to Bowen, "You got rid of Thad Crawford, didn't you?"

"The boy was legally sentenced to hang and I carried out the judge's order," Bowen said. "I just did my job."

"Ezra Hannigan's job," Irish was saying as Luke closed the door.

He paused on the boardwalk just outside, drew in a deep breath, and let it out in a sigh. He glanced over his shoulder and saw through the office's front window as Bowen put his hands on Irish's shoulders, pulled her against him, and brought his mouth down on hers. His fingers appeared to be digging painfully into the creamy bare flesh. She started to pull away as if angry, then sagged against him and twined her arms around his neck, her resistance overcome by her feelings.

Evidently, the relationship between them was a complicated one, and it was definitely one more thing that was none of Luke's business.

He recalled the way Irish had said that Bowen probably stopped at Ezra Hannigan's office. To report to him that the young rancher's hanging had been carried out successfully? Had that execution been as much a matter of following Hannigan's orders as it had been carrying out the duty of a law officer?

The situation here didn't smell quite as bad as the corpse that had been hanging up there on the gallows for a week . . . but almost, Luke thought as he headed along the street toward Mac's Place.

The lunch rush, if there had been one, was well over by this time of the afternoon. Only three customers were in Mac's Place as Luke stepped into the café. A stout, middle-aged man with a brown brush of a mustache sat at a table with a blue-checkered cloth. He had a coffee cup in front of him and was reading a newspaper. The *Hannigan's Hill Chronicle,* Luke noted.

Two men sat on stools at the counter to Luke's right, not together, but spread out with several empty stools between them. One was forking bites of pie into his mouth, while the other used half a biscuit to sop up the last of some gravy on an otherwise-empty plate. Nobody was behind the counter.

It was a nice-enough-looking establishment, but far from fancy. Ten tables with blue-checkered cloths were arranged to Luke's left. The large window in the front wall and several smaller windows in the sidewall be-

yond the tables had curtains on them, but they were
just plain white curtains pulled back to let in the gray
light of the overcast day. Two oil lamps were suspended
from chains attached to the ceiling. The floor was
plain, polished wood. The countertop was polished as
well. A blackboard with prices chalked on it hung on
the wall beside a swinging door behind the counter.
The bill of fare was no fancier than the surroundings:
steak, stew, ham, fried chicken, potatoes, beans, corn
bread, biscuits, apple and peach pie.

All three of the customers looked at Luke when he
came in, displaying varying degrees of interest. The
men at the counter, who were dressed like working
men, teamsters or livery stable hostlers or carpenters,
went back to their food. The well-dressed, well-fed
hombre at the table lowered his newspaper and gazed
at Luke with more curiosity.

The door behind the counter swung open and a man
with longish dark hair stepped through, carrying a coffeepot in his left hand. He used a thick piece of leather
to protect his hand from the heat of the handle. He
wore a faded canvas apron over a blue work shirt with
the sleeves rolled up on his forearms.

He stopped as he saw Luke and said, "Be with you
in just a minute, friend." Then he turned to the man at
the table and asked, "Need that coffee warmed up,
Judge?"

"That would be fine, Mr. McKenzie," the stout man
said.

McKenzie came out from behind the counter at the
far end, carried the pot over to the table, and topped off
the judge's cup with fresh coffee.

Luke couldn't help but wonder if the stout man was the jurist who had sentenced Thad Crawford to hang. That had to be the case, he thought, because it was unlikely a town the size of Hannigan's Hill would have two judges.

The judge went back to his newspaper. As he read, he made a "Hmmph!" noise as if he didn't much like what he was reading. That made Luke more curious about what might be printed in the *Chronicle*. He definitely wanted to pick up a copy while he was here.

McKenzie went back behind the counter as Luke strolled to the empty stool at the end. Luke sat down, undid the buttons on his jacket, and thumbed his hat back. McKenzie placed the coffeepot on a round, flat stone sitting on the counter for that purpose and came down to greet Luke with a noncommittal nod.

"What can I do for you?"

"Already got a steak fried up?"

"I do."

"I'll have that, potatoes, biscuits, and coffee."

"Two bits."

Luke wasn't offended by that. He was a stranger in town, after all. It made sense the proprietor would want to be sure he could pay before he dished up the food. Luke took a half-dollar from his pocket and laid it on the counter.

"That enough to cover some pie afterward?"

McKenzie's nod was a little more friendly this time. "And some cream to go with it, if you want."

"Bring it on," Luke said.

Chapter 5

Maybe someday his stomach would no longer clench every time a stranger came through the door, Dewey McKenzie told himself. The reaction had gotten a lot better over the past few years as he had led a peaceful existence here in Hannigan's Hill. He hoped that eventually it would go away completely.

But he wasn't going to count on that, especially when the stranger was a gun-hung, tough-looking hombre like the one who had just taken a seat at the counter.

Mac kept his voice and expression neutral as he asked the man what he wanted. A Smith & Wesson revolver was in easy reach on the top shelf under the counter. Mac hoped he wouldn't have to reach for it—he had enjoyed his time here in the settlement and didn't want it to end in gunsmoke—but he would defend himself if he had to.

He always had. That was why he was still alive.

The stranger wore two guns, ivory-handled Remingtons that rode butt-forward in cross-draw holsters. He had a sheathed knife on his belt, too. He had the rugged look of a man who could use all those weapons efficiently and wouldn't hesitate to do so. Mac might have taken him for a lawman—a real lawman, not a hired killer like Verne Bowen—but no star was pinned to his shirt.

A bounty hunter? Could be. Could well be. Mac had seen plenty of them over the years. He had learned to recognize the breed.

This fella didn't seem interested in anything other than getting a late lunch or an early supper, whatever you wanted to call it. The anticipation with which he asked about the steak and potatoes and pie made him sound like a man who had gone a while without a good meal.

Mac could provide that, if nothing else. He hoped he wouldn't have to serve up some hot lead as well.

He got a coffee cup off the back shelf, filled it, then went into the kitchen for the food. When he came back out, carrying the plate, he saw that Saul Jenkins and Charlie Hawley had left. Judge John Lee Trent was still sitting at his table, pretending to read the paper while continuing to eye the stranger.

"There you go," Mac said as he placed the food before the man. "Enjoy."

The man had been sipping his coffee. He lowered the cup and said, "Oh, I intend to. I've been on the trail for a while, eating my own cooking, and I'm ready for something better."

"Well, I hope you're not disappointed."

"I'm sure I won't be. I think I'll enjoy this steak even if it tastes like shoe leather."

Despite his wariness, Mac was a little offended by that comment. "It won't," he said. "I've never had any complaints about my steaks."

The man picked up the knife and fork that were on the plate, cut off a bite, and put it in his mouth. As he chewed, his eyebrows went up a little in surprise. After swallowing, he said, "That's one of the tenderest pieces of meat I've ever bitten into. And perfectly seasoned as well."

"Glad to hear it meets with your approval." Mac's voice was crisp.

The stranger chuckled. "I had that coming for jumping to conclusions. I've eaten in a lot of small-town hash houses. The food's usually not as good as you'll find in San Francisco or Denver or New Orleans . . . but this is."

Mac caught his breath at the man's mention of New Orleans. That was where he was from originally, but he hadn't set foot there since leaving in a hurry some fifteen years earlier. Was this stranger hinting that he knew who Mac was? Or was it just an innocent comment?

Hoping that it didn't mean anything, Mac said, "I've had a lot of practice cooking." He didn't elaborate on how he had gotten that practice.

The stranger swallowed another bite and nodded. "You could charge more for this than two bits, especially if you were in some place besides a Wyoming cow town."

"Maybe, but I like it here."

The stranger continued eating, praising the potatoes and the lightness of the biscuit as well. Between bites, he said, "The marshal recommended that I talk to you."

That surprised Mac. He and Verne Bowen weren't friends, by any means.

"He did?"

"Yeah. Said that you might be able to provide supper tonight for a prisoner I brought in."

"A prisoner you brought in," Mac repeated. "Since I don't see a badge on you, does that mean you're a bounty hunter?"

"Everybody in this town seems to be pretty quick on the uptake. That's right. Name's Luke Jensen."

Mac had run into more than his share of bounty hunters over the years. The name Luke Jensen stirred a very vague memory somewhere in the back of his mind. He was confident that he and Jensen had never crossed trails before, so he must have heard talk about the man somewhere along the way.

The look of anticipation on Jensen's face told Mac that he was expecting an introduction. Since he had been using his real name ever since he'd come to Hannigan's Hill—no real reason anymore for him not to—he might as well use it now, too.

"Dewey McKenzie. My friends call me Mac."

"Anybody who can cook like this, I hope we'll be friends."

Jensen put his fork down and extended his hand. Mac gripped it firmly. Even though he was still suspicious of the man, he realized that he felt some instinctive liking for Luke Jensen.

Bounty hunter or not.

"So you want me to fix a meal for this prisoner you brought in? He's locked up in Marshal Bowen's jail?"

"That's right."

"Real badman, is he?"

Luke laughed. "Not really. He might talk your ear off, but I'm not sure he's very dangerous beyond that, if you're worried about dealing with him."

"I'm not," Mac said.

"He's a confidence man, a swindler. He picked the wrong target for one of his schemes back east, a United States senator."

Mac whistled. "That wasn't very smart of him, was it? I imagine the senator didn't take kindly to being rooked. And being a man of some power and influence . . . at least I assume he is . . ."

Jensen nodded. "He is. And possessed of a vindictive nature, too."

"So he put out a reward for this fella you've rounded up. What are you supposed to do with him?"

"I'm going to send a wire and find out about that, just as soon as I've finished with this fine meal of yours, Mr. McKenzie."

"Mac. We're going to be friends, remember?"

"Mac," Luke said with a nod. "I expect the senator will want me to take Stallings on to Cheyenne and turn him over to the law there. Wouldn't surprise me if Senator Creed has somebody pick him up there and take him back to Ohio. Pinkerton agents, maybe."

Mac nodded. "That sounds likely. Stallings is the man's name?"

"Yeah, Ethan Stallings. He's almost a likable cuss, but not quite."

"I'll take a bowl of stew and some beans and corn bread over to him later on," Mac said.

Luke added another half-dollar to the one already lying on the counter. "That cover the food and your trouble?"

"Sure, that's fine. You said you wanted some pie? Apple or peach?"

Luke's plate was clean. "I'll take the peach," he said. "And more coffee."

Once he had dug into the bowl of peach cobbler topped with cream, Luke nodded with emphatic approval.

"If you don't mind me asking, Mac, where did you learn to cook? I know this was made with canned peaches, but it tastes fresh."

Mac grinned. "Believe it or not, I got my start as a chuckwagon cook, going up the trail from Texas to the railhead in Kansas when those cattle drives started not long after the war. I never set out to be a grub wrangler. It just sort of happened that way."

"I've never gone on a trail drive," Luke said, shaking his head, "but I didn't have any idea those cow nurses ate this well."

"I don't know that what I cooked was all that good starting out, but I learned fast and seemed to have a knack for it. I wound up going on drives all over the frontier, not just from Texas up to Kansas, but after following the chuckwagon trail for a good number of years, I decided I'd had enough of it. The old fella who started this café was looking to sell out and retire, and

I happened to be passing through town at the right time to buy the place from him. Been here ever since."

There was a lot more to the story than that, of course, but Mac didn't care to go into detail. Nobody here in Hannigan's Hill knew the whole truth about him, and he would just as soon keep it that way.

It didn't make sense to go around asking for trouble.

Judge Trent rattled his newspaper as he closed and folded it. As he stood up, Mac asked, "Is there anything else I can do for you, Your Honor?"

"You might tell that friend of yours he should be more careful about what he writes. There are laws against spreading scurrilous lies about people."

"I'm sure Albert knows that, Judge."

Trent slapped the folded newspaper down on the table he had just vacated. "You couldn't tell that from his editorials." The judge put on his hat and jerked his head in a curt nod. "Good day, Mr. McKenzie."

"Yes, sir. You come on back anytime you want."

Trent said "Hmmph" again and left the café. Mac and Luke Jensen were alone in the place now. Luke looked over his shoulder at the window where Trent was still visible as he walked away.

"The judge seemed a mite upset about something he read in the paper."

"The editor had a column in there about how it doesn't look good for the local representatives of the law to be tied so closely, businesswise, to the area's leading citizen."

"You're talking about Ezra Hannigan."

Mac frowned. "If you're new in town, how did you know that?"

"I may have only ridden in a short time ago, but I've heard talk already. I'd heard of Hannigan, too, but only as a successful rancher."

"He certainly is that," Mac said. "The Rocking H is the biggest spread in these parts. Hannigan either owns outright or has a stake in more than half the businesses here in town, too."

"But not this café."

Luke didn't make it sound like a question, but Mac answered it, anyway. "No, sir. His finger's not in that pie you just ate or anything else I serve here."

"I'm glad to hear that. Don't really care for fingers in pie." Luke paused. "The judge and the marshal work for him more than they do for the town, is that it?"

"How do I know anything I say won't get back to them?"

"As you pointed out, I'm new in town. When I came in here was the first time I ever laid eyes on the judge. I've never met Ezra Hannigan. I talked to Marshal Bowen a little, but I wouldn't say we're bosom friends. Mostly, our conversation consisted of him warning me not to interfere with the little necktie party he had going on."

"Thad Crawford."

"That's right. My prisoner and I came along just at the right time . . . or the wrong time, if you want to look at it that way . . . to witness some of that."

Mac hesitated a few seconds more, then said, "My gut tells me I can trust you, Luke. You're just passing through. You don't have any interest in stirring up trouble."

"None at all," Luke agreed. "Anyway, I'm starting to get the feeling that you folks here in Hannigan's Hill already have more than your share."

"You've got that right. This used to be a pretty good place to live until—"

The door opening interrupted what Mac was about to say. He looked up, saw a familiar figure coming in, and said, "Hello, Jessie."

Jessie Whitmore moved a few steps deeper into the café, then stopped and looked at Luke Jensen, who had turned halfway around on the stool to see who the newcomer was.

"You," Jessie said with obvious distaste in her voice.

Chapter 6

The attractive blond woman Luke had last seen going into the *Chronicle* office now stood in the café, glaring at him. She had taken his advice and put on a coat before coming up the street, he noted.

"Ma'am," he said as he lifted a hand and ticked his forefinger against the brim of his pushed-back hat. "It's good to see you again, but I suspect the feeling isn't mutual."

"Hold on a minute," Mac said. "You two know each other?"

"We spoke briefly," Luke said, "but we haven't been introduced."

"I was watching from the porch of the newspaper office," the blonde said. Mac had called her Jessie, Luke recalled. The name suited her. "This man stood by and did nothing while Bowen and his killers hanged Thad Crawford. He just rode on and didn't even look back."

"I thought we agreed that was the only sensible thing I could have done," Luke said.

"And we also agreed that I still didn't like it."

"No offense, ma'am, but my hide is more important to me than what you like or don't like."

"What can I do for you, Jessie?" Mac asked, sounding like he wanted to head this off before it turned from minor wrangling into a full-fledged argument.

"Albert wanted to know if you'd be able to help us tonight. We're going to bring out an extra edition of the paper this week."

"Because of the Crawford hanging?"

Jessie's chin lifted. "Someone has to point out the injustice of it. I'm not sure anyone else in this town is brave enough to do that."

Mac sighed and then he nodded. "Sure, I'll give you a hand," he said. "I'll come on down to the *Chronicle* office just as soon as I'm done here and close up for the evening."

"Thank you, Mac." Jessie smiled. "We'll get printer's ink running in your veins before we're done."

"I don't reckon that's very likely. I've already got too much gravy flowing through there, after all those years next to a chuckwagon campfire."

Jessie threw another chilly glance in Luke's direction, smiled again at Mac, and opened the door to go back outside. When she had closed it behind her, Mac said to Luke, "Sorry about that. Jessie's not exactly the shy, retiring type. If she's got something on her mind, she says it."

"Nothing wrong with that. I've found that a woman's opinion is nearly always just as good as a man's. Sometimes better, now and then." Luke took a sip of his coffee. "I'm guessing here, but is the lady married to the editor of the local newspaper?"

"That's right. Albert and Jessie Whitmore. They came to Hannigan's Hill not long after I did and started the paper."

"And they don't like all the power that Ezra Hannigan wields around here through the judge and the marshal."

For a moment, Mac didn't respond. Then he said, "Look, since we're alone here for the moment, I'll tell you how things are around here, Luke. But I'd just as soon you didn't repeat any of this or mention that you got it from me."

"I don't have any reason to."

"Like I said, this town used to be a pretty decent place to live. Ezra Hannigan was the biggest, richest rancher in the area, sure, and he had a stake in the town's businesses, but for the most part, he left folks alone. You used to hear stories now and then about how he cut a wide swath through here back when he first came to the area. He was one of the first settlers in these parts, and in those days, a man had to be pretty much a law unto himself if he wanted to carve anything out of the wilderness. With the Indians and outlaws around, he couldn't do anything else."

Luke nodded. "I remember those days. A man sometimes had to be pretty rough just to survive, let alone make something of himself."

"That's right. But times had changed some. The Indians haven't raised as much hell in recent years. It's sort of like Little Big Horn was a high-water mark for them, and they've been losing ground ever since. As for outlaws and rustlers, well, Hannigan put together such a salty crew that nobody wanted to cross him. It was said that most of the men who rode for him had heard the owl hoot quite a few times themselves. Taking all that into account, Hannigan didn't really need to ride roughshod over anybody anymore."

"But he did, anyway?" Luke guessed.

Mac shook his head. "Not for a while. Everything was peaceful when I got here. But then, not long after that, Mildred Hannigan took sick with a fever and died."

"Hannigan's wife."

"Yep. I wouldn't say that Hannigan changed, exactly, after that. It's more like he didn't have Mrs. Hannigan around to keep a tight rein on his worst instincts anymore. When old Judge Dunaway retired, Hannigan used his influence in the territorial capital to get John Lee Trent appointed to the position. Before that, Trent was Hannigan's partner in the general store."

"Wait a minute," Luke said. "The judge isn't even a lawyer?"

"Oh, he read for the law, years ago, but never practiced. He went into business, instead. But he knows the law well enough, I reckon. He just applies it the way Hannigan wants him to."

Luke rubbed his chin and said, "I'm guessing Bowen didn't use to be the marshal, either."

Mac shook his head. "Nope. Hannigan pressured the town council to fire Nate Driscoll, who'd been wearing the badge ever since the town was founded. He said we needed new blood in the job. That new blood was Verne Bowen, who'd been Hannigan's foreman on the Rocking H."

"This sounds like a situation as ripe for corruption as any I've ever heard of," Luke said.

"And that's the way it's worked out, too. Hannigan gets what he wants . . . and he wants everything."

"So Crawford was telling the truth about why he was being hanged?"

"You talked to him before they strung him up?"

Luke's mouth tightened into a grim line. "He begged me to help him. He said they had framed him for some soiled dove's murder, and all but accused the marshal and his men of killing the girl so they'd have an excuse to hang him."

"That's probably the way it happened," Mac said softly. "Hannigan tried to buy Crawford's ranch. It has some good water on it that Hannigan wants. But Crawford wasn't interested in selling. He started losing stock, but he still wasn't willing to let the place go."

"So they came up with a way to take it from him." Luke shook his head. "He sounded like he was telling the truth. But your friend Mrs. Whitmore was right. I rode away and let them go on with it."

"One man against seven or eight, and those men hardened killers? You couldn't have stopped them, Luke. You'd have just gotten yourself killed."

"That's what I told Mrs. Whitmore." Luke seemed to peer off into the distance for a second. "That's what I've been trying to tell myself."

For a moment, silence reigned in the café. Mac stood behind the counter, his hands resting flat on it. Luke sat on the stool, looking like a bad taste had replaced the sweetness of the peach pie in his mouth. He pushed the unfinished cup of coffee away.

"What's going to happen when the Whitmores publish their paper and condemn Hannigan?" he asked.

"Hard to say. Hannigan has left them alone so far. I reckon he's worried about pushing too hard. He has friends in the capital, and he doesn't want to look bad in their eyes. But he's a prideful man, and he'll only take so much. I don't figure he has much respect for the press, either."

"Then by helping them publish that extra edition, you might be letting yourself in for trouble, too."

"Wouldn't be the first time," Mac said.

Luke could believe that. Mac was a little younger than Luke, but still had the look of a seasoned frontiersman about him. If he had gone on those cattle drives, as he'd said, then he had fought Indians, rustlers, bad weather, and all sorts of other dangers. There wouldn't have been any avoiding them.

But hard cases like Verne Bowen and his deputies, Mac might not have faced their like before. Luke had, though. Plenty of times.

He thought he might not be moving on from Hannigan's Hill quite as quickly as he had intended.

Chapter 7

After asking Mac where the telegraph office was located, Luke left the café and walked farther along the street. In towns where the railroad had arrived, the Western Union office often was located inside the train station, but Hannigan's Hill didn't have a rail line yet. Luke didn't know if there might be a spur built here someday, but for now, the telegraph office stood between a large general mercantile and a saddle-maker's shop.

As he went in, he wondered if the telegrapher worked for Ezra Hannigan on the side, too. In this case, that shouldn't matter. He wasn't going to say anything in the wire he sent that ought to be of interest to the cattle baron.

The telegrapher stood behind the window opening in the partition that divided the room. He said, "Howdy, mister. Need to send a wire?" The man wore an eye-shade for some reason, as telegraphers often did, although he was inside and the day was cloudy, to start with.

"That's right," Luke said. He went to the counter, where a stack of telegraph flimsies and some stubby pencils lay. It took him only a minute to print out the message that he addressed to Senator Jonas Creed in care of the United States Senate in Washington, D.C. The Senate was in session at the moment, so that was where Creed would be found:

HAVE CAUGHT ETHAN STALLINGS STOP HOLDING PRISONER HANNIGAN'S HILL WYOMING TERRITORY STOP PLEASE ADVISE NEXT MOVE STOP LUKE JENSEN

The telegrapher counted out the message, told Luke the price, and scooped up the coins he pushed through the opening.

"I'll send this right now if you want to wait for a reply, Mr. . . ." The man glanced at the telegram. "Jensen."

"It may take a while to locate my party and deliver it to him, so I'm not expecting a reply right away. What's the best hotel in town?"

"Only got two, the Gem and the Northern. The Gem ain't exactly a gem, if you catch my drift. I'd stay at the Northern, if it was me."

"Thanks. What about a livery stable? Got more than one of those?"

"Nope, just the one. Next block, other side of the street. The Hannigan's Hill Livery."

"Ezra Hannigan own it?"

"Well, as a matter of fact, Mr. Hannigan does."

"What about the Northern Hotel?"

"That too. He makes sure the folks who run it keep a nice place, too."

Luke nodded as if glad to hear that. He said, "When you get a reply, you can send it over to the Northern. If I'm not there, I'll check in pretty regularlike."

"Yes, sir, Mr. Jensen."

Luke fetched the two horses from the hitch rack in front of the marshal's office and turned them over to a middle-aged hostler at the livery. Then, carrying his Winchester, his two Remingtons in holsters, he walked across the street to the Northern Hotel, signed the register for the slick-haired clerk, and got a room key from the man. The Northern's lobby was nicely furnished with several armchairs, a few throw rugs on the floor, and a couple of potted plants. The room on the second floor was small, but neatly kept, and when Luke pushed on the bed's mattress with a hand, it felt like it was in good shape. The telegrapher's recommendation had been a good one.

Luke took his turnip watch from his pocket and flipped it open. Too early to start thinking about supper, especially with the late lunch he'd had. Maybe he would take a better look around the settlement.

When he found himself in front of the Lucky Shot Saloon, he wasn't surprised. Irish Mahoney had promised him a free drink, and even if she hadn't, beautiful redheads held a powerful attraction for him.

Because of the chilly weather, the batwings were fastened back to the walls on either side of the entrance. The regular doors were closed, but Luke could still hear music coming from inside the saloon. The big front windows were steamed up so that he couldn't see very well through them, but he made out movement inside. Seemed like there was some frivolity going on. On a gray, gloomy day like this, made gloomier by the hanging he had witnessed, he could use a little frivolity, he thought.

He opened the right-hand door and went into the saloon.

The warm air pushed at him, thick with smells: whiskey, beer, bay rum, lilac water, tobacco, sawdust, and a less pleasant, faint undercurrent of unwashed flesh and human waste. The same assortment that Luke had encountered in scores of other frontier saloons. The Lucky Shot smelled a little better than some, but there was only so much you could do when a bunch of hardworking, hard-drinking men were crowded into a confined space with soiled doves, who covered up their own scents with cheap perfume.

The place wasn't packed, but it was doing good business despite the early hour. Men stood at the bar drinking, several poker games were going on, a roulette wheel spun and clicked on one side of the room, and a man played the piano that sat against one of the sidewalls, banging out tunes with more enthusiasm than skill.

As Luke looked around, he spotted four men sitting at a table toward the back of the room. They weren't playing cards. The half-empty bottle and the glasses in front of them testified that they were here to drink, and nothing else. He recognized them from Hangman's

Hill—and would have even without the badges they wore. They were some of Marshal Verne Bowen's deputies.

"Luke, there you are."

He turned to see who had greeted him and saw Irish Mahoney making her way through the tables toward him.

"Miss Mahoney," he said, nodding to her.

"I'm glad to see that you took me up on my invitation. Will you be staying with us tonight?"

"Ah, I'm afraid not. I have a room at the Northern Hotel."

A disappointed pout pursed her lips. "I'm sorry to hear that. I hoped we'd have your company all evening."

"Well, just because I don't spend the night doesn't mean I won't be here for a while. This seems to be a lively place."

"Oh, it is." She linked her arm with his and steered him toward the polished hardwood bar. "We have all sorts of things to offer for your pleasure. What do you say we start with a drink?"

"Sounds good to me."

When they reached the bar, she said to the man behind it, "Bourbon for our new friend, Grant."

"Yes, ma'am, Miss Irish, coming up," the bartender replied.

"From my personal bottle," Irish added.

Grant nodded and reached under the bar to take a bottle from a shelf. Luke saw the label and recognized it as an excellent brand. Of course, just because a label was stuck on a bottle didn't mean what was inside was the genuine article. He had a hunch that Irish wouldn't try to pass off inferior goods as the real thing, though.

Nor did she expect him to drink alone. The bartender set two shot glasses on the bar and poured a couple of fingers of bourbon into them. Irish picked up the glass closest to her and raised it.

"Welcome to Hannigan's Hill, Luke. May your stay here be a pleasant one."

"It's already improving," Luke said. He clinked his glass against hers, and they both drank. Luke's hunch had been right: The bourbon was smooth and potent and went down well. It was what the label claimed it to be.

"That's right, your visit didn't get off to a very nice start, did it? The first thing you saw was that hanging."

Luke shrugged. "I've seen hangings before. Some are worse than others. Sometimes the man being hanged has it coming."

"Do you think that was the case today?"

"I don't know the particulars," Luke said. "I've heard some talk, that's all. I wouldn't want to venture an opinion."

"But you have one. An opinion, that is."

"Opinions are like rear ends. Everybody's got one."

Irish laughed and said, "Well, you're discreet, I'll give you that. You're not going to say too much because you think I might go and repeat it to the marshal."

"The two of you seemed friendly earlier."

Irish signaled for the bartender to put bourbon in the glasses again. "We've been friendly in the past," she said as she picked up her drink. "Maybe not quite as friendly as Verne would like to be. But I stay out of the law business and he stays out of the saloon business. It's an arrangement that works out satisfactorily most of the time."

"I can see how it would," Luke said. He picked up his drink and put his hand in his pocket to dig out a coin to pay for it, but Irish put her other hand on his arm.

"Mr. Jensen's money is no good here tonight, Grant," she told the bartender. "At least not for drinks. If he wants to sit in on any of the games or partake of other . . . entertainment . . . that'll be up to him."

"Yes, ma'am," Grant said.

"I'm obliged to you," Luke said to Irish. "That's very generous."

"I could learn to enjoy your company," she said. "I'm hoping you'll spend the evening with us."

"I might just do that."

He had nowhere else he had to be. If a reply came to his telegram to Senator Creed, it would be delivered to the hotel and he could pick it up later. He wasn't leaving Hannigan's Hill until the next day, at the earliest. After talking to Mac McKenzie, he had pondered staying around for longer than that, but he was reconsidering the idea. If he involved himself in this settlement's problems, he would be just asking for trouble. The citizens needed to figure out a way to handle Ezra Hannigan for themselves.

Of course, that was going to be difficult with all the gun-wolves Hannigan had working for him . . .

He put that out of his mind for now, and when Irish

suggested that they take the bottle and move to a table, Luke didn't argue with her. They sat down, chatted idly, and sipped on the whiskey.

While they were doing that, Luke noticed one of the deputies get up from the table where he was sitting with the others. The man went over to a side door, opened it, and slipped out of the saloon into the fading light outside.

That made the skin on the back of Luke's neck prickle. He could leave the Lucky Shot, but that would feel too much like running away from potential trouble and that wasn't something he was in the habit of doing.

Instead, he said, "Tell me about the situation in town."

"What do you mean?"

"You know how it feels when a big thunderstorm is about to break? How there's something in the air that might bust loose at any time? That's the impression I've been getting ever since I rode in."

Irish shook her head. "Things around here are just like they have been for quite a while."

"That's not what I've heard. Ezra Hannigan owns half the town already and wants to own the other half. He's got his eye on all the range in these parts that he doesn't control, too."

"That's just gossip," Irish snapped.

"That hanging I saw this afternoon was more than gossip."

"Thad Crawford was tried and found guilty in a court of law."

"Do you believe he was guilty?"

"What I believe or don't believe doesn't matter a damn," Irish said. "The jury said he was guilty and Judge Trent handed down the sentence. Simple as that."

"It gets more complicated when you consider that Crawford controlled a water source Hannigan wanted. Add in Hannigan's close ties with the judge and the influence he probably wields over anybody who was on the jury. Earlier, when you were talking to the marshal, you made it sound like you thought the whole thing was pretty rotten."

Irish splashed more whiskey in her glass and tossed back the drink. "Like I told you," she said, "what I think doesn't matter."

"Or maybe Bowen set you straight and told you to be careful what you say, especially around outsiders."

Instead of flushing with anger, Irish's creamy skin became even paler. But her green eyes sparked as she said, "I won't let any man tell me what to do, not even Verne Bowen."

Luke wasn't sure he believed that, but he didn't have a chance to ponder the question. At that moment, one of the doors at the entrance opened abruptly and a bulky figure stomped into the saloon, bringing a gust of frigid air with him.

Marshal Verne Bowen glared around the room. When his gaze landed on the table where Luke and Irish sat, he started toward them and demanded in a rumbling voice, "What the hell is this?"

Chapter 8

Bowen's arrival didn't surprise Luke. He had been expecting the marshal to put in an appearance ever since he'd seen the deputy sneaking out of the saloon. He was sure the man had made a beeline for the marshal's office to tell Bowen that Luke was over here sharing drinks and getting cozy with Irish Mahoney.

It had been pretty obvious from the way Bowen treated Irish earlier that he considered her his property. Luke had no doubt that was the kind of hombre Bowen was.

As Bowen advanced on them, Irish glanced at Luke and said quietly, "I don't need any trouble in here. I don't want the place busted up."

"Won't be any trouble as far as I'm concerned," Luke replied with a shake of his head. "We're just sitting here, talking and drinking. Nothing wrong with that."

"There's a man to your right."

Luke glanced in that direction. The side door was over there, and it had been eased open again. The deputy who had left earlier was back. He leaned against the wall and crossed his arms. He had drawn his gun and held it in his right hand. Luke saw the barrel sticking up from the crook of the deputy's left elbow.

A quick look in the other direction revealed that the remaining deputies had pushed their chairs back from the table and were watching closely, ready to spring to their feet if necessary. They hadn't drawn their guns, but it would take them only a second to do so.

"You wouldn't stand a chance," Irish said. "And I'd have a lot of bullet holes to patch up, too."

Luke had to chuckle at that. "I'll try to keep the damage to a minimum," he said dryly. "No shooting if I can help it."

Bowen reached the table and came to a stop next to it. His face was flushed as his gaze swung from Irish to Luke and back to the redhead again.

"Since when do you sit and drink with every saddle tramp who rides into town, Irish?"

"I sit and drink with whoever I please, Verne," she said coolly. "This is my saloon, after all."

"It's partly your saloon. Have you forgotten your silent partner?"

Luke kept his face carefully expressionless. He had a pretty good idea who that silent partner was. Irish hadn't said anything to indicate that Ezra Hannigan had a stake in the Lucky Shot, but she'd had no reason to reveal that, either. She didn't owe Luke the truth or anything else.

Worry lurked in Irish's green eyes. "There's nothing

going on here, Verne," she insisted. "Mr. Jensen and I
were talking, that's all."

She waved a hand to indicate their surroundings.
The saloon had gone quiet when Bowen came in. The
men standing at the bar or sitting at tables just looked
on nervously, unsure what was going to happen. Poker
games, mugs of beer, and shot glasses of whiskey were
all forgotten for the moment. The girls who worked
here, all of them in short, spangled dresses, garters,
and stockings, were equally wary and appeared ready
to hit the floor if bullets started flying around. The two
bartenders held themselves in similar stances.

"With all these people around," Irish continued, "I
couldn't have gotten up to anything improper even if I
wanted to. Which I don't."

"You didn't invite Jensen up to your room?"

"I most certainly did not."

To tell the truth, Luke believed she had been hinting
about that very thing, but she'd never come out and
said it and he hadn't suggested it, either.

He said now, "Marshal, I'm not looking to cause
trouble. Like I told you, I just want to keep my prisoner
locked up until I find out what I'm supposed to do with
him. As soon as I do, we'll be out of your hair."

"You'd damned well better be. I'm already regret-
ting that I agreed to let you keep him in my jail. How
big is the bounty on him, anyway?"

Luke wasn't sure he wanted to reveal that, but it was
entirely possible Bowen had a reward dodger on Stallings in his desk. The senator had seen to it that those
wanted posters were flooded all over the frontier. So if
Luke lied, Bowen might well know it.

"Twenty-five hundred dollars," he said. That was a fourth of the amount Stallings had swindled Senator Creed out of.

Bowen gave a low whistle. "I see why you want to collect on him. That's a lot of money. More than some men will see working their whole lives."

"I've already sent a wire back east to let the man who posted the reward know that Stallings has been captured," Luke said. He hoped that would head off any ambitious idea Bowen or anybody else in town might get. "When I hear back from him, we'll be moving on. In the meantime"—he started to get to his feet—"I suppose I'll go back over to the hotel and wait."

Bowen put out a hand to stop him. "No, you don't have to do that," he said. "I reckon maybe I got a little hot under the collar for no reason. I'm fond of Irish here. As beautiful as she is, you can see with your own eyes why I get a little jealous, whether I have any reason to be or not."

"I suppose that's understandable," Luke allowed.

"So the two of you just go on talking, if you want to. Irish, I'm sorry I busted in here like this."

"Forget it," she said in a curt voice.

"Join us for a drink?" Luke said. "We'll have to get another bottle, but—"

"No, that's all right. It'll be dark soon, and I have evening rounds to make. By the way, Jensen, were you able to make arrangements to feed that prisoner of yours?"

"Mac McKenzie said he'd take him something later."

"All right, then. Sounds like everything's squared away." Bowen nodded to Irish. "I'll see you later."

"Sure," she said.

Bowen left the saloon. The piano player started pounding the ivories again, and the other customers resumed drinking, talking, and laughing. Cards were dealt and the roulette wheel spun.

Irish Mahoney said, "Don't trust him. When Verne turns calm and reasonable like that, you know he's up to something."

"I kind of had that hunch," Luke said, "but I'm glad to get confirmation that it's right. I'll keep my eyes open." He paused and then added, "I always do."

"If you have any in the back of your head, you'd better use them, too. That was a nice touch, telling him you'd already been in touch with the fellow who's offering the reward, but I wouldn't put it past him to try to figure out a way to get his hands on it."

"I intend to be careful."

Irish seemed to accept that assurance. She said, "Do you want something to eat? We can't compete with McKenzie's food, but we have some roast beef in the back, along with bread and cheese and a jar of pickled eggs."

"I had a late lunch," Luke explained. "But I've also had enough whiskey that I probably ought to put something solid in there with it."

"Wait right here," she said with a smile. "I'll bring you a sandwich."

"And maybe some coffee, if you have it."

"There's always a pot of coffee on the stove in the back," she told him.

Night settled down on Hannigan's Hill as Luke sat there for the next couple of hours, enjoying the food, the coffee, and Irish's company. She had to get up and leave the table a few times to deal with saloon business, but she was never gone for long. The Lucky Shot got busier as darkness fell. Men who worked in town had closed their shops or finished their daily tasks. Cowboys who rode for the spreads outside of town came into the settlement for some excitement. Some of them were probably Ezra Hannigan's men, Luke supposed, but he didn't know who they were.

The deputies had left. Luke wasn't sorry to see them go. They had directed unfriendly stares toward him from time to time.

Finally he decided that he ought to head back to the hotel. It was possible he had gotten a reply to his wire by now, and if the telegrapher had done as Luke asked, he would have had it delivered to the Northern.

He drank the rest of the coffee in his cup and set it down, saying, "I'd best be going."

"I know you have a hotel room," Irish said, "but if you'd like to stay, I'm sure something can be arranged."

Half-a-dozen girls were working in the saloon. Luke had seen all of them go up and down the stairs to the second floor several times while he was here, accompanied each time by a different one of the saloon's patrons. He shook his head and said, "I'm sure the young ladies are lovely and quite friendly, but I don't think that would be a good idea."

For a second, he thought she was going to offer herself in their place, but then she sat back and said, "Maybe another time."

"Maybe." Luke got to his feet. "I don't mind paying for the food."

"No, it's all on the house." Irish smiled. "Honestly, you're the most interesting man to ride into this town in a long time, Luke Jensen. I've enjoyed spending time with you."

"It's been a pleasurable evening," Luke agreed. "I'll try to stop in again before I ride out."

"I'd like that."

Luke nodded to her, pulled his hat down, and headed for the entrance. The wind had picked up and grown even chillier, he discovered as he stepped outside and pulled the door closed behind him. He paused to turn up his jacket's sheepskin collar. From the feel of the air, he wouldn't be surprised if there were a few snowflakes by morning, but he didn't think there would be an actual snowstorm.

Lights glowed in a number of buildings along the street, but he didn't see anyone else moving. The cold was keeping everybody indoors, he thought as he started walking at an angle across the street toward the Northern Hotel.

He hadn't made it halfway there when he heard a sudden rush of footsteps behind him and knew he was under attack.

Chapter 9

The men must have been waiting in the alley next to the saloon for him to emerge, Luke realized as he whirled to meet the assailants, but the thought was only in the back of his mind. His attention was focused on dealing with this threat, which he'd been halfway expecting when he left the Lucky Shot.

In the poor light, it was difficult to be sure how many men were charging at him. They were only vague shapes in the shadows. Five or six, he guessed.

He figured they were all wearing deputy badges, too, or at least had the badges in their pockets. As Irish had hinted, Verne Bowen had turned reasonable during their earlier confrontation because he'd decided to strike back later in some other manner.

This was it, Luke was sure.

Those thoughts flashed through his mind in the time it took for him to set his feet. He heard something whip-

ping through the air as the man closest to him swung
some sort of club at his head.

Luke ducked under the sweeping blow. The miss
brought the man close enough for Luke to step in and
lift an uppercut that caught him under the chin. The
punch made the man's teeth click together and rocked
his head back. He came up off the ground for a second
and fell back, right into the path of two of the other men.

That caused them to stumble and break off their
charge for a moment. But the other two were able to
veer around and continue their attack. Luke tried to
weave aside, but he wasn't able to completely avoid a
swiftly swung fist. The blow clipped him on the side of
the head, knocked his hat off, and made him take a step
to his right.

In that second as he caught his balance, a stray beam
of light from a lamp down the street illuminated the
face of the man who'd just struck him. The attacker's
hat was pulled low and a bandanna was tied across the
lower half of his face, concealing his identity. Luke
thought the others probably wore masks, too.

That did nothing to convince him they weren't
Marshal Bowen's hardcase deputies. At the moment,
who they were didn't matter. He flung up his left arm
to block another punch, but the second man crowded in
and hooked a fist to his ribs. That knocked Luke back
in the other direction, putting him well within reach of
a punch that smacked into his jaw.

The man on whom he had landed the uppercut was
still down, but the two who had tripped over him had
scrambled back to their feet and surrounded Luke. He

tried to twist away from them, but a man grabbed him from behind, pinning his arms to his sides.

"I got him!" the man told his companions.

Luke jerked his head back and rammed his skull into the man's face. The man yelled in pain as blood spurted from his nose. But his grip didn't loosen and Luke wasn't able to pull free.

Another attacker closed in from the front, fists raised and poised to dish out some punishment. Luke got his right leg up and drove the heel of his boot into the man's belly. The man doubled over and staggered back.

"Watch it!" one of the other men yelled. "Get him on the ground! We'll stomp him!"

The shouts and the other sounds of battle should have drawn some attention by now. Maybe they had, but it didn't appear that anybody was coming to investigate the commotion. They sure as blazes weren't coming to help him, Luke knew. Probably the citizens of Hannigan's Hill were too scared of Bowen and his deputies to cross them. If he was going to get out of this predicament, he would have to do it himself.

Unfortunately, even though he had managed to whittle the odds down to four to one, that wasn't anywhere near enough. These men were wiry and rawhide-tough, and they had plenty of experience at brawling, just like he did. No matter how desperately he fought, they were going to put him on the ground sooner or later, and when they did, the kicking and stomping would commence.

And he would be lucky to survive it.

* * *

Mac's Place stayed open fairly late because there was always a chance some rancher who'd come into town to pick up supplies would want supper before starting home, or a cowboy who'd had too much to drink might want a cup of coffee and maybe some pie to help him sober up.

Typically, though, Mac didn't close up himself. Alf Karlsson, a middle-aged Swede who had decided that he wasn't cut out to be a sodbuster, worked in the evenings, keeping the food warm that Mac had prepared earlier and dishing it out to any late customers. So when the supper rush was over, Mac rolled down his shirtsleeves, took off his apron, and replaced it with a lightweight coat. He filled a bowl with stew from the pot on the stove, filled another bowl with beans, set them on a tray, along with a couple of chunks of corn bread wrapped in paper, and told Alf, "I'm going to take this over to the jail for a prisoner."

He didn't need to take coffee. Marshal Bowen would have a pot on the stove and an extra cup the prisoner could use. It wouldn't be as good as the coffee Mac brewed, of course, but that was another reason not to commit crimes and wind up behind bars.

He put his hat on and left the café. The marshal's office and jail were in the next block on the same side of the street. A light burned in the office window. Mac didn't knock, just opened the door with his free hand as he balanced the tray with his other.

Marshal Verne Bowen sat behind the desk with his feet propped up. He was smoking a cigar and had a glass with amber liquid in front of him. He lowered his boots to the floor and stood up as Mac came in.

"McKenzie," he said by way of curt greeting. "Brought supper for Jensen's prisoner?"

"That's right."

"What do you think of him?"

"The prisoner? Haven't met him yet."

"I meant Jensen."

"Oh. He's all right, I suppose. We didn't really talk all that much."

There was no reason for Bowen to know that he and Luke Jensen had discussed the problems in Hannigan's Hill and the surrounding area.

"He's a bounty hunter, you know."

Mac nodded. "I got that impression."

As a matter of fact, he had good reason to dislike bounty hunters, or at least he had had good reason at one time in his life. Not in recent years, though. And no matter what Luke's profession was, Mac liked him. He seemed like an honest, forthright, capable hombre. Just the sort who would make a good citizen . . . other than having too much sense to hang around this town any longer than he had to.

Bowen puffed on his cigar and said, "I don't trust him or have any use for him. I'll be glad when he's gone, along with that prisoner of his. The man strikes me as a troublemaker."

"Well, I sure hope not, Marshal," Mac said mildly. "All right to take this on back?"

Bowen jerked a thumb toward the cellblock door. "Yeah, go ahead. It's not locked."

Mac went into the cellblock, which was dimly lit by

a candle in a holder sitting on a small wall shelf. The man in the first cell was stretched out on the bunk, but he swung his legs to the floor and stood up as Mac came in.

"Is that my supper?" he asked.

"Yep."

"About time. I haven't had much to eat today. What is it?"

"Stew, beans, and corn bread."

The prisoner's face fell. He was a compactly built man in his thirties with reddish brown hair. "I was hoping for maybe a steak."

"Folks behind bars can't be choosers," Mac said. He passed the tray through the opening in the barred cell door designed for that.

"Don't I get a spoon?"

"The marshal doesn't allow it. The chunks of beef and potatoes and carrots are big enough to fish out with your fingers, and you can drink the liquid. There's plenty of corn bread to sop up what's left."

The prisoner scowled. "What about coffee?"

"I'll tell the marshal you want some, but that'll be up to him whether he feels like going to the trouble."

"These accommodations sure leave something to be desired. I remember a hotel where I stayed in Chicago. Fanciest place you ever did see. The floor in the lobby was made out of marble, and they had these crystal chandeliers—"

Mac remembered Luke telling him that this confidence artist was the talkative sort. He didn't want to hear about any hotel in Chicago, so he interrupted and said, "Sounds like a nice place. Give the bowl and the tray to the marshal or one of the deputies when you're done. I'll collect them in the morning when I bring your breakfast."

He and Luke hadn't discussed providing breakfast for the prisoner, but Mac figured it was likely that would be the plan. As the prisoner carried the tray to the bunk and sat down to eat, Mac left the cellblock. He closed the door behind him.

"All right, Marshal, that's taken care of," he told Bowen. "The fella would like some coffee, if you're of a mind to oblige him."

"I'll get around to it," Bowen replied in a surly voice. "Maybe. You know, the least Jensen could do is offer to cut me in for a little of that reward, since I'm helping him out."

"Maybe you should suggest that." The last place Mac wanted to be was between the marshal and a bounty hunter, so he nodded to Bowen and left the office before the man could complain about anything else.

He had gone only a few steps when somebody yelled in the night, not far away.

The shout came from down the street, toward the Lucky Shot Saloon. Mac glanced back at the marshal's office. The door and the windows were closed, but even so, Bowen should have heard that yell and come out to investigate. Another man shouted something about stomping somebody.

Mac's keen eyes spotted the knot of men struggling in the shadows along the street. He wasn't sure what was going on, but from the sound of it, he guessed that several men were attacking a lone victim. That would explain the way the group was kind of bunched up in a circle that swayed back and forth. Somebody was in for a real beating.

And having been on the receiving end of such brutal violence in his life, Mac's sympathy immediately went to the man who'd been jumped.

He looked again through the front window of the marshal's office. Bowen was still sitting behind the desk, smoking and sipping whiskey. Mac knew that the smartest thing for him to do would be to go back to the boardinghouse where he rented a room and pretend he had never noticed a thing.

Problem was, he wasn't good at pretending, and he had never been one to turn his back on trouble.

Foolish or not, he trotted toward the fight. As he came closer, he made out one man lying on the ground, moving around a little, apparently only half-conscious. Four more had another man surrounded and were trying to wrestle him to the ground. As they struggled, they swayed through a small patch of light that spilled from a nearby window. Mac felt a shock go through him as he recognized the victim of the attack.

Luke Jensen.

At the same time, he wasn't all that surprised. Luke was new in town. He might have done something to make an enemy out of the marshal. Those could be some of Bowen's hired hard cases trying to get Luke down so they could stomp the guts out of him. Mac wouldn't put that past the bunch at all.

He tripped on something and nearly fell as he approached. Looking down at his feet, he saw a piece of two-by-four, about three feet long. Without thinking too much about what he was doing, he reached down, picked up the board, and stepped closer. He swung the lumber as hard as he could and whaled one of the attackers across the back.

Chapter 10

Luke barely caught a glimpse of a shadowy figure rushing up behind the men surrounding him. He thought for a split second it was another enemy joining the attack, but then a loud crack sounded as the newcomer slammed a board across the back of one of the men.

That unexpected blow knocked the man forward and made him cry out in surprise and pain. He crashed into Luke and knocked him backward. Because of that impact, the man holding on to Luke couldn't stay on his feet and fell. In fact, all five of them went down and sprawled in the dirt.

As Luke felt the grip on him loosen, he drove an elbow back into his captor's midsection. The man grunted and let go. Luke slapped his hands on the ground and pushed himself into a roll that took him clear of the tangled mess of arms and legs.

He came up and lifted a boot into the face of a man who was trying to clamber to his feet. The kick knocked the man onto his back. He slid a few inches before coming to a stop. Luke met the jaw of another man with a roundhouse right as that hombre tried to get up. He went right back down.

The man who had come to his rescue sank a fist into the belly of a third attacker, then clubbed his hands together and swung them in a crushing blow to the jaw as the man doubled over. They were all down now, except for Luke and the newcomer, and only one was very coherent. He grabbed at the collars of his companions and urged them to back off.

"Come on!" he said. "Let's get outta here!"

Slowly, awkwardly, the men shoved themselves backward, crablike, until they could stagger to their feet. Luke stood there with his fists clenched, a part of him wanting to shout defiantly at them to come on and try again.

But that would have been a foolish thing to do, since he was bruised and battered and still outnumbered, even with his unknown ally beside him. Better to let them go, which is what he did. The attackers retreated unsteadily into the shadows and then disappeared up an impenetrably black alley.

"How bad are you hurt?"

Luke recognized the voice that asked the question. He already had a hunch as to the identity of the man who had come to his aid, and that confirmed it. He turned to Mac McKenzie and said, "I don't think anything is broken. I'll be stiff and sore in the morning . . . Hell, I'm already stiff and sore . . . but that's nothing new. At my age, I'm stiff and sore when I get up every morning."

"Do you know who jumped you?"

"Not for sure, but I could make a guess."

"Yeah, so could I. Come on over to the café with me. We'll take a look and make sure you're not hurt worse than you think you are."

"How did you happen to come along and give me a hand?" Luke asked as he looked around for his hat. Seeing a dark shape on the ground that he thought might be it, he bent to pick it up. He was right, but when he straightened with the hat in his hand, his head spun crazily for a second.

Mac must have noticed that he was unsteady, because he put a hand on Luke's shoulder to brace him.

"I'd just delivered supper to your prisoner at the jail," he explained. "That's why I was in the right place at the right time."

Luke put his hat on, checked to make sure his Remingtons were still in their holsters, and said, "Might be more like the wrong place at the wrong time for you when Marshal Bowen finds out what you did."

"Let me worry about that," Mac said. "Come on."

Luke's head had stopped spinning enough so that he didn't stagger as he walked beside Mac toward the café. Mac didn't have to help him.

No customers were in the place. A middle-aged man Luke hadn't seen before was sweeping up. The fellow wore an apron and had thinning hair. A soup-strainer mustache drooped over both ends of his mouth. He stopped sweeping and leaned on the broom as he looked at Luke and Mac.

"You men look a mite rumpled up," he commented. He had a slight accent, which Luke thought was Swedish. "Did you run into trouble, Mac?"

Mac chuckled. "You could say that. Charged right into it, in fact." He nodded toward the man beside him. "Alf, this is Luke Jensen. Luke, meet Alf Karlsson. He gives me a hand around the place."

"Jensen, eh?" Alf looked a little wary. "A Dane."

Luke managed a weary smile. "Maybe if you go back far enough. My history is more Missouri Ozark hillbilly than Danish, as far as I'm concerned." He extended a hand. "It's good to meet you, Alf."

"I've heard some talk about you," Alf said as he shook hands. "You seem to have gotten on the wrong side of our local law. But that ain't necessarily a bad thing. Were Marshal Bowen and his deputies responsible for those bruises you've got startin' to show up?"

Luke rubbed his jaw, which was a little tender and swollen from the punches that had landed there. "I can't prove it, because I never saw their faces, but I'm convinced it was the deputies who jumped me."

Alf nodded. "More than likely. Bowen likes to sit back and have other folks do his dirty work for him. His boss, Ezra Hannigan, is the same way, only worse."

Mac said, "If anybody else was in here, Alf, I'd tell you to be careful about what you're saying. You don't need those sentiments getting back to Bowen."

Alf shrugged. "I ain't a-scared of Verne Bowen. He's a bully, and like all bullies, he's a coward at heart."

"That may well be true, but it doesn't mean he's not dangerous. Is there still coffee in the pot?"

"Sure. I ain't got around to dumpin' it out yet. By

now, it's liable to be strong enough to get up and walk around on its own hind legs, though."

Luke grinned and said, "That sounds like exactly what I need right now."

Mac got two cups and filled them when Alf waved off the offer of coffee for himself. Luke and Mac sat on stools at the counter. Luke sipped the potent brew and sighed in appreciation. He felt its bracing effect going through him.

"It's a little early yet, but go ahead and lock the door and pull the shades, Alf," Mac said. "I don't think we'll be doing any more business tonight."

Alf did so and turned out a couple of the lamps as well, leaving the café mostly in shadow, which was easier on Luke's eyes. Alf resumed sweeping, while Luke and Mac drank their coffee.

"Alf used to have a farm east of town," Mac explained. "He's sort of retired these days and helps me out."

Alf snorted. "'Retired,' my hind foot! It was a nice little homestead until Hannigan decided he needed it for extra range and hay."

"What are you talking about?" Mac asked. "I didn't know Hannigan had anything to do with you giving up farming."

"Well, like you said, a fella's got to be careful what he spouts off about. There's no tellin' who might hear him and go carryin' tales. There are a lot of folks in this town who are beholden to Ezra Hannigan in one way or another, and they might want to curry favor with him."

"That's true, I suppose."

Alf stopped sweeping and leaned on his broom again. "I put up with Hannigan's boys drivin' cattle across my land and tearin' up my crops. Figured that sooner or later, he'd get tired of tryin' to intimidate me and would give up on pryin' the place away from me. When they come raidin' at night and shot the windows outta my cabin, I just hit the floor and let it make me stubborner. But when they chucked a firebomb through one of those busted windows a few nights later, I'd had enough. I was able to keep the cabin from burnin' down, but just barely. If I'd been asleep . . . if I hadn't been sittin' up waitin' for trouble . . . I reckon there's a good chance I'd have burned to death and the place'd be nothin' but a heap of ashes now. I hated like hell to quit, but I knew I couldn't hold out against Hannigan."

Mac was staring at the Swede by now. "You never told me any of this," he said.

Alf shrugged. "What good would it have done to talk about it? Just a chance it'd get me in more trouble, that's all. Anyway, I packed up and left, just rode away from the place on my old mule, and came to town, lived by scroungin' and doin' odd jobs until you asked me to help you out here, Mac. I'll always be obliged to you for your kindness."

"I didn't offer you the job out of the kindness of my heart. I needed help. It's hard having to work from before dawn to well after dark every day."

"Anyway, now you know why anybody who's got crosswise with Hannigan and his bunch is a friend of mine. And as a friend, Jensen, let me give you some advice . . . Rattle your hocks outta this settlement as soon as you can. Things is only gonna get worse here, and it ain't your fight," Alf cautioned.

"Correction," Luke said. "It wasn't my fight. After Bowen sent his hounds after me tonight, and considering that Bowen works for Hannigan . . ." Luke let his voice trail off, then continued, "I don't know what my next move is. I have a job to do, and that's delivering my prisoner wherever the man who put the bounty on him wants him delivered. But after that, I might take a ride back in this direction."

Mac said solemnly, "I have to agree with Alf, Luke. You don't want to do that. Put Hannigan's Hill behind you as soon as you can, and don't look back."

"We'll see." Luke knew the other two had his best interests at heart, and if he looked at it logically, they were probably right.

But it wasn't easy to be logical when you'd been viciously attacked and you knew that men you now considered friends might be in for more trouble in the future. Luke's first instinct was to help them.

After all, that was what Smoke would do.

Mac drank the last of the coffee in his cup and said, "I told Jessie Whitmore I'd give her and Albert a hand getting that extra edition of the *Chronicle* out tonight. I suppose I'd better go and do that."

"And I should head back to the hotel," Luke said. "That's where I was going when Bowen's deputies showed up. Assuming we're right about it being them who came after me."

"I think that's a safe assumption." Mac went behind the counter, reached down for something on the shelf, and tucked a Smith & Wesson Model 3 .44-caliber revolver in the waistband of his trousers. "I'll walk over to the hotel with you."

"That's not necessary."

"It's no bother. My mind will rest easier if I do."

"I'll be glad to have the company, then."

"The place looks fine, Alf. You can head on home."

"Just as soon as I finish washin' the dishes that are in the washtub now," Alf said. He shook his head and added, "You fellas be careful. This night's got a bad feelin' to it."

Luke was glad to know he wasn't the only one experiencing that sensation.

Chapter 11

Nothing happened on their way over to the Northern Hotel. Mac tried to look both ways along the street at the same time, even though that was physically impossible. He didn't spot any movement, not even a stray dog or cat. More of the buildings were dark now, although light still spilled through the windows of the Lucky Spot and the other three saloons. For the most part, Hannigan's Hill was asleep.

As the two men paused in front of the hotel doors, Mac said, "I'll see you for breakfast at the café in the morning?"

"That depends," Luke answered. "Are your flap-jacks and bacon and eggs as good as that steak I had earlier today?"

"Better, in my opinion," Mac said with a grin. "I bake the best biscuits you'll find in these parts, too."

"I may have to take you up on that. I'll sure get some to take along with me when I ride out with Stallings."

Mac grew serious. "I meant what I said a few minutes ago, Luke. Once you leave, just keep riding. Don't come back here. There's no point in you getting mixed up in our troubles." He sighed. "Sooner or later, Ezra Hannigan's going to run all the decent people out. Once they're gone, the town will die. It may take a while, but it'll happen. Hannigan will have won . . . but what he wins won't be worth having in the long run."

"Maybe not, but a lot of folks will get hurt in that long run. Innocent folks who don't deserve the trouble that's going to rain down on them," Luke said.

"Some of us will work to keep that from happening. If Albert and Jessie can rally enough support, maybe they can keep Hannigan from taking over completely."

The words sounded a little hollow, even to Mac. He thought they probably sounded the same to Luke. Plenty of people in the settlement and the surrounding area were opposed to Ezra Hannigan's rampant greed and ambition, but the man had two dozen ruthless, seasoned gun-wolves backing any play he made, counting Bowen and the deputies. Ordinary people, no matter how many of them there were, couldn't stand up to that menace.

But they couldn't just roll over and give up, either, Mac knew. They had to keep trying to rein in Hannigan's excesses. Albert and Jessie were spearheading that effort. Not an issue of the *Chronicle* came out without including some veiled—and sometimes not so veiled—comments about how it was time for Hannigan to stop trying to crush anyone who opposed him.

Mac was sure that Albert would have some scathing

things to say about Thad Crawford's hanging in the extra edition he was working on.

And since Mac had promised to help with that, he nodded to Luke now and said, "I'll see you in the morning."

Luke returned the nod and went into the hotel. Mac turned away from the entrance and paused for a moment to survey the street again. His hand drifted toward the butt of the revolver stuck in his waistband. The feel of the smooth hardwood grip against his fingers was reassuring. Not seeing anything suspicious, he headed along the boardwalk toward the newspaper office. It was the last building on the left where the business district began.

The lamps were still burning there, of course, but when Mac tried the door, it was locked. The shade was pulled on the window in the door and the curtains were closed on the large front window that had the newspaper's name painted on it.

A sense of unease stirred inside Mac. He remembered what Judge John Lee Trent had said in the café that afternoon. Ezra Hannigan and his followers didn't like the things the Whitmores printed about them. Mac had always figured that Hannigan wouldn't move openly against Albert and Jessie because he knew it would look bad to attack the press. But that was no guarantee Hannigan wouldn't get mad enough to try something . . .

Once again, Mac wrapped his right hand around the Smith & Wesson's butt. He lifted his left and knocked on the door, not pounding but rapping hard enough to be heard inside. He leaned toward the door and listened intently.

A moment later, he heard quick, light footsteps as someone approached the door inside. The shade flicked back enough for Jessie Whitmore to peek out and see who had knocked. The light was behind her and struck scintillating reflections off her fair hair.

Mac's heart slugged heavily in his chest a couple of times. He told himself the reaction was out of relief from seeing that Jessie appeared to be all right.

Problem was, the same thing happened most of the time when he saw her. He had felt that same swift response when she came into the café this afternoon while Luke was there. It was troubling, but he tried not to let himself think about it.

She let the shade fall back into place. A second later, a key rattled in the lock and then the door opened.

"Hello, Mac," Jessie said as she stepped back to let him in. "I thought maybe you had changed your mind about helping us tonight."

"No, just had a few extra things to take care of first," he said as he stepped in, rubbing his hands together against the chilly night.

She didn't press him for details, just closed the door and said, "Come on back. Albert has the front page just about ready to run off."

Jessie twisted the key in the lock again before turning away from the door. Mac nodded toward it and said, "You don't normally keep that locked, do you?"

"Albert thought it might be a good idea tonight. We're not sure if word has gotten around town about the extra we're printing."

"You think Hannigan might have heard about it."

"We can't be sure that he hasn't."

That made sense to Mac. He had thought basically the same thing a few minutes earlier.

Jessie pointed at his midsection and said, "You don't normally do that, either."

Mac frowned in confusion for a second as he looked down at himself. Then he realized she was pointing at the Smith & Wesson sticking up from his waistband.

"I'm not sure I've ever seen you carry a gun before," Jessie went on. "Although I'm sure you must have all the time when you were going on those cattle drives you told us about."

He had shared some stories from his past as a chuck-wagon cook with the Whitmores, skipping over the more violent and outrageous parts and saying nothing about the trouble that had put him on the run as a young man and resulted in him going up the cattle trails, to start with.

"Didn't seem to be any reason to pack iron when all I was doing was running a café," he said. "Most of the time, I keep this on the shelf under the counter, just in case, but I've never needed it. Something about tonight, though . . . it just seems different."

Jessie nodded. "Albert and I were saying the same thing earlier. It's like the whole town is on edge. Thad Crawford had friends here. Most of them don't believe he could have done what he was accused of." She paused, then added meaningfully, "And everyone in town knows who benefits the most from his death."

Yeah, Mac thought. Ezra Hannigan would swoop in

like a buzzard, snatch up Crawford's spread for the unpaid taxes, and add it to his ever-growing domain.

Jessie led the way toward the door between the small front office with a counter, where merchants could come in to buy advertisements in the paper, and the larger back room, where the actual work of printing the *Chronicle* took place. The printing press dominated the room, looming like some mechanical medieval dragon.

Albert Whitmore stood at the inclined composing table, setting type in the plate for the front page. He turned his head to grin over his shoulder as he greeted Mac.

"You made it. Good to see you, Mac. I appreciate you giving us a hand."

"Happy to help," Mac said.

"Take off your coat and get an apron. Can't promise you won't get ink on your fingers, but no need for you to get it on your clothes!"

Albert wore a canvas apron, but that hadn't kept ink stains from getting on his fingers and his clothing. He clearly didn't care about his own garb, though; stains were just occupational hazards of the newspaper business.

As Mac took off his coat and started to roll up his sleeves, Albert took note of the same thing his wife had. "You're carrying a gun."

"I hope that's all right. I figured it wouldn't hurt, as tense as things have been getting around here."

"They're tense, all right," Albert agreed. "Sort of like sitting on a powder keg, I guess."

Albert Whitmore was in his midthirties, a couple of

inches taller than Mac, but more leanly built, so they probably weighed about the same. He had a friendly, slightly lantern-jawed face, topped by close-cropped brown hair. He had been in the printing and newspaper business since he was little more than a boy, he had told Mac, and he had printer's ink for blood.

"Hanging Thad Crawford like that may be what finally wakes up enough people to what's going on around here," Albert went on. "You want to read my editorial, Mac? It's over there."

He pointed with his chin toward a scarred old desk where he wrote his editorials and put together news stories. A sheet of paper lay on the desk with a pencil on top of it. Mac finished tying his apron in place and went over to pick up the editorial.

Albert wrote in a very plain, easy-to-read script. There was nothing plain about the words that had flowed from his mind onto the paper, though. The editorial strongly condemned the execution by hanging of local rancher Thaddeus Crawford, which had followed a kangaroo court trial conducted by a bought-and-paid-for judge. A jury of citizens, too terrified or too much in debt to the local powers that be, had handed in a guilty verdict, and the sentence of death had been imposed on Crawford by the corrupt judge. Crawford's life had been taken away from him on the flimsiest of evidence provided by witnesses that couldn't be trusted as far as a weak man could throw them.

The rhetoric was fiery, worthy of a politician trying to inflame a crowd of potential voters or a general attempting to rouse his troops for battle. Nowhere in the editorial was Ezra Hannigan's name mentioned, but where Albert referred to a powerful individual behind the scenes manipulating the law to suit his own ends, spinning a web like a fat, evil spider, no one who read the editorial was going to have any doubt who he was talking about.

Mac set the sheet of paper back on the desk and said, "You don't pull any punches, do you?"

"I wouldn't be a newspaperman if I didn't tell the truth."

Mac recalled some of the things printed about him in the papers back in New Orleans years earlier and said, "Well, I don't reckon that's always true." He tapped the sheet of paper with a fingertip. "Hannigan's going to be livid when he reads this."

"Why should I care what Hannigan thinks?"

"Because it would be a lot easier on you if you did, not to mention probably more profitable, too."

"Profit's not as important as the truth," Albert insisted. "And if I wanted to live an easy life, I never would have started a newspaper. Isn't that right, Jessie?"

"Of course, it is," she replied.

The sentiment was true for Albert, Mac thought. He had no doubt that his friend was sincere.

But he couldn't help but wonder how Jessie actually felt about it. Were there times when she wished her husband would have been a little less noble, a bit less of the crusader?

That was none of his business, Mac told himself firmly. Albert and Jessie both were his friends, and he was here to help them.

"What would you like me to do?" he asked.

"The front page will be ready to run in just a few more minutes. We can take turns on the press."

Mac nodded. He knew that Jessie sometimes had to turn the crank to operate the press. He was glad to spare her that tiring task.

"Right now, though, we need some more ink," Albert went on. "There's a can of it in the front room, on the shelf under the counter. Can you get it, Mac?"

"Sure. Be right back."

The lamp in the front room wasn't lit, but with the door to the brightly lit back room open, Mac had no trouble seeing as he stepped over to the counter to look for the can of ink. He spotted it on the shelf and bent down to reach for it.

That was when the front window shattered, spraying glass across the room, and Mac felt as much as heard the wind-rip of a bullet passing closely over his head.

Chapter 12

It had been a long time since anybody had taken a shot at him, but some things you never forgot. Instinct took over as Mac threw himself to the floor behind the counter.

When he landed, the Smith & Wesson was clutched in his hand and his thumb was looped over the hammer, ready to ear it back. He hadn't even been aware of drawing the revolver as he dived for cover.

More shots roared outside. Bullets came through the broken window and thudded into the wall behind the counter. Given the number of shots being fired, some of them had to be hitting the outside wall, too. The window in the door blew inward as a shotgun boomed and broken glass clinked and bounced on the floor in a glittery spray.

In the back room, Jessie Whitmore screamed. Her husband bellowed curses and then yelled, "Mac! Mac, are you all right?"

"Stay back there!" Mac shouted in reply. "Get low and stay there!"

With the heavy tables and cabinets and the printing press itself in the back room, Jessie and Albert had plenty of cover as long as they would use it. Mac hoped Albert had the sense to grab hold of his wife and keep her safe.

The gunfire continued as he crawled along the floor to the end of the counter. Staying as low as possible, he rolled toward the front wall and tried not to flinch as more slugs whipped through the air above him. When he reached the wall, he sat up with his back against it, close to the broken window. Some of the shards of glass from the floor had stuck to his clothes. He didn't worry about them for the moment.

Twisting, he reached across his body with the gun and stuck the Smith & Wesson's barrel in the bottom corner of the shattered window. He edged his head past the facing, just enough to see the indistinct shape of several men on horseback milling around in the street. Muzzle flame bloomed like crimson flowers in the darkness as they continued their assault on the newspaper office.

Mac triggered off three rounds at them as fast as he could cock and fire.

They probably didn't know he was in here and hadn't expected anybody in the office to be armed, let alone willing to put up a fight. Mac heard some startled yells, and then a fresh volley of shots erupted from the riders. He didn't think he had hit any of them, but he sure as blazes had discouraged them, he saw a moment later as the men wheeled their horses and galloped away. They threw a few final shots over their shoulders as they took off for the tall and uncut.

Mac waited to make sure they weren't going to turn around and make another pass. While he knelt there with his heart pounding, a good-sized chunk of glass that had clung stubbornly to the window frame finally let go and crashed to the floor a couple of feet from him. It was all he could do not to jump and yell when that happened.

"Mac!" Albert called again from the back. "Are you all right?"

"Yeah, I'm fine," Mac told him, "other than my ears ringing a little." The reports from the Smith & Wesson had been almost deafening in the close confines of the small front office. "What about you and Jessie?"

"We weren't hit. We hunkered down behind one of the cabinets."

Mac heaved a mental sigh of relief. With so much lead flying around, he had feared that some of it might have found one or both of the Whitmores.

He stood up and used the barrel of his gun to brush broken glass off his clothes. He risked another look and saw that the street was empty. If anyone was curious about the small-scale war that had just gone on, they weren't doing anything about it.

Glass crunched under his boots as he walked to the door between the rooms. He looked into the back room and saw Albert helping Jessie to her feet from where they had taken cover. Jessie's blue eyes were wide and her face had lost all its color. She looked terrified, and Mac couldn't blame her. Albert appeared to be a little shaken, too.

Mac saw damaged places on the rear wall, where bullets that had come through the open door had struck. He asked, "Was the press damaged?"

Albert pointed to a streak on the metal frame and said, "A bullet ricocheted off here, but I'm pretty sure that was the only one that hit it." He managed to smile. "So it'll leave a scar, but no lasting damage."

"That's good. You can still print that extra."

Jessie blurted out, "I don't know if we should."

Albert frowned at her and said, "Honey, what do you mean?"

"You know good and well that was Hannigan's men doing the shooting. If Hannigan is already mad enough at us to order an attack like that, what's going to happen *after* he reads your editorial?"

"I can't worry about what's going to happen. What I wrote is the truth, and it needs to be said."

"Who made it your sole responsibility to spread the truth? Nobody else in this town stands up to Ezra Hannigan. Why should you?"

Albert looked confused. His frown deepened. He said, "Well . . . well, somebody's got to, I guess. Whether anybody else does or not." He glanced over at Mac. "Back me up here, Mac. Sometimes a fella's just got to do what he knows is right, even if it does rile some folks up."

Mac nodded slowly. "I reckon that's true, Albert. But you can't blame Jessie for being upset and scared. It's only been a couple of minutes since a lot of lead was flying around in here."

"I know, I know." Albert stepped closer to Jessie, put

his arms around her, and drew her against him in a comforting embrace. "It'll be all right, Jessie, you'll see."

She sniffled a little, then said, "You're right, Albert. I'm sorry, I . . . I just let my emotions get the better of me for a minute. Of course, you have to do what's right and tell the truth. That . . . that's what being a newspaperman is."

"For what it's worth," Mac said, "I'm not sure those gunnies were trying to kill you. I mean, it wouldn't have bothered them if you happened to catch a bullet, Albert, but they were just emptying their six-shooters at the building. I think they meant to scare you more than anything else."

"Maybe," Albert said as he patted Jessie on the back while he continued to hold her. His expression hardened. "They stood a mighty big chance of hurting somebody, though, whether that was their main intention or not."

Mac knew he meant Jessie with that comment, and he could understand the hot anger he saw flash in his friend's eyes. Hannigan had crossed a line tonight.

The question was, now that that line had been crossed, how far over it would Ezra Hannigan go?

Mac had no idea what the answer was, and before he could ponder it, a fist knocked heavily on the front door. A familiar voice called, "Open up in there!"

Jessie lifted her head. Albert let go of her and stepped back. Both of them, along with Mac, turned toward the door.

"I guess the marshal has decided he can't go on pretending not to have heard all those shots," Albert said.

He started toward the door, but Mac put out a hand to stop him.

"Let me answer it, just in case."

He held up the Smith & Wesson to show what he meant. The revolver still held two rounds. He should have reloaded as soon as the shooting stopped, Mac told himself. There was a time he would have done that without even thinking about it. Settling down and living in a town for the past few years had caused him to forget some useful habits.

He was downright rusty.

But he was still more suited to handle gun trouble than Albert Whitmore was. He didn't expect that from Marshal Bowen, but it was better to be prepared.

For a second, Albert looked like he was going to argue, but then he nodded and gestured for Mac to go ahead. Holding the gun down at his side, Mac crossed the front room and twisted the key in the lock, where Jessie had left it after letting him in.

"Howdy, Marshal," he said as he opened the door.

"McKenzie?" Verne Bowen frowned and moved his head back a little in surprise. "What are you doing here?"

"I just stopped by to help Mr. and Mrs. Whitmore with a little chore," Mac said. "They're friends of mine, you know."

"What happened here?"

"You tell me, Marshal. All I know is that some fellas decided to use the newspaper office for target practice, I guess. They rode up and fired a couple of hundred rounds at it." Mac paused, then added, "You might have heard all the racket a little while ago."

Bowen scowled as he crowded the threshold. He carried a shotgun, but it was pointed toward the floor.

Mac hadn't forgotten that he'd heard a shotgun go off during the attack.

"Are the Whitmores hurt?"

"No, they were lucky. All of us came through without a scratch." Mac smiled wryly. "There's a lot of broken glass to clean up, though. Might draw some blood yet."

"I want to see them and make sure they're all right."

"Albert and Jessie? Sure." Mac figured it was safe enough, as long as Bowen was standing in the doorway. That would make it harder for anybody to take a potshot at them from outside. He turned his head and called, "The marshal wants to talk to you two."

They came out of the back room. "Marshal," Albert said with a nod. "Took you a while to get down here after the shooting stopped, didn't it?"

Bowen's heavy features darkened with anger. "What do you mean by that?"

"Nothing," Albert said, shrugging. "Maybe you figured there was no hurry, since you had a pretty good idea who was responsible for all this. Could be you even know them pretty well."

Jessie put a hand on his arm, as if telling him to be careful, but it was a little late for that.

"As usual, Whitmore, you're throwing around accusations when you don't actually know a thing about it. I don't have any idea who shot up your office. And I got down here as fast as I could, I'll have you know."

"Fine," Albert said. "Anyway, it doesn't matter We'll sweep up the broken glass and plaster over the bullet holes. But we'll do that after we've run the copies for tomorrow's extra edition. There'll be a new issue of the *Chronicle* on the streets tomorrow, Marshal, with a story about how somebody tried to stop me from printing the truth, to go along with my editorial."

"I reckon you can print what you want," Bowen said coldly. "That's the way things work, isn't it?"

"That's the way it works in this country. For now."

A few seconds of tense silence ticked by, and then Bowen asked, "Did you get a look at whoever did the shooting?"

"I saw them," Mac said. "Five or six men on horseback."

"Anything else you can tell me about them?"

"Not really," Mac said. "I didn't get *that* good a look at them."

That was actually all he knew, but he made it sound as if maybe he had gotten a better look at the gunmen than he really had. Let Bowen sweat about that for a while.

At the same time, Mac realized the impression he'd just conveyed might paint a target on his back. The attackers might try to eliminate him if they believed he could identify them.

He would just have to be watchful, Mac told himself. And somewhat to his surprise, the wariness that went through him at this potential threat almost felt good. He had been allowing himself to get fat and lazy. Maybe he needed some danger in his life again to hone a keener edge on him.

"What happened to the men who did this?" Bowen asked.

"They took off when I threw some lead back at them," Mac said. "I don't reckon they were expecting that."

"Hit any of them?"

"I couldn't tell you, Marshal. Mostly, I was just trying to keep my head down."

"Did you see which way they rode off?"

"East," Mac said. "But they could have gone any direction under the sun, once they were out of sight."

"Then I don't see what I can do about this," Bowen said, shaking his head. "It'd be impossible to pick up any tracks in the street."

"That's all right, Marshal," Albert said. "We didn't really expect you to track them down."

"You sometimes rub folks the wrong way, you know that, Whitmore?"

"That's my job, Marshal. A good newspaperman never lets folks get too comfortable."

"Just remember what I said." Bowen gave Jessie a curt nod. "Ma'am."

"Good night, Marshal," she responded coolly.

Mac closed the door behind Bowen. Albert sighed and said, "Mac, do you mind sweeping up this broken glass?"

"Not at all," Mac said. He chuckled. "Before I hired Alf Karlsson, I swept up in my place all the time."

"Jessie and I will get back to working on the paper."

"I'll give you a hand as soon as I finish cleaning up in here."

"I appreciate it. The broom's in the back."

Mac fetched the broom, and Albert and Jessie returned to their work. He had one other thing to do, though, before he started sweeping.

He reloaded the Smith & Wesson, including the chamber he normally carried empty.

With the way things were coming to a head in Hannigan's Hill, it might be a good idea to have a full wheel from now on.

Chapter 13

Luke had been right when he thought there might be a few snowflakes before morning. As he stepped out the front door of the Northern Hotel onto the porch the next day, he saw a few small patches of fine white pellets that stirred almost like sand when the wind blew along the street. In a month, there might be a foot of thick, wet snow on the ground, but for now, it didn't really amount to anything.

The sky was still overcast this morning, creating a gloomy pall that hung over Hannigan's Hill. Luke's breath fogged in the air as he turned to walk toward Mac's Place.

Despite the chill in the air, quite a few people were moving around this morning. Women in coats and scarves and mufflers hurried along the boardwalks to get their shopping done in the stores. Wagons and buckboards were parked in front of several businesses.

Men on horseback rode up and down the street. A hammer rang on an anvil in the blacksmith shop.

And every few yards, somebody was stopped, holding up a sheet of newsprint to read what was written on it. Luke saw several knots of people holding papers while they talked animatedly among themselves.

That single sheet, printed front and back, was the extra edition of the *Chronicle,* Luke supposed. It appeared to be causing quite a stir in the settlement.

The café's front window was fogged up, Luke saw as he approached the building. When he opened the door, warmth flowed out around him, wrapping him up in enticing aromas. The smells of bacon, fresh baked goods, and coffee drew him in.

The tables were full, as were all but two of the stools at the counter. Luke took one of them and watched Mac scurry back and forth, and in and out of the kitchen, as he took care of his customers. Luke had to wait several minutes before Mac got around to him.

"Looks like you could use some extra help in the mornings, too," Luke observed as Mac came to a stop on the other side of the counter.

Mac rested his hands on the counter and drew in a deep breath, then nodded. "It's usually a little busy at this time of day," he said, "but not like today. Everybody wants to talk about what's in the paper, and they want to do it over a cup of coffee and a stack of flapjacks."

At least one person at each of the tables had a copy of the extra edition. Several of the men at the counter were reading the sheet of newsprint, too, although quarters were a little cramped for that.

"What does your friend charge for those?" Luke asked. "He ought to be making a nice profit this morning."

Mac shook his head. "He's not charging for them, since it's an extra and it's only one sheet, front and back. Said it was more important that the community be well-informed, rather than putting money in his pocket."

"A noble attitude, but perhaps not a very farsighted one. Without making money, he can't continue publishing the paper, can he?"

"I think he figures this is a one-time deal." Mac shrugged. "And there's a little bit of spite in it, too, I reckon. Albert wants to get back at Ezra Hannigan, so getting that paper in as many hands as possible is one way he sees of doing that. You want coffee?"

"Yes, and plenty of it. Plus some of those biscuits you talked about and a pile of that bacon I smell."

"Comin' up." Mac grinned as he reached under the counter. He laid a folded newspaper in front of Luke and added, "While you're waiting, you can see what everybody's talking about."

Luke opened the paper. On the front page, under the masthead that included the *Chronicle*'s name and *Extra Edition* was a banner headline reading INJUSTICE!

Below that, in a box, printed in large type so it filled the entire front of the sheet, was Albert Whitmore's editorial condemning the hanging of Thad Crawford and excoriating the corrupt local administrators of justice,

Judge John Lee Trent and Marshal Verne Bowen. Luke, who was very well-read, despite having little formal education, admired Whitmore's skill with words. The editorial was impassioned and designed to stir up the emotions of anyone who read it, as the language wove a spell of outrage. Trent and Bowen came across as craven toadies eagerly doing the bidding of a ruthless, power-mad, cruel despot.

That despot was never given a name, but everyone in town would know Whitmore was writing about Ezra Hannigan.

At the bottom of the editorial was a line urging the reader to turn the sheet over for all the details of a cowardly attack against the newspaper, an onslaught intended to suppress the truth.

Mac placed a cup of coffee in front of Luke and added a platter of biscuits and a plate piled high with bacon. "What do you think?" he asked.

"Looks as good as it smells."

"I meant the editorial."

"Your friend has a way with words," Luke said. "If anything's going to get the town stirred up enough to fight back against Hannigan, this might do it."

"That's the problem," Mac said with a sigh. "I'm not sure even this will make folks stand up for themselves. Hannigan and his bunch have everybody around here pretty much buffaloed. And anybody who does defy him might just get hurt."

Luke had flipped the sheet over and was scanning the story on the other side. He said, "You mean the way your friends got their office shot up last night."

"Exactly. I was there, you know."

Luke frowned. "At the newspaper office? When the shooting happened?"

"Yep. You remember I promised to stop by and give them a hand with printing the paper. We hadn't gotten started yet, when all hell broke loose."

"Whitmore doesn't mention you being there."

"No point in it," Mac said. "It wouldn't change anything."

"And there's no reason for Hannigan to know about it, I suppose."

"He already knows about it. I was there when Bowen showed up, after the attackers were gone. I'm sure the marshal told Hannigan I was there, when he rode out to the Rocking H to deliver his report, either last night or first thing this morning."

Luke studied Mac for a couple of heartbeats, then said, "Did you have anything to do with those bushwhackers lighting a shuck?"

"I may have thrown a little lead in their direction and it spooked them," Mac allowed. "They wouldn't have been expecting that from Albert and Jessie."

"No, not likely. You've declared yourself on the other side now, instead of remaining neutral."

Mac gestured at the full tables and stools. "It hasn't hurt business any."

"Give Hannigan time. I've never met the man, but I have a hunch he's already planning his next move."

"Wouldn't surprise me a bit," Mac agreed.

One of the men farther along the counter called for more coffee. Mac went to tend to him, while Luke drank his coffee and dug into the food. The biscuits were every bit as good as Mac had claimed, warm, light, and fluffy. The bacon was crunchy and flavorful.

When Mac paused across the counter a few minutes later, Luke complimented him on the food and then said, "You know, I heard that shooting last night. Something told me you might be mixed up in it, and I almost headed out to see what was going on. But when I looked out the window of my room, I saw a bunch of hombres riding, hell-bent for leather, up the street, and figured they were the ones who'd been raising the ruckus. The shooting had stopped by that point."

"I'm sure that was them, all right. Everybody else in town was keeping their heads down."

Luke lowered his voice. "Bowen's deputies again?"

Mac shrugged and said, "Who knows? Could have been, or maybe some of the crew from the Rocking H. They're all cut from the same cloth, and they all take Hannigan's orders." He shook his head. "Just as well you didn't get involved, Luke. I've been telling you all along not to get mixed up in this business. And speaking of business, how's yours? Have you gotten a reply to that wire you sent yesterday?"

"Not so far. I expected that I would, before now, but maybe the senator's been busy. I hear tell, those politicians occasionally do a little bit of actual work in Washington, D.C."

Mac snorted. "Damned little, from what I know of it, and when they do, it's always something that'll help them line their pockets with other people's money."

Luke grinned. He couldn't argue with Mac's cynicism when it came to politics.

A steady hum of conversation had filled the café

while Luke was eating and talking to Mac. It came to an abrupt halt as the door opened and cold air gusted in. Luke looked over his shoulder and saw Marshal Verne Bowen enter the café, trailed by two of his deputies.

For a second, all the customers stared at the lawmen, but then the gazes switched back quickly to the food in front of them. The newspapers that were still being read were folded and dropped on the tables or stuffed inside coats. The silence that followed was awkward as Bowen and his companions just stood there. The wind continued to blow in.

Then Bowen grinned and said over his shoulder, "Close the door, Jed. What's wrong with you? Were you raised in a barn?"

With an arrogant smirk on his face, the deputy, Jed Lawrence, closed the door. Bowen walked toward the counter.

Several men who had been sitting there, lingering over cups of coffee, pushed their empty plates away and stood up. Without bidding farewell to Mac or saying anything else, they headed for the door, circling wide around Bowen and his men.

"Looks like some seats just opened up, boys," Bowen said. He and the deputies settled themselves on the vacant stools. "Morning, McKenzie."

Mac drifted toward them and said, "Marshal. What can I do for you?"

"Why, the boys and I stopped in for coffee and breakfast, of course." Bowen was jovial and seemed very pleased with himself this morning. "Everybody knows your food is the best in Hannigan's Hill."

"Thanks," Mac said.

One of the men who had left hurriedly had abandoned his copy of the *Chronicle*'s extra edition. Bowen picked it up, glanced at it, and then tossed it down disdainfully.

"You need to gather up these papers and use them for kindling," he said. "That's about the only thing they're good for. Can't trust a newspaper that reports the facts incorrectly."

"Just what facts did Albert get wrong?" Mac asked.

"That business about a gang of gunmen attacking the newspaper office. Whitmore made it sound deliberate, when all it was, was a bunch of high-spirited cowboys letting off some steam. We've all seen that plenty of times before. A fella gets liquored up and decides what he needs to do is shoot some holes in the sky."

"They weren't shooting at the sky. You forget I was there, Marshal."

"I don't forget anything," Bowen said, and under his affable pose, a look of pure venom showed through.

"They were aiming at the newspaper office," Mac went on. "I can show you the bullet holes."

Bowen had control of himself again. He said, "That's where some of the slugs ended up, sure. But it wasn't deliberate. I know that because the fellas who did it slunk back into town late last night with their tails between their legs and confessed to me. They were part of Ed Glasby's crew from the Diamond G."

Mac frowned. "Ezra Hannigan holds Glasby's note on that spread, doesn't he?"

"That's got nothing to do with anything. Like I said, they confessed. This morning, Judge Trent fined them and collected for the damages." Bowen looked pleased with himself. "Tell your friend Whitmore to go see the judge. He can collect some of that money to replace the glass those boys shot out and patch up the bullet holes. Now, how about some coffee? You do sell coffee here, don't you?"

"I'll fetch cups," Mac replied tightly.

Bowen looked over at Luke. "Are you going to be collecting that prisoner of yours today, Jensen?"

"I'm not sure yet," Luke said, "but I hope so."

"As long as you're feeding him, keep him there as long as you want." Bowen paused. "No skin off my nose. Just don't get any ideas about sticking *your* nose in any of our local business. We don't need outsiders horning in on community matters. We take care of our own problems around here."

"I'm sure you do," Luke said. He caught Mac's eye, slid a silver dollar across the counter to pay for his breakfast, and slowly and deliberately picked up the newspaper he had been reading earlier. He folded it, stuck it under his arm, and left the café, ignoring the cold, hostile stares the two deputies gave him as he went out.

Chapter 14

As Luke walked back to the hotel, he noticed blue sky showing through a few gaps in the overcast. Maybe the clouds were going to break up and clear off later today.

Or maybe this was just a false promise of better weather. Time would tell about that, the same as it did about everything else.

When he entered the lobby of the Northern Hotel, the clerk hailed him from behind the desk. "A boy just delivered this telegram for you, Mr. Jensen."

Luke suppressed the impulse to say that it was about time and took the sealed envelope from the clerk. He tore it open, fished out the message form, and read the printed words.

REMAIN CURRENT LOCATION STOP
MAINTAIN CUSTODY PRISONER STOP WILL

*CONTACT YOU WITH FURTHER INSTRUC-
TIONS STOP CREED*

"Well, son of a . . ." Luke's voice trailed off and his
jaw tightened angrily.

"Trouble?" the clerk asked.

"Just an annoyance," Luke said as he replaced the
message in the envelope and stuffed it in his shirt
pocket.

"Will you be checking out today?"

He didn't know what he was going to be doing, and
that was what was so annoying, Luke thought. Basically, Senator Creed had told him to stay put and keep
Ethan Stallings in jail here until he got in touch again.
That might be later today, or it might not be for several
days. Luke had no way of knowing. It might even be a
week or more before he heard from the senator again.

He was stuck in Hannigan's Hill until he did.

Realizing that the clerk was waiting for an answer,
Luke shook his head. "It's possible I might be leaving,"
he said, "but it's just as likely I'll be staying for a few
more days. Why don't I pay you for a couple of nights,
then."

"That'll be fine," the clerk agreed. "We're never full
up this time of year, even when a stagecoach has to
stop because the pass is closed by snow or something
like that. Glad to have you with us, Mr. Jensen. Hope
you enjoy your stay in Hannigan's Hill."

It was probably too late for that already, Luke
mused, but he kept the thought to himself.

He had considered the idea of asking Mac to pack
up a bag of food to take with them, instead of provid-

ing an actual breakfast for Stallings. But that was when he had thought there was a good chance they would be riding out this morning. Now, that that appeared unlikely, he would have to see about feeding the prisoner, after all.

Luke paid for his room for the next two nights, then headed back to the café.

He had to stop in the street to let a carriage go by. It was a fancy conveyance of the sort that wasn't often seen in a frontier settlement like this. Constructed of black wood polished to a high sheen, with plenty of gleaming silver trim around the doors, windows, and frame, it was pulled by a team of four magnificent black horses. Silver trim decorated their harness, too. Luke would have expected to see a carriage like that on the streets of New Orleans or San Francisco.

The man on the driver's seat handling the reins would have drawn some attention in a big city, that was for sure. His hawk-nosed face looked like it was carved out of copper. His black hair was pulled back into a single thick braid that hung between his shoulder blades. He wore a black suit, a snowy white shirt, and a black silk top hat with an eagle feather sticking in the band. Luke wasn't as skilled as some men were at identifying Indian tribes, but if he had to guess, he would have said the driver was a Crow.

The lone passenger glared out at Luke as the carriage rolled past. It was an oddly impersonal stare, though, as if the man wasn't directing it at Luke specifically, but rather just felt hostile toward the world at large. He would have looked the same at anyone the carriage happened to pass.

The man's face was as round and pale and hairless as the moon. He had a cream-colored, high-crowned hat on his head. Luke couldn't see any hair under it and figured the hombre was bald.

He also figured he was looking at Ezra Hannigan. He had no real reason for thinking so, other than the fact that this gent obviously was rich, based on the carriage in which he rode, but he was convinced of the man's identity, anyway.

Luke watched as the carriage came to a stop in front of an office building. The Indian driver jumped down from the box and opened the carriage door, then stepped back. Hannigan didn't want any help climbing down, Luke thought.

Hannigan wedged his thick body through the door, held on to the carriage with one sausage-fingered hand, and wielded a silver-headed cane with the other to brace himself as he stepped down. His big belly was round as a melon under a tan suit, an embroidered vest, and a white shirt. His legs reminded Luke of the stumps that would be left if a pair of good-sized trees was cut down. His trouser legs were tucked in high-topped brown boots.

With the Indian trailing him, Hannigan went into the building. He used his cane to help him get along. As Luke watched, he pondered the fact that Ezra Hannigan was a successful rancher, and, in fact, his Rocking H was the biggest spread in these parts. That meant that at one time, Hannigan had been able to sit a saddle. Not just ride, but ride hard from dawn to dark and beyond. That was the only way a man could build a successful ranch, especially in the days when Hannigan had come to this area. Wyoming Territory had been lawless back then, filled with savage Indians and ruthless outlaws. Hannigan would have needed guts, determination, and gun-handling skills to carve out his place in that rugged world.

Clearly, things had changed—a lot—in recent years. Luke doubted if Hannigan could even climb onto a horse these days, let alone ride it and do any range work.

He had people to do that, Luke was sure . . . Just as he had people to do his gun work for him.

Luke moved on toward Mac's Place. As he approached the café, a man rode up and swung down from the saddle, then looped his horse's reins around the hitch rail. He turned and gave Luke a curt nod.

"Mornin'," he said. "Are you from around here, mister?"

"No, just passing through," Luke replied. That was still true, even though it now appeared he was going to have to stay in Hannigan's Hill longer than he'd intended.

"Know anything about this here eatin' place?"

The question made Luke pay more attention to this stranger. The man wore a long buffalo coat that hung open over patched and faded canvas trousers and a faded blue bib-front shirt. A yellow bandanna was looped around his neck. His hat was battered, stained, and almost shapeless. The brim was turned up in front and pinned in place.

The most striking thing about him was the black patch over his left eye. His right eye, a muddy brown, was set deep in a weathered, rawboned, beard-stubbled face. Hair the color and consistency of straw poked out under the old hat around a pair of jug ears. The man was ugly enough that most folks would remember him.

Because of that, Luke wasn't completely surprised when something stirred in his memory. He had crossed trails with this hombre before, somewhere and sometime he couldn't recall, and probably only briefly, or he would remember.

"I've had a couple of meals here," he said in answer to the stranger's question. "The food is excellent."

The stranger nodded. "You don't never know what to expect in these cow-town hash houses. I've et in some where the grub weren't fit for the hogs."

"That's not the case here, I assure you."

The man squinted his single eye at the sign on the building's front and read the words slowly, sounding them out as if deciphering them taxed his brain.

"'Maaac's Puhlaaace.' I reckon Mac must be the feller who owns it?"

"That's right."

"What's the rest of his name? I've knowed a few Macs in my time. This feller might be one of 'em."

"His last name is McKenzie."

"What's his front handle?"

The questioning made Luke wary, but if he didn't answer, this stranger could find out what he wanted to know from many of the other people on the street. So he said, "I believe it's Dewey, but he goes by Mac."

The man chuckled. "Reckon I would, too. 'Dewey.'"

Shaking his head, he turned away. He seemed to have lost interest in the subject. But then he paused and looked over his shoulder.

"Happen to know the best saloon in town?"

"I've only been in one of them," Luke said honestly. "The Lucky Shot." He pointed across the street in the next block. "It's fine, but I don't know if it's open yet this morning."

"I'll mosey on over there and see. Probably is open. Lots of fellers wake up in the mornin' cravin' a little hair o' the dog, as they say."

He was right about that, Luke supposed. For a moment, he watched the stranger amble toward the saloon; then he went into the café.

Just in the time Luke had been gone, Verne Bowen and his deputies had departed. He'd expected them to still be there. In fact, the café was a lot less crowded than it had been only a short time earlier. Only a couple of the tables were still occupied, as well as half of the stools.

"Looks like you've had an exodus," Luke commented to Mac as he came up to the counter.

"Yeah, folks decided that they didn't have as much of an appetite with Bowen and his hard cases around." Mac shrugged. "And then the three of them left, too, once they'd scared off most of my customers. I suspect that was the real reason they came in, in the first place. Now that they know I was helping Albert and Jessie, they'll try to ruin my business. Wouldn't be the first time they've gone after somebody for standing up to Ezra Hannigan." He laughed, but the sound didn't hold any genuine humor. "Look at it this way, I tell myself, at least they didn't take me up to Hangman's Hill for a necktie party."

"What would happen if they tried?"

Mac's eyes and voice turned cold. "It would never get that far. They'd have to gun me down. And I'd take some of them with me. Verne Bowen his own self, if I could manage it."

"Maybe it'll never come to that," Luke said. "By the way, I think I saw Hannigan come into town a few minutes ago."

"Big fella who bears a resemblance to a bullfrog?"

"That would be him. He was riding in a fancy black carriage."

Mac nodded. "With an Indian driving. Yeah, that's Hannigan, all right. The Indian's name is Medicine Bear. He and Hannigan used to be mortal enemies, back in the days when his tribe was still raiding the Rocking H. But the rest of the band got wiped out by the army. Medicine Bear was badly wounded. Hannigan's wife took him in and nursed him back to health, and from then on, he was devoted to her. After she passed away, he kept working for Hannigan. At least that's the story as I've heard it from folks who have been around here longer than I have."

"He looked like a man to stand aside from."

"Medicine Bear? I agree. Hannigan's turned into a tub of lard the past couple of years, but don't underestimate him. I'm told he can still move quicker than you might think for such a big man, and he's still got some muscle under that fat."

"I'll remember that."

"No need for you to think about things like that," Mac said. "After all, you're leaving soon, aren't you?"

"I wish I knew," Luke said. He explained about the telegram he had received from Senator Jonas Creed.

"So I don't know how long I'm going to be here. Might be an hour, might be a week. But I'm not going to do anything to risk losing that bounty. Creed said to stay put, so I'm going to stay put."

"I reckon you'll need to make arrangements to feed that prisoner of yours," Mac said.

"That's exactly what I came to talk to you about. Can you handle the job?"

"Of course. I'll make sure he gets three square meals a day. I have a kid who works part-time for me, like Alf does in the evenings. He can take the trays over to the jail and fetch back the empty from the time before."

"I'm obliged to you." Luke took out a twenty-dollar gold piece and slid it across the counter. "Take the price out of that, and let me know when and if you need more."

"That ought to cover everything for a good while," Mac said as he picked up the double eagle. "What are you going to do while you're waiting to hear from the senator?"

Luke thought about it, scraped a thumbnail along his jawline, and said, "Maybe I'll spend some time at the Lucky Shot. That Irish Mahoney seemed friendly."

Mac frowned. "Verne Bowen won't care much for that. He's got the idea that Irish is wearing his brand."

"That," Luke said, "will be up to the lady."

Chapter 15

Judge John Lee Trent was closing one of the drawers in his desk as Ezra Hannigan thumped into the judge's office. From the hasty manner in which Trent acted, as well as the slightly guilty look on his beefy face, Hannigan knew the man had been drinking, even though it was a long time until noon. Hannigan's lips pursed in disapproval.

But he had to make allowances, he told himself. Not everyone was as strong-minded and able to control their appetites as he was. Not to mention the fact that he had to work with people who were weaker than he was—otherwise, there would be no one to help him accomplish his aims. Trent was valuable in his way. He followed orders and had enough of a backbone that some of the local citizens were intimidated by him.

"Ezra," Trent said as he pushed himself to his feet. He swallowed hard and put a hand on the desk to steady himself. Maybe he'd had more than one drink. "I wasn't expecting to see you in town this morning. What can I do for you?"

"I want to make sure the problem regarding the newspaper was handled in a suitable fashion." The words came out in a deep rumble, the sort of voice that had to originate from Hannigan's massive chest. It was the voice of a powerful man . . . in more ways than one.

"Yes, certainly. Glasby's riders came into town, just like they were supposed to, and I fined them and collected damages, just like the note you sent back last night with Verne suggested."

It had been an order, not a suggestion, but if Trent wanted to pretend that he was an actual jurist and not a puppet, Hannigan didn't care. As long as Trent did what he was supposed to do, it didn't matter what he told himself in order to sleep at night.

Hannigan rested both hands on the silver head of his cane and leaned on it. Trent hadn't offered him a seat, and he wouldn't have accepted if the judge had. Getting up from a chair was too difficult. Better to just stay on his feet, once he was standing. Let other people hop up and down like jack-in-the-boxes.

"Has Albert Whitmore been in to be reimbursed for the damage to his office?"

Trent shook his head. "No. I sent my assistant to let him know that he could do that. So he's been notified. He'll have no complaint coming if he chooses not to accept the money."

"Oh, he'll complain whether he has a right to or not," Hannigan said. "The man's never said or printed anything that wasn't a puling little complaint, has he?"

"He's too outspoken," Trent agreed. "It'll get him in real trouble one of these days."

"Sooner rather than later," Hannigan snapped.

Trent frowned. "Are you sure that's a good idea, Ezra? I mean, we just had that ugly business with Thad Crawford, and then the attack on the newspaper office last night . . . I mean, Glasby's men getting drunk and firing off their guns in celebration—"

Hannigan lifted his right hand and slashed it in the air. The hand was puffy, the fingers short and thick, but the gesture conveyed a considerable amount of menace, anyway.

"Stop it," Hannigan said. "There's no need to maintain that fabrication with me. We both know what happened last night and who ordered it."

With an unusual show of spirit, Trent said, "All I know for certain is what was testified to in my courtroom, Ezra. That's all I go by. And all I'm saying is that with the trouble that's already occurred in town, it might be a good idea to let things cool off a little."

Hannigan reached inside his coat and brought out a folded sheet of newsprint. He slapped it down on the desk between them and said, "Bowen told me yesterday that Whitmore was going to print an extra edition and condemn our actions. I sent a rider into town this morning to fetch a copy."

He spread his feet a little more to make sure he was well-balanced, then lifted the cane, gripped it in the middle, and shook it at Trent.

"This cannot stand, John! This . . . this insolent pup trying to raise himself to the level of a demagogue and inflame the people against me! Good Lord, this town wouldn't even exist without me. This region would not even be settled if I had not risked my life and everything that was precious to me to come in here and crush all the forces that wanted to hold back the tide of civilization! Hannigan's Hill is *my* town! The range for scores of miles in all directions is *my* range!"

"The . . . the government doesn't see it that way, Ezra," Trent faltered. "It says that the smaller ranchers have a right to be here, too, and so do the homesteaders—"

"Insignificant ants who never risked a thing, but now want to reap the benefits of others' sacrifices! I'll never give them an inch, John. Not one inch, do you understand?"

Hannigan's round face was no longer pale, but was flushed with anger, instead. He lowered the cane and rested his weight on it again as he drew in several deep breaths to calm himself. When he continued, his voice was steadier, but no less filled with fury and determination.

"As long as my wife rests beneath the soil of this land, I'll never allow anyone to challenge me. Anyone foolish enough to do so will regret it. That includes Albert Whitmore. The so-called power of the press doesn't scare me, any more than savages and owlhoots did! I wiped them out and I'll do the same to any damned fool who gets in my way now."

Trent sank down in the chair behind the desk. "You really shouldn't be telling me these things, Ezra," he said in what was almost a moan of dismay. "You do what you think is best. You always do. But I don't have to know about it, especially before it happens."

Hannigan's thick lips twisted in disdain. "Lost your nerve, *Your Honor*?"

The last two words were so packed with contempt that Trent paled. If he was tempted to respond angrily, though, he suppressed the impulse.

"I'm just saying that if you want me to continue working with you, you have to at least try to see my side of things," Trent said.

"*My* side is the *only* side. Get that through your head now, or we'll make other arrangements."

Let Trent worry about what those arrangements might be. He wouldn't like them, that was certain, Hannigan thought.

Trent looked down at the desk, sighed, and said, "What do you want me to do?"

"For now, nothing. Just hold yourself ready. I'm going to speak to Bowen. If there's any direct action to be taken, he'll do it." Hannigan started to turn away, then paused to add, "You've been helpful to me so far, John, and I appreciate that. Don't allow nerves or some misguided sense of morality to ruin things between us."

"I won't, Ezra," Trent said without looking up. "You can count on me."

"I had better be able to," Hannigan said.

Luke was headed toward the Lucky Shot Saloon when he glanced over and saw that he was passing the marshal's office. He hesitated, then gave a mental shrug and turned in that direction. He supposed it wouldn't do any harm to let Ethan Stallings know that they were

going to be here longer than either of them had anticipated. Stallings might figure that out when his breakfast arrived, but Luke didn't see any point in keeping
him in the dark until then.

Marshal Bowen wasn't in the office. The deputy
called Jed looked up from the desk when Luke opened
the door and came in. His face tightened with anger as
he recognized the visitor. He started to stand up and his
hand moved toward the gun on his hip.

For half a second, Luke thought he was going to
have to shoot the man.

Then Jed got control of himself and didn't complete
the draw, stopping it before his hand touched the gun
butt. That was a good thing, because if the gun had
started to come out of leather, Luke would have drawn
his Remingtons and blasted the deputy into eternity.
His reflexes wouldn't have allowed him to do otherwise.

"What do you want?" Jed asked.

Luke hadn't noticed it before when Jed came into
Mac's Place with Bowen and the other deputy, but the
man held himself as if he was rather stiff and sore, and
some bruises showed on his face. Were those the re-
sults of that fight in the street the night before, when
the masked men had jumped Luke?

That was entirely possible, Luke decided. He was
pretty sore himself this morning from that fracas.

"I need to talk to my prisoner for a minute," he said.
It wouldn't do any good to stir up more trouble, so he
kept his tone civil.

"If you ask me, the marshal should've told you to go

to Hell when you asked if you could lock that fella up. This is a jail, not a damn hotel, and he ain't broken any laws here."

"That's true," Luke allowed. "Just call it professional courtesy, and I'm obliged to Marshal Bowen for his cooperation."

Jed jerked a thumb toward the cellblock. "Go ahead. But if that varmint tries anything, don't expect me to come runnin' to help you."

"That's fine," Luke said. He was confident that Stallings wouldn't try anything tricky. Stallings didn't seem to have any real capacity for violence. Anyway, Luke wasn't going to give him the chance.

Stallings got up from the bunk and came quickly to the cell door when Luke walked in. "It's getting kind of late," he said. "When do I get some food and coffee? And when do we get out of this place?"

"Are you anxious to get back east so you can apologize to Senator Creed for swindling him out of that money?"

Stallings grasped the bars in the door. Instead of answering Luke's question, he asked one of his own. "Have you ever heard the old saying that you can't swindle an honest man? Creed was looking to make a fast, shady profit for himself or he never would have fallen for my scheme."

"What did you do, anyway? I never got the details."

Stallings waved dismissively. "Oh, it was a water rights deal. An honest man would've known it was too good to be true, especially since it would have bankrupted a bunch of innocent farmers if it had been real.

But Creed didn't care about that. He just wanted to put some extra money in his pocket. Hell, he swindles his constituents every day by promising them honest representation."

For all Luke knew, Stallings's bitter assessment of Senator Jonas Creed was a hundred percent accurate. But that didn't matter in this situation, so he got back to the subject at hand and said, "We're staying here in Hannigan's Hill for a while. Some breakfast should be brought over to you soon."

Stallings looked confused. "What do you mean, 'we're staying'? I thought you were going to send a wire to Washington and find out what to do next."

"I did. The senator told me to stay put with you until he gets in touch with me again."

Stallings shook his head and said, "I don't like the sound of that. Creed is up to something, Jensen."

"He's more than halfway across the country from here," Luke pointed out. "How can he be up to anything?"

"I don't know, but you mark my words, this is going to be trouble."

"Just sit down and take it easy," Luke told him. "Your food should be along soon."

As Luke turned back toward the cellblock door, he heard voices in the outer office, punctuated by a thumping sound. A deep, rumbling voice was saying, ". . . tell you, I'm not going to put up with this, Bowen. You'd better do something, and waste no time about it!"

Luke paused before stepping into the doorway and revealing that he was back here. He heard Verne Bowen say something that he couldn't make out; then Jed spoke up and interrupted the conversation between Bowen and whoever had come in with him.

"Uh, Marshal, Mr. Hannigan, excuse me for butting in, but there's a fella back there in the cellblock—"

"You mean the prisoner?" Bowen asked.

"No, sir. The fella who brought him in. Jensen."

There was no point in staying back here any longer. Luke walked out of the cellblock and into the office.

Bowen stood there with the man Luke had seen in the fancy carriage earlier. Mac had confirmed that was Ezra Hannigan. Since Hannigan had been talking when he and Bowen came into the marshal's office, Luke expected to see him out here.

"Jensen, what the hell are you doing skulking around in my jail?" Bowen demanded.

"I'm not 'skulking,'" Luke said. "And your deputy said it was all right for me to speak to my prisoner."

"Come to get him out, have you?"

"Unfortunately, just the opposite. We're going to be staying here in Hannigan's Hill for the time being, until I get more instructions from the individual who posted the reward on Stallings."

"What?" Bowen glared at him. "You're just going to keep him locked up here?"

"As long as that's all right with you."

"Well, it's not all right! I have enough problems without—"

Hannigan lifted a hand to stop Bowen's angry response. "If this man, Stallings, is a criminal, Marshal, of course, he should remain locked up. We can't have lawbreakers running loose in our town, can we?"

Bowen didn't look happy about that, but he said, "Uh, no, I suppose not, Mr. Hannigan."

Hannigan's cane thumped on the floor again as he shuffled forward and extended his other hand to Luke. "I'm Ezra Hannigan. The town is named after me."

Luke would have rather grabbed a handful of maggots, but he clasped Hannigan's hand and shook it. "Luke Jensen."

"I've heard a little about you, sir. I'm told you're a bounty hunter."

"That's my job, all right."

"Not a highly respected one, I'd venture to say."

"I never worried overmuch about such things."

A bark of laughter came from Hannigan. "Neither did I, sir, neither did I. And it hasn't held me back. I'd rather be feared than have the so-called respect of some toadying sycophant. Better for an enemy to be wary of you."

"Even better to take them by surprise."

This time, the guffaw Hannigan let out sounded more genuine. "Indeed! You can keep your prisoner here as long as necessary, Jensen."

Bowen's scowl deepened. He didn't like Hannigan speaking for him. Yet, at the same time, no one in this room had any doubt who was really calling the shots around here. To pretend otherwise was a waste of time.

Maybe trying to save a little bit of his dignity, Bowen asked, "Is there anything else you need, Jensen?"

Luke shook his head. "No, that'll do it for now. Obliged to you, Marshal."

"Forget it," Bowen snapped. "What do you plan to do while you're waiting?"

"Actually, I was on my way over to the Lucky Shot when I decided to stop here. I thought I might as well while away the time in pleasant company."

Bowen's face darkened. If Hannigan hadn't been there, there was no telling what he might have done. But he didn't want to lose control in front of his boss, so he said in a taut voice, "Yeah, you go ahead and do that. I'll be seeing you around, Jensen."

Hannigan lifted a pudgy finger to the brim of his big hat and added, "Good day to you, sir."

"Mr. Hannigan," Luke said with a nod. He circled the other men and went to the door, managing to do so without fully turning his back on them, but not being too obvious about that.

He knew Bowen already didn't like him, but he had made the marshal even more of an enemy, he thought as he walked away in the street outside. Now he and Hannigan had had a chance to size each other up, and he figured that despite the jovial façade, Hannigan regarded him as an enemy, too.

Luke didn't waste any time or energy, though, pondering what they might be saying about him right now in the marshal's office. Or what they planned to do about him . . .

He knew he would find out sooner or later.

Chapter 16

The ugly stranger with the eye patch had been right: The Lucky Shot was open and, in fact, was doing a decent amount of business despite the relatively early hour. It was a good place for getting out of the cold, and it had a convivial atmosphere. A couple of poker games were going on and half-a-dozen men stood at the bar, drinking. The roulette wheel was silent at the moment, as was the piano, but both of them would get going later, Luke knew.

He spotted the stranger he had talked to among the customers at the bar. The man saw him, too, and waved him over. Luke hesitated, but as he looked around, he didn't see Irish Mahoney anywhere in the room. Maybe it was too early for her to be up and around. So he went to the bar and joined the stranger, with a nod that wasn't quite friendly, but was pleasant enough.

"You were right," the man said. "This here is a right

nice place. I'm obliged to you for pointin' it out. Have a beer on me as my way of thankin' you."

"That's not necessary—"

The man scowled and broke in, "It ain't a matter of necessary. It's somethin' I want to do."

"Well, in that case, I'll have that beer, and you're welcome."

Luke nodded to the bartender, who filled a mug from the tap and slid it in front of him. At least the beer at the Lucky Shot was good, Luke thought as he lifted the mug in salute to the eye-patched man and then took a swallow.

"Name's Costaine," the man introduced himself. "Jack Costaine. Some folks call me Cougar Jack. You might've heard tell of me."

The name did strike a faint chord in Luke's mind, the same way that he had thought earlier he had laid eyes on Costaine before, without actually meeting the man. But the memory was vague, so he shook his head and said, "Sorry, don't think I have."

Costaine looked a little disappointed by that.

"My name is Jensen," Luke went on. He didn't supply his first name. He didn't have any desire to build a friendship with this man. He was just killing time, something he might have to do a lot of if Senator Creed didn't get back in touch with him soon.

"I'm glad to know you. You live around these parts, or are you just passin' through like me?"

"Just passing through," Luke said.

"That's right, you said you'd only et at Mac's Place a couple of times. I might go over there and try some of his grub in a little while. Want to come along?"

"We'll see," Luke said. Costaine's buffalo coat had a rather pungent aroma, so Luke wasn't sure if he wanted to share a meal with the man. He was beginning to regret even joining him at the bar.

Rescue came in the appealing form of Irish Mahoney, who appeared at Luke's other elbow and smiled up at him. He hadn't seen her come down the stairs from the second floor. She might have been in the saloon's office, through a door at the end of the bar.

"Hello, Luke," she said. "It's good to see you again. I thought you might have left town by now."

"I guess you haven't heard. I'm going to be staying for a while."

He didn't elaborate just yet on why he wasn't leaving Hannigan's Hill. Although he couldn't explain it, he had a hunch that he didn't want to say too much about his business in front of Cougar Jack Costaine.

"That's good news," Irish said. She linked her arm with Luke's. "Why don't you come and join me? That is, if I'm not interrupting anything . . . ?"

Costaine leaned forward to leer past Luke at the redhead. "No, ma'am, you go right ahead and take him," he told her, obviously having heard her invitation. "No feller in his right mind'd rather spend time with a ol' goat like me, instead of with a mighty fine-lookin' gal like yourself. I'll see you later, Jensen."

Luke picked up his beer, said, "I'm obliged to you, Jack," and let Irish steer him to a table in the back of the room.

"You're welcome," she said as they sat down. "Unless I read the situation wrong and you weren't wanting to be rescued from that . . . colorful character . . . you were talking to."

"You read things exactly right," Luke told her, "and I appreciate it."

"So he's not a friend of yours?"

"I laid eyes on him for the first time a little while ago when he rode into town. Wait, let me amend that statement. I believe I may have seen him somewhere, sometime in the past, but I can't recall where or when. So no, we're not friends. Barely acquaintances, in fact. He told me his name is Cougar Jack Costaine."

Irish shook her head. "Never heard of him. He's definitely new in Hannigan's Hill. It would be difficult to forget someone like him, once you met him. Or even saw him." She laughed. "But let's not waste time talking about such things. Tell me why you're staying for a while. I consider that a stroke of good fortune, but you may not."

"Call it a matter of business. I have to wait for a telegram."

"From the man who posted the reward for your prisoner?"

"That's an astute guess."

"It seemed like the most logical reason. So you don't have any idea how long you're going to be here?"

Luke shook his head. "None at all."

"I'll enjoy having you around while I can, then."

Luke took another drink of the beer Costaine had bought for him and then said, "I'm not sure Marshal Bowen will care much for that."

"Do you think I care what Verne Bowen likes or doesn't like?"

Luke shrugged. "It might be wise to care at least a little. From what I've seen of the marshal, he doesn't seem like the most forgiving man in the world if he believes he's been wronged."

"Verne and I have an understanding," Irish said. "We enjoy each other's company from time to time, but when we're not together, neither of us has any ties on the other."

Despite what Irish said, Luke had a feeling the "understanding" between her and Bowen went in only one direction. She was supposed to overlook whatever he did, but he probably wouldn't extend the same courtesy to her.

However, he didn't intend to put that to the test. While he enjoyed talking to Irish Mahoney, that was as far as he planned on taking it.

He had learned over the years that while trouble invariably showed up, there was no point in inviting it early.

When Mac had the breakfast tray ready to send over to the jail, he went to the front door of the café and looked out into the street. Chet Baxter, who helped him out from time to time, was usually around somewhere, and he thought he could get Chet to deliver the tray.

Failing that, he would leave the café open and deliver the meal himself. Nearly everybody in Hannigan's Hill was law-abiding, with the exception of the men who should have been the most trustworthy: Marshal Bowen and his deputies. Mac wouldn't worry about the business if he had to leave it unattended for a few minutes.

He didn't see any sign of Chet. However, Jessie Whitmore was walking along the street, and when she saw Mac standing in the doorway, she turned and came toward him.

"Good morning, Mac," she said as she smiled. "How are you today?"

"All right, I suppose," he said. "How about you and Albert?"

She looked more solemn as she answered, "Well, I don't think either of us slept very well last night. I know I didn't. That was the first time I've ever been shot at."

"It can be a mite disconcerting, all right," he allowed. He didn't mention that he'd heard bullets flying around his head so many times in his life, he didn't even think about it all that much anymore. As long as he lived through it, that was the only important thing.

He went on, "You caused quite a stir with that extra edition. I must've seen a hundred people or more reading it this morning."

"Good," she said vehemently. "Maybe it'll open the eyes of enough of the citizens that something will finally be done about Ezra Hannigan's heavy-handed behavior."

Mac wasn't going to count on that. In his experience, most people might get worked up enough about wrongdoing to run their mouths, but they wouldn't actually take a stand and fight back unless their lives, or the lives of their loved ones, were at stake. Of course, it might come to that, the way things were going around here . . .

He changed the subject by saying, "You look mighty nice today."

She blushed faintly and seemed pleased by the compliment. What Mac had said was true. Jessie wore a dark blue skirt and jacket over a frilly white blouse. A velvet choker with a gemstone on it was around her neck. Her blond hair was put up and a hat that matched the suit was perched on it.

"You look almost like you're going to church," Mac added.

"No, not church, but almost as important. The bank."

"Oh. Making a deposit?"

Jessie started to look uncomfortable, making Mac wish he had kept his mouth shut. She said, "Not exactly. You know that Mr. Grissom loaned us some money when we came here and established the *Chronicle*. We had that inheritance from Albert's grandfather, of course, but it wasn't enough. We've been paying back the loan since then."

"Uh, Jessie, you don't have to tell me about this. It's your business. I didn't mean to pry."

"Goodness, don't worry about that. You're our best friend in this town, Mac. I don't mind sharing things with you, even problems."

"Well, if listening helps . . ."

"Business hasn't been good lately. Some of the people who subscribed to the paper hadn't renewed, and we haven't been selling as much advertising. Many of the businesses here in town are reluctant to continue supporting the paper."

"Because they're afraid of Ezra Hannigan," Mac said with a frown.

"The reasons don't matter. What's important is that we're not going to be able to make the full payment on our loan this month, and I thought it would be a good idea to let Mr. Grissom know about the situation. I'm sure things will turn around and we'll catch up quickly. We just need the bank to be a little patient . . ."

"Howard Grissom's a good man, but Hannigan is the biggest stockholder in that bank," Mac said. "I don't know how much leeway he'll let Grissom give you."

Jessie's chin lifted the way it did when she was angry . . . or scared. "Mr. Hannigan claims to be civic-minded," she said. "Surely, he can understand that it's good business for a town to have a local newspaper."

"Maybe not when it's all the time talking about what a bad hombre he is."

"Albert just reports the truth."

"As he sees it."

Her blue eyes narrowed as she gazed at him. "Just whose side are you on, Mac?"

"Damn it, I'm on your side!" he wanted to yell at her. *"On your side and your husband's side. But especially on yours . . ."*

But there was no way he could say that, not without admitting feelings he didn't want to bring out into the open. So instead, he said, "Look, I want to help out. The café has done well, and I have some money saved up—"

She was shaking her head before he could finish what he was going to say. She said, "I told you, you're

our best friend in Hannigan's Hill, Mac. Taking money
from you might be the beginning of the end of that
friendship. Neither Albert nor I would want that."

"I wouldn't want it, either. I just thought that if I
could help—"

She interrupted him again. "It's sweet of you to
offer, but no." She took a deep breath, which drew more
of his attention to her bosom than he liked. "Now I'd
better get on and talk to Mr. Grissom."

"Stop back by if you want to and tell me how it
went."

"We'll see," she said.

Feeling awkward and sort of wishing he hadn't
stepped into the doorway at the moment he had, he
watched her walk on down the street toward the bank.
He hadn't known that the newspaper was having
money problems, but what Jessie had said made sense.
Ezra Hannigan had half the town buffaloed, if not
more. Mac couldn't blame people for not wanting to
get on his bad side. They had families and businesses
to take care of, too.

Mac went back into the café, picked up the breakfast tray, and carried it over to the jail. Marshal Bowen
wasn't there; one of the deputies was on duty. Mac didn't
know his name. The fellow gave him a sullen look, but
told him to take the tray to the prisoner.

"It's about time," Ethan Stallings said as he took the
food through the narrow, horizontal opening in the
barred door. "It'll be time for another meal soon. Or do
I have to wait until supper?"

"I told Luke I'd provide three square meals a day for
you. I'll get another one over here later. You may have

to wait until I can work it in, though. You're not going to get the same kind of service here you would in a hotel in New Orleans or San Francisco."

Stallings sighed and said, "I suppose not. I don't reckon you've heard any more from Jensen about when we're going to be leaving?"

"Luke doesn't tell me his business. Give me that tray from last night."

Stallings passed the empty tray through the slot. As Mac went out through the office, he told the deputy, "You can give him a cup of coffee."

"The marshal didn't tell me to do that," the man replied sullenly. "And I sure as blazes don't take orders from you, McKenzie."

"That's fine. When the prisoner starts caterwauling about it, you can deal with him, not me."

"I'll deal with him, all right. I'll bend a pistol barrel over his head if he gives me too much trouble."

Mac grew serious. "Take it easy there," he advised. "Stallings may not look like much, but don't give him a chance to jump you. We don't know what he's capable of."

"Just go peddle your hash," the deputy snapped.

Mac left the marshal's office and headed back to the café. The place had been empty when he left, but as he came in, he saw that one customer had shown up. A man in a buffalo coat and a battered old hat sat on a stool at the counter. As Mac closed the door, the man turned on the stool and said, "Well, howdy there, Dewey 'Mac' McKenzie."

Chapter 17

Mac stopped just inside the door and frowned in surprise and confusion. The old tension, the sickening feeling of never knowing when and where danger might come at him, flooded through him. He wasn't carrying a gun, but his hand ached to reach for one.

He did his best to control that response and even managed to smile a little as he said, "Sorry, friend. You seem to have the advantage on me. Do we know each other?"

"Naw, we ain't never met. But I know who you are."

That didn't make Mac feel any better.

A grin broke out on the man's ugly face. "You're the feller who cooks the best food in this whole dang town."

Relief went through Mac. He said, "I don't know who you've been talking to, but I appreciate the testimonial." He went behind the counter. "What can I do for you? I have a pot of stew simmering in the kitchen, and there's a pan of fresh corn bread in the oven."

The man grinned and slapped a hand on the counter in enthusiasm. "Now you're talkin'! Bring it on, Mac."

"Sure. You want coffee?"

"Black and plenty of it will plumb hit the spot. And by the way, it was a feller name of Jensen who told me this was the best eatin' place in town."

Mac nodded. "Yes, I know Luke."

"Luke Jensen," the stranger said slowly. "He didn't tell me his front handle. Seems like I've heard that name before, but I ain't sure."

Mac didn't say anything else. He didn't know who this man was. Maybe he was acquainted with Luke, as he claimed, or maybe he was fishing for information for some unknown reason.

Mac was certain of one thing: He had never seen the stranger in Hannigan's Hill before. With that eye patch, those rawboned features, and those big ears, he was so distinctive-looking that it would be impossible to forget him. Not to mention the buffalo coat and that old hat with the turned-up front brim.

Mac poured the coffee and set a bowl of stew and plate of corn bread in front of the stranger, who dug in with gusto and a lot of slurping and smacking. Between eager bites, the man said, "My name's Costaine. They call me Cougar Jack."

"I'm glad to meet you, Mr. Costaine. You already know my name."

"Yep, I sure do. You don't have to call me mister. If I ain't payin' close attention, I'm likely not gonna answer to it. Jack or Cougar Jack will do fine and dandy."

Costaine gulped down more stew and then said, "You know, this tastes a whole heap like the stew we used to get when I was pushin' longhorns up the trail from South Texas to Kansas. Chuckwagon stew, I reckon you could call it."

"That's where I learned how to make it," Mac admitted. "I drove a chuckwagon myself for a spell."

Costaine leaned back on the stool as his eyes opened wider. "You don't say! You reckon we was ever on any of the same trail drives?"

"I suppose it's possible," Mac said, although he considered that highly unlikely. "I don't remember you, but that was a good number of years ago."

"It durned sure was. Them days is dead and gone now, like so many of the fellers who followed those trails. Gone across the divide and ain't never comin' back." Costaine scratched his angular jaw as he frowned in thought. "I recollect one ramrod I rode for, a gent name of Flagg."

"Patrick Flagg?" Mac asked, his interest quickening.

Costaine slapped the counter again. "That's him! You knowed him?"

"He was the trail boss on the first drive I ever made. I learned a lot from him."

He had learned a lot about handling a gun from Patrick Flagg, Mac thought, but the trail boss had also taught him plenty of other things, like courage and loyalty and determination. It wouldn't be an exaggeration to say that Flagg had taken a scared boy on the run and started the process of molding him into a man. Mac had never forgotten him and never would.

Costaine sighed and said, "Ol' Flagg's done crossed over, too, or so I hear."

"That's right. A long time ago."

"A pure shame. But knowin' him, he wouldn't have wanted to wind up sitting in a rockin' chair on some porch, lettin' the years whittle him down to nothin'."

"No, probably not."

They might have talked more about the old days, but the door opened and three more customers came in, followed within minutes by several more. The midday rush was beginning, and it would keep Mac busy for a while.

Sometime during that hectic period, Cougar Jack Costaine finished his meal and departed, leaving a silver dollar beside his empty plate to pay for his meal and some extra. Mac hadn't seen the man go, and he was a little sorry when he noticed the empty place at the counter. Costaine was a colorful character, and Mac had enjoyed talking to him.

But Costaine had seemed to really like the food, so Mac had a feeling that sooner or later he would be back.

The rest of that day passed, and so did another, and still Luke hadn't heard any more from Senator Jonas Creed. He considered sending another telegram to the senator to remind him that he and Stallings were waiting here in Hannigan's Hill, but he held off on that for the time being. Creed's initial reply had made it clear that he would be in touch, and he might get annoyed if he thought that Luke was pressuring him.

Anyway, despite the air of tension that hung over the settlement, a man could get to like it here, Luke thought. The overcast had broken and the weather had warmed up somewhat under cloud-dotted blue skies. The dusting of snow from a couple of mornings earlier had melted. The snowcapped mountains to the west were clearly visible in the crisp, thin air.

Luke took all his meals at Mac's Place, so he had plenty of good food to eat. He spent quite a bit of time talking to Mac and the friendship between the two of them deepened. Most of the rest of Luke's time, he was at the Lucky Shot, playing cards, nursing drinks, listening to the piano music, and enjoying the company of the beautiful Irish Mahoney.

More than once, Luke had gone into the saloon to find that Irish was already sitting with Marshal Verne Bowen. On those occasions, he hadn't tried to intrude, instead ambling over to the bar or finding a poker game to sit in on.

Likewise, when Luke was with Irish and Bowen came in, the marshal steered clear of them. Somehow, the two men seemed to have declared an unofficial truce. Luke didn't care how it had come about; he just didn't want any trouble.

Things were quiet overall in the settlement. Luke had looked up at the hill where the gallows was located and noted that Thad Crawford's body was gone. Someone had cut it down instead of leaving it up there to serve as a grim reminder of Ezra Hannigan's power.

Luke wondered if Hannigan had ordered that. After the way everyone in town had been reading the extra edition of the *Chronicle* and talking about what had happened, Hannigan might have decided that it would be wise to back off a mite. To loosen the grip of his iron fist on the settlement, even if only slightly.

He could always crack down again later, when it suited his purposes better.

Luke was having supper in the café, sitting at the counter, when Mac came up and said, "I never did thank you for recommending this place to that fella Costaine."

Luke had to think for a second before he recalled the conversation with the stranger from a couple of days earlier. When he did, he chuckled and said, "Came in to try the food, did he?"

"That's right, and he really seemed to like it. Enough so that I'm surprised he hasn't been back. Have you seen him around town yesterday or today?"

Luke considered the question, then shook his head. "Come to think of it, I don't believe I have. And that doesn't seem like something I would overlook."

"No, he was definitely somebody you'd take notice of."

Luke shrugged. "Well, he said he was just passing through, so I suppose he picked up some supplies or whatever brought him here and then rode on. I can't say as I'll particularly miss him, now that he's gone."

"He and I had a mutual friend, you know."

"Really?"

"Yeah. Patrick Flagg. Trail boss on the first cattle drive I ever was part of. Costaine claimed he went up the trail from Texas to Kansas a few times himself."

"He might have. With that coat he wore, I had him pegged more as a buffalo hunter. But I suppose that you don't have to have hunted the creatures to wear their hides." Luke grunted. "Seems more sporting, somehow, though."

Before they could continue discussing Costaine, Albert Whitmore came in and took the empty stool next to Luke after giving him a friendly nod. He wore a brown tweed suit today, instead of his printer's apron.

"Hello, Mac. Can I get a cup of coffee?"

"Sure, but doesn't Jessie usually keep a pot on the stove down at the newspaper office?"

"She does," Albert said, "but sometimes I'm in the mood for the way you brew it. Has a little of that New Orleans flavor to it."

Mac grinned. "That's the chicory. I'd put more in it, but I kind of got out of the habit while I was driving chuckwagons. Those cowboys wanted plain old Arbuckle's as stout as I could brew it. That's what they needed most days to stay in the saddle from dawn to dusk or longer."

"I can understand that. Some days, it feels like coffee's the only thing keeping me going. Well, that and the need to make sure that Jessie's taken care of." Albert paused. "That part of it is kind of worrisome these days."

Mac was filling a cup from the coffeepot as Albert said that. Luke noticed the way the pot jerked just a little as Albert mentioned his wife's name. The motion interrupted the flow of the coffee for a split second, but it wasn't enough to spill any of the hot black brew.

"Not sure I know what you're talking about," Mac said as he set the coffeepot aside.

"I think Hannigan's put out the word to all the businesses in town, at least the ones he has his fat little fingers in. He's told them not to advertise with us anymore. The money we're taking in has dropped quite a bit. The accounts that owe us keep putting us off. I know times can be hard, but they're hard for us, too."

Mac hesitated, then said, "Jessie stopped to chat for a minute the other day when she was on her way to talk to Howard Grissom at the bank. She mentioned some of this."

Albert nodded. "She told me she'd talked to you, and that you offered to loan us some money. I hope you understand why we absolutely can't agree to that, Mac."

"Sure," Mac said. "It's usually not a good idea to mix friendship and finances."

"That's right. However . . . the next regular edition of the paper comes out tomorrow. We'll lose money on it, more than likely, but I don't want to miss an issue. When a paper starts doing that, it usually never recovers. So the *Chronicle* will be on the streets tomorrow morning as scheduled, come hell or high water. And if, as a friend, you'd like to help us make that deadline, I sure wouldn't say no to the offer."

Mac laughed and reached across the counter to clap a hand on Albert's shoulder.

"I'll be there," he promised. "Whether it's turning the crank on the press or lugging buckets of ink, I can handle that. Just tell me what to do."

"We appreciate it."

"I'll be there after I've got things squared away enough for Alf to close up."

Luke said, "What's your editorial going to be about this time, Mr. Whitmore? Hannigan seems to be keeping a low profile the past couple of days."

"That doesn't change all the despicable things he's done in the past," Albert said. "Just because a snake's gone back down in its hole for the moment, that doesn't mean it's not still there, full of venom and just waiting to come out and strike again."

That was true enough, Luke thought, but maybe it would be a good idea not to poke a stick down that snake hole. That sounded like what Albert Whitmore intended to do by continuing to editorialize against Ezra Hannigan.

Nothing he said was going to change that, though, so he didn't try. He just sipped his own coffee and told Albert, "Good luck to you."

"I'm not sure if you need luck as long as you have truth on your side."

Luke didn't believe that. Not for a second. Everybody could use a little luck. He thought it was a little pompous of Albert to say otherwise.

"I hope you'll pick up a copy of the paper in the morning," Albert went on.

"I wouldn't miss it," Luke said.

Albert finished his coffee and left. When he was gone, Mac said quietly, "Albert gets a little carried away sometimes with this whole 'power of the press' business and acting like he's on some sort of noble crusade."

"From what I've seen, he's right about Hannigan, and he's doing good work," Luke replied. "I reckon that is kind of noble. The way he talks is probably to prop himself up, as much as anything else. He must feel like the whole world is against him sometimes."

"Yeah, I imagine so. All he's got is Jessie."

"And you. You're their friend as well."

"Yeah," Mac said, sounding a little distracted as he looked out the café's front window. Luke glanced over his shoulder to see if Mac was looking at anything in particular. The street scene appeared completely normal. Mac had to be thinking about something else.

Or someone else.

Jessie Whitmore.

Luke gazed down into his coffee cup. None of his business, he told himself for what seemed like the hundredth time since he and Stallings had first ridden in sight of that gallows with its grisly adornment.

But it was as true now as it had ever been. The last thing he wanted was to poke his nose into any personal drama involving Mac McKenzie and the Whitmores . . .

Chapter 18

Mac put on his hat and coat and nodded to Alf Karlsson as he moved out from behind the counter. Only four customers were left in the café, and they already had the food they had ordered. It was unlikely anyone else would come in, but if they did, some stew remained in the pot and there were always beans ready, too. Alf could dish that up. There was pie left and, of course, coffee.

"Mac, aren't you forgetting something?" Alf asked.

Mac paused and frowned in thought. "I don't believe so."

Alf shook his head and said, "What happened the last time you went down the street to help Mr. and Mrs. Whitmore get their newspaper printed?"

"Oh," Mac said. "You're right."

He went behind the counter again and took the Smith & Wesson off the shelf. He tucked it in his waistband and let the coat hang over the gun butt.

"I don't think there's going to be any trouble tonight, but it doesn't hurt to be ready."

"George Armstrong Custer didn't think he was going to run into that many Indians, either, now, did he?"

"You have a point there," Mac agreed. He waved as he left the café.

It was a cold, clear night. His breath fogged in front of his face as he walked toward the *Chronicle* office. He kept his eyes moving, searching the shadows ahead of him and off to the sides, alert for any signs of an ambush.

Marshal Bowen knew that he had been at the newspaper office the night the extra edition was printed. That meant Ezra Hannigan knew it as well. It was possible he was being watched. They might make a move against him, even if it was just to prevent him from helping Albert and Jessie tonight and in the future.

One thing he knew for sure about Hannigan, the man held a grudge. He wouldn't like it that Mac had thrown in with his enemies. Mac had never made a secret of his friendship with Albert and Jessie, but he hadn't directly opposed Hannigan until a few nights earlier, either.

And he didn't believe for a second that flimsy story about some of Ed Glasby's hands being responsible for the shots fired at the newspaper office. More than likely, nobody in Hannigan's Hill believed it . . . but many would pretend to because it served their own interests.

All those thoughts made Mac wary as he walked toward the newspaper office. But the few people on the street on this chilly evening were clearly bent on other errands and no one approached him.

He wasn't the only one being cautious. The office door was locked when he got there, as it had been the previous time. The bullet-shattered windows had not been replaced yet; boards had been nailed up in their place.

Albert answered his knock this time, instead of Jessie, and not until he had called through the door, "Who's there?"

"It's me. Mac."

The key rattled in the lock. Albert swung the door open. In his right hand, he held an old cap-and-ball pistol.

"Come on in," he invited. "We're being careful tonight."

"Nothing wrong with that." Mac nodded toward the revolver. "Does that old hogleg actually work?"

"Yeah, it does. I rode out a little ways from town earlier today and tried it. I figured if it was going to blow up when I pulled the trigger, it ought to be where nobody else was around. It worked fine, though. I've kept it good and clean all these years. It belonged to my father."

"Did he ever use it?"

"Not that I know of," Albert said, shaking his head. He closed the door, locked it, and pocketed the key.

"Can I give you a word of advice?" Mac asked.

"Sure."

"When you call through a door like that, and you don't know who's on the other side, but it could be somebody who's out to hurt you . . . it would be a good idea to step to one side or the other. A double-barreled Greener can blow a hole right through a door like that."

Albert's eyes widened in the realization that Mac was right. "I never thought of that," he said. "But if it was some hard case like the ones who work for Marshal Bowen, mightn't he guess that I'd move aside and take that into account when he fired the shotgun?"

"Well, yeah," Mac admitted, "but at least you'd have a fifty-fifty chance of him guessing wrong which way you went."

Albert stared at him for a second and then laughed. "I'm not sure if you're joshing me or not, Mac. Still, I guess it's good, practical advice." He leaned his head toward the door to the other room. "Come on. The type is set and inked, and we're ready to start turning out copies."

Mac took off his hat and coat, placed them on the small counter, and followed Albert into the other room. Jessie stood there beside the printing press. "Hello, Mac," she greeted him.

She wore an apron like the one Albert had on, and the sleeves of her blouse were rolled up. Somehow, she had already gotten an ink smudge on her nose. Mac thought it looked downright adorable, but he caught himself before he said anything like that. Whether Jessie was adorable or not was none of his concern.

He wished he could make himself believe that.

For now, he just returned her smile and said, "I'll take the first turn on the crank. I'm ready to get to work."

"Ready to be a thorn in Ezra Hannigan's side?" Albert asked with a grin.

"That's our job, isn't it?" Mac said.

"Our job, not yours."

"I've picked my side in this fight. Too late to back out now."

Mac moved over to the press and grasped the crank handle. Jessie stayed where she was, and he was all too aware of how close she was to him. Close enough he could smell the clean scent of her hair . . .

"Go ahead and give her what she needs, Mac," Albert said.

Mac blinked. "What?"

"The crank. Give her a turn."

Mac drew in a deep breath, turned the crank, and a sheet of newsprint rolled through the press to come out on the other side with the front page of the *Chronicle* printed on it. The run of the paper's next edition was underway.

Luke studied the cards in his hand, then picked up a couple of five-dollar gold pieces from the pile in front of him and tossed them into the center of the table, adding them to the pot that was already there.

"I'll see your five and raise five," he said.

All the other players had dropped out of this hand except the owner of the local hardware store. It was a friendly, low-stakes game, but the players still took it seriously. The man pondered his cards for a long moment and then matched what Luke had put in, saying, "I'll call."

Luke laid down his three queens. His opponent shook his head and said, "That beats my jacks," before tossing his cards away. Luke raked in the pot. He was well ahead for the evening, but because of the low stakes, his winnings didn't really add up to all that much.

Even so, he had won, instead of losing, and that was worth something. He was just passing the time, anyway.

"I believe I'll take a break, gentlemen," he said as he gathered up the coins and greenbacks. "It's been enjoyable, and perhaps I'll rejoin you later."

No one objected. Luke went to the bar and told the apron to bring him a beer.

He picked up the mug and turned so that he was leaning his back against the bar as he sipped the beer. He looked across the room at the table where Irish Mahoney sat with Marshal Verne Bowen. They had been together over there when Luke came in. He had left them alone, thinking that maybe Bowen might leave later and he could talk to Irish then, but so far, the marshal looked like he wasn't going anywhere. He laughed from time to time and so did Irish.

Her gaze darted over toward the bar now and then, however, when it appeared Bowen wasn't paying attention. Luke knew she was looking at him. Was she trying to communicate that she wanted him to come over there and confront Bowen? To have it out with the marshal and settle things, once and for all? An awkward situation like this couldn't hang fire forever.

And if he had known that he was going to be here longer, he might be more inclined to do something about it. But he might have to take Stallings out of the jail and leave Hannigan's Hill on short notice, so it seemed to him that no matter how beautiful Irish was, her favors weren't worth killing a man over—or getting killed.

Then the deputy named Jed came into the Lucky Shot, looked around, spotted Bowen, and headed right for him. He wove through the tables and came to a stop beside the one where Bowen and Irish sat. Leaning over, he spoke in what appeared to be a quick, animated fashion to his boss.

Bowen listened with great interest and then jerked his head in a nod. He spoke curtly to Irish before getting up and leaving the saloon, with Jed following closely on his heels.

Irish looked considerably put out at being deserted like this. She glared toward the door where Bowen and Jed had disappeared.

Carrying his half-full mug of beer, Luke walked over to the table.

"Looks like some law business took the marshal away," he commented as he stopped beside the table. He didn't sit down.

"Maybe," Irish said. "Jed was careful not to let me hear what he was telling Verne." She gestured at the empty chair, where Bowen had been sitting. "Join me, why don't you?"

"Don't mind if I do," Luke said. He sat down and placed his beer on the table. "Did Bowen at least apologize for abandoning you?"

"He did not," Irish replied tautly. "He just said that he had to go. I didn't argue with him, of course. Wouldn't have done any good if I had. Once Verne's mind is made up . . . or somebody makes it up for him . . . he's not going to change it."

"Someone with a jaundiced view of the hierarchy around here might think you're saying that when Ezra Hannigan says jump, the good marshal asks how high."

"Something like that," Irish said.

A troubling thought stirred in Luke's head. He said, "If you had to venture a guess, what would you say Hannigan has Bowen doing tonight?"

"There's no telling. If the reason Verne rushed out of here has something to do with Hannigan, though, you can bet it means trouble for somebody."

The same thing had occurred to Luke and was making him uneasy. He had no way of knowing if Bowen had rushed out of the saloon to tend to some errand for Hannigan, but if he had, it might have something to do with Albert and Jessie Whitmore and their newspaper. The regular edition of the *Chronicle* came out tomorrow, Luke recalled Mac telling him.

Mac had also mentioned that he was going to give the Whitmores a hand when they printed the paper tonight, just as he had been there when the newspaper office was attacked before.

Those thoughts went through Luke's brain in a matter of seconds, and when they ended, he pushed his chair back.

"Oh, great," Jessie said. "Don't tell me that you're going to run off, too."

"There's just something I have to check on," Luke told her. "I hope I'll be back in a little while."

"Well, maybe I won't be busy . . . and maybe I will," she said, clearly miffed by his pending departure.

Luke would worry about her annoyed reaction later,

if he got around to it. And if this proved to be a false alarm and nothing happened. But until he knew for sure, he had more important things on his mind.

He stood up, drained the last of the beer in his mug, placed the empty on the table, and left the Lucky Shot, going out into the chilly night.

He fastened his jacket against the cold wind. It was short enough that it wouldn't interfere with his draw if he had to reach for his guns. Tugging his hat down tighter, he strode toward the *Chronicle* office at the edge of town.

He couldn't see any lights coming from it as he drew closer, but that didn't mean anything. He had noticed earlier in the day that the broken windows had been boarded up. The new glass would have to come from Laramie, perhaps even Cheyenne, and that would take a while.

He didn't see anyone moving around the building, either, but the shadows were thick and it was hard to tell what they might hide. Luke felt his nerves tightening as he approached. Even if everything turned out to be fine, he might hang around the newspaper office, anyway, at least until they finished printing tomorrow's edition.

He stepped from the street onto the porch and paused, listening intently as he heard a clanking sound from inside the building. That would be the press turning, spitting out copies of the paper. Luke didn't hear anything else, no voices, no footsteps, nothing that would indicate a problem.

But he stiffened as one of his other senses came into

play. He had just caught a whiff of something in the night air. Something he shouldn't have been smelling at this particular place and time . . .

Coal oil.

The sharp tang was unmistakable. Luke followed it toward the far corner of the building, alarm bells going off inside his head as he did so. There was no good reason for anybody to be splashing coal oil around—only bad ones.

He pressed his back to the wall as he reached the corner. With his right hand, he drew the Remington revolver that rode in the cross-draw holster, just forward of his left hip. Holding the gun up next to his head, with his thumb looped over the hammer, ready to cock it, he edged his head past the corner to take a look along the side of the building.

His keen vision spotted a couple of man-sized shapes in the shadows near the rear corner. He heard a few whispered words, without being able to make out what the men were saying. He was about to level the Remington at them and order them to move away from the wall when something happened that made a chill far icier than the night wind go through him.

Flame spurted from the head of a match that one of the men had just struck!

Chapter 19

Luke didn't waste time pondering the situation or issuing any warnings.

Instead, he aimed at the match flame and triggered three shots as fast as he could cock and fire.

The chances of one of his bullets actually hitting the flame and snuffing it out were mighty slim, but he had to try. He hoped at the very least the man holding the match would jerk back away from the slugs whipping through the air in front of his face. If he dropped the match, maybe it would fall far enough away from the wall that it wouldn't ignite the coal oil.

Luke had absolutely no doubt that the men had splashed coal oil on the wall and intended to burn down the *Chronicle* office. The fools. The absolute damned fools. No greater threat existed for a frontier town than that of uncontrolled fire.

But the building that housed the newspaper office sat by itself, Luke recalled, with an alley on one side and open ground on the other. A swift enough response probably would be able to contain the flames.

However, the would-be arsonists hadn't counted on somebody else taking a hand.

The match flame vanished as men yelled curses. Luke hadn't seen it fall, so he hoped that meant luck was on his side and he actually had shot it out. He didn't know what the men might do. Attacked by an unknown, unexpected enemy this way, they might try to flee.

Or they might stay and fight it out.

They stayed and fought.

Gun flame ripped the shadows apart. Luke ducked back around the corner as bullets chewed splinters from the trim board at the corner and sprayed them in the air. Luke drew his other gun, too, and wheeled around the corner, dropping to one knee as he did so. More flame spouted from the muzzles of the Remingtons as he sent a storm of lead scything through the alley.

Before he could tell if those shots had done any good, he heard a gun boom somewhere behind him and felt, as much as heard, a slug sizzling past his head. He twisted and fell back against the front wall of the newspaper office, spotting a muzzle flash across the street as a second shot erupted from that direction.

Luke had emptied the Remington in his right hand, but he still had a couple of rounds in the left-hand gun. He slammed them toward the muzzle flash he had seen.

That left him unarmed except for his knife, and he

didn't think that was going to do him much good in this situation, with enemies on both sides.

Even worse than that, back at the rear of the building, a man's muffled voice shouted, "Light that coal oil, damn it! Burn the place to the ground!"

The printing had gone well so far. The crank on the press wasn't too hard to turn. Mac knew he could keep going for a while. Albert planned to run three hundred copies of the paper. When the front page was done, they would switch forms and Albert would take over the cranking.

After a while, Jessie had moved away from where she was standing. Mac was both relieved and disappointed by that. It was easier to concentrate on what he was doing, without her being so close to him.

Of course, turning a crank wasn't that difficult. He had to keep an eye on the paper and make sure it fed through the press cleanly, that was all.

With the pungent aroma of the freshly printed pages filling the air, it was hard to smell much of anything else. Even so, Mac gradually began to become aware of an odd odor seeping into the room. It took him several minutes to identify it. When he did, he stiffened and stopped turning the crank.

"What's wrong?" Albert asked as he stood beside the tray, where the printed pages were stacked up.

"Do you smell something?" Mac said. "Something like maybe . . . coal oil?"

Jessie was over by the table, where she was composing another page. She lifted her head from what she was doing, sniffed the air, and said, "Why, yes, I think I do. What in the world—"

At that second, gunshots roared somewhere outside the building, but close by.

Mac grabbed the canvas apron he had donned, pulled it up, and reached under it to grab the Smith & Wesson from his waistband.

"Stay here," he snapped at Albert and Jessie. "I'll see what's going on. Albert, give me the key to the front door."

"Mac, be careful!" Jessie cried.

Albert pulled out the old cap-and-ball pistol and said, "I'll come with you, Mac."

"No, blast it! Stay here and protect Jessie."

Albert looked like he wanted to argue, but he grimaced, tossed the key to Mac, and moved over to his wife's side. He urged her toward the press, while Mac ran into the front room. The lamp there was out. He closed the door to the pressroom, which plunged this smaller chamber into darkness.

More gunshots crashed close by. Mac thought they sounded like they came from the front porch. He didn't hear any bullets hitting the building, though. Was this a different sort of attack than the previous one?

And what about that coal oil? Mac's guts twisted as he thought about the damage that a fire fueled by that stuff could cause.

More than likely, that's what somebody would use if they wanted to burn this place down.

Because of the boards nailed over the windows, he couldn't see out. Then he caught a glimpse of a flash and went over to the door. The boards had been put on, as close and tight as possible, to keep the cold air out, but there was a tiny gap between a couple of them due to a knothole, Mac saw now. He put his eye to it and peered through the opening. That gave him a view directly across the street.

Orange muzzle flashes lashed through the darkness. Somebody over there was shooting at the newspaper office, all right. He wasn't going to let them get away with that. Maybe some return fire would spook them and make them run off, like the other time. Mac put the key in the lock, twisted it, and opened the door enough to thrust the Smith & Wesson through the gap.

Shots came from Mac's left. Mac pulled back instinctively, then realized someone on the porch was firing back at the gunmen across the street. He heard shouts, but with all the guns going off, he couldn't make out the words.

Then he saw two men charge into the street, firing toward the newspaper office as they came. He couldn't tell who they were, but under the circumstances, he didn't figure it mattered. He threw the door open all the way, stepped out, and fired two shots into the ground at their feet. That made them stumble and fall, blunting their charge.

"Mac!"

The call came from the corner. Mac recognized the voice. He looked in that direction and saw Luke Jensen getting hurriedly to his feet.

"Around back!" Luke went on. "They're trying to set the building on fire!"

That was exactly what Mac had been afraid of ever

since he'd first sniffed out that coal oil. He leaped to the corner beside Luke, leaned around it, and spotted two vague shapes back there. He squeezed off a shot and one of the men cried out in pain, then stumbled away from the building.

That must have been enough to spook the other man. He grabbed his wounded companion's arm and steadied him as they ran away from the building and disappeared in the shadows.

The two who had charged into the street, and had tried to ventilate Luke, were still in the fight, though. After falling, they had scrambled back up and now they opened fire again. Slugs whistled around the two men on the porch.

A third defender appeared. Albert Whitmore stepped out of the office and the old revolver in his hand boomed and bucked. He fired twice at the attackers, one of whom cried out in pain and spun off his feet. Mac fired at the other one and was rewarded by the sight of the man flying backward as if he'd been swatted off his feet by a giant fist.

Even though it was dark on the porch, Luke was reloading by feel with practiced ease. He had holstered one of the Remingtons as he replaced the loads in the other gun. He snapped it closed and repeated the process.

"Thanks for giving us a hand, Albert," Mac said. "You'd better get back to Jessie."

"No need," Jessie said as she stepped out onto the porch, too.

She held something in her hands, and Mac was

shocked to realize that it was a shotgun. Jessie seemed much too delicate to be wielding such a weapon, but he figured that was just his conception of her, and maybe not the reality. She certainly sounded fierce as she asked, "Is it all over?"

"They were trying to burn down your building," Luke said. "There's still coal oil there in the back that will have to be cleaned up. You'll need to get some buckets of water and wet down the wall, as much as you can, to dilute the stuff."

"Mr. Jensen?" Albert said. "Is that you?"

Mac said, "It looks like Luke came along just in time to keep those fellas from burning you out."

"We're really grateful to you for that, Mr. Jensen," Albert said.

"I had some luck on my side," Luke told him. "Right now, Mrs. Whitmore, why don't you point that shotgun toward those men in the street? They don't look like they have any fight left in them, but they'll be less likely to get up and start more trouble if there's a shotgun aimed at them."

"All right," Jessie said. "I can do that."

"I'll get a bucket and fetch water from the town well," Albert said.

Mac spotted movement up the street and the glow of a lantern. "Hang on, Albert," he said. "Someone's coming."

All four of them on the porch turned to face this new potential threat. As the figures came closer, though, Mac recognized Marshal Verne Bowen in the lead. The deputy called Jed was beside him, carrying the lantern.

A couple of other deputies trailed them, and a small group of townspeople brought up the rear, curious to find out what all the commotion was about.

"That's funny," Luke said quietly. "I thought those two might be lying out there in the street with bullets in them."

"Bowen and Jed, you mean?" Mac asked.

"That's right. They were acting a little funny down at the Lucky Shot earlier. That's what made me come and check on you."

"That was a stroke of luck, then," Mac agreed. "And you thought they were behind this?"

"Seemed like a logical theory at the time," Luke said. "I'm not sure we can rule it out even now."

That was true, Mac thought. Albert and Jessie wouldn't have been able to annoy Ezra Hannigan anymore if their newspaper was destroyed.

And if they had been killed in the blaze, too . . . well, Hannigan wouldn't have shed any tears over that.

"What's going on here?" Bowen demanded as he stalked up. "Are you and your friends shooting up the town again, McKenzie?"

"Just defending ourselves, Marshal. Somebody tried to set the newspaper office on fire, and when that didn't work, they started throwing lead."

"'On fire,' you say?"

"That's right. Just go around back and you'll smell the coal oil."

"Better get that cleaned up," Bowen snapped. "Thing like that is a menace."

"I couldn't agree more, Marshal."

"Who did it?" Jed asked harshly.

Albert pointed and said, "There are two of them. I don't know about the others."

"They got away," Mac said. "One was wounded, I think. The two in the street may be dead. They haven't moved or made any noise since they went down."

Bowen and Jed looked at each other. Bowen jerked his head toward the bodies and said, "Go take a look." To Jessie, he added, "Put that scattergun down, ma'am. You're making me a mite nervous."

Jessie lowered the shotgun, but remained tense and vigilant.

Mac said, "I believe I'll take a look at those fellas, too," and stepped down from the porch to join Jed in checking on the bodies. Bowen looked like he wanted to tell him to stop, but that might have put him in a bad light in front of the townspeople, so he kept his mouth shut.

Jed held the lantern high. A couple of the townsmen had come out into the middle of the street with him and Mac. He told them, "Roll those varmints on their backs."

The townies did so. The lantern's light fell on rough, beard-stubbled faces. Mac didn't think he had ever seen either of the men before. That was a bit of a surprise. He had expected them to be more of Bowen's deputies.

But if that had been the case, Bowen wouldn't have risked everybody seeing their faces, Mac realized. He would have done something to try to keep their identities secret.

The fact that they were strangers didn't rule out the possibility of them working for Ezra Hannigan. Hannigan had a lot of men in his crew on the Rocking H, and many of them were no better than outlaws. Bowen and Jed still could have known what was supposed to happen, even though Hannigan had sent outsiders to carry out the planned destruction.

"Never saw 'em before," Jed called to Bowen.

The marshal nodded and turned to Albert. "I wonder why they wanted to burn down your office, Whitmore."

"Yeah, I wonder," Albert said. His tone of voice made it clear that he didn't actually consider that a mystery at all. "But I don't guess that matters. They failed, Marshal, and you know what that means."

"What does it mean?" Bowen asked.

"Tomorrow the latest edition of the *Chronicle* will be on the streets, as usual. And it'll have a little extra news in it that it wouldn't have had, otherwise."

Chapter 20

True to Albert Whitmore's prediction, the latest edition of the *Chronicle* was quite popular with the citizens of Hannigan's Hill the next day. As Luke walked toward Mac's Place for breakfast, he saw a number of people on the boardwalks reading the newspaper. Some were discussing what was printed in it, talking excitedly and pointing at the pages they held in their hands.

Most of the customers in the café had copies, too, Luke saw as he stepped inside and appreciated the warm air full of delicious aromas. It was late enough that the morning rush was over, but Mac appeared to still be doing steady business.

Luke took one of the empty stools as Mac delivered a meal farther down the counter. When he finished with that, he brought the coffeepot without asking and poured a cup for Luke.

"How about ham, fried taters . . . and biscuits and honey this morning?" he asked.

Luke chuckled. "I'm not going to say no to that." He sipped the hot coffee and nodded in satisfaction. "After a long night, this tastes mighty good."

"I know. I don't reckon I could keep going without it. I brew a tasty cup of coffee, if I do say so myself."

It had taken until well after midnight before the paper was printed. They had wet down the outside wall where the coal oil had been thrown, soaking it enough that the stuff was no longer a threat.

Then Albert had insisted on remaking the front page so he could include a box containing the story of the latest attack on the newspaper. Discarding the pages that had already been printed might not make financial sense, especially considering the paper was struggling, but Albert said that it was more important to get the truth out to the readers.

Luke had read the story when it was fresh off the press, with the ink still damp. Albert didn't come right out and accuse Ezra Hannigan of being behind the attempt to burn down the *Chronicle* office, but he stressed the idea that only one man in the area really wanted to silence the newspaper so that it could no longer print the truth about his high-handed and illegal activities.

The story also mentioned that the two strangers killed in the course of the attack could have been staying at one of the local ranches and had never come into town before. That would explain why no one recognized them. Which ranch the story was talking about could be left to the readers' imaginations.

Marshal Bowen and his deputies came in for some criticism, too, as the story pointed out that they were supposed to patrol the town, protect its citizens, and prevent atrocities, like this, from happening. That is, they were supposed to do those things if they were truly interested in carrying out their duties and weren't actually following the orders of someone who might not have the town's best interests at heart. Once more, Albert didn't refer to Hannigan by name, but everyone reading the paper would know who he meant.

Mac brought the plate of food from the kitchen and set it on the counter in front of Luke, who ate several bites and nodded appreciatively before looking around the room and commenting, "Your friend is something of a rabble-rouser."

"I don't reckon I'd call the citizens of this town 'rabble,'" Mac said.

Luke nodded and allowed, "That was probably an ill-considered term to use. The people around here have some legitimate grievances against Hannigan, from what I've seen. If he succeeds in putting the *Chronicle* out of business, it's just going to get worse, I imagine. He'll feel like he can get away with anything."

"He already feels like he can, or like he ought to be able to, anyway. That's why it makes him so mad when anybody stands up to him."

Luke went back to eating as a man stepped up and took the stool next to him at the counter. The man slapped down a folded copy of the paper and said, "McKenzie, I want to talk to you."

The aggrieved tone drew Luke's interest and made

him look over at the man. He saw a burly hombre of middle years, barrel-chested, with a rugged face deeply tanned from being out in the sun and weathered by the wind. The white mustache, bushy white eyebrows, and white hair under a brown hat stood out in sharp contrast to his mahogany skin. He wore denim trousers and a denim jacket over a flannel shirt.

"What can I do for you, Mr. Raskin?" Mac asked.

The man tapped a blunt finger on the folded paper. "The fella who puts this out is a friend of yours, ain't he?"

"That's right," Mac responded levelly. Luke could tell that Mac didn't know what the older man wanted, but he wasn't going to deny his friendship with Albert Whitmore.

"I want you to tell him something for me," Raskin said.

"I suppose I can do that."

"Tell him he's right as rain about Ezra Hannigan, and there's some of us in these parts who aren't gonna stand for Hannigan ridin' roughshod over everybody who gets in his way anymore."

"That story in the paper doesn't mention Hannigan."

Raskin snorted in contempt. "Hell, everybody knows what he's talkin' about. The story doesn't have to spell it out. Did you know that Hannigan made me an offer on my spread a month ago?"

Mac shook his head and said, "No, I didn't."

"It was a pur-dee insult, too. He offered me maybe fifty cents on the dollar compared to what the place is really worth. Said he only wanted it for that high meadow graze of mine. Needs it for his cows, he claims. I told him I wasn't interested in sellin', even if he was to offer me a fair price." Raskin drew in a deep breath. "My wife, our daughter, and two of our sons are buried on that place. That's where I'll be planted, too, when my time comes. I'll never leave it, except to come into town here for short spells when I have to."

"Well, I can understand why you feel that way," Mac told him.

Luke gave in to an impulse and asked the man, "How did Hannigan take it when you turned down his offer?"

Raskin looked over at him and frowned. "I don't reckon I know you, mister, and I ain't in the habit of answerin' questions from folks I don't know."

"Luke is all right, Mr. Raskin," Mac said. "I'll vouch for him. This is Luke Jensen. Luke, Pete Raskin. Luke helped fight off the attack on the *Chronicle* last night."

"Is that so?" Raskin stuck out a heavily calloused hand. "Then I reckon I'm glad to meet you, Jensen, and you can probably guess how Hannigan took it. He didn't like it at all. Nothin' that man hates more than bein' told no."

"That was my impression," Luke said as he shook hands with the rancher. "Has he done anything about it?"

Raskin snorted again. "I lost my hay barn last week. Went up in flames in the middle of the night. I'd call that mighty suspicious, especially under the circumstances."

Mac stared across the counter for a moment, then said, "You think Hannigan was responsible?"

"I don't reckon anybody else'd have a reason to do such a thing. He's the one who'd benefit if I gave up and sold out to him."

"Could something else have started the fire?" Luke asked. "Something natural, like lightning?"

Raskin shook his head. "It was a clear night. Besides, we don't get much lightnin' this time of year." He tapped the newspaper again. "You can see why I thought of Hannigan right off when I read about what happened last night. Seems like burnin' folks out is one of his favorite tactics. We're not gonna stand for it anymore. I plan to talk to some of the other ranchers and see if we can get a group together to keep an eye on things."

"Like a vigilante patrol?" Mac asked.

"Yeah, just like that. Armed men who don't mind fightin' to protect what's theirs."

Luke said, "From what I've heard, the members of Hannigan's crew are professional fighting men. No offense, Mr. Raskin, but you and your friends would be outmatched against them."

"We'll have right on our side," Raskin snapped.

"That may be true, and in an ideal world, that would count for something, but, unfortunately, in this world it seldom does when men are outnumbered and outgunned."

Raskin eyed him and said, "You got the look of a fightin' man, Jensen. It could be that we'll have to hire some gun handlers of our own. Maybe you'd be interested in throwin' in with us?"

"I'm sorry," Luke said. "I'm already here on business." He didn't offer to explain what that business was. If Raskin hadn't heard the talk around town about Luke and his prisoner, Luke wasn't going to bother supplying the information.

"If you change your mind, my ranch is eight miles north of town. Most folks around here can tell you how to find it."

Luke just nodded, seeing no point in telling the man how unlikely that possibility was.

Mac lowered his voice and asked, "Have you been talking to many people about this, Mr. Raskin?"

"A few," the rancher replied.

"Just folks you know you can trust, I hope. It might not be a good thing if talk like that got back to Hannigan."

Raskin's white brows went up. "I didn't figure you for being scared of him, Mac."

"I'm not. But I don't believe in going out of my way to hunt trouble, either."

Raskin's eyes went narrow again. "Sometimes it's better to hunt it down before *it* can hunt *you*."

Luke didn't say anything, but he couldn't disagree with that sentiment, either.

"Just tell Whitmore that things are gonna change around here," Raskin went on. "He's gonna have plenty of big stories to write soon, and they won't be about how Hannigan's gotten away with something again."

"Hang on," Mac said. "Did you tell the law about what happened to your barn?"

"What law?" Raskin asked in a scathing tone. "Verne Bowen works for Hannigan, so he's part of the problem. And the sheriff over at the county seat can't be bothered to get up off his rump, and you know it. No, things in these parts are like they always have been. The only real law is what a man packs with him."

His hand dropped to the bone handle of the gun holstered at his waist.

"Just be careful," Mac told him. "That's all I'm saying."

Raskin nodded and used his left hand to slide a silver dollar across the counter.

"Obliged to you for the breakfast. It was good, just like always. You learned a lot on those chuckwagons, Mac."

The rancher left the café. Mac shook his head slowly as he watched Raskin go.

"You think folks shouldn't fight back?" Luke asked. "That goes against everything I've seen from you so far, Mac."

"I never said that. I agree with everything Albert and Jessie have been printing in the paper. Otherwise, I wouldn't have helped them with it. And Mr. Raskin's right that sooner or later, folks have to stand up for themselves. I just worry that nobody around here is any match for Bowen and his deputies and Hannigan's crew from the Rocking H."

"I'm not sure about that. I can think of a couple of fellas who could hold their own against that bunch."

Mac frowned at him for a second, then shook his head. "No, sir. Not against those odds, we couldn't. I'll fight when I have to, to protect me or my friends, but I've seen more than my share of trouble."

"Fair enough," Luke said with a tiny shrug. "I could make the same claim about myself."

"I'll just bet you could."

The door opened just then and Jessie Whitmore came

into the café. She wore a quilted jacket, and her face was red from the cold. She walked over to the counter and rested her gloved hands on the edge of it, giving Luke a polite nod as she did so.

She had acted a little more friendly toward him the past few days. Evidently, she had gotten over some of the resentment she'd felt because he hadn't interfered with Thad Crawford's hanging. Then, the previous night, he had interrupted the arsonists in the act of setting their fire and quite possibly saved the newspaper office from being destroyed. She had to feel some gratitude toward him for that.

"Good morning, Mac," she said.

"Morning." Mac made a little gesture that encompassed the other customers in the café. "Just about everybody's got a copy of the *Chronicle* this morning. You and Albert have done well with this one."

"It's a start, I suppose. The news about what happened last night has gotten around town. Everyone wants to read the truth . . . even the ones who have to pretend to support Mr. Hannigan."

"What brings you here? Need some coffee? Something to eat?"

Jessie shook her head. "No, I've already eaten. I thought maybe you might have a pie that you'd sell me. I'd like to have one for Albert and, well . . ." She smiled. "My baking skills don't compare with yours, Mac. You're a wizard with an oven."

"When you have to make do with a Dutch oven while you're learning, the real thing seems like a luxury. I have a whole peach pie on hand. Will that do?"

"That's perfect. Thank you."

He nodded and said, "I'll fetch it," then went into the kitchen.

That left Jessie standing next to Luke as a some-what-awkward silence developed between them. Luke was all right with letting it stretch out, but it must have bothered Jessie, because she said, "I want to thank you again for what you did last night, Mr. Jensen."

"Most of it was because those fellows started shooting at me, and I've never liked that very much."

"Yes, but you stepped in first to stop them from setting that fire."

"Seemed like the thing to do at the time."

"I'm not sure where we would be now if it weren't for you and Mr. McKenzie. He's given us so much help . . ."

"He thinks highly of you and your husband."

"And we're quite fond of him, too."

"You know that Mac's in love with you, don't you?" That was the question Luke wanted to ask her. It seemed obvious to him. The way Mac looked at her, the tone of his voice when he talked about her, the tension in the air when the two of them were close together . . . It didn't take any special observational skills to notice such things.

And if he had to guess, he would say that Jessie Whitmore had feelings for Mac, too. Clearly, she was struggling against them. She loved her husband, Luke had no doubt about that, but at the same time, she was drawn to Mac.

The door to the kitchen swung open and he came out with a flat box in his hands.

"Here you go," he said as he placed it on the counter in front of Jessie. "One peach pie for my friends."

Jessie started to open the little purse she carried. "How much do I owe y—"

Mac reached across the counter and touched her hand. "Don't worry about it," he told her. "It's my treat."

"But that's not right. This is your . . . your stock in trade. You get paid for cooking for people."

"I get paid plenty," Mac said. "I can afford to do something nice for my friends."

"Yes, but I don't mind paying. If I tell Albert you gave me this pie—"

"Then don't tell him," Mac interrupted with a grin. "Shoot, if you want to claim that you baked it yourself, that's fine with me."

That made Jessie laugh as she shook her head. "I couldn't do that," she said. "He would know I was lying. On my best day, I could never bake a pie as delicious as yours, Mac—"

She was interrupted again, but it came from the café's entrance this time. The door was thrown open and a figure in a familiar buffalo coat stepped through. Cougar Jack Costaine leveled the Winchester he held at Mac and yelled, "Hands up, Dewey 'Mac' McKenzie! I'm takin' you into custody and claimin' the bounty on your head, you no-good, murderin' skunk!"

Chapter 21

The café went completely quiet after that shocking accusation. Mac didn't move as he stared at Costaine in stunned surprise. But after several seconds, he recovered enough to say, "You're making a big mistake."

"The only mistake was you thinkin' you could hide from me forever, McKenzie. I been on your trail for a long time now. Get your hands up and keep 'em up while you come out from behind that counter. I'll shoot if you don't." A leering grin stretched across Costaine's face as he peered over the rifle's sights with his one good eye. "That ree-ward dodger says the bounty's the same whether you're alive or dead, and dead's sure enough simpler."

Mac tried again. "I'm not wanted—"

"Lyin' ain't gonna do you no good, boy. You're comin' with me, one way or another."

Luke could tell that Costaine wasn't going to listen

to reason. And the fact that Costaine wanted to collect a bounty on Mac's head made the previously elusive memories click into place. Luke knew now why Costaine had seemed vaguely familiar to him. He had heard stories about a ruthless, one-eyed bounty hunter who was quick to shoot and sort things out later. Luke didn't figure there could be more than one like that on the frontier.

Mac probably had that Smith & Wesson under the counter, but he couldn't reach down and pick it up before Costaine could squeeze the trigger. Since Costaine seemed to be looking for an excuse to do just that, there didn't appear to be anything Mac could do.

So Luke did something, instead.

Costaine's attention was focused on Mac. He hadn't even glanced in Luke's direction. Luke had swiveled halfway around on the stool when Costaine came into the café. He moved his hand slightly, just enough to grasp the heavy china plate on which Mac had served his breakfast. The plate was empty except for a couple of bites of ham and fried eggs and part of a biscuit.

Costaine didn't appear to notice what Luke had just done. Luke took a breath as he saw Costaine's finger begin to whiten on the Winchester's trigger. He couldn't wait any longer.

He twisted more toward Costaine and brought his right arm around in a whipping motion as he flung the plate at the one-eyed man. The bits of food flew in the air.

At the same time, he looped his left arm around Jessie Whitmore and dove to the floor, taking her with him out of the line of fire.

Costaine saw the plate spinning at him and tried to get out of the way, but he wasn't fast enough. The heavy piece of crockery smashed into his left cheek without breaking and knocked his head back. His finger jerked the Winchester's trigger, but the barrel had ridden up as Costaine took an involuntary step backward. The blast was deafening, but the bullet went harmlessly into the ceiling above the counter.

Before Luke could scramble up, Mac slapped his left hand on the counter, vaulted on top of it, and leaped toward Costaine. He landed halfway across the room and it took only a split second for him to bound the rest of the way. He tackled Costaine as the man tried to bring the Winchester down.

The impact knocked Costaine off his feet. He crashed to the floor just inside the café's door, which was still open, so cold air blew into the room. Mac landed on top of him and grabbed the rifle barrel. He twisted the weapon out of Costaine's hands and tossed it aside.

Costaine recovered enough to drive a fist up under Mac's chin. The blow levered Mac's head back. Costaine bucked his body up from the floor and threw Mac to the side. He rolled after him and reached for Mac's throat. Before he was able to clamp his fingers around Mac's neck, Mac lifted a knee into Costaine's belly, grabbed him by the shoulders, and heaved him away.

By now, Luke was back on his feet and had one of the Remingtons in his hand. He couldn't shoot Costaine, though. Mac was in the line of fire and too many other people were in here. No doubt, most of them would have fled once the fight started, but Mac and Costaine had the door blocked at the moment. They came to their feet at the same time and began slugging away at each other. Fists thudded heavily against flesh and bone as the two battling men surged back and forth.

Costaine landed a powerful blow to Mac's solar plexus, which drove the air out of his lungs and left him paralyzed for a second. That gave Costaine time to hook his right foot behind Mac's left knee and jerk that leg out from under him. As Mac went down, Costaine sank the toe of his other boot in Mac's ribs. The vicious kick rolled Mac onto his belly. Costaine dropped swiftly on top of him and dug his knees into the small of Mac's back, pinning him to the floor. Costaine jerked a knife out of its sheath at his belt and raised the weapon as if intending to plunge the blade down into Mac's body.

Costaine froze as Luke pressed the Remington's muzzle against the back of his head. In the sudden silence, the revolver's hammer made a sinister metallic ratcheting sound as Luke eared it back.

"If that knife moves, I'll blow your brains all over this floor," Luke said.

Costaine's upraised arm trembled slightly as he fought to control his muscles. "You're helpin' a wanted man, mister," he said. "A murderer."

Mac had caught his breath enough to gasp, "That's . . . a lie! I never . . . murdered anybody . . . in my life."

"The wanted poster I got in my saddlebags says different. I been carryin' it for a long time, so I oughta know."

"Get off of me, damn it. I can explain."

Luke took the knife out of Costaine's unresisting hand. "Let's just remove that temptation," he said. "Now, since the man asked you more politely than I would have, let him up."

Costaine pushed to his feet and stepped back. Luke took the gun away from his head, but kept it pointed at him.

Mac pushed to his hands and knees and then climbed upright. His chest still rose and fell rapidly as he tried to recover. He turned to face Costaine and said, "If you have a wanted poster on me, it's old and no good anymore. Those charges were dropped a long time ago, and they were false, to start with. The man who posted the bounty has been dead for years, too."

Costaine sneered. "That's just the sort of lies I'd expect to hear from a killer."

"I'm not lying, blast it! I'm not wanted for murder or anything else."

"I don't believe you. And when I collect that reeward for bringin' you in, I'll have all the proof I need."

During the fight, the customers had jumped up from their seats and moved back against the walls to stay well out of the way. Now that things appeared to be under control again, several of them stepped forward.

One man said, "You're loco, mister. I've known Mac McKenzie for years. He's no criminal."

"That's right," another man added. "He's a respectable businessman."

"And he runs the best café in Hannigan's Hill," a third man said.

Jessie Whitmore, who had gotten to her feet as well, said, "I can vouch for Mac's character. He's a fine, upstanding man. A gentleman."

"Thanks, Jessie," Mac said with a faint smile. "Kind words from you are worth a lot."

Costaine shook a finger at the crowd and declared, "You folks've been taken in by a lyin' scoundrel. And you, Jensen, you're interferin' with an officer of the law—"

"You're no officer of the law," Luke said. "You've already admitted you're a bounty hunter. You don't have any official standing."

"Just as much as you! I know who you are. Took me a while to remember, but I recollect now that you're a bounty hunter, too."

"I've never denied that," Luke said coolly.

"You're probably after the ree-ward on this hombre your own self. That's why you want to run me off."

"I already have a prisoner. I'm not looking for another one. Besides, I believe Mac when he says he's not wanted."

"But that poster—"

"Go get it and bring it in here," Mac interrupted him. "I'll explain the whole thing." He looked around. "I'd just as soon not air my dirty laundry in front of everybody, though, so I'd appreciate it if you folks would give us some privacy. All your meals are on the house."

"You don't have to do that, Mac," one of the customers said.

"I want to. You folks stood up for me when this fella started slinging accusations around. That means a lot to me."

After several expressions of gratitude and support, the café's customers cleared out. When Jessie started to go, Mac stopped her, saying, "No, I'd like it if you'd stay, Jessie. I don't mind you hearing the story."

She hesitated, but then nodded and said, "All right, Mac. But anything I hear is off the record."

He smiled. "Albert probably wouldn't make that promise if he was here. He's too much of a newspaperman to commit to passing up a story. But you have my permission to tell him about it, and he can do what he thinks is best."

"He's your friend. He's not going to do anything to hurt you."

Luke motioned with the Remington's barrel. "Come on, Costaine. Let's get that wanted poster you keep going on about."

"I don't need your help to fetch it," Costaine snapped.

"Maybe not, but I'm going to keep an eye on you, anyway, to make sure you don't try anything."

Costaine sniffed. "You don't have to make fun of a feller just 'cause he's only got one eye."

"I wasn't . . . Never mind. Just go on."

Luke kept Costaine covered while the man went outside and fished a folded piece of paper out of one of his saddlebags. It showed the signs of a lot of handling, so Luke could believe he had been carrying it for years.

When they were back in the café, Costaine unfolded

the paper and spread it on the counter. He stabbed a finger against it and said, "See? Right there. It says plain as day that Dewey McKenzie is wanted for the murder of some hombre named Micah Holdstock down yonder in New Orleans. There's even a fair likeness of you on there, McKenzie."

Mac stood in front of the counter with Jessie close beside him. He sighed, nodded, and said, "There's no point in denying that for a while, I was wanted for Holdstock's murder. But I didn't kill him. You see the name of the man who posted the reward?"

Costaine squinted his good eye at the dodger. "Feller name of LeClerc."

"Pierre LeClerc. *He's* the one who actually murdered Micah Holdstock. You see, I was in love with Holdstock's daughter, Evangeline, or at least I thought I was. And I believed she was in love with me. But I was penniless, and Evangeline's father was a banker and one of the richest men in New Orleans. He didn't want me involved with his daughter, so he tried to run me out of town. LeClerc was there to step in, claim Evangeline for himself, and kill her father so he could take over the Holdstock fortune, all the while making it look as if I were the killer. I had no choice but to go on the run. That's how I wound up on that cattle drive from Texas to Kansas, handling the chuckwagon."

"A likely story," Costaine said.

"It's true. I had those bogus charges hanging over my head for a couple of years. Not only was the law after me, but LeClerc sent gangs of hired killers after me, too. He wanted to make sure I was shut up and could never reveal the truth. But it finally came out and caught up with him, and he died, too, up Montana way. You can look the whole thing up in the newspapers from the time, if you want to. It was a pretty big story."

Costaine glared at him. "I still say you're makin' it all up."

"You can say whatever you want. It's the truth." Mac laughed without sounding amused. "Some gent who claimed to be a writer even looked me up and talked to me about what had happened. He said he was going to write a series of dime novels based on my story. I don't know if he ever did or not, though. From what I've heard, writers are always full of big talk about what they're going to do, but then they usually never get around to it."

Luke said, "All right, Costaine, you've heard the story. Whether you want to admit it or not, you know there's no longer a reward for Mac's capture. So you might as well ride on out of here and leave him alone from now on."

Costaine looked like he wanted to argue, but Luke was still holding that Remington. In a surly voice, Costaine said, "I want my knife and my rifle back."

Mac had picked up the Winchester from the floor and set it on the counter. He pushed it in front of Costaine. Luke set the knife down beside it. Costaine sheathed the knife, picked up the rifle, and glared at Luke and Mac again before turning toward the door.

He stopped and started to reach for the wanted poster, but Luke said, "Leave it. You don't need it anymore, and I imagine Mac would rather none of those were floating around anywhere."

"Yeah, they've caused more than their share of trouble," Mac said. "I think this one's going in the stove."

"Fine," Costaine snapped. He stalked toward the door, still bristling with barely suppressed anger.

Luke didn't holster the Remington until Costaine was gone. When he had pouched the iron, he turned to Jessie and said, "Mrs. Whitmore, I apologize for handling you in such a rough manner. I hope I didn't hurt you."

"Nonsense, Mr. Jensen," she said. "You were just trying to make sure that terrible man didn't shoot me by accident. I should be thanking you for what you did, not only for me, but for Mac as well."

"I know I'm mighty obliged to you," Mac said. "That hombre was loco enough to just go ahead and ventilate me without ever giving me a chance to explain."

Jessie turned to him and said, "What a sad story. I'm sorry you had to go through all that, Mac. After your name was finally cleared, did you go back to New Orleans and look up . . . Evangeline, was it?"

"That was her name," Mac said, nodding. "But I didn't go back. She was mighty quick to believe I'd killed her father and she didn't waste any time marrying LeClerc. I figured her feelings for me were never quite as deep or as genuine as she made out they were. It's even possible that one reason she liked me was because she knew I annoyed the heck out of her father." He shrugged. "I decided there weren't any flames there I wanted to rekindle. It was better just to move on instead of trying to go back."

"It generally is," Luke said.

Mac smiled at Jessie. "So, now that you've heard it, do you think Albert will want to write about this when you tell him the story?"

"Are you sure you want me to tell him?"

"It's not really a secret. Like I said, it was in the newspapers at the time."

"But the people here don't know about it. To them, you're just Mac McKenzie, the owner of the best café in Hannigan's Hill." Jessie shook her head. "I don't know what I'll do."

"Better go ahead and tell him," Mac advised. "He's going to hear about Costaine coming in here and causing trouble. Everybody in town will hear about that." He rested a hand on her shoulder for a second. "Might as well get the truth out there. That could prevent more trouble in the future, maybe."

"Well . . . all right. If you're sure."

"I'm sure." Mac picked up the box with the pie in it. "Now you'd better get on back to the paper. Albert's probably wondering where you've gotten off to."

"All right. Thank you, Mac. For the pie . . . and for trusting me with the truth."

"Should've done it before now," he said gruffly. "I just never saw any reason to bring it up. All those bad things are in the past. Dead and gone."

Jessie nodded solemnly and left the café, carrying the pie box. Luke watched her go and then said, "I wish you were right about all the bad things being 'dead and gone.' But I don't know if that's true. Costaine didn't really seem convinced."

Mac sighed. "I know. He's liable to cause more trouble in the future, on top of all this mess with Hannigan and Bowen and the others. I am glad of one thing, though."

"What's that?"

"I'm glad you threw an empty plate at Costaine and didn't chunk that pie at him. I'd hate to see a perfectly good pie get ruined on a varmint like that."

Chapter 22

If the Lucky Shot was the best of the half-dozen saloons in Hannigan's Hill, Kildare's Tavern was the worst. It was a dingy hole-in-the-wall, barely large enough for a twelve-foot bar, a couple of tables that wobbled because their legs were uneven, some rickety chairs, and a cast-iron stove. The front window beside the door was so grimy, it barely let in any light, so on an overcast day like today, the shadows were thick inside the tavern. A couple of flickering lanterns did little to dispel them.

Cougar Jack Costaine didn't care. The gloom matched his mood as he stood hunch-shouldered at the bar, glaring down into the glass of whiskey around which he had wrapped the fingers of his left hand.

Both tables were occupied. A gray-whiskered man in a threadbare suit sat at one of them. His head rested on the table, with his face turned to the side. He snored softly as drool formed a puddle under his open mouth.

Two cowboys played cards and nursed beers at the other table. Costaine had overheard enough of their conversation to know that they were unemployed at the moment, and this was a bad time of year to be looking for riding jobs. It was an even bet whether they might starve to death before spring came with its roundups.

Costaine wondered if he might be able to talk them into throwing in with him in return for a share of the reward when he brought in Dewey McKenzie. Both cowboys packed guns. Whether they could actually use them or not was another story. But at least they were warm bodies and might be able to keep Luke Jensen occupied while Costaine went after McKenzie.

The bartender, who Costaine assumed was the proprietor of Kildarc's, moved along the bar in front of him and asked, "Are you going to drink that, my friend, or just continue studying it for a while? I do believe you've probably figured out all its secrets by now."

Costaine lifted his gaze from the drink. The bartender was a short man, with a freckled face and graying red curls under a derby hat. The apron he wore had been white once, but was now gray, like the day, and Costaine's state of mind. Costaine picked up the shot glass, threw back the raw liquor, and thumped it, empty, on the bar.

"You Kildare?"

"Aye, that I am."

"Well, fill it up again, Mr. Kildare."

"I'll be seein' some silver or gold first."

Costaine frowned across the hardwood. "You think I ain't good for it?"

"Don't take it as me passin' judgment on you, lad.

This is a cash business. I'm willing to spot a man one drink, especially if he looks like he needs it, and you do. But beyond that, I need to see the color of your money."

Grumbling, Costaine dug a silver dollar out of his pocket and tossed it on the bar. Kildare caught it deftly on the bounce. He reached under the bar for the bottle he had poured from before and splashed more liquor in Costaine's glass.

Instead of drinking it right away, Costaine leaned forward, lowered his voice, and asked, "Can you tell me anything about those two fellers sittin' at the table? The ones who look like cowhands?"

Kildare tipped his head to the side to look past Costaine. He said, "I've seen them around some. They're just drifters, as far as I know."

"Can they handle those guns they're packin'?"

"How the hell would I know?" A look of alarm appeared on Kildare's face. "You're not about to shoot them, are you? What did they ever do to you?"

"Hush!" Costaine said. "I ain't fixin' to shoot nobody. I just might have a business proposition for 'em, that's all. If they don't mind a little trouble."

Kildare shook his head. "You'd have to ask them, friend. I wouldn't venture a guess."

Costaine thought about it, then said, "Gimme that bottle and a couple o' glasses."

"That'll cost you another three dollars."

Scowling, Costaine ponied up the money. He snagged the half-empty bottle by the neck, juggled his own glass and the none-too-clean pair of empty glasses Kildare placed on the bar, and turned toward the table.

The two cowboys looked up at him, their gazes a mixture of surprise and trepidation, as he set the bottle and glasses on the table in front of them.

"Do we know you, mister?" one of them asked warily.

"No, but I'd be pleased to make your acquaintance. That's why I brung over this bottle. Call it a get-to-know-you gift."

"We're obliged to you," the other cowhand said. He used his foot to push an empty chair out. "Sit down and join us."

"Don't mind if I do. Name's Costaine. Folks call me Cougar Jack."

"Why do they do that?" the first man asked. "Did you tangle with a catamount once?"

"Maybe lost your eye that way?" the second man said.

"Well, no." The real story behind the name was a mite embarrassing, so Costaine didn't want to go into it. He didn't want to explain how he'd lost the eye, either. He went on, "But don't worry none about that. What do they call you fellers?"

"I'm Hank Zachary," the first cowboy said.

"Andy Clement," the second man supplied.

Costaine poured drinks for both of them, then said, "Did I hear you boys sayin' something about how you're lookin' for work?"

"That's right," Zachary said. "If you know of some ridin' jobs, we're sure in the market for them. We were working on a spread, over east of here a ways, until the foreman got a burr under his saddle and fired us."

"And it was for something that wasn't even our fault," Clement added. "It was over a saloon gal who preferred our company to his."

"Why, that don't seem fair a'tall," Costaine said. "A lady's got a right to make up her own mind when it comes to suitors, don't she?"

Both cowboys laughed. "Well, Dinah wasn't exactly what you'd call a 'lady,'" Zachary said.

"Not hardly," Clement said.

"But, yeah, the boss shouldn't have fired us for that. We always done our jobs."

"I don't doubt it," Costaine said. "Can you use those hoglegs on your hips?"

That abrupt question made both men look surprised again. Zachary said, "I wouldn't call us gunfighters, or anything like that, but we've been in a few shootin' scrapes."

"Some Comanches jumped us down in the Panhandle, about five years ago," Clement said. "We had to shoot ourselves outta that little dustup."

"And we tangled with some rustlers once, while we were ridin' nighthawk," Zachary said. "So we've smelled powdersmoke more'n once, if that's what you're askin'."

Costaine nodded and said, "I might know of a job for you, then." He didn't figure either of these cow nurses was anywhere near good enough to match up with Luke Jensen, but they'd probably be cool-headed enough to skin their irons and force Jensen to deal with them. Costaine could hang back, and while Jensen had his hands full killing these two, that would give him the opening he needed to drill the rival bounty hunter.

With Jensen dead, he could take McKenzie. Costaine was sure of that.

And more than likely, he wouldn't even have to pay Zachary and Clement anything, since they'd both be dead. It seemed like the perfect plan to Costaine.

McKenzie and Jensen had thought he'd accept some loco story about Mac being framed for that murder. What kind of idiot did they take him for?

Before he could explain about the job to the two cowboys, the door into the tavern opened and a tall, lean figure came in. His coat was open enough for the badge pinned to his shirt to be visible. The man looked around the room, which didn't take long, because the tavern was so small.

"Hello, Deputy," Kildare said. "Something I can do for you?"

The lawman ignored the question and came toward the table where Costaine was sitting with Zachary and Clement.

"Your name Costaine?" he demanded as he came to a stop beside them.

"That's right." Costaine was as wary as the two cowboys had been earlier. Generally, star packers didn't have much use for bounty hunters. Costaine had had run-ins with quite a few of them over the years.

"I need you to come with me."

"What for?"

The deputy didn't look happy about having his statement questioned. He probably wasn't used to being asked to provide explanations.

He put his hand on the butt of his gun and said, "Marshal Bowen wants to talk to you."

"Is this about what happened at the café? Because I was within my rights to do what I done—"

"Take it easy, Costaine," the deputy cut in. "You're not under arrest. Like I said, the marshal just wants to talk to you. He told me to bring you to his office, so that's what I'm going to do." He shrugged. "What happens along the way is up to you."

The deputy had a lean, hard-eyed face and a hawk's beak of a nose with a thin mustache under it. Costaine recognized a killer when he saw one and knew that this man wouldn't hesitate to do whatever was necessary to carry out his orders. So it made sense to cooperate with him.

"Sure, Deputy, I'll go with you. Never figured on doin' otherwise. I was just curious what business the marshal could have with me."

"Come along and find out."

Zachary said, "What about those jobs you were offering us, Costaine? Does that deal still go?"

"We'll have to wait and see, boys," Costaine said as he got to his feet. "Maybe I'll look you up later."

"Damn it," Clement said. "Just when it starts to look like our luck might turn around, the whole thing falls apart. Hank, we oughta just chuck it all and ride on down to Mexico before the weather gets too bad. If we're gonna be broke and starvin', I'd rather it was someplace warm."

Costaine didn't have a lot of coins in his pocket, but he dug out a five-dollar gold piece and dropped it on the table. "Get yourselves a good meal, fellers," he told them. "Consider that a down payment, maybe, on what you'll make later if we do strike a deal."

Zachary scooped up the coin. "Thanks, Cougar Jack. We're obliged to you."

Costaine nodded and left the tavern with the deputy.

"What were you up to with those two saddle tramps?" the deputy asked as they walked toward the marshal's office.

"Nothin' important. I thought I might get 'em to help me out with a little chore."

"Capturing Mac McKenzie?"

Costaine looked over sharply at the man beside him. "So this *is* about what happened at the café?"

"McKenzie seems to have gotten friendly with that Jensen hombre. He's pretty tough."

"So am I," Costaine said, mustering up as much bravado as he could.

The deputy just grunted, which annoyed Costaine even more. He suppressed that annoyance as they walked the rest of the way to the marshal's office and went inside.

The burly man behind the desk stood up and said, "I'm Verne Bowen. You must be Costaine." He chuckled. "I don't think there's anybody else in these parts who matches your description."

Costaine hooked his thumbs in his gun belt and planted his feet. He knew he wasn't the best-looking hombre to ever come down the pike, but Bowen had no call to make snide comments like that about his appearance.

"No offense, Marshal, but just what is it you want with me?"

Bowen came out from behind the desk and said, "I

heard about the fracas you had in Mac's Place a while ago. There's talk about it all over town."

"McKenzie's a wanted man. I had a right to try to take him into custody and claim the ree-ward. I got a wanted poster—" Costaine stopped short and grimaced. "I had a wanted poster with his name and picture on it. He's wanted on murder charges down in New Orleans. If you go through the dodgers you got on hand, you might find the same one."

"That's just it, Costaine. I don't give a damn about some Louisiana murder charge, whether it's true or not. I have problems of my own with McKenzie and that new friend of his, Jensen." A shrewd look came over the marshal's face. "So I thought that since we both have a grudge against those two, maybe we ought to work together and do something about it."

Chapter 23

What the marshal suggested made sense, sure enough. As Costaine heard him out, he was more and more inclined to accept Bowen's invitation to join forces.

That would be a mighty odd sensation, Costaine thought, working with a lawman, instead of competing with him for a prisoner, but Bowen made it clear he had no interest in claiming the reward on Mac McKenzie.

"Some folks are making things difficult for an associate of mine," Bowen explained, "and McKenzie has been helping them. So has Jensen, since he and McKenzie became friends. I'd like to see to it that neither of them causes any more trouble."

"You mean you want 'em dead."

"I didn't say that. I'm the marshal of this town, blast it. A sworn officer of the law. I can't just go around executing people, unless it's a sentence properly handed down by a judge."

"Oh, I get you," Costaine said, nodding slowly and solemnly. "You want them took care of, but . . . what's the word . . . discreetly."

Jed, who had brought Costaine to the office, still stood behind him. In a sharp voice, he said, "Don't get mouthy, bounty hunter."

"Wasn't meanin' to. I just like to make sure I'm clear on a thing before I agree to it."

"If you're interested," Bowen said, "here's what we'll do. Jed will take you to meet with my associate. He'll want to talk to you before you become part of our group."

Costaine squinted his lone eye at the marshal. "So you're sayin' this other feller is the real boss?"

He knew that question would annoy Bowen, more than likely, and judging by the marshal's scowl, it did.

"You ask too many questions, Costaine. Do you want to work with us or not? If you don't, then you need to get out of town. I'd be glad to have Jed escort you."

"Happy to do that, Marshal," Jed said with a soft but menacing edge to his voice. Costaine realized that if he said he wanted no part of this proposed alliance, Bowen didn't intend to let him live. Jed would ride out of town with him and shoot him in the back the first chance he got.

"Sure, I'll go meet this other feller. What's his name?"

"Don't worry about that," Bowen said.

Costaine let that evasion pass. Out of curiosity, he had read the extra edition of the *Chronicle* a few days earlier. He knew that Bowen, like everybody else around here, was under the thumb of a wealthy rancher named Ezra Hannigan. He was sure that was who the deputy would take him to meet.

"When is this gonna happen?" he asked.

"Nothing wrong with right now, is there?"

"Not a damn thing," Costaine said. "Come on, Deputy, let's go."

"Marshal?" Jed asked.

"Go ahead," Bowen ordered. "Take him out to the Rocking H and then get back here, just in case anything else happens."

Costaine's horse was saddled and ready to go, tied at the hitch rack in front of Mac's Place, where he'd left it when he went into the café. He cast a wary eye toward the building as he retrieved his mount. He didn't see McKenzie or Jensen anywhere, so he supposed they weren't waiting to ambush him.

Costaine led his horse to the livery stable, where Jed had said he would meet him. His timing was good, because the deputy brought his horse out of the barn just as Costaine got there.

They mounted up and rode out of Hannigan's Hill, heading north. Both men were silent for a few minutes, and then Jed said, "You rode into town several days ago. If you were after McKenzie all along, why'd you wait until today to make a move against him? And where have you been? I haven't seen you around, and it's part of my job to keep up with strangers who come into town."

"It is if you're actually tryin' to do a lawman's job, I reckon."

Jed glared over at him. "Do you try to get under everybody's skin, mister, or does it just come naturally to you?"

"I believe in speakin' my mind," Costaine said. "Always have. Anyway, I like to take my time and do things deliberate-like. Once I'd met McKenzie, and knew I had the right feller, I decided to lay low for a while and figure out the best way to go about takin' him into custody. I made camp out yonder in the hills so I could think it over."

Jed stared at him. "And the best plan you came up with was marching into the café and pointing a rifle at him?"

"It woulda worked if that varmint Jensen hadn't been there and stuck his big nose into my business," Costaine insisted. "Wasn't no way I could have planned for that."

Jed just shook his head and didn't say anything else.

Costaine wasn't sure how far they rode, but it took a while to reach their destination. He saw a lot of cattle along the way. They came close enough to some of the animals for him to read the Rocking H brand burned into their hides.

"This feller Hannigan must have a mighty big spread," he commented. "He has a heap of cows, that's for sure."

"Nobody said anything about Hannigan."

"What do you take me for?" Costaine asked. "I know you and the marshal work for Hannigan. He's the one that newspaper feller is feudin' with. Hannigan's the big skookum he-wolf around here, and he don't like it when folks stand up to him. That's what this is all about, ain't it?"

Jed eyed him for a moment and then said, "Maybe you're not as dumb as you look, Costaine."

"O' course, I ain't. Wait . . . I mean . . . Well, what the hell do you think you're doin', insultin' me that way?"

"Just speaking my mind, the way you claim to."

"Sometimes that gets folks' dander up. You best just be careful when you go spoutin' off like that."

"I'll remember that," Jed said, but he didn't sound too impressed or worried about what Costaine might do.

The deputy was just like everybody else, Costaine thought. The hombre underestimated him. But one of these days, he was liable to discover that he'd been wrong to do so.

They came in sight of the ranch headquarters, which backed up to a low, wooded hill to the west. A small creek ran between brushy banks to the east. In between was a large, sprawling frame house, which rose two stories. Beyond it was a huge barn with attached corrals on three sides, a long bunkhouse, a cookshack, a smokehouse, a blacksmith shop, and a couple of other buildings that were probably used for storage. It was an impressive layout, Costaine thought, just the sort of spread that ought to belong to the most successful rancher in the area. This was no greasy sack outfit.

Somebody must have spotted them coming, because a couple of men on horseback came out to meet them.

Both riders had pistols on their hips and Winchesters in saddle sheaths. They had the hard-faced, squint-eyed look of men who were ready for trouble.

These two were gun-wolves, not regular cowboys. Their hands weren't all scarred and calloused, Costaine saw when they reined in. They worked with guns, not ropes.

"Who's this, Jed?" one of the men asked as they all came to a stop, facing each other about fifteen feet apart.

"His name's Costaine. He's a bounty hunter."

The second member of the welcoming committee stiffened in his saddle. His hand moved toward the butt of his gun.

"Take it easy, Mitch," Jed went on. "He's not looking for you or anybody else out here. He came to Hannigan's Hill on the trail of Mac McKenzie."

"McKenzie?" the first man repeated. "The fella who runs the café in town?"

"That's right. Turns out he used to be wanted for murder. Had a nice little reward on his head."

"He still does," Costaine snapped. "That yarn he spun about his name bein' cleared was a pack of lies."

"That doesn't matter," Jed said. "Marshal Bowen thought Costaine might make a good addition to the crew out here, so he sent me to introduce him to Mr. Hannigan."

Costaine said, "Wait a minute. You figure I'm gonna be nothin' but a ranch hand? I figured the marshal was gonna make me a deputy if Hannigan goes along with that."

"*Mister* Hannigan will decide what to do with you,"

the first man said, "and so will I. My name is Carl Munson. I'm the ramrod out here. I'm not sure we need another hand . . . especially a crippled one."

Costaine bristled. "You say that because I got only one eye? I can see just fine to shoot with it, if you're of a mind to find out."

Munson glared and leaned forward a little in his saddle. His hand drifted toward his gun.

Jed said sharply, "Take it easy, both of you. You go gunning each other, and Mr. Hannigan won't like it. Neither will Marshal Bowen. Let's just all go on about our business."

Munson continued giving Costaine a hostile stare, but after a moment, he said, "Fine. Go on to the house." He moved his horse aside, as did the man called Mitch. Then Munson said, "Costaine? That's your name?"

"Yeah, that's right. Cougar Jack, some folks call me."

"If the boss says you're hired, Costaine, then you're hired, and there's no bad blood between us, as far as I'm concerned. But if you're not riding for the Rocking H, well, then, I'll take you up on that challenge anytime you want."

"Fine by me," Costaine said with a jerk of his head.

Jed said, "You banty roosters can scratch the dirt at each other some other time. Come on, Costaine."

As they rode toward the house, Costaine asked, "Is that feller Munson fast on the draw? I don't reckon I've heard of him."

"He's fast enough that he's about my age. That tell you what you want to know?"

"Yeah, I expect it does."

Men who thought they were slick with an iron, but

really weren't, nearly always died at a young age when they found out just how wrong they were. So Munson was dangerous, more than likely . . . but so was he, Costaine told himself.

A short, gnarled, white-bearded man came out of the ranch house and waited for them on the porch. "Is that Hannigan?" Costaine asked.

A bark of laughter came from Jed. "Not hardly. That's Jasper Smith. Used to be a wrangler until he got too stove-up. Mr. Hannigan moved him into the house to take care of things there. There was a woman who did the housekeeping and cooking and looked after Mrs. Hannigan, but after she passed on, Mr. Hannigan fired the woman. Said he didn't want any more blasted females underfoot. If you ask me . . . which you sure as hell didn't, and you didn't hear this from me . . . he was afraid that with his wife gone and some other woman in the house, he'd be tempted to make improper advances, and he didn't want to risk that."

Costaine frowned. "But if his wife's dead, then there wouldn't be nothin' improper about it."

"He doesn't see it that way. I figure he wants to stay faithful to his wife, whether she's still around or not. Ezra Hannigan's kind of a complicated gent, Costaine. You never know which way he's gonna jump. So you'd be wise to watch what you do and say around him."

"I'm obliged to you for the advice, I guess."

As the two riders came up to the porch, Jasper Smith called a greeting. "Howdy, Jed. What brings you out here from town, and who's this fella?"

"He's what brings me from town," Jed replied as he reined in. "This is Jack 'Cougar Jack' Costaine. Marshal Bowen sent him to talk to Mr. Hannigan. He thinks Costaine would be a worthwhile addition to our little group."

"Ain't so little," Smith said. "There's a couple dozen of us, remember?"

"Well, Costaine will be one more, if Mr. Hannigan goes along with it."

"Light down and come on in, then," Smith invited. "The boss is in his library."

"'Library'?" Costaine said under his breath.

"That's right." Both men swung down from their saddles. "Mr. Hannigan is a big reader. You'd be well advised not to make any comments about it."

"Ain't nothin' wrong with readin'." Costaine patted his saddlebags. "Why, I carry around some o' them dime novels about scouts and Injun fighters and the like. You know, to help pass the lonely nights on the trail."

"Fine. Just concentrate on why you're out here."

"To get some help roundin' up that no-good murderer McKenzie. And if I can help you fellas with your deal at the same time, well, so much the better for ever'body. That's why I'm here."

Jasper Smith led them down a hall in the ranch house to a set of double doors. The old-timer knocked, and when someone responded, he opened one of the doors to say, "Boss, Jed Lawrence is here with a fella Marshal Bowen thinks you ought to talk to."

"Bring them in, then," a deep voice rumbled.

Smith stepped back to let Jed go in first. Costaine followed him. The man waiting for them inside the library was big, Costaine saw right away, although since he was sitting behind a vast desk, it was difficult to tell just how big he was. He seemed to radiate power as he placed his thick-fingered hands flat on the desk and frowned at the visitors.

"Deputy Lawrence," he said. "You have someone with you?"

"That's right, Mr. Hannigan." Jed moved aside and motioned for Costaine to step forward. "This is Jack Costaine. He rode into town hoping to take Mac McKenzie into custody."

"You're a lawman, Mr. Costaine?" Hannigan asked.

Without being told to, Costaine took off his battered old hat with its pinned-up brim and held it in front of him. "Not exactly," he answered Hannigan's question. "There's a ree-ward for McKenzie's capture, and I figured I'd collect on it."

"Ah." Hannigan nodded slowly. "You're a bounty hunter."

"Yes, sir, I reckon you could say that."

"And McKenzie is a wanted man? I must say, that surprises me. He always struck me as a rather inoffensive sort."

Jed said, "Tell that to the fellas he's shot over the past few days."

"I'm aware that I was laboring under a misapprehension," Hannigan snapped. "Tell me about the charges against him. I find this rather intriguing."

Costaine explained about the murder charge hanging over Mac McKenzie's head, then said, "Now he claims the whole thing ain't true and that his name was cleared years ago, but I never heard nothin' about that, and I think he's lyin'."

"That certainly seems like something a guilty man would say," Hannigan agreed.

"Yes, sir. I'm gonna take him into custody, anyway, and get in touch with the authorities in New Orleans and let them sort it out. Marshal Bowen seemed to think you might be interested in helpin' me do that."

"He did, did he?" Hannigan scowled. "This bounty on McKenzie's head . . . is it payable dead or alive?"

Costaine couldn't help but smile. "Yes, sir, it surely is. And I like the way we seem to be thinkin' along the same lines."

Hannigan raised his right hand and said, "Hold on, sir. Don't get ahead of yourself. I won't deny that McKenzie has allied himself with my enemies, but I have other problems besides what's going on in town. In some respects, those problems are more pressing than anything that involves McKenzie. So . . ."

He took hold of a silver-headed cane, which was leaning against the desk, and used it to help push himself to his feet. He was even more imposing standing up.

"If we're going to discuss a possible alliance, Mr. Costaine, the question becomes . . . what do you bring to the table? What can you do that will help me with my problems?"

The query took Costaine by surprise, but he recovered quickly and said, "Why, whatever it is you need me to do, I reckon, Mr. Hannigan."

The big man grunted and a thin smile appeared on his moonlike face. "I'm very glad to hear that," he said, "because I'm planning to take action this very night against an individual who has become a very annoying thorn in my side. A man by the name of Pete Raskin . . ."

Chapter 24

The overcast hung on stubbornly, so that night, the moon and stars were hidden behind a thick blanket of clouds as Costaine, Munson, the gunman called Mitch, and eight more of the Rocking H crew rode toward Pete Raskin's ranch.

"What is it we're fixin' to do?" Costaine asked as he rocked along in the saddle beside Munson.

The foreman snorted. "If you're nothing but a babe in the woods, you're the ugliest one I ever did see, Costaine."

"What do you mean by that?"

"I mean, you know good and well what we're going to do tonight, or at least you ought to be able to figure it out. Raskin stands in the way of the boss's plans. That's our job, removing obstacles."

"Gonna pay him a visit and spook him into leavin' these parts, eh?"

"We already tried that. He lost his hay barn last

week. Burned right to the ground, it did. But Raskin didn't get the message, no. Instead, he went to town and started runnin' his mouth off about it, claiming that what happened was the boss's fault and trying to stir folks up against him."

"But was he right? Did you fellers burn down his barn?"

Munson shrugged. "It doesn't matter whether we did or not. Raskin can't get away with going around talking against Mr. Hannigan. That's just going to cause trouble, and we're not gonna allow it."

Costaine wasn't sure what Munson meant by that, but he supposed he would find out before the night was over. He didn't ask any more questions.

That didn't mean Munson was finished talking, though. He seemed to have forgotten about the earlier friction between them at their first meeting. He sounded almost friendly as he went on, "One thing about Mr. Hannigan, he won't stand for folks getting uppity. He's one of the men who built this country. Hell, I'd say that nobody did more to settle this part of Wyoming than Ezra Hannigan. People need to give him the respect that's due him. Instead, they talk bad about him—like the fella who runs the newspaper in town."

"McKenzie's friend, ain't he?"

"That's right. Whitmore's his name. He's all the time writing things in his paper about how the boss is a bad man and has to be stopped from doing the things he wants to do. Like hanging that fool who stole from him."

"I don't reckon I heard about that," Costaine said. "Did you string the varmint up?"

William W. Johnstone and J.A. Johnstone

"Not us," Munson said. "He was tried and found guilty. Judge Trent passed sentence on him, and Marshal Bowen and his deputies carried it out." The foreman snickered. "Just like the law took care of Thad Crawford. He wouldn't be reasonable when Mr. Hannigan wanted to buy his water rights, so he wound up at the end of a hangrope, too."

"But legally."

"Well, sure. I mean, did Crawford really kill that soiled dove he was accused of killin'? That's not for me to say. The jury said he did, and the judge said he'd hang for it. And that's what happened. Anybody who says anything else is just trying to cause trouble and ought to be stopped." Munson's voice hardened. "Whatever it takes to shut them up."

Costaine felt a sense of unease growing inside him. From the sound of what Munson was saying, Ezra Hannigan was a law unto himself around here. Munson wouldn't come right out and say that Thad Crawford had been framed and had been hanged for a crime he hadn't committed . . . but you could take Munson's comments that way, if you wanted to. You sure could.

Likewise, Munson hadn't admitted that he and the other members of Hannigan's crew had burned down Pete Raskin's hay barn, but he hadn't denied it, either. And according to Munson, anybody who even brought up the possibility that Hannigan was connected to any wrongdoing ought to be shut up, by any means necessary.

Costaine didn't believe that Mac McKenzie was no longer wanted. He didn't like McKenzie, and by extension, he didn't like McKenzie's friends and allies, including that Jensen hombre and the man who published the newspaper. But they ought to have the right to say what they wanted. That was the way things were supposed to work. Some powerful gent like Ezra Hannigan didn't have the right to keep folks from expressing their beliefs, whether he liked what they were saying or not.

It all looped back around on itself and made Costaine's stomach squirm when he thought too much about it. His usual solution when something like that happened was to not think about whatever it was. He tried that now, pushing away the worries that nagged at his brain.

Munson just wouldn't shut up, though. He said, "Whitmore's gonna be sorry he didn't take the hints we've been giving him. I don't understand it, myself. A man with a wife as pretty as the one Whitmore has ought to be worried about protecting her, not spouting off about what somebody else is doing." Munson shrugged. "Well, he had his chances, and he sure as hell can't claim otherwise. When he's dead, maybe his wife can go to work at the Lucky Shot. I'd pay to spend some time with her, that's for damn sure, as long as the price was reasonable. Shoot, for a gal who looks like her, I might even pay a little more than the going rate."

"Wait," Costaine said. "You're gonna kill that newspaper feller?"

"I didn't say that, did I?"

"Well, no, but—"

"Something could happen to him, though. Somebody might break into that house behind the newspaper office, where he and his wife live, and shoot the place up, and then they might take sledgehammers to the printing press, so it wouldn't be anything but a pile of rubble that could never be used again. Then, for good measure, they might drag that high-and-mighty news-paperman up Hangman's Hill and leave him dangling from the gallows so that everybody in these parts could look up there and know that it's not smart to say bad things about Mr. Hannigan, and it's even more foolish to print them in a newspaper."

It was a cold night, the way most of them were this time of year in Wyoming, but the ice in Cougar Jack Costaine's veins had nothing to do with the temperature.

Munson could talk around it and play coy all he liked, but Costaine could draw only one conclusion from this conversation.

He had fallen in with a bunch of snake-blooded killers.

Pete Raskin and his late wife, Clara, had had four sons and two daughters. Two of the boys were dead, one falling victim to a fever when he was eight years old, the other killed in an Indian raid when he was twelve. One of the girls had died in that same Indian fight. The other girl, grown now and married, lived in Laramie with her storekeeper husband and their family.

The two surviving sons, Lafe and Chuck, in their twenties now, were still here on the ranch, working the spread with their pa.

Lafe was the best cook out of the three of them, so

he usually rode back to the house first to prepare supper, while his father and brother finished up the day's chores and then came in a little later. They had followed that familiar routine today, then cleaned up after the meal, sat by the fireplace, and smoked their pipes as they talked over the day, and finally turned in.

At least the two younger men did. Pete Raskin lay in his bed for a while and then got up, unable to sleep. He had been restless every night recently since his barn had burned. He knew Ezra Hannigan was behind what had happened, and he was equally convinced that Hannigan wasn't through causing trouble for him. The man would try something else, especially when he found out that Raskin had been in town talking against him and trying to convince the citizens that something ought to be done about Hannigan's behavior. Hannigan wouldn't like that, not one bit.

And there were plenty of folks in the settlement who would be happy to tell him all about it if they believed it would benefit them. Raskin remembered a time when everybody looked after their neighbors; now too many people were just out for themselves.

He pulled his trousers on over the long underwear he'd worn to bed, stamped his feet down in his boots, put on his sheepskin coat, without donning a shirt over the underwear, and took down his Winchester from where it hung on hooks on the wall beside the door.

He was able to do all that without lighting a lamp, since he knew every inch of the house he had built more than thirty years earlier. Then he pulled the latch-string on the front door and stepped out onto the porch, taking a deep breath of the frigid night air.

Right away, the sound of hoofbeats came to his ears.

It sounded like a good-sized group, and the riders were coming closer. Raskin wasn't sure how far away they were; sounds could be deceptive out here, especially at night. But he knew they were bound to be here soon, and was just as convinced that they were up to no good, even without knowing who they were.

Raskin wheeled around quickly. He hadn't closed the door yet, so he was able to call through the opening, "Lafe! Chuck! Get up, boys! Trouble comin'!"

He didn't know for a fact that the nocturnal visitors were bent on trouble, but it seemed like a safe bet, given everything that had happened lately. Raskin turned back to the railing around the porch and levered a round into the Winchester's chamber.

He glanced at the flower bed in front of the porch, empty now in the winter. But to tell the truth, he had neglected it since his wife died, and he felt bad about that. The flowers Clara had grown had been her pride and joy, and he should have done better about maintaining them. He just hadn't been able to find it in his heart to do so, once she was gone.

That thought flashed through his mind in the time it took him to lift the rifle to his shoulder.

Then torches burst into flame in front of him, blooming like crimson flowers in the darkness. Smaller spurts of muzzle flame came from several guns. The swift rataplan of hoofbeats grew louder. The attackers were charging full speed at the house now. As Raskin opened fire with the Winchester, the torches sailed into the air, spinning in blazing circles as powerful throws carried them toward the house.

Heavy footsteps sounded as Lafe and Chuck, wearing long underwear and barefooted, emerged from the house. They also clutched Winchesters.

"Cut loose your wolf, boys!" Raskin roared at his sons. They joined him in shooting at the attackers, firing as fast as they could work the rifles' levers.

But as much lead as the Raskins were throwing, more of it was coming back at them. Bullets buzzed like angry hornets around Pete Raskin's head and thudded into the walls of the house behind him. So far, he and his sons hadn't been hit, but that couldn't continue.

It didn't. Lafe reeled back and made a high-pitched keening sound of agony. His brother called his name and grabbed his arm. Chuck's strong grip kept Lafe from falling, but clearly, the young man was hit hard.

"Get in the house!" Raskin ordered. "Get back!"

He cranked off three more rounds, while Chuck was helping Lafe through the door. Then the Winchester's hammer clicked on an empty chamber. Raskin ducked after his sons, but as he was passing through the opening, what felt like a giant fist punched him in the back of the left shoulder. He staggered, but stayed on his feet and made it through the door to kick it closed behind him.

A bullet had caught him in the shoulder. How bad it was, he couldn't tell. His left arm was already starting to go numb. While he could still use it, he grasped the Winchester in his left hand and used the right to take fresh cartridges from the box kept on the table underneath the hooks where the rifles hung when they weren't being used. He thumbed the cartridges through the loading gate as he listened to Chuck helping the wounded

Lafe stretch out on the sofa. Lafe complained that he was going to get blood on the furniture, but his brother told him not to worry about that.

They had plenty of other problems to worry about, Raskin realized. With all the shooting going on, he had lost track of those torches after they'd been thrown toward the house.

Now, as he sniffed the air and smelled smoke, he knew that at least some of them had landed on the roof and had set the place on fire.

Last time, they had burned down his barn. This time, the stakes were higher.

Life and death.

Chapter 25

Costaine hung back when Munson, Mitch, and the others attacked the Raskin ranch. Not so far that it was obvious he wasn't taking part in the raid, but far enough that he hoped to avoid any of the shots Raskin and whoever else was in there fired in defense of their home. He was still willing to take help from Ezra Hannigan, and Hannigan's men, in capturing Mac McKenzie, but he couldn't bring himself to pitch in and assist with burning out an innocent man and his family.

Maybe Munson wouldn't notice that he wasn't shooting. He could always claim later that he had taken part. With all the gunplay that was going on, Munson couldn't prove otherwise, Costaine told himself.

The men charged with throwing the torches had flung the burning brands with strength and accuracy. Three of them had landed on the ranch house's roof, and the small fires they had started spread and joined together, and a column of flame erupted into the cold night sky, almost blinding in its fierce glow.

Exultant shouts came from several of the raiders. They had their quarry where they wanted them. Raskin and his companions could stay inside and meet a fiery end as the house burned down around them, or they could try to come out shooting and run right into a withering storm of bullets.

Even knowing what was waiting for them outside, not many men could stand around and wait for flames to consume them. There was something in the human spirit that refused to surrender the last little bit of hope. The brain clung to a tiny shred of longing for life and urged doing *something*, no matter how doomed the effort might be.

What it came down to was that most frontiersmen, if they had to cross the divide, would rather cross it with a gun in their fist and a snarl of defiance on their lips.

That was the way Pete Raskin and his sons came out of their house. One of them was wounded and the other two supported him between them. They all had guns and the revolvers roared and bucked as they charged into the open.

Costaine couldn't see them all that clearly because of the smoke in the air, but he was able to make out what happened. A crashing volley came from Munson and the others. Raskin and the other two stumbled as bullets ripped through them. Blood must have flown through the air, although it was too dark to see that. The three men somehow stayed on their feet and continued to stumble forward, but the guns in their hands sagged. Costaine could tell how hard they were struggling to raise the weapons and fire again, but then another round of shots came from the attackers.

Flesh and blood could only do so much, no matter how determined the spirit was. Slugs pounded the three men and drove them off their feet. The blaze on the roof reached the walls, and the burning house turned into an inferno that cast its hellish glare over the three sprawled, motionless forms that lay just in front of what might have once been flower beds . . .

The killers sat on their horses and watched as the ranch house burned to the ground. It really didn't take that long, not as long as you might expect for a home and the lives of the people who had lived there to be completely consumed.

Costaine drifted up next to Munson, who didn't seem suspicious of him. He hoped that meant no one had noticed that he hadn't taken part in the raid.

But he hadn't done anything to stop it, either, and that knowledge sort of gnawed at his guts. Costaine knew that as one man, there wasn't much he could have done, if anything. That certainty didn't make him feel any better.

After a while, Munson said, "We'd better make sure Raskin won't be running his mouth anymore."

Costaine didn't see how it was even remotely possible that the rancher had survived. He and the other two had been shot to pieces.

Flames still danced, here and there, amid the rubble. The glow they cast was enough for Costaine to see the lifeless, staring eyes of the three men on the ground. Oddly enough, their faces were unmarked. Costaine could see the resemblance between the older man, who he assumed was Pete Raskin, and the two young ones. Munson had mentioned that Raskin had two sons. This had to be them. The family had died together.

"Well, the boss won't have to worry about Raskin anymore," Munson said as he leaned on his saddle horn and looked down at the corpses. "He'll be glad to hear that." He straightened and lifted his reins. "Come on, let's head back to the ranch."

Costaine said, "I reckon I might go back to town."

Munson looked at him. "You reckoned that, did you?"

"Yeah. I left a few things in my hotel room I'd like to fetch."

That was a lie. Costaine didn't even have a hotel room in town. But he didn't want to go back to the Rocking H tonight.

"I'll ride out to the ranch again tomorrow, now that I know where it is," he went on. "Then Mr. Hannigan and me can talk about corralin' Mac McKenzie."

Munson just grunted, as if he weren't sure that conversation would ever take place. But Costaine let it pass. He just wanted to get away from these men.

When Munson didn't say anything else, Costaine added, "I done my part, you know. I kept my word."

"Sure," Munson said. "That's fine. Go on back to town. We'll see you tomorrow."

Costaine nodded. "So long, boys." Even though it sickened him to do it, he added, "Good work tonight."

"Yeah."

Munson and the others sat and watched Costaine ride away. His muscles were tense because he didn't like having his back to that bunch. Part of him expected to feel a bullet smash into him at any second.

But nothing happened, and eventually, darkness swallowed them up. When Costaine looked back over his shoulder, he couldn't see them anymore. All he could make out was the faint glow of the dying fire where the Raskin ranch house had been.

Costaine wasn't sure what he was going to do next. He considered not even stopping at the settlement. Maybe he ought to just keep going and find some other fugitive with a bounty on his head. There were plenty of them out here on the frontier. A hunter like Cougar Jack Costaine would never run out of outlaws to track down.

But the thought of McKenzie putting one over on those folks in town and getting away with murder just didn't sit right with Costaine. It wasn't only the money. He didn't like lawbreakers. There were too blasted many of them for the sheriffs and the marshals and all the other badge-toters to handle. It fell to men like him to clean up the ones who might otherwise escape justice.

The ones like Mac McKenzie.

No, he couldn't turn his back on that, Costaine decided. And he couldn't allow Munson and those other men to get away with the violent atrocity they had carried out tonight. He had to do something about it.

The question was, what could he do . . .

And would it wind up getting him killed, too?

The trail he was following ran between a pair of ridges up ahead. The night was so dark, he could barely see the ground rising on both sides of him. But he heard a horse moving and then a moment later spied a shape coming to a stop in the trail, blocking his progress. He could make out that it was a man on horseback, but that was all he could tell.

Costaine reined in, put his hand on the butt of his gun, and called, "Who's that?"

"Costaine?" a familiar voice asked. "Is that you?"

Costaine recognized the voice as belonging to Marshal Verne Bowen. He hadn't expected to run into the lawman out here in the middle of nowhere, this far from the settlement of Hannigan's Hill.

"Marshal? What are you doin' out here?"

Bowen nudged his mount forward a few steps so that Costaine could see him better now. The marshal said, "I was checking on you. When Jed got back to town, he told me that Mr. Hannigan was sending you on a job tonight with some of the other men. I wanted to see how well you carried it out."

"Why, it all went fine, I reckon," Costaine said. He figured he'd better try to bluff his way through this unexpected encounter. He had wondered exactly how much Bowen knew about what Hannigan was doing. Was he in any respect still a real lawman, or was he just another of Hannigan's hired gun-wolves? If Costaine told him about the murders of Pete Raskin and his sons, would Bowen do anything about it?

Costaine had enough respect for the law, despite all the times he had bent it himself, that he hated to think Bowen was completely corrupt.

"Raskin and his boys are dead?" Bowen asked harshly,

dashing Costaine's hope that the man might still have some small shred of honesty and decency inside him.

"Yeah," Costaine replied in a sullen voice. "Yeah, they are."

"You got in there with the others and did your part?"

"What do you think?"

Bowen shifted slightly in the saddle. Costaine heard the leather creak. A second later, the marshal said, "I think you stayed back and didn't do a damned thing, like the coward you are. I know that's what you did. The more I thought about it, the more I worried that I made a mistake about you, Costaine. You're not the sort of man the boss needs working on his crew, after all. That's why I decided to keep an eye on what you did tonight and find out for sure."

Costaine stiffened as Bowen's words lashed at him. So Bowen had been spying on him the whole time. Anger welled up inside him. Without thinking about what he was doing, he blurted out, "I don't mind puttin' the fear o' God into a man, but what happened tonight was cold-blooded murder! Raskin and his boys never had a chance. No, I didn't help gun 'em down! They didn't have that comin' just because they don't go along with ever'thing Ezra Hannigan wants."

"That's exactly what they deserved," Bowen said coolly. "They were fools, and they paid the price for that foolishness."

Costaine leaned forward and said hotly, "Folks don't think much of bounty hunters, but, blast it, we serve the law just like you're supposed to, Bowen. But you're nothin' but a crook! I see it now. That newspaper fella in town is right about Hannigan, even if he is friends with McKenzie. Hannigan's got to be stopped, and I'm gonna tell him that!"

"You're not going to tell anybody anything, you stupid son of a—"

The tone of imminent danger in Bowen's voice warned Costaine. Before the marshal could finish his threat, Costaine yanked his pistol out of its holster, jabbed his boot heels in his horse's flanks, and sent the animal lunging forward.

Bowen must have already drawn his gun because as soon as Costaine made his move, a shot roared and a tongue of flame, nearly a foot long, licked out toward the bounty hunter. Costaine had leaned instinctively to the side as he tried to charge past Bowen, so the shot missed. He triggered his own gun, but it was too dark to tell if he hit the corrupt marshal.

Bowen fired again as Costaine flashed by. This time, the slug tore through the thick buffalo coat and hammered into Costaine's body. He gasped in pain as the bullet's impact twisted him in the saddle. Feeling himself slipping, he grabbed desperately at the horn with his left hand and hung on for dear life as he thrust the gun in his other hand behind him and fired three more shots in Bowen's general direction.

Then he was well beyond Bowen and the horse underneath him was running freely and swiftly through the night. Costaine pulled himself into a position where he was mounted more securely. He tried to holster his revolver, but his muscles didn't seem to work exactly how he wanted them to and he fumbled with the weapon. It slipped out of his grasp and fell. He knew he couldn't stop and turn back to try to retrieve it.

All he could do was keep going.

A rifle cracked several times behind him. Bowen was shooting after him, but the marshal was firing blindly. None of the bullets found their target.

Pain from Costaine's wound washed through him. His head spun crazily. He was able to stay in the saddle, but that was all he could manage. He didn't know where the horse was going and couldn't have found the strength to guide the animal even if he was able to make his thoughts work that coherently.

All he could do was try to get away from Bowen. More shots blasted, hoofbeats pounded behind him, and darkness closed in around him as the deadly race continued.

Chapter 26

This waiting had gone on long enough, Luke decided. He didn't care if Jonas Creed was a United States senator. The man couldn't just leave him hanging like this. Already, Luke had been in Hannigan's Hill for almost a week. Ethan Stallings had been stuck in jail the same amount of time.

Of course, Stallings was out of the cold weather and was eating Mac McKenzie's excellent cooking, three meals a day, so he didn't have all that much to complain about, to Luke's way of thinking, but even so, this situation needed to be resolved.

Luke sent another wire to Washington, requesting those further instructions from Senator Creed that he had assumed would be forthcoming days ago.

The reply came back surprisingly quickly:

REMAIN IN PLACE STOP MEN COMING
TO TAKE CUSTODY OF PRISONER STOP DO

NOT TURN STALLINGS OVER TO ANYONE
ELSE STOP CREED

Luke spread the telegraph flimsy on the counter in Mac's Place so that the man standing opposite him could read it. Mac frowned and said, "When are these fellas coming to pick up Stallings supposed to get here?"

"Your guess is as good as mine," Luke said, not bothering to keep the disgust out of his voice. "But until they do, I'm stuck here. At least I am if I want to claim that reward."

"Hey, it's not that bad. You've made some friends . . . and you have a good place to eat."

Luke chuckled. "That's what I keep telling myself."

Mac leaned to the side to peer past Luke out the front window.

Luke noticed that and asked, "Something going on out there?"

"A fella just rode by, hell-bent for leather," Mac said. "I think I recognized him as Hal Burks. He has a little spread a few miles outside of town. I wonder what's brought him here in such a big hurry."

Luke looked around the café, which was empty at midmorning except for himself and Mac. "I reckon you can go find out without risking the loss of much business."

"That's true." Mac left his apron on as he came out from behind the counter and headed for the door.

Luke joined him. A thin haze of dust still hung in the air from the hooves of the horse that had just galloped past. Mac looked down the street and pointed at a horse tied at the hitch rail in front of the marshal's office. The animal's sides were heaving from a hard run.

"That's Burks's horse," Mac said. "Looks like he went to see Bowen."

"The marshal and I don't get along that well," Luke said. "Maybe I'd better stay here. But you can go see what it's about, if you want to."

"Appears that several other people are headed to the marshal's office to find out the same thing."

Luke had noticed that, too, and figured the rancher might have shouted out his news to attract more attention as he raced into town. He nodded toward the other side of the street and said, "There goes your friend Albert. He must be after a story."

Albert Whitmore was trotting along the opposite boardwalk toward Bowen's office. Mac said, "Yeah, I know that look. He's like a hunting dog that catches a scent. He smells news and he's determined to find out what it is."

"Go on," Luke told him. "I'll stay here and keep an eye on the place for you."

Mac started along the street, then paused and glanced over his shoulder.

"There'd better be some pie left when I get back," he said.

Luke grinned. "You think I can eat every bite of pie in the place?"

"I'm just saying, that's all."

"Go see what's going on. Your pie is safe."

* * *

Albert saw Mac coming and slowed down so that Mac was able to join him as they both reached the marshal's office.

"What's this all about, Albert?" Mac asked. "Do you know?"

Albert shook his head. "All I know is that I was coming out of the general store when Hal Burks galloped past, yelling something about all of them being dead."

"All of who?"

"I have no idea, but I intend to find out."

The door into the marshal's office stood open, allowing a hubbub of excited voices to escape. Mac and Albert went in and found half a dozen of the townspeople crowded into the area in front of Marshal Verne Bowen's desk. Hal Burks was in the forefront of that group.

Bowen stood behind the desk with his hands raised. In a loud, irritated voice, he said, "Everybody just calm down and be quiet. Burks, the way you're gabbling, I can't tell what you're talking about. What are you trying to say, man?"

"They're all d-d-d-dead, I tell you," Burks said. He was a small, middle-aged man with a stammer that came out when he was excited or upset. Mac had known him for several years and liked him well enough.

"Who's dead?" Bowen asked.

"Pete Raskin! Pete and his boys, Chuck and Lafe. I s-s-s-seen 'em layin' there, with a b-b-b-bunch of b-b-b-bullet holes in 'em. They was shot to doll rags and the house was burned down!"

Bowen glared at him. "You're loco! Who would do a thing like that?"

"You know good and well who'd commit such an atrocity, Marshal," Albert said from the rear of the group. Mac cast a warning glance at his friend, but Albert ignored it. "Your boss is bound to be responsible. Your real boss, not the people of this town you're supposed to be working for!"

The cluster of folks in front of the desk parted quickly, almost as if they were getting out of the line of fire. That might not be such a far-fetched possibility. Bowen leaned forward, smacked a fist down on the desk, and roared, "Be damned careful what you're saying, Whitmore! I won't stand for any more of your lies!"

"What am I lying about?" Albert demanded. "What did I say that's not true? Are you claiming Ezra Hannigan didn't send his crew of killers after Pete Raskin and his sons?"

"I just heard about this, damn it." Bowen spread his hands. "I don't know the details. If something actually happened to Raskin and his boys—"

"Oh, it h-h-h-happened, all right," Hal Burks said. "I seen 'em with my own eyes."

"I'll have to ride out there and take a look before I know what really happened," Bowen went on. "But I'm not sure I ought to. I'm the marshal of Hannigan's Hill. Raskin's ranch is out of my jurisdiction. As a newspaperman, you ought to know a little about the law, Whitmore."

"Don't lecture me about the law," Albert said. "You're

the only lawman in this part of the county. You know the sheriff ignores us down here except at election time. But it's a waste of time talking to you. You just do what Hannigan tells you to do, whether it's legal or not!"

"Keep it up, mister," Bowen snapped. "Keep it up and I'll throw you in jail for spreading lies about one of our leading citizens. Don't think that just because you publish that rag of a newspaper you can get away with saying whatever you want."

"I don't have to be a newspaperman to say what I want. I'm an American citizen so that gives me all the rights I need. You can't shut me up." Albert waved a hand at the other townspeople, who had gathered in the office. "You can't shut any of us up! We have a right to speak!"

"Well, go do it somewhere else!" the marshal bellowed. "This is still my office, and I've got a right to tell you to get the hell out of it!"

"Are you going to investigate the murders of Pete Raskin and his sons and the burning down of their ranch house?" Albert demanded.

"I don't have to answer your damn questions. Get out, I tell you!"

Bowen was trembling with rage. Mac saw the way the marshal's hand hovered over the butt of his gun. Bowen wanted to draw the weapon and blast a hole through Albert. He couldn't do that while Albert was unarmed, not in front of this many witnesses. Although Mac couldn't guarantee that Bowen wouldn't lose control, he was so furious . . .

Mac put a hand on Albert's arm and said quietly,

"Come on, let's go." To Burks, he added, "Art, come on over to the café with us. I want to hear all about what you saw, and I'm sure Albert does, too."

"That's right, I want the whole story," Albert said.

"You're gonna p-p-p-put me in the paper?" Burks asked.

"Of course, if you tell me what you saw."

Burks bobbed his head in a nod. "Sure, let's g-g-g-go."

Bowen pointed a finger across the desk. "You'd better be careful what you say, Burks. There are laws against lying about folks."

"I don't figure on lyin', Marshal. I'm just gonna t-t-t-tell Mr. Whitmore what I saw with my own two eyes, that's all."

Mac moved his hand from Albert's arm to Burks's shoulder and steered the man out of Bowen's office. Albert was on Burks's other side. The rest of the crowd followed them into the street. Several men called out questions.

Albert told them, "Just be patient, folks. I think this story warrants another extra edition of the *Chronicle*. It'll be on the streets first thing tomorrow morning and you can read all about it."

That seemed to satisfy their curiosity for the moment. Mac and Albert led the rancher toward the café. Mac asked, "Would you rather have this conversation in your office, Albert?"

The newspaperman chuckled. "My office doesn't have pie and coffee, Mac. Well, it has coffee, but not the equal of yours. Just don't tell Jessie I said that."

"Don't worry, I don't intend to."

"I know it ain't lunchtime yet," Burks said, "but I could go for a p-p-p-piece of pie."

Mac grinned. "We'll see what we can do about that."

Luke was sitting at the counter when they came in. He waved a hand toward several pies sitting on the shelf next to the door into the kitchen and said, "See? All of them are fully intact." He raised the cup in his other hand. "I did help myself to the coffeepot, though."

"And you're welcome to it," Mac said. "Hal, this is Luke Jensen. Luke, I don't believe you and Hal Burks have met."

"No, we haven't." Luke stood up and shook hands with the man. "Pleased to meet you, Burks."

"Likewise, M-M-M-Mr. Jensen."

Mac poured coffee for himself, Albert, and Burks. Several of the townspeople who had been in the marshal's office had followed them to the café and came inside now, taking seats at the counter and a couple of the tables. They wanted coffee, too, so Mac was kept busy for a few minutes taking care of them. A few asked for slices of pie, too. This was good business for this time of morning, smack-dab between the breakfast and lunch rushes.

It was just too bad folks had had to die in order to generate this crowd.

Mac came back to the counter, where Albert had been waiting to talk to Burks until Mac could listen, too. He said, "All right, Mr. Burks, tell me everything you can about what you found this morning."

Burks nodded, took a sip of coffee, and said, "I was ridin' into t-t-town to talk to Walt Jackson over at the blacksmith shop. I need to bring my mule team in to have 'em reshod. I know some fellas d-d-don't put shoes on their mules, but I do a lot of work on rocky ground with my team, so I like to k-k-keep 'em shod. Saves wear and tear in the long run."

Mac could tell that Albert was getting impatient already and wanted Burks to get to the meat of his story. But most fellas had to be allowed to proceed at their own pace when they were talking, so Mac just nodded and smiled encouragingly at the rancher. Burks's speech impediment was easing as he calmed down, so they didn't want him to get upset again.

"Anyway," Burks continued, "the trail took me past Pete Raskin's place, and before I ever got there, I smelled sm-sm-smoke. When I saw that the house was gone, I pulled my rifle out and galloped on in. It looked like somethin' from b-b-back in the days when the Injuns was raidin' around here." He shook his head. "But then I saw the bodies, and they didn't have no arrows pincushioned in 'em. Just bullet holes. It was Pete and his boys, Lafe and Chuck. I'd say each one of them had been shot at least six t-t-times."

"That's terrible," Albert said. "So they were dead when you got there?"

"Oh, yeah. Dead as could be. Shot up like that, there wasn't nothin' else they could be. And I'd say they'd b-b-been that way since sometime last night."

"Did you bury them?" Mac asked.

Burks shook his head. "No, sir, I didn't, and I feel bad about that now. But I thought I ought to get on into town and tell the law about it." He made a disgusted sound. "Not that it did a d-d-damned bit o' good. Verne

Bowen didn't care what happened to Pete and his boys. Didn't care a lick!"

Albert said, "He probably knew all about it already. I wouldn't be surprised if he was aware of the plan before the Raskin place was attacked."

"You can't know that for sure," Luke observed, "but my hunch is that you're right. It seems to me that with each new outrage he gets away with, Ezra Hannigan becomes bolder."

Mac nodded. "That's the way it usually works. Hannigan already had a pretty high opinion of himself. By now, he must feel pretty near unstoppable."

"He's going to find out he's wrong about that," Albert said. "He'll be easier to deal with if he doesn't have the pretense of the law on his side. When I publish that extra edition in the morning, there'll be an editorial on the front page calling for the ouster of Marshal Bowen and all his deputies. They have to be removed from office even if we have to form a vigilante group to do it. I'm also going to send a letter to the chief United States Marshal down in Denver and request that a deputy marshal be sent here to arrest Hannigan, Bowen, and the others and restore law and order. That will be in the editorial as well."

"It might take more than one marshal to do a job that big," Luke said dryly.

"I suppose that would depend on the man with the badge."

Mac said, "If you print those things, you'll be putting the biggest target so far on your back, Albert. Hannigan has attacked you twice already. We know that whether we can prove it or not. You and Jessie could have been killed in either of those incidents. Hannigan won't leave it to chance now. He won't be satisfied with maybe scaring you off. He's going to want you dead."

"He wouldn't dare . . ." Albert began, but then his voice trailed off. He let out a hollow laugh and shook his head. "I was about to say he wouldn't dare attack the press like that, but given everything that's happened so far, that would be a foolish thing to say. Clearly, he doesn't care about public opinion anymore. All he cares about is power. He has it, and he'll do anything to hang on to it."

"And he'll always be hungry for more," Luke added.

"I suspect you're right," Albert said. He looked from Luke to Mac. "You both are. But I've tried everything. I started out by trying to shame Hannigan into ceasing his high-handed behavior. I condemned his actions. I urged him to change his behavior. Nothing has worked. So it's time to call for direct action and to take such action by contacting higher authorities. If Ezra Hannigan wants war—"

"If Hannigan wants war, he's a lot better equipped to fight it than you and your friends here in town are," Luke said. The words were blunt enough to make Albert frown.

"So, are you saying we should just roll over and surrender? We should let him win?" Albert shook his head. "Things have gone too far for that. We have to stand up for ourselves now, or we never will."

As worrisome as that thought was, Mac knew his friend was right. At this point, nothing short of force was going to stop Ezra Hannigan.

Hal Burks said, "I wish I hadn't ridden off and left Pete and his boys out there like that. There are wolves around. Somebody needs to bury them."

"You have an undertaker here in town, don't you?" Luke asked.

"We do," Mac said. "But Ezra Hannigan owns the undertaking parlor, and the fella who runs it for him won't go against his wishes."

Luke made a face. "So the hombre's not going to be in any hurry to retrieve the bodies, then, is he?"

"Not likely."

Burks said, "I'll ride back out there and b-b-bury 'em. It's the least I can do, since I'm the one who found 'em."

"I'll come with you and lend a hand," Luke offered.

Mac said, "I would, too, but I've got to tend the café."

"That's fine. The two of us ought to be able to dig three graves without much trouble. It hasn't been cold enough yet to freeze the ground, thank goodness," Luke commented.

Burks said, "I'm obliged to you, Mr. Jensen. We can get shovels from the general store. I'll go do that right now and meet you outside in a few minutes."

Luke nodded. Burks left the café. Albert had taken a piece of paper from inside his coat and began scribbling notes on it with a pencil.

"Working on that editorial already?" Mac asked.

"I have to get my thoughts in order."

Luke picked up his coffee cup and drank the last of the strong brew in it. While he was doing that, Mac leaned forward over the counter and said quietly, "Be careful out there, Luke. I noticed that a few of my customers have left quietly in the past few minutes. I can't rule out the possibility that one of them might have heard everything that was said and lit a shuck to tell Bowen all about it."

"And Bowen will pass that along to Hannigan," Luke said. "But either way, those men still need burying."

"Just don't make me have to ride out there and dig any extra graves," Mac said.

Chapter 27

As Luke and Hal Burks rode out of Hannigan's Hill a short time later, Luke noticed a low line of clouds to the northwest, hanging over the range of mountains in that direction.

"Looks like there might be a storm headed our way," he commented.

"Well, it's ab-b-b-bout time," Burks said. "We usually get the first decent snowfall of the winter around n-n-now."

"It's a good thing we're going to lay those unfortunate souls to rest while we can, then."

"Yeah, I'd want somebody to do the same for me if'n I was gunned down like that." Burks scratched his chin. "You really think Mr. Whitmore's gonna get a bunch of vigilantes together and throw Marshal Bowen and his d-d-deputies out o' their jobs?"

"You tell me," Luke said. "You know Whitmore and, more importantly, you know the people of Hannigan's

Hill a lot better than I do. Is it likely that Whitmore can make good on what he's vowing to do?"

Burks thought about it for a moment and then said, "I reckon he'll try. Mr. Whitmore's a stubborn cuss. Once he's convinced he's right about something, he'll give it all he's g-g-got. What I ain't sure of is how much help he's gonna get from the folks in town, though."

"You don't believe they have the courage to stand up to Hannigan and his hired guns?"

"You got to remember, it's the ranchers, like me and Pete Raskin and Thad Crawford, who have had the most trouble with Hannigan. We're the ones he wants to p-p-push out so he can control all the range around here. Other than bein' pushed around and harassed some by Bowen and his deputies, most folks in town haven't been put into a corner where they had to fight. There's plenty of resentment about Hannigan ownin' so much of the business in town, but as long as people can go on about their day-to-day lives without bein' interfered with, they ain't likely to get in a fightin' mood."

Luke nodded and said, "Unfortunately, I think you're probably right. Albert Whitmore may have a bigger job ahead of him than he thinks he does."

"He's bitin' off more than he can chew by hisself, that's for durned sure."

"Well, he has some help," Luke pointed out. "Mac will stand with him, and since Mac and I are friends, I suppose I will, too. And those ranchers you were talking about may support him as well. Still, once someone is as entrenched as Hannigan is, it's hard to dig him out of his hole."

"Speakin' of holes . . . there's the Raskin place up

yonder. You can see what's left of the house. The barn burned down a week or so ago and Pete hadn't started rebuildin' it yet."

"More of Hannigan's work?"

"Pete sure thought so. That's what he was tellin' everybody in town who'd listen."

"And that may well be what got him killed," Luke mused. "A tyrant like Hannigan doesn't like having his activities exposed in the light of day."

As they drew closer, Burks spurred his mount forward and yelled angrily as he rode toward the sprawled corpses. Buzzards abandoned their feast and rose into the sky with an ungainly flapping of their black wings. The carrion birds were incredibly graceful when they were gliding on air currents high above the earth, but awkward in everything else they did.

As Luke came up to join Burks, where the rancher was dismounting near the bodies, Burks said, "I reckon it's lucky no wolves come along and dragged 'em off. The buzzards ain't been at 'em too b-b-bad yet. Still and all, it's a mighty grim job we got in front of us, Mr. Jensen."

"Call me Luke. And yes, laying to rest men who have been gunned down unjustly is a chore that never gets any easier."

Luke swung down from the saddle and took the shovel that Burks handed him. The graves of Pete Raskin's wife and three other children were in a neatly tended plot near a grove of trees behind where the ranch house had stood. Raskin and his sons would be laid to rest next to their loved ones. Luke began to dig.

From time to time, Luke glanced toward those clouds over the mountains. They were moving closer, but not getting in any hurry about it. They had darkened from a pale blue, barely distinguishable from the sky, to a more threatening shade. The breeze, which had been steady all morning, fell away to nothing, leaving an oppressive, heavy feeling in the atmosphere. The sun was still shining, and with no air moving, a cloying heat began to develop as Luke and Hal Burks worked. Luke took off his jacket as beads of sweat popped out on his face and trickled down his weathered skin.

"Worries a man when it gets to feelin' all ominous like this," Burks commented as he paused to lean on his shovel and rest for a moment. "If it was summer, I'd say there was a b-b-big ol' thunderstorm comin'. Maybe even a cyclone. At this time of year, though, we don't get such storms."

"Down in Texas when they see a cloud like that, they call it a blue norther," Luke said. "The wind behind it is going to blow hard and be mighty cold. Might be some snow in with it, too."

Burks nodded. "Could be. Don't expect it'll hit until tonight, though, or maybe even tomorrow. We've got plenty of time to finish d-d-diggin' these graves." He shook his head. "Too bad we didn't bring a preacher with us. I never was much of a hand for t-t-talkin', and these boys oughta have words spoke over 'em when they're laid to rest."

"I can say a few things."

"You didn't even know 'em."

"That's right, I never met them," Luke said. "But they were fellow human beings, and I feel their loss whether I knew them or not. 'Each man's death diminishes me, for I am involved in mankind,' John Donne wrote. 'Therefore, send not to know for whom the bell tolls, it tolls for thee.'"

"Don't reckon I know the fella," Burks said, "but he sounds pretty smart, if a mite on the gloomy side. Well, that's enough of a break. We'd best get back to d-d-diggin'."

They soon finished the graves, taking turns on the third one. Burks had thought to fetch some blankets from the general store, along with the shovels. They wrapped the bodies in the blankets, covering up the faces frozen in strained lines of death, as well as hiding the damage done by the buzzards.

Carefully and respectfully they placed the men in the graves, then took off their hats as Luke recited Psalm 23 and said a brief prayer that the spirits of Pete Raskin and his sons would be received into Heaven. Luke was not a particularly religious man at heart, at least not any organized religion, but no man could spend years riding the lonely trails of the frontier and not develop some sort of relationship with a higher power. Besides, the words helped Hal Burks, who had been friends with these men.

With that done, they put their hats on and began shoveling dirt back into the graves. By now, it was the middle of the afternoon, and Luke was keenly aware that he had missed the midday meal. He wasn't sure what Mac had been planning for that day's menu, but he knew the food would be good, whatever it was.

An early supper when he got back to town would take care of the rumbling in his belly, he told himself.

He forgot about that instantly and completely as he glanced toward the east and spotted a lone rider heading toward the Raskin place. Luke wasn't sure who that might be. Could be someone from town or just a drifter passing through this way. But he said quietly to Hal Burks, who had his back toward the stranger, "Rider coming in, Hal."

Burks stopped shoveling and turned to look. "Don't recognize the horse," he said, "but whoever it is, is still a ways off. Reckon it could be one of Hannigan's men?"

"Checking on the aftermath of last night's attack? It's possible."

"Gimme that shovel you're holdin'. I think it'd be b-b-better if you had both hands free, just in case."

Luke gave Burks the shovel and walked over to where they had left their horses tied to a small bush. He thought about pulling his Winchester from the saddle sheath, then decided to leave it where it was and rely on the Remingtons, instead, if he needed to. So far, the distant rider didn't appear to pose any threat.

In fact, the horse was ambling along so slowly that Luke wasn't sure what would get there first, the stranger or the clouds drifting down from the northwest. As Luke watched, he realized the horse was veering a little from side to side, too. It seemed like the rider wasn't controlling his mount. He was just letting the horse go wherever it wanted.

They were close enough now for Luke to see that the man in the saddle was slumped forward. He called to Burks, "Hal, I think that man is hurt!"

"Looks like you might be right. Reckon he's lookin' for help?"

"I'm not sure he's looking for anything. I'm not sure he's even conscious."

The thought crossed Luke's mind that the fellow might even be dead and just hadn't gotten unbalanced enough to topple out of the saddle yet.

Or maybe his corpse had been tied into the saddle to serve as a warning for whoever found him . . .

A startled exclamation burst from Luke's lips as he recognized the battered old hat with the pushed-back brim and realized that the man had a black patch over his left eye.

"That's Costaine!" he told Hal Burks.

"Who?"

"Cougar Jack Costaine. He's a bounty hunter who came to town looking to collect a reward on Mac McKenzie."

"What! Mac's a wanted man?"

Luke glanced around at his companion. "You haven't heard about that?"

"I ain't b-b-been in town for a while. I can't hardly believe that good ol' M-M-Mac is an owlhoot. I eat in his café every time I go to the settlement."

"He's not an outlaw," Luke said. "It was all a misunderstanding, although Costaine seemed to have a hard time getting that through his thick skull. I was hoping he'd given up and left town."

"Well, somethin's wrong with him. He's hurt or sick or dead, judgin' by the way he's ridin'."

Luke agreed. He said, "Get your rifle out, Hal. I

don't think there's going to be any trouble, but we need to be ready just in case there is. I'm going to find out what's happened to Costaine."

"Be careful. Don't reckon it's an ambush. There's too much open ground around that. No place for bush-whackers to hide. But it could still be a t-t-trick o' some sort."

Luke filled his right hand with a Remington as he strode forward to meet the horse and rider. Costaine's head drooped forward. Luke couldn't tell if his eyes were closed, but even if they weren't, he didn't seem to be seeing anything.

As he closed in, Luke saw that Costaine's buffalo coat hung open. He spotted a dark stain on the flannel shirt underneath it. Luke had seen enough bloodstains to know what he was looking at. Costaine was wounded, at the very least.

The horse didn't seem to notice Luke until he was about twenty feet away. The animal tossed its head and stopped short, then moved a couple of skittish steps to the side. As long as the horse had been moving at a steady, if erratic, pace, Costaine had swayed back and forth only slightly.

Now, in response to the horse's reaction to Luke, Costaine tilted to his left. He didn't grab the saddle horn or try to stop himself in any other way. Instead, he toppled off the horse's back and crashed to the ground.

Costaine's left foot was still in the stirrup. Luke holstered the Remington, spoke softly to the horse, and moved forward, not rushing so as not to spook the animal worse, but not wasting any time, either, and caught hold of the headstall to keep the horse from bolting. The reins were looped around the horn. Luke got them, too, and when he had a firm grip, he transferred the reins to his left hand and used his right to free Costaine's foot. Then he led the horse several yards away so there was no chance it would step on the fallen man.

"Hal, come take this horse," he called to Burks.

The rancher hurried over to take the reins from Luke. "Is he dead?"

"Don't know yet. That's what I'm about to check. He's got a lot of blood on his shirt, though."

Costaine had landed on his side. Luke knelt beside him, took hold of his shoulders, and carefully rolled him onto his back. The buffalo coat fell open even more. The stain on Costaine's shirt went around his left side. The way the blood had dried, getting the garment off him might not be easy. It might have to be soaked off before Luke could tell just how badly the other bounty hunter was wounded.

But Costaine was alive. Luke could tell that much. His chest rose and fell in a shallow, ragged rhythm. Air rasped in his throat as he breathed. Luke would have been doubtful that a man could lose as much blood as Costaine appeared to have lost and still survive, but evidently, Costaine was a tough hombre.

Tougher even than Luke thought, because at that moment, his eyelids fluttered up and down a few times and then stayed open. He peered up at the sky, not seeming to see anything, but then his gaze swung to Luke's face. Dry lips writhed for a second before he was able to husk out, "J-Jensen . . ."

"Who shot you, Costaine?" Luke asked as he leaned closer. If Costaine was going to cross the divide, as it appeared he might do at any moment, maybe Luke could at least find out who was responsible first.

Somehow, the answer didn't surprise him. "Bowen," Costaine whispered. "That no-good . . . son of a . . . Bowen!"

Chapter 28

One of the deputies was on duty at the marshal's office and jail when Mac came in carrying the tray with Ethan Stallings's midday meal on it.

"Got lunch for the prisoner," Mac said.

The deputy stood up and came around from behind the desk. "What's he eatin' today?"

"Beans, ham hocks, and corn bread. And a bowl of deep-dish apple pie."

"Dadgum it!" the deputy said. "Prisoners around here eat better than I do. On my salary, I can't afford to eat that fancy café food every day."

The fare didn't seem all that fancy to Mac, and with the graft that the local lawmen collected, he doubted if the deputy couldn't afford to eat whatever he wanted.

On the other hand, maybe Bowen got the lion's share of all the payoffs and protection money and the deputies really did have to make do with the marshal's leavings. Mac didn't know the details of the corruption that had taken over Hannigan's Hill.

"Well, take the grub on in," the deputy said disgustedly, with a wave toward the cellblock door. "He's already got a cup of coffee he was yellin' for, a while ago." He stood up. "Wait a second. Got to make sure you're not tryin' to smuggle anything in there."

The deputy patted Mac's pockets and took a good look at the food, stirring the spoon around in the bowl of beans and ham hocks. Satisfied that Mac hadn't hidden a Colt in there, he nodded and waved toward the door.

Mac went into the cellblock. Ethan Stallings was sitting on his bunk, but he got up to come over and take the tray when Mac handed it through the slot in the door.

"I'm obliged to you, McKenzie," Stallings said. "I have to say, being locked up in this town has one advantage. This is the best jail food I've ever eaten."

Mac smiled. "Been locked up in a lot of different jails, have you, Stallings?"

"Well, not that many." Stallings took the tray back to the bunk and sat down. "I take it as a point of pride that I haven't been arrested all that many times."

"So you've been mostly successful at swindling people?"

Stallings laughed. "Of course. That's because I know how to pick my targets. I only go after the greediest, most corrupt individuals I can find. They're the ones who are the easiest to fool. All you have to do is let them think they're getting away with something or putting one over on somebody else. Then they'll eat right out of your hand and swallow everything you tell them."

Mac nodded and said, "I can see how that would work, all right."

Stallings's face grew serious as he asked, "Listen, McKenzie, how would you like to make more money than you'll ever see slinging hash in this little cow town?"

Mac frowned at the confidence man for a moment and then laughed. "Just how loco do you think I am? You explain to me about how you play on folks' greed in order to trick them, and then you turn around and try to bribe me to help you escape?"

"I didn't offer you a bribe."

"That's what you were leading up to, though, wasn't it?"

Stallings shrugged and then laughed. "I guess maybe my timing wasn't the best," he admitted. "But you can't blame a fellow for trying. Even in here, I've learned a little about you. I've overheard the deputies talking about how that one-eyed bounty hunter, Costaine, was after you, and how you were wanted for murder at one time. So you know what it's like to have every hand against you, to be on the run for something you didn't do."

"Are you saying you didn't bilk that senator out of ten thousand dollars?"

Stallings made a face and said, "Well, I can't deny I did that, and I've done plenty of other things I suppose crossed the line." A faraway expression settled over his features as he went on, "But that wasn't always the case. When I was young, I got blamed for some things I didn't have anything to do with. Being wrongly accused like that, it makes you feel like there's no point in trying to do the right thing. People are always going to believe the worst of you, no matter what you do."

"That's a mighty cynical way to look at life. If I thought that way, I should have just gone ahead and become a murderer and an outlaw, since that's what I was accused of."

Stallings shrugged. "Maybe you should have. You might have been better off."

"I don't see how. I never would have been able to settle down here in Hannigan's Hill and open Mac's Place."

Stallings had started eating. He swallowed a spoonful of beans, washed it down with coffee, and said, "You have friends here?"

"Some."

But the only ones he was close to, Mac had to admit when he thought about it, were Albert and Jessie Whitmore.

"A girl, maybe?" Stallings prodded.

Jessie's image popped into Mac's mind again, but he shook his head, both to banish that thought and to answer Stallings's question.

"No girl."

"So really all you do is work. You show up at the same place every day and do the same thing. And then the next day, you do it again, without any real hope that it'll ever change."

"You make it sound pretty monotonous," Mac said.

"That's because it is! But you take me, now." Stallings patted his chest. "Most of the time, I never knew where I was going to be or who I was going to be with from one day to the next. If I did stay in one place and see the same people for a while, it was because I was setting something up."

"Swindling them, you mean."

Stallings ignored that. "And when I was doing that, there was always an element of danger, a threat of being found out, to spice things up and keep them interesting. You've been on the run, McKenzie. Probably found yourself in some pretty wild scrapes."

"A few," Mac admitted. More than he liked to think about, actually.

"Be honest. Did you ever feel more alive than when you were skating right on the edge of disaster? When you knew you had to rely on your wits and your nerve to survive?" Stallings laughed. "You don't get that sort of excitement baking corn bread, I'll bet!"

"Maybe not," Mac conceded, "but that doesn't mean I want to go back to that sort of life. I'd have to be loco to say that I'd rather be on the run."

"You're probably right. But you can't deny there are moments when you'd like to experience some of those thrills again."

This conversation was making Mac uneasy enough that he didn't want to continue it. He said, "Enjoy your meal. I'll pick up the tray and the empty bowls when I bring your supper, as usual."

"Wait a minute, McKenzie." Stallings set the tray aside on his bunk and stood up. He came over to the bars and jerked his head toward the door between the cellblock and the marshal's office. "What's that deputy doing?"

Mac frowned. "What are you up to?"

"Just see what he's doing, if you can. But don't let him notice."

Casting a wary look at Stallings, Mac thought about the request for a second and then eased over to the doorway. He was just curious enough about what Stallings had in mind that he was willing to play along . . . for now.

Mac paused just inside the door and listened. He heard the deputy breathing, and the sound's regularity was enough to make him suspect the man might be asleep. Mac risked a look and saw the deputy leaning back in the chair, with his hat tipped forward over his eyes and his feet resting on the desk, crossed at the ankles. He had dozed off, all right, and as long as no one came in, or he didn't lose his balance and fall over backward, he probably wouldn't wake up for a while.

Mac went back to the bars, where Stallings waited, and said quietly, "He's asleep. You have something to tell me you don't want him to hear? If you think I'm going to help you escape, you might as well forget—"

Stallings shook his head and interrupted, "That's not it. Listen, McKenzie, I like you. I'm not telling you some story. You've fed me well, and you've always treated me civil when you came in here. I'd just as soon nothing happened to you, and it's not just because you're a damned fine cook." He laughed softly. "Although that's one more thing on your side, I have to say."

"Get on with it, whatever it is," Mac told him.

"All right. Listen." Stallings leaned closer to the bars

and Mac followed suit. "My hearing is pretty good. I've heard Bowen talking to those deputies. I don't know the details, but they're planning something for tonight. Something bad for you and your friends, that couple who publish the newspaper. They're going to come out with an extra edition, aren't they? Like they did right after Jensen and I rode in here?"

Mac hesitated. Stallings seemed sincere enough. But that was his stock-in-trade, wasn't it? He had to appear genuine in order to put over whatever pack of lies he was using to swindle his current mark.

Mac was determined he wasn't going to be one of those marks.

"If you're telling me that Hannigan and his men don't like what the newspaper has been saying about them, I already know that."

"This is worse than that. Bowen rode in from Hannigan's ranch and talked to Jed and some of the other deputies. He said that after tonight, the Whitmores won't be a problem anymore, and neither will you, if you're helping them." Stallings wrapped his hands around the bars. "I think they're going to try to kill the newspaper folks, McKenzie, and you, too. That's what it sounded like to me."

Mac's heart began to beat a little faster in his chest. "There have been attacks on the newspaper before."

"Yeah, I heard about those. And Bowen said something about bringing along sledgehammers this time. What would they use sledgehammers for, unless it was to beat that printing press to pieces?"

That made sense, all right. If they killed Albert and

destroyed the press, the *Chronicle* would be out of business, and any other newspaperman would think twice before coming in here and opposing Ezra Hannigan.

Mac couldn't set aside his natural suspicion of Stallings, though. Stallings must have been able to see that in Mac's expression because he said, "I know you think I'm trying to work some sort of angle here, McKenzie. But ask yourself . . . what could I possibly hope to gain by telling you about this?"

Mac turned that question over in his head and had to admit that Stallings had a point. The only thing that would actually benefit the prisoner was to be turned loose, and keeping Mac and the Whitmores from being killed wouldn't accomplish that. Unless he thought that Mac would be so grateful, he'd help him escape . . .

That wasn't going to happen. Stallings was actually Luke Jensen's prisoner. He had pretty much confessed that he was guilty of the crime with which he'd been charged, and he was going to remain behind bars, no matter what else happened. He had to be aware of that.

So, did that mean he was telling the truth about Bowen and the deputies plotting to attack the newspaper office again?

Stallings grinned. "You get it, don't you? You know I'm being honest for a change." He chuckled. "You don't know how unnatural it feels for me to do that!"

"Maybe," Mac allowed. "What I can't figure out is what you get out of telling me?"

Stallings spread his hands and said, "I get to keep eating that good food you bring over here. I told you, that's a big mark in your favor. I figure I'll deal with my other problems later."

Mac didn't know what he meant by that, but at that moment, he heard some sputtering coming from the office. A couple of thumps sounded as the deputy's feet came down on the floor. A few seconds later, the deputy appeared in the doorway and looked confused as he raked his fingers through his hair and blinked bleary eyes.

"You still here, McKenzie?" he asked. "I figured you'd be gone by now."

Stallings said, "We've been swapping recipes, Deputy. You know how it is when a couple of fellows who like to cook get together."

The deputy scowled. "Get back to your bunk and finish eatin'. McKenzie, get away from those bars. You two shouldn't have been that close together. You didn't try to slip him a gun or anything, did you?"

"You know better than that, Deputy," Mac said in a mild voice. "You searched me, remember? Besides, I don't even know this hombre except for his name. I don't have any reason to help him." Mac smiled. "And he's a steady customer, or, rather, Luke Jensen is. I'm getting paid good money for every meal I deliver. Why would I want to interfere with that?"

"Yeah, I reckon that makes sense." The deputy gestured curtly. "Get on about your business."

Mac nodded to Stallings, who had returned to the bunk and picked up the tray, as ordered by the deputy. "I'll see you this evening."

"I'm looking forward to it," Stallings said. "Just

don't forget what I told you about the temperature getting too high in the oven, McKenzie. You know what happens when it does. Everything gets ruined."

"Yeah, it does," Mac agreed. "I'll try to keep the heat turned down to a reasonable level." He paused. "Wouldn't want things to burn."

Chapter 29

Being as gentle as they could, Luke and Hal Burks carried Cougar Jack Costaine over to the trees behind the burned-out ranch house, not far from where they had buried Pete Raskin and his sons. Luke hadn't put his jacket back on, so he wadded it up to make a pillow of it and placed it under Costaine's head and shoulders when they stretched him out on the ground.

"Fetch a bucket of water from the well, if you don't mind, Hal," Luke asked of his companion.

"Sure. Is he still alive?"

"He appears to be. I wasn't sure if moving him would finish him off. He's being stubborn about dying, though."

Burks hurried off to get the water. Luke hunkered on his heels in front of the unconscious Costaine, pushed the buffalo coat back, and used his knife to cut away as much of Costaine's flannel shirt as he could.

When Burks got back, Luke took the bandanna from around Costaine's neck and soaked it in the bucket of water. Then he began squeezing it out so that it moistened the cloth stuck to Costaine's flesh by dried blood. He continued doing that until the blood loosened enough for him to peel away the cloth and expose the ugly, black-rimmed hole on the left side of Costaine's torso, just under the ribs.

Luke studied the bullet wound's position for a moment and then told Burks, "Help me turn him on his side for a minute."

"You lookin' to see if the bullet came out?"

"Judging by where it hit him, it might have. And it might have missed anything too vital as well."

They took hold of Costaine and rolled him to his right. Luke saw the blood on the man's back and knew the bullet had gone through. That was good, although it was possible Costaine might have lost enough blood to kill him, anyway.

"Let's leave him on his side," Luke said. "We need to get this coat off him and clean both of those wounds. You don't happen to have a bottle or a flask of whiskey in your saddlebags, do you?"

"No, I sure don't."

Luke smiled. "Well, that doesn't matter, because I do. We can use it to disinfect those bullet holes, and if Costaine regains consciousness while we're working on him, he's likely to need a slug or two of it to dull the pain as well."

For the next half hour, Luke worked on patching up Costaine as best he could under these conditions. He wanted to get Costaine in good enough shape to take him to the settlement. Luke didn't know if there was a doctor in Hannigan's Hill; the subject hadn't come up in any of the conversations he'd had with Mac or Irish Mahoney. But either way, Costaine's chances would be better if they could get him to town.

"I don't mean to be nosy," Burks said, "but isn't this the fella who tried to kill Mac McKenzie?"

"He wanted to take Mac into custody, but he would have been willing to do it dead or alive."

"Then why are we workin' so hard to save his life?" Burks held up a hand before Luke could answer. "Is this another of those 'ringing bell' things?"

"You mean asking 'for whom the bell tolls'?" Luke shrugged. "Not really, although you could certainly take the connectedness of mankind into account. No, Costaine said something before he passed out that I want to ask him about. He said that Marshal Bowen is the one who shot him."

"Bowen! Why would he shoot a bounty hunter?"

"That's what I'd like to know."

Costaine began moaning and stirring around while Luke was swabbing the bullet wounds with whiskey. His eyelid fluttered, but didn't open. He didn't regain consciousness.

When Luke was finished and had bound pads of cloth torn from one of his spare shirts over the wounds, he and Burks lifted Costaine and carefully propped him against a tree trunk. A groan came from deep within the one-eyed bounty hunter.

Costaine finally opened his eye and was able to

keep it open as he struggled to focus. After a moment, he was able to fix his bleary gaze on Luke's face. He rasped some words that Luke couldn't make out.

Leaning closer, Luke asked, "What did you say, Costaine?"

"I'm . . . in Hell . . . ain't I?"

"No, you're still in Wyoming," Luke said. "Not all that far from Hannigan's Hill, in fact."

Costaine tipped his head back against the tree trunk. "When I seen you, Jensen . . . I figured you was dead, too . . . and we both wound up . . . in Hades."

"Why would you think I was dead?"

"Because Bowen plans on . . . killin' you . . . He's mostly after . . . McKenzie and that newspaper feller . . . but he figures you'll . . . pitch in to help McKenzie . . . and he can get rid o' you, too." Costaine's tongue came out and scraped over his dry lips. "Goldang it, I . . . I'm thirsty . . . You got anything . . . to lubricate a man's tonsils?"

"Try some of this," Luke said as he lifted the flask. It still had a little whiskey in it, and he dribbled some of the liquor into Costaine's mouth. Costaine sucked it down eagerly and licked his lips again.

"That's . . . mighty good stuff . . . not reg'lar . . . panther piss."

"I'm glad you approve of my taste in whiskey. How do you know Bowen is planning to do those things?"

"He said so. Him and . . . his deputies. And Hannigan. That dang . . . big ol' bullfrog . . ."

Luke knew from that description that Costaine had indeed met Ezra Hannigan. He asked, "What were you doing with Hannigan and Bowen?"

"Figured I would . . . throw in with Hannigan . . . get his help with . . . corralin' McKenzie."

"Blast it! Are you still hanging on to that loco idea about McKenzie being a wanted man?"

"I got . . . the reward dodger . . ."

"It was withdrawn. All the charges against Mac were dropped."

"I'll believe it . . . when I see it."

Luke could tell it wasn't going to do any good to argue with Costaine, and he still wanted to find out a few other things.

"If you were working with Bowen and Hannigan, why did Bowen shoot you?"

"Hannigan said—" Costaine choked and couldn't get any more words out. He coughed, and Luke expected to see blood come from his mouth. It didn't, though, which was a good sign. "Gimme . . . some more . . ."

Luke tipped the flask to Costaine's mouth again without waiting for him to finish the request. Costaine swallowed a couple of swigs of the fiery stuff, then was able to continue.

"Hannigan said . . . I had to prove myself . . . before they'd trust me. Figured I had to . . . play along. They sent me . . . with a gang o' killers . . . to raid a ranch—"

Hal Burks had been listening intently to what Costaine was saying. Now he leaned down sharply and demanded, "Are you sayin' you were part of the bunch that murdered Pete Raskin and his boys?" Burks's face flushed with fury as he asked the question. Luke was ready to hold the rancher back, if he had to.

"That's what they . . . wanted me to do . . . but I

couldn't . . . gun those fellers down . . . in cold blood . . . I had . . . no part in killin' them . . . or burnin' the house . . ."

"But you didn't try to stop them, either, did you?" Burks snapped.

"Couldn't . . . There were too many of 'em . . . They woulda just killed me . . . along with Raskin and his sons . . ."

Luke said to Burks, "I know what he's talking about. I had to deal with the same thing the day I rode into Hannigan's Hill. Bowen and his men were hanging Thad Crawford. I couldn't do anything to stop them."

"Well, that . . . that's different," Burks said.

"Not really. I won't defend Costaine for getting involved with snakes like Bowen and Hannigan, to start with, but once he was, he couldn't do anything other than what he did."

"Which was nothin'," Burks said bitterly.

Costaine said, "You're right . . . mister. It was . . . eatin' at me . . . too. I was gonna . . . talk to Bowen . . . Hoped he wasn't as crooked . . . as I thought . . . but then he stopped me . . . on the way back to town. He'd been . . . spyin' on me . . . makin' sure I wasn't gonna . . . double-cross 'em . . . and seen that I didn't take part in . . . the attack. He tried to . . . kill me . . ."

"He came pretty close, I'd say," Luke commented.

A raspy chuckle came from Costaine. "Yeah . . . He ventilated me real good . . . but I got away from him . . . He must've . . . thought I was a goner . . . My horse carried me . . . into some wild country . . . Lord knows I didn't have no idea . . . where the critter was goin'. I remember . . . fallin' off . . . must've passed out . . .

and when I come to, this mornin' . . . I didn't know where I was . . . but the hoss . . . was close by . . . Called him over . . . grabbed hold of the stirrup . . . got myself up and . . . in the saddle . . . then started ridin' . . . Didn't know where . . . Didn't know nothin' . . . until I woke up a little while ago . . . with your ugly face peerin' down at me . . . Jensen."

"You're a fine one to be calling somebody else ugly, Costaine," Luke said.

A grin of sorts stretched Costaine's mouth. "There are some ladies . . . hither an' yon . . . who'd disagree with you."

"That's neither here nor there. What we have to figure out now is what we're going to do with you." Luke lifted his head as a gust of wind blew through the grove of trees. He felt the chill in it and knew that blue norther was getting closer.

"Wait." Costaine managed somehow to lift a hand. He clutched at Luke's arm. "I didn't tell you . . . all of it yet . . . Bowen and his deputies . . . and that crew of gun-wolves . . . from Hannigan's ranch . . . I got a hunch all of 'em are gonna be in town tonight . . . They're gonna go after . . . the newspaper folks . . . and McKenzie, too . . ."

Luke frowned in thought and tugged at his earlobe. "Albert Whitmore plans to put out an extra in the morning about what happened here at the Raskin place, and it'll include the strongest editorial yet calling for action against Hannigan and Bowen. They won't want that paper to hit the streets. The Whitmores will be working tonight to get it printed, and I'm sure

Mac will be helping them. Both previous attacks against the *Chronicle* have taken place at night . . ."

Laying it all out in words like that, the thing made sense, and the warning Costaine had given them about the plans Hannigan and Bowen had made locked right into place with all the rest. Luke had no doubt now that Costaine was telling the truth.

That cold puff of air a moment earlier had been more than a gust. The wind was blowing steadily now and definitely had an edge to it. Luke checked his jacket to make sure Costaine hadn't bled on it, then put it back on.

The chill seemed to have braced Costaine and perked him up some. His voice was stronger as he asked, "What are you gonna do, Jensen?"

"Get back to Hannigan's Hill and warn Mac and the Whitmores. It might be best if Whitmore gave up the idea of that extra edition, and he and his wife got out of town for the time being. They'd be safer that way."

"You really think he'll do that?"

Luke shook his head. "It seems unlikely to me. Whitmore is smart enough to realize there's a big target on his back, but he may not be aware that Hannigan and Bowen are zeroing in on it." He looked at Burks. "Hal, do you think you can get Costaine to town?"

Burks nodded. "I was gonna head back to my ranch, but I reckon I can take care of that chore, instead."

"You feel strong enough to ride, Costaine?" Luke asked the man.

"Yeah. Especially if you give me another swig o' that Who-hit-John."

Luke handed him the flask. "Keep it for now. I'll be wanting the flask back, though, when this is over."

Costaine tipped the flask to his mouth and swallowed more of the whiskey. He sighed in satisfaction and then asked, "When do you reckon that'll be?"

"I hate to say it, but it's beginning to look as if this affair won't be over until Hannigan and Bowen are dead . . . or all their enemies are."

Chapter 30

The cold wind blowing down the main street of Hannigan's Hill kicked up a dust devil in front of Mac as he hurried toward the newspaper office. He had left Chet Baxter looking after the café and knew the young man wouldn't mind staying a while, so he figured it would be a good idea to go ahead and have a talk with Albert and Jessie Whitmore.

He had his doubts about it accomplishing anything, though. Albert had known all along that crusading against Ezra Hannigan's iron-fisted rule was going to cause trouble and make him some dangerous enemies. Simply knowing that Hannigan and Bowen might be planning to kill him wouldn't be enough to make him back down.

Mac just hoped the potential threat to Jessie might be enough to make Albert see reason.

As that thought went through his head, Mac stopped short on the street. He felt as if someone had just punched him in the gut. He stood there for a long moment as his forehead creased more and more in a frown.

Then he said aloud, "Mac, what the hell is wrong with you? What happened to you?"

He knew the answers to those questions. Years of peace and quiet had happened to him. Owning and operating a reasonably successful business had happened to him. Living a normal life and putting behind him all that time spent running and fighting for his life had happened.

He had gotten the Smith & Wesson from the shelf under the counter when he stopped by the café after leaving the marshal's office. Now, without thinking about what he was doing, his hand moved to the gun's smooth walnut grips and closed around them. The feeling was a familiar one, and welcome as well. When he'd been forced to fight recently, all those old habits and instincts had come back to him instantly.

Why was he trying to suppress them now?

"Gonna be a cold night, isn't it, Mac?"

The question took him by surprise. He let go of the revolver and turned his head to see who had spoken to him. Stan Dawson, who worked at the livery stable, was walking past. Stan wasn't a close friend, but he ate at the café a couple of times a week and was enough of an acquaintance that it wasn't unusual for him to speak to Mac when they met on the street, as he had just now.

Mac nodded and said, "Maybe. But I've got a feeling it may be a hot night at the same time."

Dawson paused and frowned in confusion. "What do you mean by that?"

"Never mind," Mac said as he waved off the question. "Take care of yourself, Stan."

"Uh, yeah. You too."

Dawson went on his way and so did Mac. He stepped out of the street onto the boardwalk and found himself in front of the Lucky Shot Saloon just as Irish Mahoney emerged from the building and turned toward him. The stunning redhead wore a simple green dress, with a darker green jacket over it, the sort of more respectable outfit she would wear to do some shopping instead of running the saloon.

"Hello, Mac," she greeted him with a smile. They were just acquaintances, too, and that knowledge made Mac realize he didn't have any actual close friends in Hannigan's Hill except for Albert and Jessie . . . and his friendship with them was complicated. More complicated than he liked to think about.

"Miss Mahoney," he said. "What brings you out?"

She laughed. "Why, Mac, you make it sound as if I live in a cave or something. I just thought I'd pick up a few things at the store before the weather turns bad. One of my bartenders insists that the bone in his big toe tells him a storm is on the way, and I've found his predictions to be pretty reliable."

Mac nodded and said, "A man's bones sometimes know, that's for sure." He paused and then risked asking, "Have you seen Marshal Bowen today?"

"As a matter of fact, I haven't," she replied with a slight shake of her head. "Are you looking for him? If you are, you're going in the wrong direction."

She nodded toward the marshal's office and jail.

"No, I just realized I hadn't seen him today. I've been over to his office twice already."

"Yes, of course, delivering meals to Mr. Jensen's prisoner. Do you know how long he's going to be there?"

"Don't have any idea, and as far as I know, Luke doesn't, either. Some fellas are supposed to be coming here to pick up Stallings and take him back east, but I don't know when they're going to get here."

"I'll hate to see Luke leave," Irish said boldly. "He's livened things up around here, hasn't he?"

Mac supposed that was true, although as far as he could tell, it was Albert Whitmore who had really stirred things up in Hannigan's Hill. Luke had been on hand for some of the trouble, but hadn't caused it.

Albert had only told the truth, Mac reminded himself. It was Ezra Hannigan's reaction that had sparked the attacks on the newspaper and the murders of Pete Raskin and his sons.

"Luke is a good fella, seems like," Mac said in response to Irish's comment. "But I have a hunch he won't be around long, once he's claimed his reward for that prisoner. He doesn't seem like the sort of hombre who stays in one place any longer than he has to."

"I'm afraid you're right. That man has drifting in his blood. I've known too many like him not to recognize the type." Irish gave Mac a shrewd look. "In fact, I would have said the same urge to roam is in your blood, Mac. I'm a little surprised you've stayed in Hannigan's Hill this long."

"I have a business here. I've put down roots, as they say."

"Some men's roots only go down so far, and they're easily torn out." Irish smiled and shook her head. "Ah, well, what am I going on about? You'd expect that sort of blather, given my name, wouldn't you? I'll let you get on about your errand, whatever it is, and I'll go on about mine. Goodbye, Mac."

"Ma'am," he said, nodding, since he didn't have a hat on at the moment and couldn't pinch the brim.

Luke ought to be getting back from the Raskin place soon, he thought as he moved on toward the *Chronicle* office. He hoped his friend hadn't run into more trouble out there.

Jessie was behind the counter in the front room, with a ledger book open in front of her, when Mac got there. Mac supposed she was trying to figure out just how far in the red the newspaper was. The door into the pressroom was closed, which was unusual.

"Hello, Mac," Jessie said as she looked up at him. She tried to smile, but the effort wasn't very successful. "How are you?"

"I'm fine. How about you?"

She set aside the pencil she was holding. "All right, I suppose."

"Where's Albert?"

Jessie nodded toward the closed door. "In there working on his editorial for the extra edition. He made me leave him alone. He was so worked up, he said he was afraid he might talk to himself while he was writing and use some language a lady shouldn't hear."

That made Mac laugh. "That doesn't sound like Albert. He's always been a gentleman, no matter how worked up he was. I'm not sure I've ever heard him swear."

"That just goes to show you how upset this whole business has him." Jessie closed the ledger. "What's going to happen, Mac? Mr. Hannigan has probably heard about the extra by now. He's not going to let us publish it without doing something to try to stop it, is he?"

Mac said, "There's no way of knowing." He took a deep breath and plowed ahead. "I came to talk to you and Albert about a rumor I've heard, though, about that very thing."

Jessie's eyes widened. "Oh, that doesn't sound good. What is it?"

"Maybe I ought to wait until I can tell Albert about it at the same time—"

"Tell Albert what?" The door between the rooms had swung open while Mac was talking. Albert stepped into the front room, with a curious expression on his face.

"There's talk that Hannigan and Bowen are planning something to keep you from publishing that extra edition."

"You mean like shooting up the place or burning it down?" Albert laughed. "They've already tried both of those things and failed. That hasn't stopped the newspaper. It hasn't even slowed us down."

"You need to take this seriously, Albert," Mac said. "They're talking about killing you."

"Which could have happened twice already."

Mac shook his head. "They won't stop this time, and it won't be just a few hired hard cases causing the trouble, either. If what I've heard is true, Bowen, his deputies, and most, if not all, of Hannigan's crew from the Rocking H will be coming after you. That's a damn army of killers, Albert."

Jessie's face had gone pale. Mac hated to scare her like this, but she and Albert needed to be aware of the odds they were facing.

"They're planning to kill you, Albert, and then take sledgehammers to the press so no one can ever use it again," Mac went on. "As for Jessie, well, I don't know what they have in mind, but you can be sure it won't be anything good."

"They'll have to kill me, too," she said. "Whatever they do, I'll be right at Albert's side."

She was trying to sound brave, Mac knew, but her voice trembled a little. Despite that, he was sure she meant what she said. He had no doubt that she would fight to protect the newspaper, just like Albert would. And it was entirely possible she would force Hannigan's men to kill her, too.

Mac didn't intend to let that happen.

Neither did Albert, evidently, because he put his hand on Jessie's shoulder and said, "I think you ought to leave town, at least for tonight. You're friends with Elvira Denton. You can go stay at the Denton ranch for the time being. I can print the paper by myself—"

"Absolutely not. Do you honestly think I'd run out on you like that, Albert?"

Mac said, "When I started down here, I was going to tell both of you to leave town, to forget about printing that extra. That's the smartest thing for you to do, and you know it."

Albert began, "Mac, I'm not going to give in—"

Mac held up a hand to stop him. "I know you're not. And the more I thought about it, the more I realized I'd be disappointed in you if you did. Somebody's got to stand up to Hannigan and his bunch, and even though you appointed yourself to the job, there's nobody better suited to it than you. But you can't do it by yourself."

"I know I can count on you."

"And Luke, too, I reckon, when he gets back. But the three of us—"

"Four," Jessie broke in. "I'm not running away."

Mac looked at her and said, "I agree with Albert. I really wish you would go stay with your friend out of town, at least for tonight. But I didn't figure you'd ever agree to that."

"I won't," she said as her chin lifted in defiance.

"But even if there are four of us," Mac continued, "that's not enough. Hannigan can send between thirty and forty men against us. We won't stand a chance against odds like that. Not by ourselves."

"But what else can we do?" Albert asked.

Mac drew in a deep breath and said, "It's time for the people in this town to learn to stand up for themselves."

Chapter 31

The wind wasn't exactly howling out of the north-west by the time Luke reached the settlement, but it was blowing hard and cold at his back. The sun was lowering in the west and the onrushing clouds would soon swallow it up, even before it had a chance to drop behind the mountain peaks. Luke couldn't tell if those clouds had snow in them or just colder temperatures. Time would tell about that.

Luke reined to a stop in front of the *Chronicle* office and swung down from the saddle. The door of the newspaper office opened before he got there, but it was Mac McKenzie who stood in the doorway to greet him, not either of the Whitmores.

"I'm mighty glad to see you, Luke," Mac said. "I was afraid you and Hal might have run into trouble out there at the Raskin place, especially if any of Hannigan's men hung around to see who might show up."

Luke shook his head. "We didn't see anything like

that. We were able to bury Raskin and his sons without any more trouble." He paused. "But then someone else came riding up while we were there."

"Who might that be?"

"Cougar Jack Costaine."

Mac's eyes widened in surprise. "Costaine! What was he doing out there?"

"Trying not to bleed to death," Luke said. "He'd been shot. And according to Costaine, Marshal Verne Bowen was the one who pulled the trigger."

"This sounds like a story I want to hear," Mac said. "Come on in."

Mac closed the door behind them to keep the warmth from the stove inside the office. The door between the rooms was open. Luke heard the Whitmores talking quietly to each other in the pressroom, but couldn't make out what they were saying.

"I have something to tell you as well," Mac said, "but it can wait a few minutes while you fill me in about Costaine."

"All right." Luke launched into the tale of how Costaine had ridden up to what was left of the Raskin ranch, wounded and not really aware of where he was or what he was doing. By the time Luke reached the part where Costaine talked about Hannigan and Bowen planning to launch an all-out attack on the newspaper, Mac was staring even more than he had been earlier.

"I think there's at least a chance Costaine will pull through," Luke concluded. "Burks is bringing him into town so he can get better medical attention, but I thought I ought to ride on ahead and warn you and the Whitmores. Is there a doctor here in town? The subject hasn't come up before and I haven't noticed a doctor's shingle hung out anywhere."

Mac nodded. "Yes, there's a doctor. Hiram Mosely. He's rather elderly and a little on the shaky side."

"Not a good way to be for a sawbones."

"But at least he doesn't drink," Mac went on. "If Hal can get him here alive, I think he can take care of Costaine." A humorless chuckle came from him. "I don't know what to hope for. If Costaine is still convinced there's a reward out for me, maybe it would be better if he didn't make it."

"Better for you. Not for him."

"Well, yeah, you can look at it that way. I'm sure Costaine does. But there's something else we need to talk about. I can confirm what Costaine told you about the plans Hannigan and Bowen have made."

"How can you do that?" Luke wanted to know.

"Because your prisoner overheard Bowen talking about them to some of the deputies."

"Stallings? You got this from Ethan Stallings?"

"Yes, when I took him his food in the middle of the day."

Luke shook his head. "Stallings is a confidence artist. A swindler. He lies for a living."

"Sure. But what would it benefit him to lie to me about what Hannigan and Bowen are planning?"

Luke squinted at his friend. "Did he ask you that same question?"

"Yeah, as a matter of fact, he did. But he's right, you know."

"Well, maybe," Luke admitted. "I can't think of anything he'd get out of it, either, unless he figures I'd be grateful enough to let him go. I might be obliged to him, but probably not twenty-five hundred dollars' worth."

"Costaine told you the same story about Hannigan and Bowen," Mac pointed out.

"Hard to get around that, isn't it? I think we have to accept that they're coming after the Whitmores tonight. They're going to kill Albert and wreck the press. They won't be careful about trying not to hurt Mrs. Whitmore, either." A grim smile tugged at Luke's mouth. "And they want both of us dead, too."

"Oh, yeah," Mac said, nodding. "They'll be glad to see us gone."

"So I guess the question now is, what are we going to do about it? We can stockpile enough guns and ammunition to fort up in here for a while, but I doubt if we can hold them off for long. And if it looks like it's going to turn into a siege, they'll just burn us out. They're not trying to be subtle about this anymore."

"If we're going to stand off an army of gun-wolves, we're going to need help," Mac said. "I've already been going around town asking men I know I can trust if they'll throw in with us."

"And how much luck have you had so far?"

Mac made a face. "Well, not much. Alf Karlsson said we can count on him. Chet Baxter, who helps me out at the café sometimes, is thinking about it, but I'm not sure he's willing to risk his life. Everybody else I've talked to, they all say they have families and businesses to consider, and they wouldn't promise anything. I think they're worried that even if they survived the fight, Hannigan would have a grudge against them afterward and would make their lives miserable."

"Nobody's giving us any odds on surviving, I take it."

"They figure that standing up to Hannigan is a lost cause. And it very well may be. Five or six guns against forty isn't very good odds."

"How do you get five or six? Seems like four is all we can count on: you, me, Whitmore, and Karlsson."

"Jessie insists she's not leaving," Mac said. "She intends to fight right alongside us."

Luke shook his head. "That's not a good idea, no matter how you look at it. If she's here, it'll just be a distraction for her husband." Luke lowered his voice. "And for you."

Mac frowned and said, equally quietly, "Now's not the time to go into that. Albert and I both tried to convince her to get out of town and go stay with friends. We didn't do any good."

"If she won't listen to the two of you, she certainly won't listen to me. I suppose we'll just have to proceed on the assumption that she'll be involved." Luke frowned in thought and scraped a thumbnail along his jawline. "I think we have to cut down the odds while we have a chance. I suppose Bowen and his men are in town?"

"I haven't noticed Bowen being around all day. Several of the deputies are in town, though. I've seen them." Mac cocked his head a little to the side. "What did you have in mind, Luke?"

"I believe I'm going to pay a visit to my prisoner."

* * *

Judging by the time on the turnip watch in Luke's pocket, the sun was still up and would be for another hour or so, but the thick, dark gray clouds obscured it to the point that shadows were already beginning to gather in the alleys. He turned up the collar of his jacket as he walked toward the marshal's office and jail.

The hawk-faced deputy—Jed was his name, Luke recalled—was on duty when Luke got there. He gave Luke a suspicious frown as he stood up behind the desk.

"What do you want, Jensen?"

"I need to talk to my prisoner."

"What about?"

"That's between me and the prisoner," Luke said.

Jed scowled to show he didn't like the idea, but then shrugged and said, "All right. Take off your guns and that knife and leave them here on the desk. I'm not letting you go back there with any weapons."

"I could have a derringer hidden in my boot, you know. Or a dagger."

"Are you trying to make me run you off without talking to Stallings?"

"I'm just saying it would be easier if you let me hang on to my guns and came back there with me so you can keep an eye on me. What I need to discuss with the prisoner won't take but a minute."

With obvious reluctance, Jed said, "Fine, come on. Just don't get in the habit of doing this, blast it."

"I'm pretty sure this will be the only time I need to," Luke assured him.

Jed went to the cellblock door, unlocked it, and opened it so that Luke could go in first. As Luke entered the cellblock, Ethan Stallings stood up from where he was sitting on the bunk and came to the bars.

"Have you heard from Senator Creed again?" Stallings asked. "Are his men here yet?"

"I haven't seen them, and there's been no further word from the senator," Luke said. He was aware, without actually looking around, that Jed was behind him and to the right. "I wouldn't be trying to hurry things along if I were you, Stallings. It's unlikely this whole affair will end well for you."

"You should talk to your friend McKenzie," Stallings said.

"Mac and I have spoken recently."

Stallings glanced at Jed and asked, "Did he tell you what I told him?"

Jed stepped forward, glared, and demanded, "What the hell is this all about? Jensen, you said this would take just a minute."

"You're right, it's time," Luke agreed. The deputy was within arm's reach now as Luke used his right hand to palm out the Remington in the cross-draw rig on his left hip. Twisting toward Jed with eye-blurring speed, Luke slammed the big revolver into the side of the deputy's head.

Jed didn't have a chance to react before the blow fell. He dropped like a poleaxed steer.

"What the hell!" Stallings said.

"Keep it down," Luke told him. He bent and snagged the Colt from Jed's holster, stuck it behind his belt. Then he pouched his own iron. After unlocking the cellblock door, Jed had hung the big ring of keys on his belt. Luke helped himself to them and tried a couple of keys before he found the one that unlocked the next cell. He needed only a moment after that to grab hold of Jed under the arms and drag the senseless deputy into the cell.

Luke was ready to clout Jed again if he needed to, but the crooked lawman didn't regain consciousness until after Luke had tied him securely hand and foot with some rope he found in the office and gagged him with his own bandanna. Just to ensure that Jed wouldn't be going anywhere, Luke used one of several sets of handcuffs hanging from a peg on the office wall to attach one of his wrists to the bars between his cell and Stallings's.

"I don't know what you're doing, Jensen," Stallings said, "but if it ends with you letting me out of here, I'm all for it."

"That's not going to happen," Luke told him. "Maybe I thought you just needed some company for a little while."

"I think you're up to more than that, but I guess I'll have to wait and see." Stallings laughed. "I'm what they call a captive audience."

Jed started to stir around and make some noises. His eyes opened, and when he realized where he was and how he was tied, gagged, and handcuffed, he tried unsuccessfully to sit up, making furious, muffled sounds as he did so. Luke figured he was getting cursed out, good and proper, and didn't care in the slightest.

"You should consider yourself lucky I didn't just cut your throat while I had the chance," he told Jed. "Believe me, I considered it. That would have been much simpler and more effective."

Jed made more incoherent noises.

"That bunch was already out for your blood," Stallings said. "This isn't going to make them like you more."

"I'm not trying to make them like me. I'm just trying to survive. This is the first step."

But it wouldn't be the last. Luke left Stallings and Jed locked up and went back out into the frigid dusk settling over Hannigan's Hill.

Chapter 32

Luke spotted Irish Mahoney standing at the bar as soon as he walked into the Lucky Shot. It wasn't hard to miss her, with her red hair, her opulent gown that revealed a considerable amount of cleavage, and the crowd of men around her.

A card player at a nearby table called to Luke, "Shut that damn door! You're letting the cold air in."

Luke was already closing the door behind him. He headed for the bar.

Irish saw him coming and said to her group of admirers, "Sorry, boys. We'll continue this later."

Some of them looked annoyed, but most just seemed disappointed that she was abandoning them. That didn't stop her from moving away from the bar to meet Luke.

She slipped her arm through his and said, "Come on over to my table and have a drink."

"I've earned the displeasure of every man in here by monopolizing your attention."

"They'll get over it. They were trying to talk me into singing a song."

"I didn't know you were a singer," Luke said. "You haven't broken into song even once when I've been around."

She tipped her head back and laughed. "I'm no Jenny Lind or Lillie Langtry, but I can warble a bit. To be honest, I think the men enjoy watching me sing as much as they do listening to me, though."

"Maybe you'll favor me with a song one of these days."

"I'd be happy to."

"I'll hold you to that." They had reached the table. As Luke held Irish's chair for her, he went on, "Unfortunately, that has to wait. There are far less pleasant issues to deal with."

"I heard you went out to the Raskin ranch with Hal Burks to bury poor Pete Raskin and his sons." Irish's flirtatious attitude, which was probably a habit with her, had disappeared abruptly. "Things are getting bad around here, Luke. I don't know what's going to happen next."

"I have a pretty good idea. I don't know if you want to hear about it, though."

"Why not?"

"Your relationship with Verne Bowen."

Her red lips tightened. "I don't have a relationship with Verne, except maybe in his head. Anyway, I'm not sure that he feels the same way these days. I haven't seen him since yesterday, and even then, it was just for a few minutes. If he doesn't have time for me, then I sure don't have time for him, either."

"If you feel that way, you might want to hear what he's planning."

"If you're worried I'll betray a confidence, don't be. Even if I wanted to go running to Verne with something, I wouldn't know where to find him."

"What about his deputies?"

"What about them? I know where two of them are right now." Irish looked toward the stairs. "Up on the second floor with a couple of my girls."

"Now that's interesting," Luke said as he leaned forward in his chair. "Have they been up there long?"

Irish shook her head. "Not really."

"They're probably still occupied, then."

She shrugged and said, "You never know about things like that. But maybe."

"Can you show me which rooms they're in?"

"Luke, what the devil is going on here?" Irish asked as a worried frown put creases on her forehead.

Luke didn't answer for a moment. He had to take stock of what his gut was telling him about whether or not he could trust this woman. Her connection with Verne Bowen made it seem that he shouldn't, but at the same time, he sensed that her growing dislike for the corrupt marshal was genuine.

Instead of answering her question directly, he asked one of his own. "How do you feel about Albert and Jessie Whitmore?"

That seemed to surprise her. She said, "Why . . . I like them just fine, I suppose. Having them here to publish the paper has been good for the town. And I have to admit I've gotten some enjoyment out of seeing the way Albert's editorials make Ezra Hannigan squirm.

If anybody's ever gotten too big for his britches, it's Hannigan."

"Saying things like that can get you in a lot of trouble in this town. That's basically what the *Chronicle* has been saying about Hannigan."

With a defiant toss of her head, Irish said, "Hannigan doesn't scare me. And neither does Verne Bowen anymore. Both of them can just go and—"

"They're going to attack the newspaper office again tonight," Luke broke in, keeping his voice low enough that no one except Irish could hear what he said.

"What do you mean, 'again'?"

"They were responsible for the two violent incidents in the past week."

"I thought some of Ed Glasby's cowhands were the ones who shot up the newspaper office. That's what you're talking about, isn't it?"

"Glasby's men were forced to confess to the shooting, but they're not the ones who did it. I'm convinced Bowen and some of his deputies actually carried it out. And the men who tried to burn the office down were hired hard cases who'd been working on the Rocking H."

"Can you prove those things?"

Luke shook his head. "No, but I know they're true."

Irish thought it over for a moment and then nodded slowly. "I think I believe you. They certainly sound like things Hannigan would order. He's been a cruel, ruthless man for a long time. His wife dying just took the reins off him."

"That's my impression, too. Anyway, there'll be an all-out attack on the newspaper tonight while the Whitmores are printing that extra edition they have planned for tomorrow. The gun-wolves from the Rocking H will join forces with Bowen and his deputies. The plan is to kill Albert Whitmore, wreck the printing press, and put the *Chronicle* out of business for good."

"Poor Albert and Jessie won't stand a chance," Irish said. "And neither will anyone who's helping them, like you and Mac McKenzie."

Luke smiled. "I'm trying to improve the odds against us, at least by a little. If two of the deputies are upstairs . . ."

"Come on," Irish said, getting to her feet. "I think I know what you mean. I'll show you the rooms."

Luke knew what every man in the Lucky Shot had to be thinking as Irish led him up the stairs. They would be filled with a mixture of jealousy, resentment, and anger, with maybe just a touch of admiration thrown in.

But they wouldn't have any idea what Luke was actually on his way upstairs to do.

The corridor, dimly lit by a couple of oil lamps in wall sconces, had a carpet runner on the floor, so their footsteps were relatively quiet as Luke and Irish approached one of the doors that opened into the rooms where the soiled doves conducted their business. Irish nodded toward the door.

Luke whispered, "Will it be locked?"

Irish shook her head. "The girls know not to lock the doors. If a customer gets too rough and they have to yell for help, they want whoever responds to be able to get in quickly."

As Luke drew the right-hand Remington, Irish added, "Dora's not going to get hurt, is she?"

"I'll do everything in my power to make sure she's not," Luke promised.

Irish sighed. "I'd like a better guarantee, but I guess I'll have to take what I can get."

"Don't worry," Luke told her. He grasped the cut-glass doorknob with his left hand and turned it slowly and carefully. He eased the door inward.

The man and woman inside were still busy. The man didn't realize anything unusual was going on, until the young woman looked up past his shoulder and gasped in surprise at the sight of Luke looming over the bed. Before the deputy could react, Luke pressed the Remington's muzzle against his head, just behind his left ear.

"You should slide over and let the young lady up," Luke suggested. "At this angle, a .44 round ought to go straight through your head and miss her by a good margin, but I'd hate to take a chance."

"J-Jensen? Is that you?"

Luke didn't answer the question. He said, "Just do as you're told, friend, and you might live through this."

The deputy pushed himself up on his knees, allowing the young woman to scramble out of the bed. Luke didn't let her nudity distract him.

As soon as she was clear, he reversed the gun and smashed the Remington's butt against the deputy's skull. Naked and in an awkward position, there wasn't a thing he could do about it. He pitched forward, face down on the bed, out cold.

"I need something to tie and gag him," Luke said.

"Why don't you let me take care of that?" Irish suggested. "His friend's in the room across the hall."

Luke considered the idea for a moment, then nodded.

"Just make sure he can't get loose."

"Oh, don't worry, he won't."

Luke nodded and moved past her to the door of the room across the hall. He was reaching for the knob, when it turned and the door opened.

The second deputy was tucking his shirt into his trousers as he stepped out of the room. Eyes widening in shock, he stopped short when he saw Luke and clawed at the gun on his hip.

Luke struck first, wanting to keep things quiet. The Remington in his hand crashed into the deputy's jaw, shattering it and driving him off his feet. The man started to let out a gibbering moan of agony as he landed on his knees, but the toe of Luke's boot thudded against his head in a swiftly swung kick and knocked him out.

The soiled dove inside the room made a little whimpering sound, but Irish called to her, "Don't worry, Ida Beth, everything is all right."

That accounted for three of Bowen's deputies. Luke wasn't sure how many more were in town. And given the number of men at Hannigan's command, whittling the odds down by three didn't amount to much.

But it was a start, Luke told himself.

"Do you have any idea where I can find the other deputies?" he asked Irish.

"I'm afraid I don't. They could be almost anywhere in town. But I'll keep these two stashed here so you won't have to worry about them for a while."

He put a couple of fingers under her chin and tilted

her head up so he could look into her green eyes. "You know, if this doesn't end well, Bowen will probably find out how you helped me. That's going to make it very difficult for you to continue living here and running your business."

"You let me worry about that," she told him. "Something has to be done. If Hannigan gets away with murdering the Whitmores, this town isn't going to be a fit place to live, anyway. Sooner or later, people have to stand up for themselves."

"I'd like to think so, but I'm not convinced enough of your fellow citizens agree with you."

Irish said, "If everything you've told me is true, we'll know by tomorrow morning, won't we?"

Chapter 33

Luke looked around the main room of the Lucky Shot before he left, just to make sure that no more of Bowen's deputies had wandered into the saloon while he was upstairs. Not seeing any of them, he went outside, planning to search up and down the main street of Hannigan's Hill and try to find any of the other crooked lawmen he could.

The overcast had caused a thick early twilight to descend over the settlement. It wasn't fully dark yet, but the alley mouths were black maws and the lights inside the buildings stood out brightly. The cold wind had a raw bite to it. Because of that, not many people were on the street.

Luke looked toward the marshal's office and saw movement. The door opened and two men went inside from the boardwalk. In the brief moment when lamplight shone on their faces as they entered the office, he recognized them as two more of Bowen's deputies. Then the door closed behind them.

If they went into the cellblock, they would see Jed lying there trussed up like a hog going to market.

Luke broke into a run toward the marshal's office.

He didn't want to attract attention, but he had no choice except to hurry along the street and across to the other side. A passerby called, "Hey, what's wrong?"; Luke ignored him. He bounded onto the boardwalk and drew his gun as he flung the door open and charged into the marshal's office.

One deputy stood beside the desk, while the other was at the door to the cellblock. He had opened it and still had his hand on the door's edge. A heavy thumping sound came from within the cellblock.

That would be Jed banging his bound feet on the floor, Luke figured. Jed had heard the office door open and close and was trying to attract attention.

Those thoughts flashed through Luke's brain in a fraction of a second. He knew what was going on, but the deputies had to be pretty confused right about now. Both of them stiffened and started to reach for their guns.

"Don't do it," Luke warned them as he leveled the Remington at them. He drew his other revolver with his left hand so he could cover both men at the same time. He eared the hammers back so all it would take was a little pressure on the trigger to send .44 rounds smashing through them.

"Jensen, what the hell are you doing?" the man by the desk demanded.

Luke ignored that question. "Use your left hands and take your guns out, slow and easy," he ordered.

"You'll be sorry you're doin' this, whatever it is," the deputy at the cellblock door threatened.

"I'm already sorry I ever rode into this place, to start with, so I'm not too worried about what happens from here on out. Now lose those guns, like I told you."

When the men had reached across their bodies and gingerly removed the Colts from their holsters, Luke went on, "Put them on the floor and kick them toward me. Do it now, and don't give me any trouble."

They bent and followed his orders. When they had used their feet to slide the guns toward him, Luke stepped over the Colts and motioned, with the left-hand Remington, toward the cellblock.

"Get in there."

Now they were starting to look a little worried. Maybe they thought he was going to march them into the cellblock and then gun them down. The idea of killing them was tempting, just as he had told Jed earlier, but Luke wasn't in the habit of murdering folks in cold blood. Instead, he would force one of them to tie and gag the other; then he'd knock out that one and finish the job himself. Stashing them here wasn't foolproof, but it was the best he could do under the circumstances.

Staying back far enough that neither of them could jump him, Luke herded the two deputies into the cellblock. He had taken the keys with him when he went over to the Lucky Shot earlier. He holstered the left-hand Remington, took the keys from his jacket pocket, and tossed them to one of the men as he said, "Open the cell where your friend is."

Jed was thrashing around as much as he could while tied up that way. Muffled curses came out around the gag. Luke ignored him and kept his attention on his two newest prisoners.

Even so, he wasn't fast enough when the man with the keys darted behind the other deputy, where Luke couldn't get a shot at him, whirled around, and flung the heavy key ring at Luke's face as hard as he could.

Not wanting to fire and draw even more attention, Luke ducked and leaned to the side, so the keys struck him on the left shoulder and bounced off. That didn't do any real harm in itself, but the distraction was enough to pull the gun in his hand out of line with his captives.

The deputy closest to him launched himself in a flying tackle that took Luke around the waist. The impact drove him backward off his feet.

Crashing down on his back like that knocked the breath out of him and left him stunned for a second. He tried to slash with the revolver at the head of the man who had tackled him, but the other deputy stepped forward and kicked Luke's wrist. The vicious strike sent the Remington flying out of his grip. The gun hit the floor and slid, spinning, through the open cellblock door into the office.

The deputy who had landed on top of Luke tried to knee him in the groin. Luke's muscles began working again and he was able to twist his hips to the side just in time. The knee rammed against his thigh, instead. He shot his right fist straight up and caught the deputy under the chin. That rocked his head back.

Luke grabbed the front of the man's shirt and heaved him to the side. That freed him momentarily, but unfortunately, the other deputy was waiting for an opening. He swung another kick that thudded into Luke's ribs and sent pain shooting through him. Luke rolled to try to get some room, but came up hard against the bars of Ethan Stallings's cell.

The other man was back up on his feet. Both deputies waded in, stomping and kicking. Luke covered up as best he could and reached for the other Remington.

It wasn't there.

He hadn't had a chance to loop the keeper thong over the hammer when he holstered the weapon a few minutes earlier. It must have fallen out when he hit the floor and probably had gotten knocked off to the side during the fight. Luke still had his knife, but he couldn't get it when he was busy trying to keep the two men from stomping his head in and his guts out.

Suddenly he caught a glimpse of help from an unexpected source. Stallings reached through the bars of the cell door and caught hold of a deputy's coat collar. Stallings jerked the man toward the door with enough force to make the deputy's head bounce off the iron bars. Stallings grabbed the stunned deputy, yanked him closer again, and pulled him against the bars, where he could reach around the man's neck and lock an arm across his throat.

"I've got this one, Jensen!" Stallings said.

That evened the odds as long as Stallings could hang on to the deputy. As the other man tried to kick Luke again, Luke's hands clamped around his ankle. A quick heave sent the man reeling backward, off-balance. Luke leaped up and went after him, landing a swiftly thrown punch to the middle of the man's face.

Blood spurted hotly over Luke's knuckles as the deputy's nose flattened under his rock-hard fist. Luke crowded in and hooked a left into the man's belly. That bent him forward and put him in perfect position for the looping right that Luke threw. The punch landed with a sound like an ax splitting a chunk of wood. The deputy's knees buckled and he dropped to the floor.

Breathing a little hard from the exertion—he wasn't as young as he'd once been—Luke bent, took hold of the man's coat, and dragged him deeper into the cellblock. Spotting both his guns, he picked them up and watched as Stallings continued choking the other deputy.

The man was flailing around as much as he could with Stallings holding him against the bars like that, but as Luke looked on, his struggles began to weaken. The deputy's tongue stuck out and his face was beginning to turn a bluish shade of purple. His eyes rolled up in their sockets and every muscle in his body sagged at once. He would have fallen if Stallings wasn't holding him up.

"He's out cold," Luke told Stallings. "You can let him go, or you can hang on and he'll be dead in another minute or so. It doesn't matter much to me which you do."

Stallings released the unconscious deputy and let him slide to the floor.

"I'm not a murderer," he said. "Although I suppose I would have killed him to save your life."

"Not that I'm not obliged to you, but I can't help but wonder why you'd do that for me."

"You didn't rough me up when you took me into custody, and you treated me decent while we were out on the trail. You didn't have to do either of those things."

"You didn't put up a fight, so there was no reason to get rough. Same thing while we were traveling together. You cooperated and didn't try anything. I promise you, things could have gone a lot harder for you if you'd given me trouble."

"So you see, I'm not such a bad fellow," Stallings said. "And I've proven I'm willing to help you. You've got a big fight on your hands. Let me out of here and I'll be glad to pitch in and help you. I meant what I said . . . I'd fight to save your life."

Luke looked through the bars at the prisoner for a moment and then chuckled. "You know, I almost believe you," he said.

Stallings frowned and looked offended. "It's the truth," he insisted.

"Maybe so. But even if it is, you're still not getting out of there. You're going to stay locked up until Senator Creed's men get here and tell me what they've got in mind."

"You're assuming that you'll still be alive when Creed's men ride in. With the odds you and your friends are facing, you can't be sure of that."

"Nothing's sure in this life," Luke said. "Maybe you'd better just spend your time hoping that I do make it, because after what you just did, I don't reckon Marshal Bowen and his men will feel too kindly toward you in the future."

That made an alarmed look appear on Stallings's face. "I didn't even think about that," he admitted. "I just acted on instinct when I saw them trying to stomp you to death."

Luke got busy tying and gagging the two unconscious deputies. Inside the other cell, Jed had stopped writhing around and trying to curse through his gag. He just lay there and looked daggers at Luke.

A few minutes later, the cell door clanged shut, with three crooked lawmen locked up now. Luke had handcuffed the two new prisoners to each other and fastened another set of cuffs to the bars, as he had with Jed. None of them would be going anywhere on their own.

"What do I do if Bowen or one of the other deputies shows up after you leave?" Stallings asked.

Luke shrugged. "There's nothing you can do. They'll free these three and get the whole story from them. So there's no point in you trying to lie."

"When they hear that I helped you . . ."

"I doubt if they'll do anything tonight," Luke said. "They're going to be too busy trying to eliminate the Whitmores, Mac, and me. So, either way, you ought to be safe until morning. Even after that, if I don't make it, there's a good chance they'll leave you alone, anyway, because Bowen will want to turn you over to the senator's men and claim that reward."

Stallings shook his head and said, "You really know how to make a fellow feel better, Jensen."

With a grim smile, Luke left the cellblock, unbarring the rear door and going out that way. He stuck to the back alley for a short distance and then went up a dark passage between two buildings. When he stepped out onto the street again, he paused to look around. His breath fogged in front of his face as he did so. The temperature had dropped quite a bit already. He figured it would be below freezing before morning.

With three deputies locked up in the jail, and two more of them captives at the Lucky Shot, he had more than likely accomplished all he was going to be able to do before the trouble started. He probably ought to get back to the newspaper office while he still could, he decided.

He had just turned in that direction when he heard the sound of many drumming hoofbeats not far away. A large group of riders was headed toward town. They were almost here and getting closer by the second. That could mean only one thing.

Ezra Hannigan's men were coming to wipe Albert Whitmore, his friends, and his newspaper off the face of the earth!

Chapter 34

With no time left to lose, Luke turned and broke into a run toward the *Chronicle* office. As he did so, the group of riders swept into town from the other end. In the cold darkness, he couldn't tell how many of them there were, but he estimated at least two dozen men on horseback were pounding toward him.

At least one of them spotted him, too, because a man bawled, "It's Jensen! Get him!"

The riders charged toward Luke even faster now. Orange spurts of muzzle flame split the darkness as they opened fire. Luke didn't know if they wanted to ride him down and trample him or shoot him full of holes.

Probably some of both.

One thing was for sure. He didn't have time to reach the newspaper office before they caught up to him. So he abandoned his plan to fort up at the *Chronicle* with Mac and the Whitmores and darted toward the closest alley, instead. As he ran, he drew both Remingtons and returned fire, partially turning to trigger one revolver and then the other. The long-barreled guns boomed and bucked in his hands.

He felt as much as heard the wind-rip of several slugs passing close to him. Glass shattered in a nearby window. He hoped the citizens of Hannigan's Hill were hunting holes right now. Unless they were going to try to help fight off Hannigan's hired killers, they needed to keep their heads down.

Luke squeezed off two more shots and then ducked into an alley. Bullets thudded into the walls around him. He didn't fire again as darkness closed around him. He didn't want to give his enemies a good target.

Bumping heavily into something in the thick shadows, he realized it was a barrel. It felt like it was empty, but it might still stop a bullet. Luke crouched behind it and pressed his back against the wall as he started thumbing fresh rounds into his guns to replace the ones he'd fired.

"He went down that alley," a man called in the street. Luke recognized the voice now. It belonged to Verne Bowen. "Some of you go after him. We can't afford to have him running around loose while we're dealing with the others."

Someone replied, but Luke couldn't make out the words. Bowen responded angrily, "Go get him, I said!"

A grin as cold as the night air stretched across Luke's face. Bowen's lackeys didn't want to come down this dark alley after him. Well, he couldn't blame them for that, he thought.

Enough of a glow filtered into the alley mouth from

the street for him to see the two men who entered the alley. They split up instantly and hugged the walls on each side so they wouldn't be silhouetted. Luke could have shot at them when they first started toward him, but he held his fire. He heard faint sounds as they edged toward him. He wasn't holding his breath, but he breathed shallowly and quietly enough that it wouldn't be obvious.

Out in the street, the rest of the riders thundered past. Luke knew they were on their way to the newspaper office and wasn't surprised when he heard gunfire erupt again a minute later. He hoped Mac and the others were ready for trouble. The attack was coming earlier in the evening than they had anticipated. The shots directed at him should have warned them that something was up, though. They should have been able to hear those blasts even inside the office.

Unless Whitmore had started operating the press already, Luke thought. In that case, they might not have noticed that trouble had ridden into town . . .

He couldn't do anything about that at the moment. His own hands were full as two killers stalked him in the darkness.

Albert and Jessie were still setting type, while Mac stayed in the front room and kept an eye on the street. The glass still hadn't been replaced in the door and window, but Mac had used a knife to carve out several loopholes where the barrel of a gun could be thrust through and fired.

Those openings allowed him to see what was going

on outside, too, although it was always a little nerve-wracking to place an eye up to them. You never knew what might be waiting right on the other side to poke at you.

So far, everything had been quiet, but the evening was young yet. Mac figured that it would be later before Hannigan and Bowen tried anything, when most of the good folks in the settlement had turned in for the night already.

Footsteps sounded on the boardwalk outside. Mac had the Smith & Wesson tucked in his waistband, and he held a shotgun at the ready. A loaded Winchester lay on the counter in easy reach. He lifted the scattergun's twin barrels toward the door as the footsteps stopped and somebody rapped on the panel.

"Mac, it's just me."

Mac recognized the voice that called to him. It belonged to Alf Karlsson.

"Chet's with me," Alf went on. "We're alone, if that's what you're worried about. Nobody forced us to come up here and trick you."

Mac had considered that very possibility. And just because Alf said that he and Chet hadn't been brought here at gunpoint didn't make it true.

But he knew that Alf had promised to join in and help defend the newspaper office, and Chet had been considering it. Mac's gut told him they were alone.

He wasn't going to trust that hunch completely, though. He twisted the key in the lock and took several quick steps back from the door. Training the shotgun on it, he called, "It's open. Come on in."

The knob turned and the door swung inward. Alf

stood there and chuckled as he saw the shotgun pointed at him. He had a Spencer repeating rifle tucked under his arm.

"Yah, that's just the welcome I expected we'd be gettin'. Ain't that right, Chet?"

"That's what you said, all right," Chet replied. He followed Alf into the front room. He was around twenty, a pudgy young man, with a round, friendly face and curly fair hair. The old Henry rifle in his hands and the holstered revolver on his hip looked very much at odds with his otherwise-harmless demeanor. Mac wondered how well he could actually use the weapons.

"We closed the café," Alf said. "I hope that's all right. We sure weren't doing much business. Everybody's staying close to home tonight. They may not know for sure what's fixin' to happen, but I reckon there's something in the air that has folks spooked."

Mac could understand that. He had felt the same sensation when he walked down here to the newspaper office earlier. People on the street were moving a little faster than usual, and looking over their shoulders, as if worried that trouble might be coming at them without any warning.

And they might well be right about that.

"Lock that door again," Mac said.

Chet reached back and started to close the door, but before he could do so, a shot blasted somewhere outside and a bullet struck the edge of the door panel, chewing splinters from it and spraying them in the air. Chet yelped in surprise and pain and jumped back with the door still open. Pounding hoofbeats sounded from up the street.

Alf Karlsson was closer to the door than Mac. He leaped toward it and slapped it closed. As he did so, a bullet punched through the board that was nailed where the window had been. It clipped Karlsson on the upper left arm and the impact knocked him halfway around.

Pale and reeling from the pain of the wound, Karlsson still managed to twist the key in the lock. He pulled the key out and tossed it to Mac, who plucked it deftly from the air.

"Chet, are you all right?" he asked.

Blood oozed from a couple of scratches the flying splinters had left on the young man's face, but he nodded and said, "Yeah, I think so. None of it hit my eyes."

Bullets continued thudding against the walls outside as Mac hurried over to Alf Karlsson.

"Don't fuss over me," the older man said. "Just shoot those *jävla skitstövlar*!"

Mac had no idea what those words meant, but he assumed they were some sort of Swedish profanity. Whatever it was, it probably described right down to the bone the hombres who were shooting at the newspaper office.

Jessie appeared in the doorway to the pressroom and said, "Oh, my goodness, Mr. Karlsson, you're hurt! And Chet, you are, too."

"Aw, I'll be fine," Chet insisted. "Maybe you can help Alf, though, Miz Whitmore."

Mac put a hand on Karlsson's uninjured shoulder and steered him toward the pressroom. "Let Jessie tie up that arm for you," he urged. "Then you can get back out here and help us fight."

"All right," Karlsson agreed with obvious reluctance. As he went over to Jessie, another bullet penetrated the board over the broken window and whistled through the room to strike the back wall.

"Stay low," Mac urged them as Jessie and Karlsson vanished into the other room. "Chet, you be careful, too."

Chet backhanded blood off his face, which now wore a fierce expression that belied his usual jovial attitude. He slid the Henry's barrel through one of the loopholes and said, "Just let me get one of those varmints in my sights."

A second later, the rifle cracked, so he must have found a target. Mac picked up the Winchester from the counter and left the shotgun lying there. He went to another of the loopholes and thrust the rifle barrel through it. He saw a muzzle flash across the street and squeezed off a shot toward it. The Winchester's kick against his shoulder was satisfying. He worked the lever to throw another round into the chamber, changed the angle of his aim slightly, and fired again.

Even though it had started earlier than they'd expected, the battle was on.

The two gunmen were close enough now that Luke could smell them. Or one of them, anyway. He didn't know if the odor came from both of them. But the one coming slowly and carefully down the alley, on the same side as Luke, would be bumping into that barrel any second now.

He felt it shift slightly when that happened. The gunman let out a little "Oof," then said, "What the hell—"

That was as far as he got before Luke straightened from his crouch, thrust the right-hand Remington over the top of the barrel, and pulled the trigger.

The gun roared, the sound deafening in the close confines of the narrow alley. In the split-second glare from the flame that leaped from the muzzle, Luke saw the would-be killer fly backward, with his arms flung out to the sides, as the .44 slug plowed into his chest at close range.

At the same time, from the corner of his eye, he spotted the other man across the alley, close to the wall of the building on that side. He tried to twist toward Luke, but the Remington in Luke's left hand blasted so closely behind the first report that the two shots sounded almost like one.

The second man fired his gun, but it was just his finger jerking spasmodically on the trigger. The muzzle flame licked out toward the ground as the bullet struck near his feet. With a groan, the man slid down the wall.

Luke moved out from behind the barrel. He kept his guns pointed, roughly in the direction of the men he'd just shot. He felt a little bad about gunning them down without warning like that, but he reminded himself of what had happened to Pete Raskin and his sons and knew he wasn't going to lose any sleep over killing these men. They had signed on to do Ezra Hannigan's dirty work, to kill ruthlessly and in cold blood whoever and whenever Hannigan commanded. Now that same sort of fate had come back around to them . . . as it did to so many men who took up the gun as a way of life.

It was the ending that would come to him someday, more than likely, Luke knew.

Neither of the men he'd shot made a sound as he backed away down the alley. He was confident they were dead or soon would be. Two more of the enemy down.

But Bowen still had plenty of men to throw into the fight, and judging by the thunderous volleys of gunfire coming from the far end of the street where the newspaper office was located, that was exactly what he was doing.

Chapter 35

When Alf Karlsson returned to the front room, with a bandage tied around his wounded arm, Mac told him to blow out the lamp sitting on the counter.

"We don't need the light to shoot at those varmints," Mac added. His cheek was nestled against the smooth wood of the Winchester's stock. "It shines out through these loopholes, too, and gives them something to aim at."

"Yah, smart thinking," Karlsson agreed. With a puff of breath, he put out the lamp and then hurried to join Mac and Chet. He pushed the Spencer through a loophole between those that the other two were using. "Are they forted up across the street in that old hardware store?"

"That's right, and there are some up and down the street, too, firing at angles toward us." Mac squeezed off another round, then paused to listen. "It sounds like Albert and Jessie have the press going!"

"Aye, the extra edition is being printed even as we speak!" A sharp crack punctuated Karlsson's words as he fired the Spencer and then worked the trigger guard, which also served as the rifle's loading lever. "The question is, will it ever hit the streets of Hannigan's Hill?"

Chet said, "We really oughta change the name of this town if we live through all this."

Mac laughed. "That's not a bad idea." He sent a bullet whistling toward another muzzle flash. A couple of slugs thudded against the board near the loophole in return.

Chet yelled, "They're charging from this side!"

Mac tried to angle his Winchester in that direction, but couldn't turn it far enough. He yanked the rifle out of the loophole he'd been using and ran across the room to a loophole to the left of Chet's position. As soon as he had the barrel through the opening, he started firing the Winchester, cranking off rounds as fast as he could work the rifle's lever until the hammer fell on an empty chamber. A yard to his right, Chet did the same thing.

Then the young man cried, "They fell back! We turned 'em away, Mac!"

He had just let out that exuberant exclamation when the ugly sound of a bullet striking flesh filled the room. Chet grunted. Mac heard a heavy thud beside him and knew it was the young man falling to the floor.

Alf Karlsson must have heard enough to know what had happened, too, because he said, "Chet! Are you hit?"

"Cover the street, Alf," Mac said, his voice sharp with the tone of command. He was as worried about Chet as the older man was, but they couldn't afford to let down their guard completely. "I'll check on him."

Down on one knee beside Chet, Mac reached out, found the young man's shoulder, and shook him gently.

"Chet," he said. "Chet, how bad is it?"

No answer came. That grim silence made Mac swallow hard as he fished a lucifer out of his pocket and snapped it to life with a flick of his thumbnail. The door to the pressroom was pushed up, not completely closed but almost, and not much light from there penetrated the front room. The glare that flared up from the match was more than enough to reveal what had happened, though.

And Mac knew he would never forget the sight of that ugly black hole in Chet Baxter's forehead, about an inch above his left eye. Blood formed a small pool around the back of the young man's head as it rested on the floor. The bullet had bored right through his brain and exploded out the back of his skull, killing him instantly.

Mac was too shocked and saddened to curse. Karlsson glanced over in time to see Chet's lifeless face before Mac shook the match out and dropped it. He erupted in fervent Swedish, but whether he was cursing or praying, Mac didn't know. Maybe some of both.

What he did know was that if Hannigan's men attacked them from different directions at the same time, they couldn't hope to turn those assaults away, especially now that they had lost one of the defenders. It was only a matter of time until the newspaper office was overrun.

Mac wondered fleetingly where Luke Jensen was. Luke had planned to join them here before the attack began, but Hannigan's forces had struck earlier than expected. Luke would have been somewhere out in the settlement when the shooting started.

And that might inadvertently turn out to be a blessing, Mac realized. With Luke roaming around, he could strike at the attackers from different angles. He might even be able to convince some of the townspeople to join the battle and help him.

For now, Mac told himself as he left Chet's side and went back to the loophole where he had stationed himself, he and Alf would just have to hold out and hope that somehow help was on the way.

After reloading the Remingtons, working in the dark with practiced ease to do so, Luke went to the alley mouth and peered out at the main street, being careful not to show himself too much as he did so.

He looked in both directions. Down at the end of the street where the newspaper office was located, bright muzzle flashes on both sides created a flickering, hellish glare in the night. Hundreds of rounds were going back and forth. Luke wondered if Mac or anyone else in the office had been hit. Whoever was in there, they appeared to be putting up a spirited defense.

He saw the flank attack and was ready to take a hand, even though the range was a little long for handguns, but a thunderous volley from inside the office turned back the charge. The group of gun-wolves broke apart as some of them stumbled and fell, downed by shots from inside the office. The unharmed men grabbed their wounded companions and dragged them back into the shadows, out of the line of fire.

What he needed, Luke realized, was to be on top of the newspaper office. It had a flat roof with a short wall around it that would give him some cover. Not much, but anything was better than nothing. If he could reach the roof, then by moving from side to side, he could cover the entire front approach to the newspaper office and the back as well, if necessary.

Almost every building in Hannigan's Hill was dark now. People had blown out the lamps and hunkered down to wait until the shooting stopped. Only a few windows glowed here and there. Even the Lucky Shot was dark, Luke saw. He passed in front of the saloon and had just reached the corner, when he heard boot leather scrape the boardwalk behind him.

Whirling, he started to bring his guns up, but didn't know if he was going to be in time. A man stood in front of the saloon aiming a rifle at him. Bowen must have posted someone to keep an eye out for Luke, and the man had slipped behind him. Time seemed to slow down as Luke's Remingtons rose, but the guns couldn't come level before flame spat from the rifle's muzzle . . .

With a huge boom and the jangle of broken glass, the front window of the Lucky Shot exploded outward. The unexpected blast struck the rifleman just as he squeezed the trigger. He got his shot off, but the double load of buckshot, which slammed into him and shredded his flesh, smashed him off his feet into the street and threw off his aim just enough that the bullet sizzled past Luke's ear rather than blowing his brains out.

He held his fire, since there was no need to shoot. The man who had gotten the drop on him, and nearly put his lights out, would never be deader. Instead, out of instinct, Luke swung his guns toward the front doors of the Lucky Shot as they opened.

Irish Mahoney stepped out of the saloon. She had broken open the double-barreled shotgun she held and was slipping fresh shells into the weapon as she said, "You owe me the price of a new window, Luke, but I didn't reckon you'd mind."

"Not at all," Luke said. His voice was level and steady despite how close he had just come to dying.

"Or maybe I'll just let you buy me a drink and we'll call it square," Irish went on. She snapped the shotgun closed. The smile she wore vanished and she grew serious as she went on, "I'm in this now. I might as well give you a hand in the rest of the fight."

"It could be pretty dangerous," he warned her.

"You think living in this town wasn't already dangerous? Or anywhere in these parts, for that matter? Never knowing when Ezra Hannigan would take it in his head to get rid of you and steal everything you worked so hard for?" Irish shook her head. "That's no way to live. People worry too much about being safe and not enough about staying free."

Luke nodded in agreement. "Come on, then, but if you have a coat handy, you might want to put it on. You're not really dressed for the temperature out here."

That was true. The gown she wore was low-cut and revealed a considerable expanse of bosom and shoulders. Irish nodded, retreated into the saloon for a moment, and came back out wearing a quilted coat buttoned up to her neck. The scenery wasn't as good now, Luke mused, but it was too dark out here to fully appreciate Irish's charms, anyway.

"I hope you have plenty of shotgun shells in the pockets of that coat," he told her as she joined him on the boardwalk.

"I stocked up," she said. "What are we doing next?"

He nodded toward the far end of the street where muzzle flames still lanced back and forth. "I'm going to try to get on top of the *Chronicle* building. We'll have a better field of fire from up there."

"I know where there's usually a ladder to be found."

"You're good to have around in more ways than one."

"I'll take that as a compliment, since I'm sure that's the way you meant it."

Luke let Irish lead the way since she knew the town better than he did. She took him down another narrow passage between buildings and then along the rear alley, until she paused and said, "There's the ladder, right where I thought it would be. The roof of old man Timmons's saddle shop leaks, so he has to climb up there all the time to repair it. He told me he got in the habit of just leaving the ladder back here."

"Bad luck for him, but fortunate for us."

Luke didn't see the ladder at first. The shadows were very thick back there. She told him it was lying down and leaning against the wall. He was able to feel around and find it from that. It felt fairly sturdy when he picked it up and followed Irish.

They were almost at the newspaper office, but four men appeared in front of them, coming out of one of the openings between buildings. They stopped short and a couple exclaimed in surprise.

Then crimson flowers bloomed in the darkness as they opened fire.

Luke knew the men had to be some of Hannigan's hired killers who had come back here to try to get in the office's back door. They started shooting in surprise when they found someone already in the alley.

He called, "Irish, get down!" and dropped the ladder. His hands swept the Remingtons from the cross-draw rig.

The shotgun boomed as Irish touched off one barrel. She hadn't dropped to the dirt as he'd told her. She stood her ground, instead, and blasted a second load of buckshot along the alley as Luke moved up beside her and slammed bullets from both revolvers toward the enemy.

The poor light made for wild shooting on both sides. Luke expected to feel a bullet smash into him, but even though he heard several slugs whining past, none of them found him. As muzzle flashes stopped coming from the men facing them, he held his fire.

"Are you hit?" he asked Irish in the eerie silence following the gun-thunder.

"I'm fine," she told him. After all those shots had assaulted his ears, her voice sounded a little far away and muffled. He gave a little shake of his head to clear the cobwebs. The stink of burned gunpowder still filled his nose, though.

"I think we got them all," Irish said.

"It appears so. More may be coming, though, if they heard the shooting back here and figured out that their friends ran into trouble."

"Then we'd better get up on that roof, if we're going, and pull the ladder up after us!"

That sounded like a good suggestion to Luke. He holstered the Remingtons, picked up the ladder, and set it against the wall.

"Can you climb in that gown?" he asked.

"A little late to be worrying about that now." Irish laughed. "Anyway, just hide and watch me."

In fact, even carrying the shotgun, she went up the ladder with a lithe agility that didn't surprise Luke. He waited until she reached the top and had stepped over the short wall onto the roof. Then he followed and, as she had suggested, pulled up the ladder after him so that no one else could use it to get the drop on them.

Irish was sitting on the roof as she reloaded the shotgun. Luke knelt beside her and filled the Remingtons with fresh cartridges.

"Stay low," he told her. "They may not know we're up here right now, but they sure will as soon as we start shooting. You go to the left corner and I'll take the right. Anybody you see moving around down there is fair game. Everybody except for Hannigan's hired killers will be lying low tonight."

"All right." Irish paused. "Thanks for letting me come with you, Luke."

"With odds like these, I wasn't about to turn down help!"

Irish lifted the shotgun, and even in the dim light, Luke was able to make out the reckless grin that appeared on her face.

"Then let's cut those odds down some more, why don't we?" she said.

Chapter 36

Mac was thumbing fresh rounds through the Winchester's loading gate, when Jessie appeared in the doorway between the rooms and said anxiously, "Mac, there was some shooting out back a couple of minutes ago, and now I swear that someone's on the roof!"

Mac hadn't heard any shots behind the building, but with his and Alf Karlsson's rifles going off constantly in here, it was difficult to hear anything other than the constant cracking reports. As he finished reloading the Winchester, he said, "Alf, hold your fire for a second."

Karlsson stopped shooting. In the silence that followed, Mac looked up toward the ceiling and listened. He heard footsteps and knew Jessie was right: Somebody was moving around up there.

For a second, Mac considered putting a few slugs through the ceiling, but he hesitated, not knowing for sure who was on the roof.

Then shots sounded up there, coming from the front corners of the building. Rapid blasts from what sounded like a pair of handguns were punctuated by the heavier, less frequent booming of a shotgun. No bullets or buckshot punched through the ceiling, so Mac figured the shots had to be directed outward.

That meant the people up there were allies. He wouldn't be surprised if one of them turned out to be Luke Jensen.

"I think they're on our side," he said. "Let's get back to work, Alf."

"Yah, we got scores to settle," Karlsson said. A second later, the Spencer cracked and bucked against his shoulder.

Mac realized Jessie was still standing in the doorway. She was staring at Chet Baxter. Mac had taken off his coat and draped it over the young man's head and shoulders to cover up the fatal wound and Chet's vacant gaze.

"I . . . I didn't know Chet had been hit," she said at last. "Is . . . is he . . ."

"He's dead, Jessie," Mac said. "But it was quick. A single bullet to the head. He didn't feel anything."

"People always say that. But how do they know? How do they know what it feels like?"

He heard a hysterical edge creeping into her voice, and to ward it off, he said, "How's the press run on that extra edition coming along?"

Jessie took a deep breath and lifted her stunned gaze from Chet's body. "It's almost done. We'll have the paper finished soon and ready to distribute, first thing in the morning."

Mac nodded and said, "I'm glad. Folks around here need to be able to read the truth. Reckon you'd better go help Albert?"

Jessie swallowed hard. "Yes, of course." She turned back into the pressroom and pushed the door almost closed behind her.

Since the frontal assault didn't seem to be doing much good, Mac wondered if and when the attackers would resort to fire again. He wasn't going to be surprised if Bowen tried to burn them out.

Maybe not, though, with the wind blowing as hard as it was, he told himself as he considered the possibility. Ezra Hannigan wouldn't like it if a blaze got out of hand and burned down the whole town. He had too much of a financial stake in the settlement to want that.

So fire would be a last resort and they were probably safe from that desperate tactic for a little while, Mac decided . . . but there was no telling what Verne Bowen might do if he got frustrated enough.

He emptied the Winchester again, firing steadily and methodically at the muzzle flashes he spotted along the other side of the street. He began to wonder how long their ammunition was going to last. He had brought a good supply over here and stashed it earlier in the day, and Albert and Jessie already had several boxes of shells on hand, but sooner or later, they were going to run out.

Shots continued coming from the roof. Whoever was up there was helping the defenders hold off Hannigan's men, but they wouldn't have a limitless supply of ammunition, either. Something needed to happen, something that would even the odds and change the course of this battle . . .

But at this point, Mac wasn't sure what it was going to be.

Luke would have liked to have a rifle up here, but he didn't mind making do with the Remingtons. The settlement's main street was wide enough that the range to the buildings on the other side, where Hannigan's gunwolves were forted up, was pretty far for a handgun, but not insurmountable for a man with Luke Jensen's abilities. He picked his shots, took his time, and had been rewarded more than once by the sight of a man toppling forward in a window when he had raised up too far to take a shot at the newspaper office.

Irish fired the shotgun in a deliberate fashion as well. Luke figured the odds of her hitting any of Hannigan's men at this range were pretty small, but as long as she kept spraying buckshot in their direction, they had to worry about the possibility and that forced them to keep their heads down more.

Movement in the street to his right caught Luke's eye. A couple of men were trying to dash across. Probably in another attempt to reach the back of the newspaper office. Luke put a .44 round in the ground just in front of them, on the very slim chance they weren't Hannigan's men. If they weren't, that ought to make them turn back.

But when they immediately fired back at him on the run, he knew they were part of the enemy and responded accordingly. The right-hand Remington blasted, followed a split second later by the one in his left hand, and both men spun off their feet as Luke's bullets ripped through them.

He ducked back down as a fresh wave of gunshots from across the street struck the low wall or whistled overhead. Looking over at Irish, who was sitting down with her back against the wall while she reloaded the shotgun, he said, "Are you all right over there?"

She didn't answer. As Luke watched, his forehead creasing in a frown, the shotgun slipped out of her fingers and slid to the roof beside her. Irish leaned forward and toppled over.

Luke bit back a curse, holstered the Remingtons, and crawled over to her as quickly as he could.

"Irish," he said. "Irish, blast it, are you hit?"

Still, no response from her. Luke reached for the front of the quilted jacket, thrust his hand into the gap between two buttons, and searched for Irish's heartbeat. At the same time, he tried to make sure she was breathing.

Her chest rose and fell in a shallow rhythm. He felt the beating of her heart against his palm, too.

But he found something else: a wet, sticky area on her left side. He remembered the way those bullets had flown around them during the shoot-out in the alley, right before they climbed up here onto the roof. Irish had claimed that she wasn't hit in that fight. Either in the excitement of the moment, she hadn't noticed that she was wounded—as implausible as that sounded, Luke had known it to happen—or else she had concealed that fact from him on purpose, not wanting to hold him back from helping Mac and the Whitmores.

Whatever the case might be, eventually she had lost enough blood to make her pass out. Luke needed a place to lay her down and good light to determine just how badly she was injured. He could drape her over his shoulder and climb down the ladder, maybe head back to the saloon and check her out there. But that would mean abandoning the defense of the newspaper office.

Luke was trying to figure out his next move, when a new sound came to his ears. He lifted his head to listen, being careful not to raise it above the top of the wall, and heard the swift rataplan of hoofbeats growing louder as what sounded like a large group of riders approached Hannigan's Hill in a hurry.

"What in blazes?" Luke muttered to himself.

The riders appeared at the far end of the street and reined their mounts to a halt. Luke couldn't make out who they were or how many of them had just ridden up. But they sat their saddles for a long moment, as if sizing up the situation in the settlement. Hannigan's men seemed not to have noticed their arrival. The hired killers continued their assault on the newspaper office.

Then with a strident yell, one of the newcomers kicked his horse into motion and charged forward. The others followed close behind him. Gunfire erupted from the riders as they thundered along the street.

However, these shots weren't directed at the newspaper office. Instead, the riders poured lead into the building across the street, where Hannigan's forces had holed up, as well as targeting the other spots where riflemen had taken cover to fire at the *Chronicle*. Muzzle flashes gave away the hiding places of those men.

This bold, unexpected strike continued as the newcomers leaped off their horses and carried on with the deadly barrage at close range. The constant flashing of gun flame lit up the night with a garish glow that flickered as if it came from the very fires of Hell itself.

In that glare, Luke spotted a figure on the opposite boardwalk he hadn't expected to see: Cougar Jack Costaine. The one-eyed bounty hunter in his battered old hat and buffalo coat was unmistakable. Guns bucked and blazed in both of Costaine's fists as he exchanged shots at close range with Hannigan's men.

Luke had the sudden thought that Costaine was the one who had let out the wild whoop as he led the charge down the street. Luke wasn't sure who the other newcomers were, or how Costaine had gone from a wounded man on the verge of death to a fighting fury, but the unforeseen arrival of the bounty hunter and his companions was just what was needed to turn the tide of this battle.

As the gun-storm raged like a whirlwind across the street, Luke hurried to the back of the building, picked up the ladder, and lowered it to the ground so that it leaned securely against the wall. He picked up Irish as carefully as he could, carried her to the ladder, and cradled her against his chest as he began to descend. His left arm was tight around her, and her head rested loosely on his right shoulder.

It was awkward getting down to the alley that way, but Luke managed. He had just reached the bottom of the ladder, stepped off it onto the ground, and someone behind him yelled, "Jensen!"

Recognizing the hate-filled voice of Marshal Verne Bowen, Luke twisted around, kept his left arm around

Irish's unconscious form, and grabbed for a gun with his right hand. Some instinct told him that Bowen would get off the first shot, so Luke continued the turn to put his own body between Irish and Bowen's gun.

Flame geysered from a gun muzzle a dozen feet away. Luke felt the bullet tug at his jacket. He had a Remington in his fist now, and the long-barreled .44 blasted back at Bowen. Luke didn't know if he hit the renegade marshal, but Bowen didn't fire again. Instead, Luke heard a rush of fleeing footsteps. If Bowen was hit, it wasn't bad enough to keep him from lighting a shuck out of here.

At that moment, someone threw the back door of the newspaper office open. The twin barrels of a shotgun protruded. A female voice demanded, "Who's back here? Speak up or I'll shoot."

"Hold your fire, Mrs. Whitmore," Luke said. "It's Luke Jensen. I have a wounded woman here and need some help."

Jessie Whitmore lowered the shotgun and stepped out into the alley. "Who is it?" she wanted to know.

"Irish Mahoney from the Lucky Shot. She and I were just up on the roof trading bullets with that bunch across the street."

"We heard people moving around up there and hoped they were on our side." Jessie turned her head and called, "Albert! Help me." To Luke, she said, "Bring her in here."

She stepped back so Luke could carry Irish into the newspaper office's back room. Albert Whitmore was there to give Luke a hand. Together they carried Irish into a tiny side room, which Jessie directed them to. It had a cot in it that Albert used sometimes for a nap when he worked all night.

They lowered Irish onto the cot, and Jessie set the shotgun aside to say, "I'll see what I can do for her. If there's a chance later, you might send the doctor over to take a look at her."

Irish was still unconscious and her face was pale and drawn, but to Luke, her breathing appeared fairly regular. He thanked Jessie and then turned as Mac and Alf Karlsson hurried into the pressroom.

"Luke, it's good to see that you're all right," Mac greeted him. "You are all right, aren't you?"

Luke nodded. "I've heard a lot of bullets singing tonight, but none of them got me. Irish is wounded, though. Don't know how bad."

"I'm sorry to hear that." Mac looked a little confused. "Did she just happen to get caught in the line of fire?"

"Not hardly. She saved my life a little while ago by blasting one of those gun-wolves who had the drop on me, and then she was up on the roof with me just now trading shots with Bowen and his bunch." Luke grimaced. "Speaking of Bowen, he was out back just a few minutes ago, but he took off after trying to gun me down. I don't know if he was planning to try to get in here or just leaving a sinking ship like the rat he is."

"That ship's done sunk, yah," Alf Karlsson said. "When those other fellas came storming in, they knocked all the fight out of Hannigan's men. The ones who are still alive, that is."

"The fight's over?" Luke asked. He became aware now that he didn't hear any more shooting from the street.

"That's right," Mac said. "Some of that hardcase crew from the Rocking H surrendered, and the rest are dead or next thing to it. I thought you said Costaine was wounded, Luke. He led that bunch of ranchers in like he was General Custer, only the fight turned out different this time."

"All I can tell you is that he looked to me like he was on death's door the last time I saw him out at the Raskin place. Who are those men who rode in with him?"

Alf Karlsson supplied the answer. "I saw Hal Burks and some of the other small ranchers. Looked to me like Costaine and Burks rounded up all the hombres Hannigan has been trying to push off their land for the past year."

Luke nodded and said, "It was only a matter of time until they realized they had to start fighting back. At least that was what I hoped they would figure out."

Someone pounded on the front door just then. Cougar Jack Costaine shouted, "Hey, anybody left alive in there?"

Luke left the Whitmores tending to Irish. He was worried about her, but there was nothing else he could do for her at the moment. Jessie and Albert would take care of her as best they could. He went with Mac and Karlsson into the front room.

Mac unlocked the door and opened it. As Mac stepped back, Costaine stomped into the room with a gun still in each hand. He looked at the three men and said in apparent amazement, "You ain't all shot to pieces?"

"I thought you were," Luke replied.

"My new pard, Hal, patched me up and was gonna bring me straight on into town, but then he got the bright idea of stoppin' at some of them other greasy sack outfits like his'n to see if those boys wanted to bust up Hannigan's grip on these parts, once and for all." Costaine threw back his head and let out a bray of laughter. "I had a drink at ever' place we stopped. I'm runnin' on rotgut! Done replaced all the blood I lost with whiskey. Seems to be workin' just fine so far."

Luke shook his head in amazement. He figured Costaine would collapse sooner or later when the liquor's effect wore off, but for now, the man seemed to be going strong.

Costaine went on, "Have any of you fellers seen that double-dang skunk of a Verne Bowen? I was hopin' to settle up with him for shootin' me, but he ain't among them we took prisoner and his carcass ain't layin' around, neither."

"He was in the alley behind this building just a little while ago," Luke said. "We threw some lead at each other. His missed, but I don't know about mine. It sounded like he took off in a hurry, though, so he didn't seem to be hurt bad."

"Where do you reckon he went?"

"If I had to guess," Mac said, "I think it's likely he headed back to the jail. He has to know we'll be coming after him, and that's the place where he'd be most likely to fort up."

Costaine nodded. "Let's go root him outta there. I got me a bone to pick with Verne Bowen."

"I think we all do," Luke said.

For one thing, this wouldn't be over until Bowen was accounted for. As long as he was alive, he represented a threat to the peace and stability of the settlement.

Especially if he made it to the jail and turned loose those deputies Luke had locked up . . .

Chapter 37

Seething with fury, Verne Bowen paused at the mouth of an alley and looked across the street at the marshal's office and jail. A lamp burned inside the building, its yellow glow visible through the window, but no one moved around outside and he didn't spot any movement inside, either. The place looked deserted.

Where the hell were Jed and the other deputies? There were fully half a dozen of them unaccounted for. He hadn't seen any of them all evening. They were supposed to have taken part in the attack on the newspaper office.

Bowen didn't think they would have run out on him, especially Jed, who had sided him ever since they got their start robbing stagecoaches up in Dakota Territory, but he didn't have any explanation for their disappearance.

Bowen pressed his back against the wall and took

several deep breaths to settle his nerves. All his plans were on the verge of falling apart. He wasn't wounded, that was something to be thankful for, but that blasted Luke Jensen had come close. In fact, numerous bullets had come all too close to Bowen tonight. Luck had been with him so far, but how long would it last?

Maybe it was time for *him* to cut and run. He had some money stashed in the office in a locked metal strongbox. He could grab it, get his own horse, maybe steal a couple of extra mounts, and then put Hannigan's Hill behind him, once and for all. After what had happened tonight, Ezra Hannigan's grip on this area probably was broken for good.

Bowen never would have thought those hardscrabble ranchers would ever find the backbone to fight back . . . but they had. And once that iron fist had slipped, it might never be able to close again.

He was about to step out of the shadows in the alley and dash across the street, when he heard the rattle of hoofbeats and wheels approaching. Looking to his left, Bowen saw Hannigan's fancy carriage rolling along the street, with top-hatted Medicine Bear on the driver's box, as usual.

What in blazes was Hannigan doing in town tonight? Maybe he didn't trust his partner, Bowen thought. Maybe he'd come to check up on Bowen's efforts to deal with Albert Whitmore.

Whatever the reason, Hannigan was here, and he often carried a considerable amount of cash on him, Bowen recalled. He decided to add however much Hannigan had to his stake.

Medicine Bear brought the ostentatious carriage to

a stop in front of the marshal's office. Hannigan was looking for him, Bowen thought. Well, he'd found him, although the big man probably wouldn't be very happy about how this encounter was going to turn out.

Bowen left the alley and ran across the street. Medicine Bear, who had swung down from the driver's seat, heard him coming and turned quickly toward him. The Indian reached under his coat. Bowen knew he carried both pistol and tomahawk, since his job wasn't just to drive Hannigan around, but to protect the wealthy rancher as well.

"Take it easy, Medicine Bear," Bowen called. "It's just me, Verne Bowen."

Medicine Bear grunted and took his hand out from under his coat.

From inside the carriage, Hannigan said, "Confound it, help me out of here."

Medicine Bear turned back to the vehicle and opened the door. Hannigan clambered out with the Indian's assistance. When he was standing beside the carriage, he thumped his cane against the ground and demanded, "What have you got to say for yourself, Bowen? Has the matter been taken care of? Is Albert Whitmore going to give me any more trouble?"

Bowen hated the way Hannigan talked to him, as if he were just another servant. The two of them were partners, to Bowen's way of thinking. He had risked just as much or more in this enterprise of theirs.

But somehow, Hannigan had always managed to get his fat hands on the lion's share of the profits, hadn't he? All while looking down on the men who did the real work. Maybe back in his heyday, Ezra Hannigan had been an hombre to stand aside from. But things weren't like that now, and they hadn't been for a long time.

Despite the anger he felt, Bowen didn't want to have this showdown on the street. He even made his tone a little more servile than usual as he said, "Let's go on in the office, Mr. Hannigan, and I'll tell you all about it."

Once they were inside, he would take Medicine Bear by surprise, Bowen decided. The warrior was a dangerous man and he wasn't going to take any chances with him. A swift bullet to the head, when Medicine Bear wasn't expecting it, would take care of things. Hannigan might put up a fight, but his days of being dangerous were behind him.

Bowen hoped that was the case, anyway.

He motioned for Hannigan and Medicine Bear to go ahead of him. The three men stepped up onto the boardwalk. Medicine Bear opened the office door and moved back so that Hannigan could go in first.

Bowen motioned for Medicine Bear to follow Hannigan into the office. He wanted to go in last so he would be behind the Indian and could take Medicine Bear by surprise. But as Bowen went into the office, he heard Hannigan's startled exclamation, along with shouts from the cellblock.

"Hey, whoever is out there! Let us out! Help!"

With a shock, Bowen recognized Jed Lawrence's voice. He said, "What the hell?" and pushed past Medicine Bear and Hannigan. The cellblock door was locked, but he had an extra set of keys in his pocket. Before taking them out, he put his face to the barred window and peered through. From this angle, he could see the legs of several men thrashing around in the second cell on the left. Their feet were tied together, but that didn't stop them from kicking and flailing to make more of a racket.

"Settle down in there!" Bowen bellowed. "I'll have you loose in a minute."

For the time being, at least, he abandoned his plan to kill Medicine Bear, rob Ezra Hannigan, and probably dispose of Hannigan, too. He sensed that there might still be a chance to turn things back to his advantage. If he was able to kill Albert Whitmore, Luke Jensen, and Mac McKenzie, wreck the newspaper, and eliminate those problems, Hannigan would be grateful to him. In that case, Bowen wouldn't have to just salvage what he could and flee. He could press on with his vague intention of taking over completely someday.

He might even turn Jessie Whitmore over to Hannigan. The old goat had been without a woman for a while now, and Jessie was damned attractive.

The chances of success depended on moving swiftly and decisively. Bowen took the extra keys from his coat pocket, unlocked the cellblock door, and went in to see what he might find.

Jed and two other deputies were bound, hand and foot, and handcuffed to the cell bars. The other deputies were gagged, and Jed had a soggy bandanna around his neck indicating that he had been, too, but had finally worked the gag loose.

"Get me out of here, Verne," he rasped.

"Who did this?" Bowen asked. "Jensen?"

"Damn right it was Jensen." Jed's eyes swung toward the next cell, where Ethan Stallings stood backed against the wall, his face pale. "With help from that no-good son of a—"

"Wait a minute, wait a minute," Stallings broke in, talking fast. He lifted both hands, palms out. "It looked like Jensen might win if I gave him a hand. What the hell do you think I'm going to do in a case like that? I figured if I helped him, he'd be grateful enough to turn me loose."

Bowen grunted. "Not Jensen. He's too stubborn to do that."

"I wish somebody had told me that," Stallings said bitterly. "What I really wish is that I could get him in the sights of a gun."

"Maybe that can be arranged," Bowen said as he unlocked the door of the cell where his deputies were.

"Hold on," Jed said. "You can't be talking about turning this treacherous little weasel loose, Verne."

"It sounds to me like he's got as much of a grudge against Jensen as any of us do," Bowen said as he bent over to unlock the handcuffs on Jed's wrist.

"But you can't trust him."

"I didn't say anything about trusting him." Bowen looked around and saw that Hannigan and Medicine Bear had followed him into the cellblock. He said to the Indian, "Come in here and cut these ropes off them."

Medicine Bear moved to do that, while Bowen finished unfastening the handcuffs. Bowen helped Jed stand. The deputy was unsteady at first because his feet had gone numb from being tied up.

"Gimme a gun," Jed said as the effects of his captivity began to wear off. "I'm going to settle the score with Stallings."

"Forget it. We need him on our side. There are only four of us."

"Six," Hannigan said. "Whatever you're planning, Bowen, Medicine Bear and I will join you."

Bowen frowned. "Are you sure that's a good idea, Mr. Hannigan?"

"Do you think I can't help fight my own battles?" Hannigan sounded offended. "By grab, I was fighting rustlers and savages when you were still just a petty thief!" He reached under his coat and brought out a heavy old revolver with ivory grips. "I haven't forgotten how to use this, you know."

Bowen nodded. "Well, all right. If that's the way you feel about it, sir, then you'll be coming along, too."

"Of course, I will," Hannigan snapped.

And with any luck, he'd be killed in the inevitable fight, Bowen thought. That would save him the trouble of doing it later.

He turned toward the other cell, and Stallings heaved a sigh of relief. "I was hoping you'd see the logic of my suggestion, Marshal. I want to get even with Jensen, too. Just give me a gun and I'll do anything you say."

"You're not getting a gun. It's too much of a risk. You can forget about that. But we've got a use for you, Stallings." Bowen smiled coldly. "You're going to be the bait in the trap that will mean the end of Luke Jensen and Mac McKenzie."

Chapter 38

Luke, Mac, Costaine, and Hal Burks walked down the street toward the marshal's office and jail. Alf Karlsson and some of the ranchers had remained behind at the *Chronicle* to protect Albert and Jessie Whitmore as they finished getting the extra edition ready to be distributed in the morning.

The other men who had ridden into town with Costaine and Burks were guarding Hannigan's hired gunmen who had survived the battle and surrendered. That group had been herded into the Lucky Shot.

Irish was resting on the cot in the *Chronicle*'s back room. Jessie had stopped the bleeding and cleaned up the wound, which didn't appear life-threatening, as long as there was no internal bleeding and the bullet hadn't struck anything vital. But determining if those two things were true was beyond Jessie's medical capabilities, so all she could do was try to keep Irish resting comfortably until the doctor could be found and brought there.

Luke intended to do that, but with Bowen unaccounted for, and the potential for more trouble if he found and freed his deputies, Luke figured he and his companions needed to finish mopping up first. That was why they were headed for the jail.

Without breaking stride, Mac said, "Look, isn't that Hannigan's carriage in front of the marshal's office?"

"It sure is," Burks said. "I've seen him ridin' around the country in that fancy rig plenty of times, lordin' it over everybody else like he was a king or something."

"If he's a king, he's about to be deposed," Luke said. "After tonight, he'll be weakened enough that he won't be able to hold on to power. He should be arrested and charged with murder for the deaths of Pete Raskin and his sons, but he may have been too slick to ever give a direct order like that. There should be something that will land him behind bars, though, if we can get an independent lawman in here."

Costaine said, "You and me are bounty hunters, Jensen. Don't we count as, what do you call it, officers of the court?"

Luke let out a grim chuckle. "That's a pretty far stretch, Costaine. I'm not sure we could get away with it."

Burks said, "If Hannigan's grip on the settlement actually is broken, and the members of the town council don't have to be afraid of him anymore, I'll bet they would be willing to appoint one of you fellas as marshal to replace Bowen. That'd give you some legal standing. Of course, that wouldn't happen until after all this is over . . ."

"Might look better in the long run that way, though," Mac agreed.

"And you'd be the obvious choice for the job, Mac," Burks said.

"Me?" Mac's eyes widened. "I'm a cook, I'm not a lawman. Never have been, never had any desire to be one."

"We can hash that out later," Luke said. "No pun intended. Right now—"

"Isn't that your prisoner?" Mac interrupted.

Luke looked along the street and spotted a man scurrying through a patch of light that spilled from a nearby window. He appeared to be trying to make it from one patch of shadow to the next, but he didn't move fast enough. The man threw a frightened glance over his shoulder and Luke saw his face.

Mac was right. Somehow, Ethan Stallings had gotten out of jail.

That probably meant Bowen and those deputies were lurking around somewhere, too. But at the moment, Luke wanted to corral Stallings before the confidence man got away again. Stallings was still worth twenty-five hundred dollars to him.

"Stallings, stop!" Luke called as he broke into a run after the escaped prisoner. "Hold it right there!"

Stallings paused at the mouth of an alley. Luke figured he would plunge into the thick darkness, but instead, the slender figure stood there, hesitating as if torn about his next move.

What Stallings did surprised Luke completely. He

turned to face Luke and the others, who were following closely behind him, and yelled, "Jensen, get back! It's a trap!"

Luke threw on the brakes as shots blasted from the alley, tongues of muzzle flame licking outward. Stallings pitched headlong onto the boardwalk, but Luke couldn't tell if he was hit or if he was just trying to get out of the way of all that flying lead.

As bullets kicked up dust in the street in front of him and whipped through the air around him, Luke lifted the Remingtons and returned fire with both revolvers. Beside him, Mac, Costaine, and Hal Burks spread out and started shooting as well. Gun-thunder welled up and filled the street. The cold wind swirled clouds of acrid powder-smoke around Luke and his companions. Gouts of muzzle flame tinged the smoke crimson and orange.

Gunmen erupted from the alley, firing wildly as they charged. Luke's Remingtons ran dry as Verne Bowen came at him, shrieking curses and firing a Winchester as fast as he could work the rifle's lever.

Luke was about to try to dive out of the way of that withering barrage, when Ethan Stallings scrambled up, leaped off the boardwalk, and tackled the crooked marshal from behind. Bowen outweighed Stallings by quite a bit, but Stallings had the element of surprise on his side and knocked Bowen forward off his feet. Bowen managed to hold on to the rifle and twisted around to slam the barrel against the side of Stallings's head. Stallings rolled limply to the side.

Bowen came up on his knees and aimed the Winchester at Stallings. Luke crashed into him before he could pull the trigger. Both men sprawled in the dirt. Bowen lost his grip on the rifle. Luke planted a knee in Bowen's chest and hammered a right and a left fist to his face. Bowen kicked a leg high, hooked it on Luke's shoulder, and levered him off.

The two men rolled apart and came up at the same time. Bowen clawed a Colt from the holster on his hip, but as he brought the gun up, Luke threw the knife he had just pulled from its sheath at his belt. The throw had enough force behind it that the blade penetrated deeply into Bowen's throat when it struck.

Bowen's eyes widened in horror as he felt the cold steel sever his windpipe. He gasped and gurgled and tried desperately to fire a shot, but the revolver slipped from his rapidly weakening fingers. The blood that gushed from his mouth was black in the dim light. Making a grotesque strangling noise, he swayed for a second and then pitched forward on his face.

A few yards away, Ezra Hannigan leveled an old revolver at Mac and bellowed, "How dare you!" The gun belched fire, but Mac was already weaving aside, so the slug ripped past him. The rifle in his hands cracked. Hannigan rocked back as the slug drove into his chest. Mac twisted to his right as he jacked the Winchester's lever. Hannigan's driver, Medicine Bear, had his arm pulled back with a tomahawk gripped in his hand. Mac fired just as the man threw the tomahawk. That was enough to make the throw go wide as the bullet tore through Medicine Bear and spun him halfway around. The Indian staggered, pressed a hand to his chest, and then collapsed.

In the middle of all the gunfire, Cougar Jack Costaine added to the racket by whooping at the top of his lungs as he traded shots with the deputies. He cut down Jed Lawrence and wounded another man, and finally Hal Burks had to grab him and shout, "Hold your fire! Blast it, Costaine! Those other fellas are tryin' to give up!"

Luke heard that and saw that it was true. The deputies who were still on their feet had thrown their guns down and had their hands in the air. Bowen, Hannigan, and Medicine Bear all lay, unmoving, on the ground. Mac checked them, holding his rifle ready if he needed it, and then shook his head as he looked at Luke.

That left Ethan Stallings to account for. Luke looked around, fully expecting to see no sign of the confidence man. Stallings had had time to light out while the fight was going on.

Instead, Stallings stood beside a hitch rack with a grin on his face. The clout to the head Bowen had given him didn't seem to have done any real harm.

He said, "My plan worked, Jensen. They thought they were luring you into a trap, but instead, I drew them right into one."

Luke looked at him intently, remembering the way Stallings had stood there at the edge of the light, trying to figure out what to do next. He was convinced that it hadn't been Stallings's intention all along to double-cross Bowen and Hannigan, no matter what the man said now. In all likelihood, Stallings hadn't known what he was going to do until that very instant . . .

But in the end, he had done the right thing. Not only that, but during the battle, he might well have saved Luke's life by tackling Bowen that way. Luke told himself he ought to remember that, although he didn't know what it might mean for the future.

What he knew was that Ezra Hannigan's reign of terror was over. No longer would Hannigan's pet judge sentence men to death simply because Hannigan wanted it that way, and the town's corrupt lawmen would no longer drag those victims out to Hangman's Hill and string them up. True law and order could rule in these parts again.

Mac angled the rifle back across his shoulder and nodded to the corpses lying in the street. "We'd better get back to the newspaper office," he said. "Albert's got a lot of work to do, and he could probably use a hand."

"What do you mean, 'a lot of work'?" Luke asked.

"The death of Ezra Hannigan is big news around here." Mac smiled faintly. "He's going to have to re-make the front page of that extra edition and print it again."

Chapter 39

As it turned out, Albert Whitmore decided not to do that. It would have been too expensive, and the newspaper was already operating pretty close to the bone. The *Chronicle*'s next regular edition was due to be published in a couple of days and would be a special one, telling in detail the story of everything that had happened.

It would be a tragic tale, in a way, because Ezra Hannigan had been a pioneer and, truthfully, had helped settle this area, overcoming all manner of hardships to do so. In the end, though, that history didn't excuse his wanton cruelty and his descent into lawlessness.

The question of who would be the settlement's next lawman was still up in the air, but the surviving members of Hannigan's gang of hired killers were locked up in the jail, anyway. The undertaker and his assistant were busy tending to the bodies of those killed in the battle, and probably would be occupied with that grisly task for several days.

Irish rested in her own comfortable quarters on the second floor of the Lucky Shot. The doctor had confirmed that she ought to recover from her wound, although she would have to take it easy for a good while.

Cougar Jack was also recuperating in a room on the saloon's second floor, being fussed over by the soiled doves—and loving every second of it. As he had said, even though he wasn't handsome by any normal definition of the word, many women seemed to find him attractive. With such pretty nurses, he'd be up and around in no time, he insisted.

Judge John Lee Trent seemed to have left town at some point, probably after word started getting around that Hannigan and Bowen were dead. No one had seen him leave, nor did they know where he was going, but it seemed unlikely that the judge would ever show his face around these parts again.

Nor did anyone know who would inherit the Rocking H or Hannigan's business interests in town, although his partners would keep those enterprises going for the time being, and the honest hands on the ranch would continue their jobs. Somebody would have to look into all that . . .

But it wasn't Luke Jensen's job.

He sat in Mac's Place the next day, lingering over a cup of coffee. The café was busy, with all the tables and the stools along the counter occupied, and everybody in the room seemed to be reading the extra edition of the *Chronicle*.

On the other side of the counter, Mac picked up the

pot to warm Luke's coffee and asked, "What did you do with Stallings?"

"The cells in the jail were full of Hannigan's men, so I locked him in one of the rooms at the Lucky Shot."

Mac raised an eyebrow. "Seems like that might be easy to escape from."

"Not as easy as you'd think. I nailed the window shut, and Irish has one of her bouncers sitting in a chair right outside the door, in case Stallings tries to pick the lock. I don't think he'll be going anywhere."

Mac leaned on the counter and said, "You know, we might have run right into that ambush if he hadn't warned us."

Luke nodded. "I know."

"And he could have gotten killed double-crossing Bowen like that."

"Yep, he could have." Luke took a sip of his coffee. "What are you getting around to, Mac?"

"Not a thing," Mac replied with a shake of his head. "I wouldn't stick my nose in your business, Luke. Just talking, that's all. I figured you'd be thinking about things, that's all."

"I've been thinking, all right—"

Mac nodded toward the front window and interrupted. "Looks like you might not have any more time to ponder. A group of hard-looking strangers just rode past. You're still expecting those men Senator Creed sent, right?"

Luke set his coffee cup down and stood up. "Yeah, I am," he said, "and I reckon I'd better go see if that's them."

"I'll come with you," Mac said. He pushed open the swinging door to the kitchen and called through it, "Alf, keep an eye on things. I'm stepping out for a minute."

"Yah, sure," Alf Karlsson replied.

Mac took off his apron, got the Smith & Wesson from under the counter, and stuck it in his waistband, then came out from behind the counter.

Luke raised his eyebrows at the sight of the gun. "You expecting trouble?"

"It never hurts to be prepared. I sort of forgot about that for a while. Town living will do that. Softens a man up."

"I wouldn't know," Luke said. "I haven't stayed in one place for very long since I left my pa's farm, and that was nearly thirty years ago."

"That's a long time to drift."

"I'll settle down again . . . one of these days."

Mac just grunted in disbelief at that as he fell in step beside Luke and they left the café. The riders Mac had spotted, eight in number, had reined their horses to a stop in front of the marshal's office. One man had dismounted and stood at the office door, trying it. It was locked, and when he discovered that, he turned away with a disgusted look on his face.

"Can we help you?" Luke asked as he and Mac walked up.

"That depends," the man said. "Are you the marshal of this burg?"

He was a square-jawed hombre, with a narrow mustache over a thin-lipped mouth. His eyes were cold enough to put a skim of ice on a bucket of water. A glance at the men who were still mounted told Luke they were all cut from the same cloth.

"Well, you see, there isn't a marshal here right now. The fella who held the job was killed last night," Luke answered.

The stranger's eyes narrowed. "He have any deputies?"

"Several, but most of them are dead, too. The ones who aren't are locked up in there."

"What the hell are you talking about?"

"The marshal and his deputies were all crooked. They went on a rampage last night, and the citizens rose up and put an end to it," Luke explained.

"Sounds like a riot to me. Somebody needs to call in the army."

"Let them," Mac said. "There's plenty of evidence that the marshal and his men were in the wrong. They were murderers and criminals."

The stranger gave a curt shake of his head. "Well, none of this is any of my business. I'm looking for a man named Luke Jensen."

"That's me," Luke said.

The man looked him up and down and nodded. "My name's Ransom. Senator Creed sent me to take charge of a prisoner you have, Jensen." Ransom jerked his head toward the door. "Is he locked up in there?"

"Plan to take him back east to stand trial, do you?"

A humorless smile tugged at Ransom's thin lips. "That would be a waste of time and money. No, we saw the gallows already waiting on the hill, just outside town. We'll go ahead and take care of matters, here and now."

Luke's jaw tightened in anger. After a second, he said, "Does Senator Creed know what you're planning to do?"

"Does he know?" Ransom laughed. "Mister, it was his idea. That fella picked the wrong man to swindle. Now, are you going to turn the prisoner over to me or not?"

"Well, you see, that's a problem." Luke glanced over at Mac, who gave him a nearly imperceptible nod. "Ethan Stallings was killed last night in all the commotion. There was a lot of shooting and he caught a bullet."

"What! Stallings is dead?"

"Dead as can be."

Ransom regarded Luke intently for a long moment, then asked, "What would you do if I said I didn't believe you?"

"Why, I might not take kindly to being called a liar. I might not take kindly to that at all."

Mac had shifted slightly so that he was turned more toward the men still on horseback. His hand hung innocently enough at first glance, but it wasn't far from the butt of the Smith & Wesson.

Luke continued squarely facing Ransom.

"Did you not notice that the odds are four-to-one against you and your friend, Jensen?" Ransom asked. "And those aren't normal odds, either, considering who you're facing."

"I could say the same thing about normal odds," Luke replied in a calm, flat voice. He knew that he and Mac were walking the knife edge of death, and they might well be doing it for a man who didn't deserve it.

But they had made their stand, and they weren't the sort to back down.

Regardless of what else happened, that same knife edge would claim the man called Ransom, and judging by the look that slowly appeared in his eyes, he knew it, too. He drew in a deep breath, made a slight motion to his men, and said, "Well, if you say Stallings is dead, I suppose there's nothing we can do about it except go back and tell Senator Creed that justice has been done. Maybe he'll be satisfied with that."

"That seems like the best course of action to me," Luke said. "I mean, you fellas get paid for running this errand either way, don't you?"

"Yeah, that's true. But you don't get that reward, Jensen. Not without proof that Stallings is dead."

Luke shrugged. "He's already buried, and I don't feel like digging him up."

"Your choice." Ransom stepped down from the boardwalk and went to his horse. He paused, and for a second, Luke thought the man might try spinning around and going for his gun. Instead, Ransom swung up into the saddle and said, "You know, if the senator isn't satisfied with what I tell him, he's liable to send me and my associates to look you up again, one of these days."

Luke shrugged. "I reckon the senator will do whatever he feels like he has to."

"He usually does." Ransom turned his head and told his companions, "Let's get the hell out of here."

As they rode off, Mac watched them go and said, "You reckon they'll be back?"

"They might be," Luke admitted. "But I got the feeling Ransom didn't think it was worth risking a bullet. He can go back and tell Creed that Stallings is dead, without it costing him a thing."

"Do you think Creed will believe him?"

"Hard to say, but he won't have any reason not to."

"You realize, you cost yourself a big chunk of money," Mac pointed out.

"There's more money out there waiting to be made," Luke said. "Besides, Stallings may have saved my life."

"And that's worth twenty-five hundred dollars to you?"

Luke laughed. "I don't know about that. But it's worth *something,* anyway."

Luke unlocked the door, opened it, and said, "Come with me, Stallings."

Ethan Stallings emerged from the room on the second floor of the Lucky Shot with a worried frown on his face. "I saw some strangers ride in, a little while ago," he said. "They were Creed's men, weren't they? You're going to turn me over to them."

Instead of answering that, Luke motioned with his head and said, "Come with me."

Stallings was a little wild-eyed, as if he might try to make a break for freedom, but he moved down the hallway as Luke indicated. They came to another door. Luke knocked on it and called, "You decent, Costaine?"

"Never!" he replied. "But come on in, anyway."

Luke opened the door and gestured for Stallings to

go in first. Costaine was propped up in the bed with pillows behind his back and a big grin on his rawboned face. Bandages swathed his barrel-chested torso. One of the saloon girls sat on a chair beside the bed, putting her clothes back in order and looking surprisingly embarrassed for a soiled dove.

"You're supposed to be resting and recuperating," Luke said to Costaine. "You got shot almost to pieces, you know."

"Nothin' restores a man's vitality better than embracin' life in all its glories," Costaine said.

"Well, I'm not going to argue medical matters with you. You know Stallings here."

Luke pointed to Stallings with a thumb.

"Know who he is, sure enough," Costaine answered, confirming with a nod. "We ain't been what you'd call introduced."

"Well, just in case you ever get it in your head to go after the reward on him, he's not wanted anymore."

Stallings turned his head quickly to stare at Luke in surprise.

"In fact," Luke went on, "although you wouldn't know it to look at him, Ethan Stallings is a dead man. He was killed last night in the fight with Hannigan and Bowen. So there's no reward for him anymore. Just like Mac McKenzie. You understand what I'm saying, Costaine?"

"I understand you, all right. You're turnin' this varmint loose."

Luke looked at Stallings and said, "He saved my life and the lives of several other men, and he risked his own hide doing it."

"Jensen, I . . . I don't know what to say," Stallings said.

"Say that you're going to change your name and go straight and stop swindling people. Even if you don't mean it, you can say that, anyway, so maybe every night on the trail from now on, I won't kick myself for being so damned softhearted."

A grin broke out on Stallings's face. "Sure," he said eagerly. "If you're giving me a second chance, I'm going to take advantage of it. A fresh start, maybe in California. I've always wanted to see that country out there."

"Fine," Luke said. "Just make sure I never have to come after you again." He turned back to Costaine. "And I don't ever want to hear that you've gone after him, either."

"Well," Costaine said, "I don't reckon you got to worry about that, Jensen. My bounty-huntin' days is over."

That took Luke by surprise. "You're giving it up?"

"I sure am. I been talkin' to Miss Irish—she come to visit me and make sure I'm bein' took care of all right, and danged if we didn't kinda take a shine to each other—and we came up with the idea of me stayin' on here and bein' the marshal. She says she can talk the town council into givin' me the job without any trouble. They need an honest man wearin' the badge for a change, and hell, nobody else wants the job."

Luke nodded. He knew that Mac McKenzie's name had been bandied about as a possibility for marshal, but he also knew Mac had absolutely no interest in pinning on a lawman's badge.

"All right, Costaine. It sounds like you'll have your hands full keeping the peace around here, so I don't have to worry about you going after Mac or Stallings."

Costaine leered at the saloon girl sitting beside the bed. "Oh, I'll have my hands full, all right, even before I start wearin' that dang tin badge!"

Luke found Mac waiting for him downstairs in the saloon. Mac leaned against the bar, nursing a beer. Just like in the café, numerous copies of the *Chronicle*'s extra edition were in evidence, being read avidly by the Lucky Shot's customers.

"I figured you'd gone back to the café," Luke said as he joined Mac at the bar.

Mac took a sip of the beer. "Alf can handle things just fine. I think he'd like more responsibility, and I'm going to give it to him. In fact . . . I'm going to give him the café."

Luke looked sharply at his friend. "You're going to do what?"

"Give him the café. Oh, I'll let him pay me a little bit for the place, because Alf's too proud to just take it as a gift, even though I'd be more than willing to do that."

Luke shook his head and said, "What in blazes brought this on? I thought you loved that café."

"I did . . . for a while. And after being on the run for a few years like I was, it felt mighty good to settle down . . . for a while." Mac smiled. "But my feet are starting to get itchy again. Maybe I wasn't ready, after all, to put down roots and stay in one place for the rest of my life."

Luke regarded him for a long moment and then said, "It might be different if there was a woman . . . a special woman . . . that you wanted to settle down with."

Without looking away from the mirror behind the bar, Mac said, "Yeah, it might be different, all right. But that's not going to happen. Not here in . . . whatever they change the name of the town to."

Luke mulled that over for a few seconds and then nodded. "That's none of my business. But I think I know what you mean. After this, your friends will be more successful than ever with their newspaper. And busier as well, I expect. Anything that might interfere with that is . . . a needless complication."

Mac drained the rest of his beer, thumped the empty mug on the bar, and said, "That's exactly what I was thinking."

"If you're not going to be in the eatery business anymore, what are you going to do?"

Mac smiled again. "Actually, I thought I might give bounty hunting a try. It might be nice to be on the other side of that line of work for a change. You be interested in having somebody ride with you for a while, Luke?"

"You know," Luke said, "I just might be."

Turn the page for an explosive preview!

**JOHNSTONE COUNTRY. THE ULTIMATE
KILLING GROUND.**

**There are a million ways to die in the Black Hills of
Dakota Territory—but only one way to make it out
alive if your name is Buchanon: with guns blazing . . .**

The hills have eyes . . .

The Buchanons are no strangers to hard times—or
making hard choices. After losing a hefty number of
livestock to a killer grizzly, Hunter Buchanon is
forced to sell a dozen broncs down in Denver for
some badly needed cash. Everything goes smoothly—
until he's ambushed on the way home. The culprits are
a murderous bunch of prairie rat outlaws, as dangerous as any Buchanon has ever tangled with. But
Hunter is hell-bent on getting his money back. Even if
it means pursuing the thieves into Dakota Territory—
where even deadlier dangers await . . .

Meanwhile, Angus Buchanon has agreed to guide
three former Confederate bounty hunters into the
Black Hills, on the trail of six cutthroats who robbed a
saloon and killed two men in Deadwood. This motley
trio of hunters are as cutthroat as the cutthroats they're
after. And it doesn't take long for Angus to realize they
mean to slaughter him as well at the end of the trail . . .

One family of ranchers. Two groups of cold-hearted
murderers. So many ways to die.

Chapter 1

Hunter Buchanon whipped his hand to the big LeMat revolver jutting from the holster around which the shell belt was coiled on the ground beside him.

In a half-second the big revolver was out of its holster and Hunter heard the hammer click back before he even knew what his thumb was doing. Lightning quick action honed by time and experience including four bloody years during which he fought for the Confederacy in the War of Northern Aggression.

He didn't know what had prompted his instinctive action until he sat half up from his saddle and peered across the red-glowing coals of the dying campfire to see Bobby Lee sitting nearby, peering down the slope into the southern darkness beyond, the coyote's tail curled tightly, ears pricked. Hunter's pet coyote gave another half-moan, half-growl like the one Hunter had heard in his sleep and shifted his weight from one foot to the other.

Hunter sat up slowly. "What is it, Bobby?"

A startled gasp sounded beside Hunter, and in the corner of his left eye he saw his wife, Annabelle, sit up quickly, grabbing her own hogleg from its holster and clicking the hammer back. Umber light from the fire danced in her thick, red hair. "What is it?" she whispered.

"Don't rightly know," Hunter said tightly, quietly. "But something's put a burr in Bobby's bonnet."

Down the slope behind Hunter, Annabelle, and Bobby Lee, their twelve horses whickered uneasily, drawing on their picket lines.

"Something's got the horses' blood up, too," Annabelle remarked, glancing over her shoulder at the fidgety mounts.

"Stay with the horses, honey," Hunter said, tossing his bedroll aside then rising, donning his Stetson, and stepping into his boots. As he grabbed his Henry repeating rifle, Annabelle said, "You be careful. We might have horse thieves on our hands, Hunter."

"Don't I know it." Hunter jacked a round into the Henry's action, then strode around the nearly dead fire, brushing fingers across the top of the coyote's head and starting down the hill to the south. "Come on, Bobby."

The coyote didn't need to be told twice. If there was one place for Bobby Lee, that was by the side of the big, blond man who'd adopted him when his mother had been killed by a rancher several years ago. Hunter moved slowly down the forested slope in the half darkness, one hand around the Henry's receiver so starlight didn't reflect off the brass and give him away.

Bobby Lee ran ahead, scouting for any human polecats after the ten horses Hunter and Annabelle were herding from their ranch near Tigerville deep in the Black Hills to a ranch outside of Denver. Hunter and Annabelle had caught the wild mustangs in the Hills near their ranch, and Annabelle had sat on the fence of the breaking corral, Bobby Lee near her feet, watching as Hunter had broken each wild-eyed bronc in turn.

Gentled them, rather. Hunter didn't believe in breaking a horse's spirit. He just wanted to turn them into "plug ponies," good ranch mounts that answered to the slightest tug on the reins or a squeeze of a rider's knees, and could turn on a dime, which was often necessary when working cattle, especially dangerous mavericks.

Hunter and Annabelle needed the money from the horse sale to help make up for the loss of several head of cattle to a rogue grizzly the previous summer. Times were hard on the ranch due to drought and low stock prices, and they were afraid they'd lose the Box Bar B without the money from the horses. They were getting two hundred dollars a head, because they were prime mounts—Hunter had a reputation as one of the best horse gentlers on the northern frontier—and that money would go far toward helping them keep the ranch.

Hunter wanted desperately to keep the Box Bar B not only for himself and Annabelle, but for Hunter's aged father, Angus, and for the boy they'd adopted when Nathan's doxie mother had died after riding with would-be rustlers, including the boy's scoundrel father, whom Hunter had killed.

The boy was nothing like his father. He was good and hardworking, and he needed a good home.

Hunter moved off down the slope but stopped when Bobby Lee suddenly took off running and swinging left toward some rocks and a cedar thicket, growling. The coyote disappeared in the trees and brush and then started barking angrily. A man cursed and then there were three rocketing gun reports followed by Bobby's mewling howl.

"Damn coyote!" the man's voice called out.

"Bobby!" Hunter said and took off running in the direction in which Bobby Lee had disappeared.

"They know we're here now so be careful!" another man called out sharply.

Running footsteps sounded ahead of Hunter.

He stopped and dropped to a knee when a moving shadow appeared ahead of him and slightly down the slope. Starlight glinted off a rifle barrel and off the running man's cream Stetson.

"Hold it right there, you son of a horse thief!" Hunter bellowed, pressing his cheek to the Henry's stock.

The man stopped suddenly and swung his rifle toward Hunter.

Then Henry spoke once, twice, three times. The man grunted and flew backward, dropping his rifle and striking the ground with another grunt and a thud.

"Harvey!" the other man yelled from beyond the rocks and cedars.

Harvey yelled in a screeching voice filled with pain, "I'm a dead man, Buck! Buchanon got me, the rebel devil. He's over here. Get him for me!"

Hunter stepped behind a pine, peered out around it, and jacked another round into the Henry's action. He waited, pricking his ears, listening for the approach of Buck. Seconds passed. Then a minute. Then two minutes.

A figure appeared on the right side of the rocks and cedars, moving slowly, one step at a time. Buck held a carbine across his chest. Hunter lined up the Henry's sights on the man and was about to squeeze the trigger when something ran up behind the man and leaped onto his back. Buck screamed as he fell forward, Bobby Lee growling fiercely and tearing into the back of the man's neck.

Hunter smiled. Buck screamed as he tried in vain to fight off the fiercely protective Bobby Lee. Buck swung around suddenly and cursed loudly as he flung Bobby Lee off him. The coyote struck the ground with a yelp and rolled.

"You mangy cur!" Buck bellowed, drawing a pistol and aiming at Bobby.

Hunter's Henry spoke twice, flames lapping from the barrel.

Buck groaned and lay over on his back. "Ah, hell," he said, and died.

"Good work, Bobby," Hunter said, walking toward where the coyote was climbing to his feet. Hunter dropped to a knee, placed his hand on Bobby Lee's back. "You all right?"

The coyote shook himself as if in an affirmative reply.

"All right," Hunter said, straightening. "Let's go check on—"

The shrill whinny of horses cut through the silence that had fallen over the night after Hunter had shot Buck.

"Annabelle!" Hunter yelled, swinging around to retrace his route back to the camp. "Come on, Bobby! There must be more of these scoundrels!"

The coyote mewled and took off running ahead of Hunter.

Only a minute after Hunter and Bobby had left the camp, the horses stirred more vigorously behind where Annabelle sat on a log near the cold fire, her Winchester carbine resting across her denim-clad thighs. She'd just risen from the log and started to walk toward the string of prize mounts when a man's voice called from the darkness down the hill behind the horses.

"Come here, purty li'l red-headed gal!" The voice was pitched with jeering, brash mockery.

Annabelle froze, stared into the darkness. Anger rose in her.

Again, the man's voice caromed quietly out of the darkness: "Come here, purty li'l red-headed gal!" The man chuckled.

Several of the horses lifted their heads and gave shrill whinnies.

The flame of anger burned more brightly in Annabelle, her heart quickening, her gloved hands tightening around the carbine she held high across her chest. She knew she shouldn't do it, but she couldn't stop herself. She moved slowly forward. Ahead and to her left, thirty feet away, the horses were whickering and shifting, pulling at the ropes securing them to the picket line.

Annabelle jacked a round into the carbine's action and moved toward the horses. She patted the blaze on the snout of a handsome black horse, said, "Easy, fellas. Easy. I got this."

She stepped around the horses and down the slope and stopped behind a broad-boled pine.

Again, the man's infuriating voice came from down the slope beyond her. "Come here, purty li'l red-haired gal. Come find me!"

Annabelle swallowed tightly and said quietly, mostly to herself: "All right—if you're sure about this, bucko . . ."

She continued forward, taking one step at a time. She had no spurs on her boots. Hunter's horses were so well-trained they didn't require them. She made virtually no sound as she continued down the slope, weaving between the columnar pines and firs silhouetted against the night's darkness relieved only by starlight.

"Come on, purty li'l red-headed gal," came the jeering voice again. "Wanna show ya somethin'."

"Oh, you do, do you?" Annabelle muttered beneath her breath. "Wonder what that could be."

She headed in the direction from which the voice had come, practically directly ahead of her now, maybe thirty, forty feet down the slope. On the one hand, that she was being lured into a trap, there could be no question. Hunter had always told her that her redheaded anger would get the best of her one day. Maybe he'd been right.

On the other hand, the open mockery in the voice of the man trying to lure her into the trap could not be denied. She imagined shooting him, and the thought stretched her rich, red lips back from her perfect, white teeth in a savage smile.

She took one step, then another . . . another . . . pausing briefly behind trees, edging cautious looks around them, knowing that she could see the lap of flames from a gun barrel at any second.

"That's it," came the man's voice again. "Just a bit closer, honey. That's it. Keep comin', purty li'l redheaded gal."

"All right," Annabelle said, tightly, loudly enough for the man to hear her now. "But you're gonna regret it, you son of a b—"

She'd smelled the rancid odor of unwashed man and raw whiskey two seconds before she heard the pine needle crunch of a stealthy tread behind her. She froze as a man's body pressed against her from behind. Just as the man started to wrap his arm around her, intending to close his hand over her mouth, Annabelle ducked and swung around, swinging the carbine, as well—and rammed the butt into her would-be assailant's solar plexus.

The man gave a great exhalation of whiskey-soaked breath, and folded.

Annabelle turned farther and rammed her right knee into the man's face. She felt the wetness of blood on her knee from the man's exploding nose. He gave a wheezy, *"Mercy!"* as he fell straight back against the ground and lay moaning and writhing.

Knowing she was about to have lead sent her way, Annabelle threw herself to her left and rolled. Sure enough, the rifle of the man on the slope below thundered once, twice, three times, the bullets caroming through the air where Annabelle had been a second before. The man whom she'd taken to the proverbial woodshed howled, apparently having taken one of the bullets meant for her.

Annabelle rolled onto her belly and aimed the carbine straight out before her. She'd seen the flash of the second man's rifle, and she aimed toward him now, sending three quick shots his way. The second shooter howled. Annabelle heard the heavy thud as he struck the ground.

"Gallblastit!" he cried. "You like to shot my dang ear off, you wicked, red-haired hussy!"

"What happened to 'purty li'l red-haired gal'?" Annabelle spat out as she shoved to her feet and righted her Stetson.

She heard the second shooter thrashing around

down the slope, jostling the branches of an evergreen shrub. He gave another cry, and then Annabelle could hear him running in a shambling fashion downhill.

"Oh, you're running away from the 'purty li'l red-haired gal,' now, tough guy?"

Anna strode after him, following the sounds of his shambling retreat.

She pushed through the shrubs and saw his shadow moving downhill, holding a hand to his right ear, groaning. He'd left his rifle up where Anna had shot him. "Turn around or take it in the back, tough guy," she said, following him, taking long, purposeful strides.

"You're crazy!" the man cried, casting a fearful glance behind him. "What'd you do to H.J.?"

"What I started, you finished."

"He's my cousin!"

"*Was* your cousin."

He gave another sobbing cry as he continued running so awkwardly that Anna, walking, steadily gained on him as she held the carbine down low against her right leg.

"You're just evil is what you are!"

"You were after our horses, I take it?"

The man only sobbed again.

"How'd you get on our trail?"

"Seen you passin' wide around Lusk," the man said, breathless, grunting. "We was huntin' antelope on the ridge."

"Market hunters?"

"Fer a woodcuttin' crew."

"Ah. You figured you'd make more money selling

my and my husband's horses. At least you have a good eye for horse flesh."

The man gained the bottom of the ridge. He stopped and turned to see Anna moving within twenty feet of him, gaining on him steadily—a tall, slender, well-put-together young lady outfitted in men's trail gear, though, judging by all her curves in all the right places, she was all woman. He gave another wail, moonlight glinting in his wide, terrified eyes, then swung around and ran into the creek, the water splashing like quicksilver up around his knees.

He'd likely never been stalked by a woman before. Especially no "purty li'l red-headed gal."

Anna followed the coward into the creek. "What's your name?"

"Oh, go to hell!"

"What's your name?"

He shot another silver-eyed gaze back over his shoulder. "Wally. Leave me be. I'm in major pain here!"

Now that Anna was closing on him, she could see the man was tall and slender, mid- to late-twenties, with long, stringy hair brushing his shoulders while the top of his head was bald. He had small, mean eyes and now as he turned to face her, he lowered his bloody right hand to the pistol bristling on his right hip.

"You stop there, now," he warned, stretching his lips back from his teeth in pain. "You stop there. I'm done. Finished. You go on back to your camp!"

Anna stopped ten feet away from him. She rested the Winchester on her shoulder. "You know what happens to rustlers in these parts—don't you, Wally?"

He thrust his left arm and index finger out at her. "N-now, you ain't gonna hang me. You done blowed my ear off!" Wally slid the old Smith & Wesson from its holster and held it straight down against his right leg. "Besides, you're a woman. Women don't behave like that!"

He clicked the Smithy's hammer back.

"You're right—we don't behave like that. Not even we 'purty li'l red-headed gals'!" Anna racked a fresh round into the carbine's action, raised the rifle to her shoulder, and grinned coldly. "Why waste the hemp on vermin like you, Wally?"

Wally's little eyes grew wide in terror as he jerked his pistol up. "Don't you—!"

"We just shoot 'em!" Anna said.

And shot him.

Wally flew back into the creek with a splash. He went under and bobbed to the surface, arms and legs spread wide. Slowly, the current carried him downstream.

Anna heard running footsteps and a man's raking breaths behind her. She swung around, bringing the carbine up again, ready to shoot, but held fire when she saw the big, broadshouldered man in the gray Stetson, buckskin tunic, and denims running toward her, the coyote running just ahead.

"Anna!" Hunter yelled. "Are you all right, honey?"

He and Bobby stopped at the edge of the stream. Both their gazes caught on the man bobbing downstream, and Hunter shuttled his incredulous gaze back to his wife. Raking deep breaths, he hooked a thumb over his shoulder. "Saw the other man up the hill. Dead as a post." Hunter Buchanon planted his fists on his hips and scowled his reproof at his young wife. "I told you to stay at the camp!"

Anna strode back out of the stream. She stopped before her husband, who was a whole head taller than she. "We purty li'l red-headed gals just need us a little bloodletting once in a while. Sort of like bleeding the sap off a tree."

She grinned, rose up on her toes to kiss Hunter's lips, then ticked the brim of his hat with her right index finger and started walking back toward the camp and the horses. "Come on, Bobby Lee," she said. "I'll race ya!"

AVAILABLE NOW!

Johnstone Country. Where Outlaws Shoot. And Legends Shoot Back.

When a cattle train bound for Texas is ambushed by bloodthirsty rustlers, legendary mountain man Smoke Jensen vows to get the cattle back, get the killers who stole them—and get revenge for the blood they spilled. . . .

The completion of a new railroad line from Colorado to Texas is a dream come true for Smoke Jensen and the other ranchers of Big Rock. But this dream turns into their worst nightmare when the first herd they load onto the train is stolen by a vicious gang of kill-crazy rustlers. This is no ordinary train robbery. It's an inferno of slaughter that includes the friendly rancher who volunteered to take Smoke's place on the trip. Now Smoke is saddling up and riding out—to get the prairie rats who murdered his friend. . . .

Smoke isn't the only one who's after these merciless killers. A pair of undercover lawmen from Texas have managed to infiltrate the gang by pretending to be dangerous outlaws. While Smoke is trying to track down the stolen herd, the undercover lawmen pretend to plot with the gang to rob more cattle trains. But there's a hitch in the lawmen's plan. To make sure they're really on board, the gang wants them to prove their loyalty—by eliminating their biggest threat: Smoke Jensen. . . .

NATIONAL BESTSELLING AUTHORS

WILLIAM W. JOHNSTONE
and J.A. Johnstone

THE ANGRY LAND
A Smoke Jensen Novel of the West

On sale now, wherever Pinnacle Books are sold.

Visit our website at
KensingtonBooks.com
to sign up for our newsletters, read
more from your favorite authors, see
books by series, view reading group
guides, and more!

BOOK / / CLUB
BETWEEN THE CHAPTERS

Become a Part of Our
Between the Chapters Book Club
Community and Join the Conversation

Betweenthechapters.net